JACKIE

JACKIE

A Novel

Dawn Tripp

RANDOM HOUSE NEW YORK

Published in the United States by Random House, an imprint and division
of Penguin Random House LLC, New York.

RANDOM HOUSE and the HOUSE colophon are registered trademarks
of Penguin Random House LLC.

LIBRARY OF CONGRESS CATALOGING-IN-PUBLICATION DATA
Names: Tripp, Dawn Clifton, author.
Title: Jackie: a novel / Dawn Clifton Tripp.
Description: First edition. | New York: Random House, 2024.
Identifiers: LCCN 2023034227 (print) | LCCN 2023034228 (ebook) |
ISBN 9780812997217 (hardcover) | ISBN 9780812997224 (ebook)
Subjects: LCSH: Onassis, Jacqueline Kennedy, 1929-1994—Fiction. |
Kennedy, John F. (John Fitzgerald), 1917-1963—Fiction. |
LCGFT: Biographical fiction. | Novels.
Classification: LCC PS3620.R57 J33 2024 (print) | LCC PS3620.R57 (ebook) |
DDC 813/.6—dc23/eng/20240122
LC record available at https://lccn.loc.gov/2023034227
LC ebook record available at https://lccn.loc.gov/2023034228

Printed in the United States of America on acid-free paper

randomhousebooks.com

2   4   6   8   9   7   5   3   1

First Edition

For my father

Author's Note

Jackie is a novel, a work of fiction inspired by the life of Jacqueline Kennedy Onassis. It is the story of a woman who projected a myriad of selves and who was, at her core, a deeply private person, with a nuanced and formidable intellect. It is also the story of a love affair, a complicated marriage, and the fracturing of identity that comes in the wake of unthinkable violence. A lover, a mother, a wife, Jackie reckoned with the decades-long challenge of living in the glare of the public eye, learning to harness the power surrounding her, to forge an authentic life and emerge as her true self: a brilliant, fiercely creative woman who grew up to be an artist and whose medium was fame.

E. L. Doctorow once said, "The historian will tell you what happened. The novelist will tell you what it felt like." In *Jackie,* that interstice is what I wanted to explore—the space between what took place and what she might have felt; what happened to her and how the world perceived it versus how she might have experienced it.

I came to Jackie's story through a photograph. It's not a well-known image, but to me it was striking. A black-and-white photograph of Jackie and Jack, in the summer of 1957, at the airport. Her back is to the camera, her skirt filled with wind, a triple strand of pearls around her neck. She is standing with Jack in a doorway. He leans in toward her, perhaps to say something, perhaps to kiss her goodbye. It fascinated me—that photograph and the intimacy captured between these two young people. It was clear they had little idea they were being photographed. The moment was private, a faint tension between them, a stiltedness or a longing held in check, something said or left unsaid, and, also, a vulnerability, a tenderness. I found it a moment of heartbreaking beauty, a leave-taking. Jack might have been setting off on a campaign trip. Jackie was pregnant by then with Caroline. I studied this photograph, and to me, it was like fire. Over the next few days, I wrote several different passages about it, longhand, from both Jack's and Jackie's perspective. In *Jackie*, they each remember the photograph years after it was taken, and it matters to each of them for different reasons and in different ways.

Who was Jackie? Who were Jack and Jackie together, before they were myth? When they were just two people, not well known—young, newly married, with all the incipient joys and thorns that come with a complex love affair. Who were they? As people? Who was she?

I printed out that image, their bodies in shadow, their faces close, a bright rush of the white sky behind. The vulnerability in that tentative intimacy became the heart of this novel. I researched for years before I felt I could begin to write. The story seemed too immense at first, too public. So much had already been written. But the deeper I moved into the research, the more I began to feel how incomplete our collective understanding of Jackie might be. Doris Kearns Goodwin, who knew Jackie, once said: "Culturally something happened between her and the decade that she lived in. . . ." This statement, for me, was a key. I found it exhilarating—the possibility of creating a novel that could be an extended interrogation of Goodwin's words.

I read many, many books about Jackie, Jack, Bobby Kennedy, and other historical figures featured in this novel. A list of works I found particularly helpful is in the Sources section at the end of the book. I also read countless articles, magazines, newspapers. I read letters and spent time at the JFK Library. I went to see places where Jackie had traveled. I read poems she loved. I read lines of Caroline's and John's about their mother's passion for books and literature. In the introduction to a collection of poems I read to my sons years ago, Caroline reflected on how she inherited a love of poetry and language from her mother, and how that love gave rise to her desire to instill a similar love in her own children, "not only because of the pleasure it will bring, but because the power of ideas, and the ability to express them, is the greatest power we have." Those words stayed with me. They said something not just about Jackie but also about a driving belief that she had passed on to her children.

Looking at photographs, even iconic photographs—Jackie and Jack on a sailboat before they were married; Jackie holding Caroline as a baby with her little teeth digging into her mother's string of pearls; Jackie in a white column dress, whispering with Jack in a White House corridor; Jackie and Bobby in the years after Jack was assassinated; Jackie riding her bike alone in Aquinnah—I began to wonder not about those images per se but what might have happened directly before a photograph was taken, what might have happened directly after. I began to seek out photographs that captured her when she might not have known the camera was on her: a photograph of her swinging Caroline through the surf; another of her kneeling next to John, their backs to the camera as they watch Jack leave in a helicopter from the lawn. There was a moving, free simplicity in those candid images. What might she have been thinking, feeling? There were so many facets of her—those she projected, and those projected onto her. Jackie, Jacks, Jacqueline, Miss Bouvier, Mrs. Kennedy, Mrs. Onassis, Jackie O.

At the same time, I felt that almost everything I read or learned seemed to miss dimensions of what was most human and, in doing so, missed a kind of magic. I became more curious about her apparent contradictions: her instinctive strength; her cool, at times leveling wit; her vulnerability, empathy, and warmth; her hunger for solitude and the freedom it allowed; her formidable will, her tenacity, her passion for literature, adventure, art, architecture, history; the magnitude and scope of her intellect; her fragility, fear, and how she responded to grief. The tensile relationship she had with power.

Early on, it became clear to me that her love for her children and her identity as a mother were fundamental to her character, as was her determination to construct—with measure and intention—a relatively normal life for Caroline and John and to nurture in them a spirit of inquiry and a sense of responsibility to the larger world. I saw this reflected not just in her words about her children but in their words and care for her as she aged. I was fascinated by her desire to explore, observe, learn; by her faith in the power of art and literature as forces of social change. I realized that if I wanted to write about Jackie, I needed to absorb historical sources and nonfiction accounts, and then I needed to leave it—all of it—to enter the story in a new way, to try to capture the spirit of a bold and brilliant young woman who falls in love, builds a family, endures unthinkable violence and shattering loss. A woman who rises out of that broken dark to create a legacy, who seeks to embrace life, love, work, and continues to grow, with purpose and grace—taking risks, making mistakes, often deeply public ones. That was the story I became riveted by, a story told through a human lens, which felt close to emotional and psychological truth.

Jackie's moments of irreverence were interesting to me, but I expected those, no matter how unexpected the swerves in her humor were. What I found revelatory was her passion, her genuine warmth, and the unique bond between her and Jack. Looking closely at candid photographs of Jack and Jackie—including that 1957 photograph and other moments of intimacy when they might not have known they were being observed—I felt how they were aligned, conspiratorial even. There was something deeply beautiful and real between them, an integrity in how they understood each other—with all their strengths, flaws, willfulness, play. Something resonant and irrevocable in the love that existed between them.

Jackie described herself once as "an outsider." I love that she bit her nails and read *everything*. That she loved the books of theologian Reinhold Niebuhr, as well as the novels of Irish writer Edna O'Brien. She memorized whole stanzas of Tennyson's "Ulysses" and would devour books of poetry to find lines she'd give to Jack to integrate into his speeches. She often explicitly stated she would prefer to erase her own authorship. In her career as a book editor, she didn't like her name to be in the acknowledgments. That was interesting to me, and given all that's been written about her, it felt new and integral to a holistic understanding of a woman and her complicated relationship with power—a woman who'd been written into myth and who had, at certain stages of her life, taken a role in forging that myth even as she was living it. I wondered how Jackie's love of art, literature, and stories might have given rise to an instinct to incarnate art and myth through her own life. Throughout this novel, I wanted her to strike against that boundary between self-as-subject, as a perceiving, sentient being, and self-as-object, constantly being watched, deconstructed. I wanted to render the consequent sense of disconnect that can come with that split and how a woman might have worked to reconcile various dimensions of who she was and what she wanted with how the world saw her. She was clear, in her own intention, that the White House restoration was about restoring an integrity—a beauty and grace—that might express the past and future ideals of a nation, *not* its exact historical past. That process of the restoration felt aligned with what I sought to do in this exploration of her story.

Throughout this novel, lines or fragments of things Jackie said or wrote that are found in the public record inspired lines of dialogue and interior thought. In *Jackie*, I've attempted to capture her spirit by reimagining her voice, her thoughts, and conversations between her and others in her circle of family, friends, and acquaintances. Since this is a work of historical fiction, I adapted anecdotes and verbal exchanges that have previously appeared in biographies, published interviews, speeches, forums, and other writings. On occasion, some of Jackie's actual words from these sources are woven into the dialogue and story. Less frequently, short phrases from other sources are in the narrative. Examples of this include, but are not limited to, two lines on page 17 adapted from Jackie's entry for *Vogue* magazine's Prix de Paris contest; exchanges in Parts II and III drawn from Norman Mailer's articles about Jack and Jackie; exchanges in Part IV drawn from published interviews conducted by Theodore White, Arthur Schlesinger, William Manchester, and The Warren Commission; lines of dialogue on page 274 as well as other scenes in Parts III and IV inspired by Clint Hill's moving memoir *Mrs. Kennedy and Me*. Memoirs like Mr. Hill's provide insight into the care and respect consistently integral to Jackie's close relationships. I wanted to explore scenes and anecdotes chronicled by people who knew Jackie and who experienced firsthand the complex nuances of her heart, wit, vulnerability, and intellect—the intimate *realness* of her as a human being—and I wanted to re-imagine those moments from her point of view as she might have experienced them. These are only a few examples of how published nonfiction sources have been useful in my creative process. Other works are highlighted in the Sources section at the back of this book. My use of statements that the historical record tells me were made and my reference to incidents or events that did happen are not intended to change the entirely fictional nature of this book.

There are many stellar, insightful nonfiction works written about Jackie. I believe that fiction, when it hews to the historical record, can access a different kind of truth, an experiential truth that allows us to enter the emotional heart of a story. Historical accounts are interpretations too, dependent on the selection and elision of facts, how facts are ordered and assembled, what is emphasized, where the gaps or lacunae fall. Scholarship is not static; it is an evolving body, and the historical record may always be incomplete. Truth is kaleidoscopic, continually changing according to our perspective and as new documents and understandings come to light. Women have rarely been at the center of historical narratives. Fiction can be a means of cutting past the surface of what we think we know, to reshape our collective understanding of a person, an era, a life.

JACKIE

To live past the end of your myth is a perilous thing.

—ANNE CARSON

November 22, 1963

They will tell her they found no heartbeat, no breathing, no pulse.

In the hallway where she sits, a glacial coolness—white tiles along the wall, the black linoleum floor. Clint stands near her, that precise distance an understanding between them. Others cluster in uncertain knots, voices anxious, hushed, bowed heads, someone walks away, someone else comes back. A nurse pushes through.

Three and a half seconds—that's all it was—a slivered instant between the first shot, which missed the car, and the second, which did not.

If she had been looking to the right.
If she had recognized the first sound for what it was.
If she had not been complaining in her head about the heat, how it seared her eyes, how close their hands and blurred faces came as the car took a turn, how they pressed in.
If she had not been thinking of how she wanted to put her sunglasses back on and why did he always insist? *So they can see you, Jackie. Let them see you.* She had been too focused on all that and

wondering how she could slip away from the grueling heat into the cool promise of the tunnel ahead—

A hypnotic burst of sunlight off her bracelet as she waved.

And the roses were there, on the seat between them, roses spilling toward the floor, she kept pushing them back so they wouldn't fall.

Later, she won't be able to get the roses from her mind—the petals soaked, his blood, stems broken under her knees. Three times that day someone pushed roses into her arms—yellow roses each time, until they reached Dallas. There, the roses were red.

She will say this again and again, later. Each time she is asked to tell the story of those hours, and even when she is not asked, she will tell it. She has not yet begun, but when she does, she will describe the dark, wet iridescence of those roses crushed in the white-hot glare of hate as she leapt up to grasp a piece of his skull flying away.

Sometimes—also later—she will wonder aloud to Bobby how in those few seconds her mind could have witnessed so much and at the same time remembered so little.

They killed him over that bill.
She knew it.
The civil-rights bill he wanted to get passed.
That's why they killed him.

. . .

The morning they had left the White House—Thursday, only the day before—Jack was relaxed. He told her his back felt better than it had in years. "So what will we do stuck at Lyndon's ranch?" she asked him. Kenneth was doing her hair. Jack had come into her room and was standing behind her, off to the side. He caught her eyes in the mirror and shrugged.

"We should ride," he said.

Before Jack left the room, he gave her a document. "If you want to know what my life is like, read this."

"For Texas?"

"No," he said. "I asked Neustadt to study the missile crisis and draft a report, map where things went awry."

She glanced at it. SKYBOLT AND NASSAU—*American Policy-Making and Anglo-American Relations.* **Top Secret** typed in the top and bottom left corners.

He stood in the room, like he was waiting for something.

"I'll read it," she said.

He touched his jacket pocket, his fingers tapping against the dark-blue fabric.

"I'm also going to give Macmillan a copy," he said. "I'm thinking about it, anyway. Why don't you bring it along, take a look, and let me know if that's a good idea."

"Sure," she said.

As if satisfied, he left the room.

Her mind was on the speech she had to give in Spanish to the Latino group in Houston. She put the Skybolt report in the pile of last-minute things to be packed.

Once, years ago, at a party, you left with another woman. She was blond, in a silver dress, her body like a fingernail of moon. We were married by then. This was the first time it happened. I felt myself move outside of myself, watching you leave with that woman, aware of others in the room turning toward me, as I tried to empty my face into the face of a wife who knew and did not care.

. . .

In the Parkland Hospital corridor, she sits in the metal folding chair and smokes. She is cool and still as they scuttle around—feet, voices, that awful hospital smell.

She wonders where her coat is, then realizes she's wearing it. She looks down at her lap, her skirt—then wishes she hadn't.

She looks back up through the moving stream of them. She looks at the opposite wall.

"Mrs. Kennedy, shall we go into the restroom and get cleaned up?"

"We've brought you a new set of clothes to change into."

They keep saying things like that.

When the doors to Trauma Room 1 open, the corridor goes still. She turns to the doctor stepping out, his face telling her what she already knows—it couldn't be otherwise, no matter how much wanting. She gets up as if this is how it was always meant to happen. This is the script and Jack knew it and now she has to play her part.

She goes to walk past the doctor, even as others fold in to block her way. She pushes through. She is stripped to nothing now— just a woman in the shape of a blade slipping through a line of men past the doctor through the operating-theater doors to the body laid out that is hers, naked under a sheet, her lips to his feet, her face to his beautiful face. It is no less beautiful now. She takes the ring from her finger and twists it onto his littlest finger. It stops at the first knuckle, which upsets her, but she leaves it, his lovely shattered head. They've turned the shattered part away, his eyes open still. Not blank yet.

We are made of stars and I loved you from the first moment I saw you. I loved you even knowing it would break something in me.

...

In the suite at the hotel the night before, someone had filled the walls with a collection of borrowed art. Sixteen exquisite pieces—a Monet, a Van Gogh, a Prendergast.

He had made a little doodle on a pad of paper near the phone, the drawing of a sailboat, sail filled with wind; you could tell it was moving. Up in one corner was a shape.

"Is this a bird?" she asked. "A kite, or a boxy cloud?"

"It's the sun," he said.

"No, it's not the sun," she said. "What is it?"

"I couldn't quite decide. Something in flight." He was lying on the bed. "Hey," he said then. "Come here."

The world is shadowless, time bent. No before or after, just that hard brutal sound when everything slowed and your head jerked back, your hands toward your throat, that puzzled look on your face. I remember that. I remember thinking you looked as if you had a headache.

. . .

"Mrs. Kennedy, Vice President Johnson is going back to Washington, and he would like you to go with him."

Clint, her Secret Service detail, is saying this to her. She is in the hospital corridor. Outside the closed door of Trauma Room 1. The team of doctors is doing something else in there. They told her but she can't remember now, so she is waiting, seated again in the metal folding chair. She looks up, and Clint's eyes are as young and raw and dark as she has ever seen them.

"Mr. Hill, please explain to Vice President Johnson that I'm not going anywhere without the president."

"Yes, Mrs. Kennedy," he says, and steps away.

Leaving their house in Virginia earlier that week, she had gone back through, checking rooms for last-minute things. She found the *Book Review* with Jack's markups, the books he wanted circled. It was folded and had fallen under the sofa, just an edge of it poking out. She found John's toy helicopter, a spilled set of crayons. A rogue sock.

Once, years ago, in Hyannis Port, before we were married, there was a flood of light through the window and children tumbling over one another in their little white shorts, grass-stained. I was looking for you. I crossed through the living room. You and your father and Bobby were talking in another room down the hall, you didn't know I was there; I heard your father say my name and I stopped, listening as the three of you discussed the assets I brought to the table—the illusion of wealth, the pedigree, the beauty (enough but not too much)—and then the liabilities—a little too highbrow, too French. I felt a wave of nausea, listening, as the three of you talked about me like I was a piece of territory to be inspected, parsed, acquired for gain. I glanced across the room toward the door that led out to the front yard, the driveway, my car.

But there was you.

And then your father was there, coming into the room, with you and Bobby behind him. Your father stopped when he saw me sitting there. He knew I had overheard.

. . .

They wheel an empty casket in from outside. Bronze. Up on a metal dolly with small rubber tires. O'Donnell and Powers step in front of her. *What are you doing?* she almost asks, then realizes they're trying to shield her, to block her view as it goes by. A doctor urges her to leave.

"Do you think seeing a coffin could possibly upset me?" she says. "I've seen my husband die, shot in my arms. His blood is all over me. How can I see anything worse than what I've seen?"

The doctor seems to shrink into his white coat. Baffled, embarrassed, something like that. She doesn't have space in her brain to wonder or care. Dave Powers is in an argument with the medical examiner, who's saying they have to hold the autopsy here in Texas, according to state law. Their voices rise, bouncing off the linoleum, they start to yell in the hallway. Powers explains that the vice president and Lady Bird Johnson are waiting at Love Field for Mrs. Kennedy, and Mrs. Kennedy is waiting for the president, and the medical examination can be held at the Capitol, no matter what the stupid Texas law has to say about homicide and jurisdiction.

She stops paying attention. At a certain point, the casket with the large handles glides out of Trauma Room 1. She knows he is in it, and it is time to go; he is leaving and she will leave with him. The casket is cool to the touch, and she walks out with it to the hearse. When Clint asks her to come ride in a car behind, she has to explain, "No, Mr. Hill. I'm going to ride with the president." She climbs into the back of the hearse with Jack, and Clint climbs in with her. They ride with their knees scrunched up to their chests. She knows there is more room inside where Jack is.

I should not have allowed you to come here.

The casket will not fit through the door of the plane; they tilt and try to wedge it in on an angle. She watches from the bottom of the steps. She can feel the heat rising off the tarmac. The crust of his blood on her stockings. She could tell them this won't work at all, it will never fit. The men at the top holding the casket exchange words, but from the base of the steps she can't make them out. Clint glances back at her. A warning look she recognizes a moment before they break the handles off, that awful sound of metal ripped from wood. Then they jam the coffin through the door. She walks up the stairs and follows it into the plane.

They do not take off. They have to wait, apparently, for a judge who will do the swearing in. On the bed in the Presidential Cabin, someone has laid out a dress for her, stockings, a jacket. Two blue Air Force One towels next to the clothes. Her face appears in the bathroom mirror, streaked with blood. She soaks a tissue and begins to wipe it off. No. A mistake. She should have left it. His blood, her face, this bathroom mirror that was theirs a few hours ago and is not now. There's a light knock on the door. Lady Bird comes in and offers to have someone come and help her get cleaned up.

"What if I had not been there?" she says to Lady Bird.
One glove—her right glove—white this morning, now is dark,

lacquered in blood. Her left glove is missing. Where did she leave her left glove?

"Let's get you changed," Lady Bird says gently.

"No," she says. "I want them to see what they have done to Jack."

Later, she will not remember saying it out loud.

"Lady Bird, could you please send in Mr. Hill and Mr. O'Donnell? I have to give instructions to send to my mother and Miss Shaw, about the children."

The judge who will perform the swearing in is a peanut, tiny even in her brown-and-white polka-dot dress. The heat in the plane is stifling, bodies and hot air all crushed and caught in that over-stuffed low-ceilinged space—too many, too much—and the eagle is still flying on the carpet, its wings pinched down by all their feet. Someone has realized they don't have a Bible. "The nightstand in the bedroom," she whispers to O'Brien, who is standing beside her. He leaves to go find it. The photographer has already climbed up onto the couch and is angling his lens down at them. Light nicks his spectacles as he pushes back against the curve where the wall of the plane meets the ceiling, hunching his shoulders, troll-like, trying to get them all in. The engines have snapped to life—a whirring, drowning sound, and someone's hand is at her elbow. Lyndon. He wants her to stand next to him. They are all pushing back into the tight-as-sardines-in-a-can crowd. She shuffles her feet in the direction they want her to move and looks down at her hands. They look wrong, odd and new, a pale band of lighter skin at the base of her ring finger.

"You don't have to go out there," Kenny O'Donnell had said to her ten minutes earlier, in the bedroom. He was tense, taut with grief, furious at the unthinkable that had just shredded meaning out of his life.

"I think I owe that much to the country," she had answered.

. . .

On the flight, she sits with Jack and the Irish in the rear of the plane—O'Brien, O'Donnell, Powers. The crew has taken out the seats to make room for them. She does not take her hand off the coffin. The smell of soup someone is eating somewhere sickens her.

How do I do it? How will I, can I, do it? Turn the mess of our lives with its brazen mistakes and disorder into some tenable history I can relate to the children, as if all along we had it in our control?

They are grumbling now about Johnson and why did he need to take the oath of office in Dallas? Couldn't he have waited? He told them he asked Bobby and said that's what Bobby told him to do, which Bobby would never have said. They break off, realizing she's watching them, listening. There is blood on Dave Powers's suit. For a moment she stares at it, then she tells them about Abraham Lincoln's funeral and the book in the White House library and she asks if one of them could make sure Pam has remembered to message J. B. West to go and find it so they can use it to plan.

"We are going to have a funeral like Lincoln's," she says. "There was a riderless horse, and I need to reread exactly what they did with the horse—the tack, how it was led. We will do that."

As the flight continues, they tell her stories about Jack. They drink whiskey, and she sips at hers to be polite because they've insisted on pouring her a glass as if she is one of them now. They are the widowers and she is his residual. Dave Powers tells her about Jack's last visit to Joe in Hyannis Port. He'd driven out to the Cape after the fundraiser in Boston the night before, after the visit to Harvard and to Patrick's grave. He had spent the day at the house with his father. Dave describes how Jack kissed his father goodbye. She can almost feel Joe's cheek under her lips; she can almost smell a bolt of salt wind. She takes another sip of whiskey, lets it burn in her throat.

"Dave, you have known Jack all your life," she says. "What will you do now? What will happen to you?"

His eyes are angry, almost desperate. "You want to know something, Jackie. I don't give a damn."

There's a report of a storm ahead. Severe weather, she's told. Possibly tornadoes. Through Mississippi and Arkansas. The pilot is going to try to climb over it.

"Fine," she says. "Have you ever noticed how fast the dark comes on when you are flying west to east?"

PART I

There's no one thing that's true. It's all true.

—ERNEST HEMINGWAY, *For Whom the Bell Tolls*

Growing up, I never had flying dreams or dreams of being onstage. I wanted to ride horses on an empty coast. I wanted to be Sappho, or invisible, or the circus queen who ran off with the daring young man on the flying trapeze.

I loved art, ballet, horses, and dogs. I had skinned knees and braces on my teeth, but there were writers like Chekhov and Shaw on a shelf in the room where I had to take naps. I never slept but sat on the windowsill reading. My heroes were Mowgli and Scarlett O'Hara. Later, there were poets—Virgil, Tennyson, Edna St. Vincent Millay. I loved to dance but didn't care for dancing school. By the time I was twelve, I was taller than most of the boys. Clumsy and dull, they could never keep rhythm, too fast on the waltz, too slow on the foxtrot. I kept my back straight, eyes over their heads, keeping time with the circling walls. And as those rooms spun, I dreamed of France. I wanted to grow up to write stories in a garret apartment in Paris; I wanted to smoke rolled cigarettes, date artists and aristocrats, drink grasshoppers, and dance in clubs on the West Bank until midnight.

I wanted to walk home alone by the Seine and be no one.

That was the future I'd marked off for myself. I could see it, almost breathe it. That was the edge of life I was standing on when I was twenty-one, the night I met you at the Bartletts'.

You were not part of that future. But that night there was something in you that I recognized—something hurtling, disparate—the ranging curiosity, incisive intellect. You were good-looking, of course. Your golden swagger could bend a room. I eschewed that. It smacked of arrogance. That night, though, there was something else in you I saw: something deeper, more fugitive and fragile, a kind of curious hunger to break on the world like a star.

You were not my kind of adventure. Too American. Too good-looking. Too boy. Too much about politics and new money.

Your life, I told myself, was not the life I was looking for.

Spring 1951

"He's a kind of cheerful lightning," Charley Bartlett tells me.

"I've already met your congressman," I say. "On a train when I was still at Vassar."

"And?"

"He was a flirt. We rode the same train for a while. I was the only girl in the car. I was reading and I wasn't going to waste an hour I wouldn't get back for a man like that."

"Like what?"

"The kind who loves a game and will leave it once he's won."

Now I've been rude. Silence on the line. Then Charley says, "Jack's better than that."

"No, Charley," I say. "You're better than that."

Charley Bartlett. Smart, kind, a wonderful writer. He was what my stepbrother Yusha called "an intellectual beau." Charley tried to introduce me to Jack Kennedy at a wedding the summer before. A ritzy night on Long Island, lanterns strung through the trees. I was talking with a prizefighter when Charley came over and led me by the arm through the giant crowd to where he thought Kennedy was, only to discover he'd left on the heels of some girl.

"Aiming for the Senate," Charley says to me now on the phone. "He'll need a wife, and he's not the buttoned-up boy next door."

"I'm looking at a job in New York," I say.

"You should still meet him."

I don't answer right away. It all feels a little dull and preordained—that life the young Georgetown set moves in, like fish lazing from one circle to the next.

Still, a week later, a Sunday in May, I drive from my mother's house down Chain Bridge Road, toward Georgetown. A warm evening, the cherry blossoms have gone by, the leaves already darkening to their summer green. There are narrow tree-lined streets, three shallow stone steps, the brass knocker, and my hand on it, then Charley is crossing the living room to greet me, his wife, Martha, emerging from the kitchen, with a tall glass of what looks like some rum thing. Five months pregnant, radiant, red hair piled on top of her head, she hands Charley the drink, takes my arm, and leads me past the Sheraton armchairs and framed prints onto the terrace, where the others mingle. All people I know, or know of. Pat Roche, whom I competed against at horse shows; her husband, Jeff, who has some connection to Palm Beach; Hickey Sumers, who works at *Glamour*. Altogether, a party of eight. Still missing one.

Seven-fifteen when he finally shows up, an apology muttered to Charley. His eyes catch mine, then he glances at Hickey, who looks like she's ready to purr. He's taller than I remember from the train, but still that odd magnetic sunlight blown around. I watch as the others move toward him. He doesn't look my way again until later, when he backs up and, by accident, steps on my heel.

"Sorry," he says.

"Oh, I'm fine."

"Miss Bouvier."

"Congressman."

"We've met before?"

I feel the air tighten. "Yes."

"Remind me."

"On the *Marylander*, maybe?"

"You were heading back to school. Vassar, was it?"

I feel a quiet thrill. He knows, and this is a bit of a game. "Yes, Vassar."

"I remember, you were reading."

"Jackie's a tremendous reader," Charley says. He and Martha have appeared and we're the four points of a diamond—Charley, Martha, Kennedy, me.

"And now she's leaving us for Europe," Martha says. "She's won the Prix de Paris."

"Actually, no," I say. "Those are separate. I'm going to Europe for the summer with my sister, Lee. The Prix de Paris hasn't yet been announced."

"What do you get if you win?" Kennedy says. I can tell by how he asks: He likes to win.

"A job at *Vogue*," I say. "I'd start in the fall, six months in New York, then six in Paris."

"She's being humble," says Charley. "They've practically offered it to you, Jackie."

I feel heat in my face and force a smile, the best I'm able to manage right then.

"I'm afraid I dealt my chances a blow in one of the essays. They asked for a self-description, and I might have been too honest."

"What on earth did you say?" Martha asks.

I smile at Jack. "I explained that one of my worst faults is that I get very enthusiastic over something at first, then tire of it halfway through."

An awkward silence, then Kennedy laughs—a free, bold laugh. Poor Martha, poor Charley—they are good and earnest and kind. Standing there like a pair of hard-boiled eggs with perfect smiles drawn on their round faces, and Jack Kennedy is just looking at me, his eyes still laughing. One hand fiddles at the pocket of his baggy sports coat.

"How many essays did you say you wrote for this thing?" he says.

"I didn't say. But there were eight. Short."

"That's a few more than a few. Eight essays to win a prize you're not sure you want?"

"It's like foxhunting," I say. "You don't really want to kill the fox, but it's satisfying to know you can bring down what you're after."

He laughs again.

"You like France?" he says. "On the train, I remember, you were reading a book on French art." He pronounces it with a heavy Boston accent. *Aht.*

"Malraux," I say. "I'm quite smitten with André Malraux."

"Why?"

"His first job was in the antiquarian book trade. He wrote the article that brought Faulkner to the Nobel committee. He won the Prix Goncourt, then spent the prize money scouring Arabia for the lost city of the Queen of Sheba."

"A French Lawrence."

"And he admired Lawrence, unlike most of the French."

"Who still blame Lawrence for the breakdown of French imperial power in Syria."

"Exactly. Malraux was no false hero."

This stops him for a moment, like the words sink in deeper than I intend. I remember then what I'd heard about his older brother, Joe Kennedy. How Joe was the one destined for politics. He was a Navy pilot, killed in action. His plane blown up over the English Channel.

It chills me for a moment. It's sudden and violent, that kind of loss; I soften toward him.

Martha and Charley are talking to other guests now.

"Do you read French?" Kennedy says.

I tell him that when I was a child, my mother used to make us speak French at dinner. We'd play a game with matches. Each of us started with ten. If you said a word in English, you'd throw a match away. Whoever still had a match at the end won.

"Did you usually win?" he asks.

I always won. I don't tell him this. I don't have to. He knew before he asked.

"My mother played French records to try to teach us French," he says.

"Did it work?"

"What do you think?"

"Do you always answer a question with a question, Congress-man?"

Once, on an elementary school report card, my teacher wrote: *Jacqueline is a darling child, the prettiest little girl, very clever, very artistic, and full of the devil.*

Be more ladylike, my mother always told me. Less witty. Less know-it-all. Less. Make a man feel he's smarter than you. Men don't like it the other way around.

For the rest of that night, I take more care. I lob questions to Jack Kennedy and the other men about Joe McCarthy's Un-American Activities Committee, the Rosenberg case, and Presi-dent Truman's recent dismissal of General MacArthur. *What is your view? Oh, how brilliant! I would never have seen it that way.*

Jack Kennedy seems to know all sorts of trivia about every person in the room. He asks Pat Roche about her uncle who sits on the Atomic Energy Commission. He asks Jeff about a mutual friend from Palm Beach. He is politicking, almost like he can't help it.

At the same time, he seems oddly nervous, constantly touch-ing the pocket of his sports coat or pushing back his hair. The hem of his pants hovers above his ankles. He's at once detached and weirdly self-conscious. He doesn't rest on one person or topic for long. He seems easily bored. His sense of humor re-minds me of my father's.

I sip my drink. The ice cubes, softened, clink against the glass.

This time of year—spring—when I was a child, we'd pack up the apartment in New York and move to Lasata, my grandparents' house in East Hampton—stables for the horses, brass names on the stalls, the tennis court, a grape arbor. My grandmother's gar-den wound through the boxwoods. You'd turn a corner and come upon a statue or a sudden stretch of daisies and bachelor but-tons. My grandmother would glide through the garden rows in her long dress and sun hat, a basket over her arm with her spade and shears. She'd name the types of roses for me, their English names, Latin names, while my grandfather, in his high collar and brown tweed jacket, roared down the gravel driveway, heading to town in his old red Nash convertible. I'd glimpse him as he whooshed by, his mustache waxed to unyielding points. He kept his hearing aid off as he drove; he loved to feel the vibration of the floorboards and how the wheels took the ruts in the road. I read poetry with him in the afternoons when I came home from swimming at the Maidstone Club. Once, he came to see me ride in a show at Madison Square Garden. He jumped up and down in the stands, yelling at the horse, cheering me on. His nickname was "The Major," and when he died, the loss left cracks through my heart.

I turn my wrist, quietly check my watch. After 8:00. Soon Martha will corral us inside for casserole—chicken and peas, perhaps—pressed napkins and wedding china. I'll make it through dinner, then leave directly after. Plead a headache. I don't like being set up with Jack Kennedy, I've decided. I appreciate his intelligence, of course, and sense of humor, but there's something about the way he looks at me, like he thinks he can just peel me open. I don't like the flush of heat in my face, that sense of my skin alive. It's how he looks at every woman, and I don't like that.

"Have you read the new Faulkner?"

I glance around. Hickey is leaning in to whisper something to Loretta.

"Jackie?"

"What?"

And he is there, that amused look again, like it's all a game and would I like to play? I feel my pulse race.

"Have you read the new Faulkner?" he says again.

"On my nightstand, I think. A bit down the stack."

"After?"

"I'm reading a first novel now. *Lie Down in Darkness.*"

"I saw that review. Who's the author?"

"William Styron."

"That was it."

His hand rakes the flop of hair from his face, and he's just looking at me like he's waiting for me to say more, and I'm look-

ing back at him, waiting for another question, because I've completely fallen out of the conversation, and now there are
others—Charley, Pat—watching the two of us to see where this
will go and how it might end. No one says a word. Just a funny
starched silence.

"Shall we head in for dinner?" Martha says brightly.

"Yes," someone answers. Beyond the French doors in the new
night, the patio lights bounce down, striking off the stone terrace, as the clock inside chimes the quarter hour, and Jack Kennedy is just standing there, looking at me, still waiting, that little
smile. Six feet of casual stardust.

. . .

"What was he like?" Lee asks the next morning at breakfast.

"More awkward than I expected," I say. "In need of a haircut
and a square meal."

"Rich," my mother says, drinking her orange juice. "Irish, and
something of a Lothario."

"Lothario was Spanish," I say.

"And your father hates his father."

"Which hardly matters." I reach for a piece of toast. "I have no
plans to see him again."

My sister glances at me, that slightly wicked look so altogether
Lee, her face with its delicate bones and structured beauty—the
kind of beauty that feels almost irretrievable, autocratic, because
as a woman you're told it's precisely the type of beauty you're
supposed to want and be.

The phone rings. My mother leaves the room to answer it.

Lee sets her coffee cup down.

"Come on, Jacks," she says. "Tell me. What was he really
like?"

The reception room at *Vogue*. High ceilings, tall windows, a shiny black floor. Large potted plants mixed in with white wicker furniture. Elegantly coiffed women drift by, carrying notebooks and clipboards. Two young secretaries, slim and graceful, sit behind equally graceful Chippendale desks, kitty-corner to one another. One of them hands me an employment form. I sit down on one of the sofas.

- Permanent address?

I write my mother's and Hughdie's address at Merrywood in Virginia. *I am only the poor relation,* I could scribble in the margin. *Yes, we come from once-upon-a-money.*

- Spouse? None
- Minor children? None
- Religion? Catholic
- Can you type? Yes
- Take shorthand? No
- Do you own a house? No
- Are you communist? No
- Have you ever joined a group plotting to overthrow the government? Not today

I sign the bottom of the form, hand it back, and return to the sofa to wait.

The managing editor, Carol Phillips, comes out.

"We're so happy to have you on board, Jackie," she says. "Your writing's exceptional. We all agreed. I particularly love the piece about your grandfather, the violets with the rain, the swish of traffic outside. You brought us right into that room."

She leads me through a maze of offices. I meet the personnel director of Condé Nast, then the art director, who's laying out portraits by Irving Penn for the July issue.

"I love Penn's work," I say, looking over the photographs.

"Any in particular?" Carol asks.

"His *Twelve Beauties*. His still life with the ace of hearts and the black chess piece knight. His Marlene Dietrich." I smile. Who wouldn't love Irving Penn's Dietrich?

Laid out on the worktable are portraits Penn made of a baker, a fishmonger, lorry washers.

"It'll be called *Small Trades*," the art director says.

Yes, I think. The people we don't see. There's a portrait of a young Black man in an oilcloth hat with a cart and a hand-chalked sign: HOT CHESTNUTS GOOD FOR THE BRAIN TRY A BAG.

Kennedy would love this.

It startles me. Why would he be there, in my thoughts?

I turn to Carol. "I'm just so thrilled," I say. "I wish September were tomorrow."

I take a taxi to my father's apartment on East 74th. The doorman lets me in. It's after noon. My father is sprawled sound asleep in navy boxers on the living room couch. A small card table propped open, a plate with a sandwich and a knocked-over glass that's rolled to the edge. I sit down beside him and stroke his face. His hair is wild, a stiff disarray with leftover oil and God knows what else.

"Daddy, wake up," I say. "I'm here."

He rolls toward me, his eyes bloodshot, that doomed movie-star swagger.

"Don't you have an interview?" he murmurs.

"I already went."

"My best girl," he says. "I'll get dressed and be there soon."

We go to brunch at Schrafft's.

"So my Jacks will be back in New York," he says over eggs Benedict and grits. "Which means she'll be with me."

I smile and pick through a side of creamed spinach. He is aging. I can see it in his face—heavy lines around his eyes, deeper creases on his cheeks. I don't have the heart to tell him how the *Vogue* office, that high-ceilinged, airless space, unsettled me, everything so perfect and neat, the Chippendale desks, wicker couches, and stylized women.

"Fashion has always been more Lee's world than mine," I say.

"You can bend any world to yours," my father says. "They've offered the job, right?"

"Yes."

"And you accepted?"

"I did."

He slices his knife through his poached egg; the yolk runs into the hollandaise.

When Lee and I were children, after our parents divorced, our father came for us every Saturday in his sharp black Mercury, the top down. He'd keep his fist on the horn until our mother yelled down at him and we skipped out. There were carriage rides through Central Park and extra scoops of ice cream. Urbane, impeccably dressed, roguish. Autograph seekers would mistake him for Clark Gable. *It's the part in your hair, Daddy,* I'd tease him. *Arrow-straight. Just like you.* That made him roar. He taught us how to flirt. He loved parties and racetracks and girls. An unspectacular athlete and gambler, he sunbathed in his apartment window to keep up his tan. He told us we should not only work hard but be the best. *And by the way,* he'd add, *don't forget: All men are rats.*

"Johnny Husted almost proposed," I say. My father's spoon stops en route to his mouth.

"Almost?"

"He was fishing."

"But you didn't bite."

"No."

"That's my girl." He raises his Bloody Mary to me, then drains it. "Is Johnny the one in New York?"

"Yes."

"Why not, then? Play hard to get, then say yes. You have my blessing, as long as you'll be in New York." He smiles at me, his dark eyes shining. "Another drink?"

"No."

"You've only had one."

"I still have half a glass left."

"There's a lot to celebrate." He flags the waiter. "When do you and Lee leave for Europe?"

"The week after next."

"Your plans for the crossing?"

"Third class on the *Queen Elizabeth*."

"Your stepfather can't spring for first?"

"We'll ignore the signs and infiltrate."

He makes a face. I steer the conversation away from the subject of money. "We'll dock at Southampton, then go to the Savoy. I'll let Lee have two or three days of dinner dances in London, then I want to buy a little car, a Hillman Minx if I can find one. We'll drive it all over England and onto the boat train to Paris."

"Because my girl loves her France."

"Your Bouvier France."

"Exactly." He scoops up a spoonful of grits.

"I want Lee to fall in love with Paris," I say. "I'm going to take her to all my old haunts." Dancing at L'Elephant Blanc in Montparnasse, visiting the Luxembourg Gardens and the portrait of my beloved *salonista* Madame Récamier at the Louvre.

"Don't forget the Kentucky Club," my father says.

Dark and smoky, even by day, jazz blaring.

"That's right," I say. "Lee's first existentialist nightclub."

My father pauses for a moment, then, "You love Paris, don't you?"

How to explain it? When I lived there for my junior year abroad, it was like living two lives. The city had been shattered by the war. Coffee and sugar were still rationed. Heat was scarce. We could only take one bath a week. I studied bundled up in a coat and gloves. That winter, I boarded with a comtesse who'd been in the Resistance; her husband had died in a labor camp. I'd fly from her apartment in the 16th arrondissement to my classes at Reid Hall. After class, I'd meet my friends at the little café on Rue de l'École. The world had begun to roar back. Jazz spilling from open windows. Fierce debates about postwar politics and the role of philosophy and art. We went to plays in basement theaters and took weekend trips to the south of France on third-class trains. There were free hours in the afternoons when I sat in the Jardin des Tuileries painting copies of the impressionists—Degas, Monet, Manet—that I'd invariably tear up. There were long spring evenings when the daylight just lasted and I walked through the city, that sense of my mind touched by the fire I so often feel in a foreign place—unbound, no family, no social circle with its demands, just a self alone in the world. I'd walk for hours on those evenings, looking down alleyways and narrow streets like I could take a turn down one and step through a doorway into an entirely new life.

"Yes, I love Paris," I tell my father.

"Don't love it so much you don't come back," he says. "Will you take Lee to Spain?"

"Pamplona."

He dusts his lips with a napkin. "The running of the bulls."

"Because there's no book I love more than *The Sun Also Rises*. And nobody lives their life all the way up, except you, Daddy, and the bullfighters."

He laughs. He calls for the check, flirts with the waitress, then gives her a tip.

"Or should we have one more drink?" he says.

"No more drinks."

"See, Jacks, if you're in my city, how easy it will be to keep me in line. What time is your train?"

"I have two hours."

"Let's walk in the park."

"I'd love that."

He touches his mustache, brushing some invisible thing from one end. "When you and your sister are gone," he says, "be sure to write to your mother."

"I know. Or she'll imagine me dead."

"Or married to an Italian."

He laughs at his own joke. There's often a joke at my mother's expense tucked in. He excuses himself to go to the "the gents'." I watch him thread among the tables, the graceful stroll, the light easy on his shoulders; he pauses every so often to greet someone, exchange a few words. I play with the lines of a made-up poem in my head. Lee and I have done it since we were children. I'd start with a line, she'd add one, we'd go back and forth. Sometimes I made little drawings to go along with them. My father has stopped at a table to talk to a couple. His hand rests for a moment on the wife's shoulder—always the actor, always the player—a brief gallant wave, then he's off again. He passes the bar, takes a right turn, and disappears.

Oh, we're not at all what you think we are
We've traveler's checks and a little car

When I lived in France for that college year abroad, my friend Paul de Ganay took me to parties at the home of Louise de Vilmorin, who was once engaged to Antoine de Saint-Exupéry. In her drawing room, silk coverings sheathed the walls. There were banquettes under each window, long ebony tables, and malachite elephants. The conversation was smart and quick, with currents of French and English, and extraordinary guests. Rita Hayworth, Orson Welles, French filmmaker Jean Cocteau.

One night, Paul introduced me to a woman named Pamela Churchill. A horsewoman. We were talking about the shows at Olympia and Bath when she suddenly stopped.

"Did Paul say you live near Washington?" Pamela asked. "You must know the Kennedys."

"Of them," I said.

"Kick was my best friend. She died, I'm sure you heard, in a terrible plane wreck. They went into a dive in the Cévennes Mountains. Kick had such life. Everyone loved her."

I nodded. I hadn't actually heard this.

"And her brother," Pamela continued. "Not the oldest who was killed in the war but the next one. Jack. A congressman now. He came to visit Kick once. We all piled into her old station wagon and drove to Ireland to find the original Kennedys. He called me in London one night and said, 'I think I need a doctor.' I brought him to Lord Beaverbrook's doctor, the best I know. Jack was ill for days, you can't imagine how ill, and I sat by his hospital bed as the life just drifted in and out of him. The doctor said it was something in his constitution and he might not live three years."

"I don't know Jack Kennedy," I told Pamela Churchill that night, which was only partly true. By then I'd met him on the train. I decided that didn't count. I didn't want to go into it. There was something about him even then that got under my skin, which I did not have language for.

My father is on his way back. He stops to chat up one of the waitresses. The prettiest one, I'll tell Lee later, and we'll laugh about that and roll our eyes—*So Black Jack*—but it will remind us both of those harder, more ruined spaces in our childhood we don't like to dwell on.

Oh, we're not at all what we seem to be . . .
No one could be wronger, much wronger than he

I stand up; the air in the room feels gauzy, strange, like the reasonable world has begun to dissolve in the heat of the midafternoon.

"Ready, my best girl?"

"Yes," I say. He takes my arm, and we walk outside into brilliant city sunlight. We cross the avenue, heading north to the park. When he realizes he's out of cigarettes, I offer him one of mine.

"Too light for me, sweet Jacks. I'll go buy a pack. Wait for me here. I'll just be a moment."

He'll take longer than he's promised. He always does. He'll get caught up with something or someone. Eventually he'll be back, unfazed that so much time has passed. There's a bench ahead in the shade. I sit down. A man on a bicycle rides by. A woman with a little dog on a leash—pug nose, bright eyes. A breeze moves through the trees. Dry leaves, leftover from last fall, chase one another in circles. It's something I've loved since I was young, how leaves seem to have a free unseen life beyond the pressure of the wind. Sitting on that bench alone in the warm shade, watching those dry leaves circle, I feel my mind settle.

Once, in Europe, I went with some friends to a painter's studio, in a courtyard off a sleepy street. While the others sat around smoking cigarettes, he made a portrait of me. Rough, abstract. I was long angles and fierce lines. I loved it.

I don't want that job at *Vogue*. I've known it, haven't I, for days. Maybe since that night at the Bartletts' when Jack Kennedy said, "Eight essays to win a prize you're not sure you want?" He said it with that smile.

I don't want the job at *Vogue* with its smart, hard, beautiful women and the men who cage them into glossy prints. And I don't want a predictable post-debutante life of charity teas and manicured nails. I don't want to stay stuck for long at Merrywood or even Hammersmith Farm—its soft-boiled heaven so easy to lose yourself to. I don't want to grow up to fall into bourbon old-fashioneds and half-nibbled codfish balls. I want to be the artist, not just the figure he drew into raw lines. I want to be the painter, the writer, the scholar. I want to devour books, knowledge, art. I want a life soaked in adventure. I want to never be bored.

I decide it then. How I'll frame it for my mother: *At* Vogue, *Mummy,* I'll say, *there are no boys. In that entire office building, not one eligible man.* That will terrify her. I'll stay in Washington for now, and while she shops for a suitable husband for Lee, I will get a job. Something with edge. A position at the CIA, or journalism. Maybe the *Times Herald.* It isn't the *Post,* but it's known for always having room for smart young women who want to learn on the job and are willing to work a lot for not much. It's a place to start. I can move into the bedroom that used to belong to my stepbrother Gore, with its view to the river. I can ride and read and write. I can keep dating Johnny Husted, who lives too far away to really matter. I can go to dances and parties when I feel like it and plead a deadline when I don't. I can start to map the rest of my life. Quietly. No one has to know. To everyone else, it will all look the same on the surface.

The leaves keep swirling. They blow over my feet. Leaf bits and dust wrap like hennaed lace around my ankles.

I don't want to be the dust or the leaf or the girl or the cog. I want to be the wind that makes them spin.

February 1952

A light flash of recognition when he sees me.

"You again," he says.

"And you."

"Must be fate."

"It's hard to be a bolt from the blue in this town."

He is holding a drink. With his free hand, he pushes that mop of hair off his forehead. I've heard he spends weekends in Palm Beach. He leaves on Friday, skips out of Congress at two, and flies south for golf, parties, and whatever else a man like Jack Kennedy does.

We're at John White's basement apartment on Dumbarton Ave. Ground-level windows set into the walls above our heads, dark panes wet with rain and streetlight. Floor-to-ceiling book-shelves. The room is filled with smoke and the snap of ice cubes melting in tumblers.

He looks flustered for a moment.

"Weren't you in Europe?" he says.

"I was, with my sister; now I'm back."

"You were moving somewhere—New York?"

"I didn't."

"I see. You didn't get that job?"

"I did."

"You didn't take it?"

"Do you know who else is coming?" I say.

"Bill Walton."

"I heard he isn't writing for *The New Republic* anymore."

"Not since he started painting."

"Do you paint, Congressman?"

He nods, an awkward look. "When I'm laid up," he says. "Or bored."

"Are you?"

"Am I?"

"Bored."

"Right now?" He smiles. "No."

I'm aware of my hands folded on my bag, the ring on the hand underneath.

"How do you know John White?" he says.

"I'm working at the *Times Herald* now."

"I heard that. You're one of Frank Waldrop's girls. You like it?"

"Being a reporter seems a ticket out into the world."

"You have a column, right?"

"You've read it?"

"Sure." But I can tell by how he says it that isn't quite true.

"You've skimmed it once or twice?"

He laughs. "White was their star reporter when my sister worked for Waldrop."

"Kathleen."

"Kick." His eyes shift when he says her name, the grief precise on his face. Then it's gone. "You must be pretty good if Waldrop gave you a column."

"The first day I showed up, he peered at me over the rim of his glasses, across that massive desk. I thought he was going to fire me before I started."

"And I bet when he hired you, he said, 'Now, don't come back in a week and tell me you're engaged.' That's what he said to Kick."

"Actually no. I got, 'Just remember, Miss Bouvier, your job is to say over and over, "Thank you very much," and draft an impeccably polite letter when I tell you to curse out a bastard.'"

"That's a good Waldrop," he says. "So John White still hangs around the paper?"

"Every few days on his way to the State Department, he'll drop by to sit on the edge of my desk, those wild tattoos snaking out of his shirtsleeves."

"Make it hard to type?"

I smile. "We go for lunch once a week to the Hot Shoppe and gossip. I love his stories. None about you, Congressman. At least that I can remember."

A pause, then he says, "I didn't expect you'd have interest in stories about me."

It was John White who told me how Jack Kennedy once described a broken-down jeep in the war. *That fucking fucker's fucked.*

"He's that vulgar?" I'd said.

White just shrugged. "That's straight-up talk in the middle of a war."

It was also John White who told me the story of Jack and a blond Danish reporter, a former Miss Denmark nicknamed Inga Binga. Inga Arvad was Kick's roommate, and they were a foursome—Kick and John White, Jack and Inga. Jack was working for Naval Intelligence at the time, and Inga was head over heels for him, but she was married. What's more, she'd known Goebbels and Göring and had once been invited by Hitler to sit in his private box at the Olympic Games.

"Heavens," I said, "how did it end?" And John White told me that when a photo of Inga with Hitler surfaced at the FBI, Joe stepped in and got Jack transferred to a desk job in South Carolina. Lovely Inga was heartbroken. She got a divorce, tossed herself at Hollywood, and married a millionaire cowboy.

"I think we should keep up the pretense," Jack Kennedy is saying now.

"Of?"

"Meeting again for the first time."

To keep me a novelty. New.

John White is at my elbow. He takes my glass of water and hands me a glass of wine. "I'm sure it's not the best you've had, Jackie, but it's the best I've got." He looks at Jack. "Whatever you're angling for, pal, you missed your chance. She's fallen into the sad trap of a diamond ring. Yale fellow, right, Jackie? Works on Wall Street?"

"Johnny Husted."

"I'm entirely thrown over," White says.

"Well, congratulations," Kennedy says. "So how long will you keep working at the paper?"

"What's that supposed to mean?"

"Won't you quit now that you're engaged?"

"Why would I?"

"Most girls would."

"I like journalism. Just because a woman chooses to marry doesn't mean she has to hang her life up on a coat hook. Weren't you a journalist once, Congressman?"

"It was fun. But I didn't have the leverage I wanted. In politics, I can get things done."

"You like history."

"I do."

"News today is tomorrow's history. You know what words can do."

"Look how well I've taught her," White says.

I'm annoyed with them both for their presumption. Kennedy is looking at me, though, a raw electric light in his eyes. I just stare back. There's no reason, anymore, to be discreet. I can do what I want. Say what I want. Be as scathing as I want. I'm marrying someone else. Oddly, that was my first thought when Johnny Husted offered me his mother's ring at the Carlyle: It was out of the blue and exactly what I swore I didn't want, but it suddenly occurred to me that if the marriage question was neatly settled, to a perfectly respectable catch, I might not be more trapped but free.

Once, at a party in Newport, there was a boy I flirted with. He was brutally handsome and knew it. I sat next to him on a long sofa set between two potted ferns. He lit a cigarette for me. I listened and oohed and aahed after every stupendously brilliant and arrogant thing he said, and when he finally shut his mouth, I gave a little swooning sigh and went to stub my cigarette out, just brushing his hand with the lit end. He jumped, that boy, spilling his drink right down the face of his white shirt. I pretended it was a terrible accident.

A part of me now wants to tell Jack Kennedy this, to see how he'd react, what he'll say, if he'll frown or, more likely, get that little smile. I like that smile. More than I want to.

"So what do you do," he asks, "when you're not making up questions for the paper about Chaucer and Marilyn Monroe?"

"I make little drawings to go with my questions."

"Cartoons?"

"Sometimes."

"What have you got for the coming week?"

"Do you think a wife should let her husband think he's smarter than she is?"

"Never."

I wish you wouldn't smile at me like that, I want to say.

"Would you like to sit down?" he says.

Leather couches, drink rings and cigarette burns, a sizable hole on one arm patched with fabric tape. Bachelor couches. I set my drink on the low coffee table, move the ashtray closer, and rest my cigarette on the edge.

"I do like history," Kennedy says. "I always have. Mostly British."

"Not American?"

"I like reading about the Civil War." He smiles then. "And the Federalist Papers."

I laugh. "Oh, that's good. Why?"

"They were an argument for the Constitution, written when the country was up for grabs."

"Now, though, looking back, it doesn't seem like things could have unfolded any other way."

He looks at me. "That's right," he says. "So what else do you do for fun?"

"I ride."

"Horses? I'm allergic."

"Seriously?"

"Would you ask me to go riding if I weren't? Do you like the ocean?"

"I love the ocean. And I love to dance."

"I have a bad back."

"Would you ask me to go dancing if you didn't?"

He smiles. "Old football injuries are unforgiving."

"I imagine the war didn't improve things. It sounded dramatic—your boat rammed by a Japanese destroyer. You saved your men, were shipwrecked, then written up in *The New Yorker.*"

"John Hersey was kind in that piece." He looks a little embarrassed, though. I'm curious why. "So when's the big day?" he says.

"What day?"

"You're getting married. The wedding?"

"We've talked about June."

"That's right around the corner."

I glance at him. Something light and teasing in his voice.

When Johnny Husted proposed, I almost put him off. I explained I wasn't going to leave my job. I love my work. The interviews I get to do with random people in the street. I walk up to strangers and ask if I can photograph them. I ask them questions about topics in the news. I ask for their views on politics, the arts, their marriages and children. I weave snippets of their answers into my *Inquiring Camera Girl* column. There's life in that work I don't want to give up.

Jack Kennedy is just looking at me, like he's waiting for me to say something; the waiting sharpens the air. That look in his eyes throws me a bit. I don't want to talk about my engagement, or Johnny, or how, after we left the Carlyle on the night he proposed, with the huge ring on my left hand, Johnny assured me that of course I could keep working, at least until we had children. I don't want to talk about how that night the snow was falling on Madison Avenue, thick flakes whisked by the gusts, and Johnny kept a tight comforting grip on my arm like he was tucking me right into place. Johnny's a good man, all the right clubs, a terrific dancer; he wants to make me happy. I'm making a good choice, I keep reminding myself, a sensible choice that will be at once an anchor and freedom. "He is kind and safe and good, like Hughdie is to Mother," I told Lee. Lee laughed, "Johnny is far better-looking than Hughdie." A part of me wants to joke with Jack Kennedy about this. I have a feeling he'd laugh, and I like to make him laugh, but he has a more serious look on his face now, like he might be about to ask something more important, and the silence between us feels steep and unfinished.

Then John White is there, with Bill Walton and John's sister Patsy. I feel my face flush like they've caught us at something, when of course there is nothing, but I shift away from Kennedy toward the other end of the couch. Bill Walton sits down in the space between us.

"How are you, Billy Boy?" Kennedy says. They're friends. I like Bill Walton, very much. I met him at a dinner, where we learned we both knew Gore Vidal, my stepfather Hughdie's stepson from an earlier marriage. "We joke about all those steps," I told Bill Walton once. Originally from the Midwest, Bill is a journalist and an artist. Stunningly smart, kind, with a broad square-cut face, he's the sort of person I trust, though I don't know him well. Several weeks ago, at another party, we talked about how someday we'd go barhopping together in Provincetown.

"Say, Bill," Jack says now, "is the rumor of a new Hemingway book true?"

Gore has told me stories of Bill Walton and Hemingway, how they met during the war through photographer Robert Capa. Bill was working as a war correspondent for *Time*, training to parachute into Normandy. Hemingway tagged along. They were at the Battle of Hürtgen in 1944. Hemingway saved Walton's life, pushing him out of a truck they were driving moments before it was strafed. When France was liberated, they drank at the Ritz Bar in Paris. Walton watched Hemingway's marriage unravel, right down to the night the writer showed up at his wife's hotel room, naked, drunk, a bucket on his head, banging on her door with a mop. It seemed like such a big life, drawn in bold broad strokes and furious colors across a huge canvas. My father had a dimension of that in him, and a knack for the reckless.

The talk has shifted to the conflict in Indochina. I've dropped the thread. I watch Jack Kennedy. He listens, mostly. He has a curious way of asking questions but rarely offering his own view. His fingers move, touching his collar, pockets, hair, almost a nervous tic. The conversation swings back to lighter things; Bill Walton jokes that he quit his job at *The New Republic* for Lent to take up abstract expressionism because it seemed to be the language that made sense in a postwar world.

He has a kind of careless, distant radiance. That's how I'll describe Jack Kennedy to Lee.

He asks his questions, drawing stories and opinions out of everyone else until the air ripples and burns, and he just sits there, long legs stretched out, that boyish rugged awkwardness that seems like an act but maybe isn't.

He is alone, the way I am alone.

The thought startles me.

"So what are your plans as senator?" John White's sister is asking Jack now.

"I have to win first."

"He'll win," John White says. "People want some new fire to believe in."

"Some say the world will end in fire," Kennedy says. The others laugh politely.

"Some say in ice," I say. Robert Frost.

He looks at me, that smile again. "It's a good poem, isn't it. Jackie." A slight pause before he says my name, which sends a shiver through me and, for a moment, the air drops out of the room.

Later that evening, as I fish around in my bag for matches, John White comes up to me and holds his lighter out.

"You're extraordinary," he says, snapping the lighter closed, "but that game you're playing with Jack Kennedy is a game even you can't win."

"No game there I want," I say.

"Ah, Jackie, that's playing too well."

I exhale and glance toward the sofa, where Patsy and Bill Walton are still sitting, talking with Jack. He nods, listening, but his eyes are on me. When he sees me looking over, he smiles—that same look he gave me when I first came in, as if this is all some glorious joke we've colluded on.

Nearly midnight when I cross back over the Chain Bridge to my mother's house, heading slowly up the drive, the crunch of gravel under the tires, the house rising from the trees. I make scrambled eggs in the kitchen, eat them at the counter, and leave the pan to soak. I don't feel tired, but I climb the stairs to bed. On the landing, I nearly trip over the moonlight. Delirious, it rakes through the window and over the mute ground outside, the fields and hills, wavering pale bars of it falling across the sill to the floor, like the night has been ransacked, everything untethered, blown around.

. . .

"I'd love to talk," I say when John White swings by my desk at the paper. "But it will have to be another time. I'm late."

"Aw, come on," he says. "Let's see what questions you're taking out into the streets today."

"My notebook's already in my bag," I say, but he picks up an earlier draft on my desk and reads the first few questions aloud: "*Do you consider yourself normal? When did you discover that women are not the weaker sex? Are wives a luxury or a necessity?*"

He skims silently, a smile as he nears the end.

"*Do a candidate's looks influence your vote?*" he reads slowly. "And last but not at all least: *The Irish author Sean O'Faolain claims that the Irish are deficient in the art of love. Do you agree?*"

He sets the paper down.

"I notice a shift," he says.

I just look at him.

White shakes his head. "He dislikes being alone, Jackie. He surrounds himself with friends and family. He doesn't like to be around any one person for more than a few hours. Women are prey, but he does respect them in a certain way, if they're a certain type. It's double-edged. He's coming by my place again next Thursday."

"I have to leave now," I say. "I have to be at the Hill by eleven."

"Are you free Thursday?"

"No."

"He's understated, but don't let that fool you. And I told you once, he's ruthless when there's something he wants."

I point to the middle button on his tweed jacket. "That button's hanging by a thread, John. Pop it off before you lose it." I drop my pencils into the drawer, close it, then open it again and take out two.

"You like him," he says.

"I'm engaged, John."

"To a good catch who's too dull for a girl like you."

"That's an awful thing to say."

"You like Jack Kennedy."

"I appreciate that his mind never seems to let up."

"Like yours."

"We're nothing alike, John. If I was drawing a man like that, I'd draw a tiny body and an enormous head. I have to go."

"What about Thursday?"

"I am very busy Thursday."

"You are lying, Jackie Bouvier."

"*Honi soit qui mal y pense*," I say.

"What does that mean?"

"Shame on him who evil thinks."

I almost walk out the door without my camera. I smile at John White as I walk back to my desk, pick it up, then leave.

A long wolf whistle as I walk out of the building. Two boys from the fourth floor. The redheaded one and the one with the scrubbed prep school face. Heading up the stairwell, they lounge around the banister, watching me.

I don't go to John White's that Thursday. Johnny Husted is coming down from New York, a quick trip to D.C. We have dinner together. The next morning I drive him to the airport. A blinding rain. The windshield wipers sweep the world left to right to left, and as we drive, I tell him I think we should postpone the wedding. He asks if "postpone" is what I really mean. We reach the airport; I leave the car running. I get out to see him off. He pulls his collar up against the rain, sets his hat. "I'm sorry, Johnny," I say, slipping his mother's ring off my finger. I drop it into his pocket. "I'm so sorry."

"He wasn't good enough for you," my mother says when I tell her.

"Or rich enough for you?"

"He just wasn't enough." She looks at me over the rim of her teacup, the curved edge of china against her face. "This isn't about that skirt-chaser, is it?"

There's a photograph of my parents that someone took when they were still married. Black Jack leans against a fence, rakishly gorgeous as he was back then, in a summer-weight suit. He's holding hands with a woman who sits on the fence beside him, while my mother sits near them facing away—smartly dressed in her riding gear, a stoic turn in her face, pretending not to know what she knew.

"In a world of money and power, Jackie," my stepbrother Gore said once, "sex is something you do, like tennis."

We'd been talking about how badly, and publicly, our parents and stepparents behaved. I realized Gore was inviting me to see how wit might take the edge off pain.

"That may be true, Gore," I answered. "But it's quite a bit nicer for everyone if each point of the match isn't documented in *The New York Times*."

~

Spring 1952

Another May. Another dinner party at the Bartletts'. Peonies bursting from the centerpiece, conversations, laughter. Another warm spring evening spilling through the door propped open to the terrace.

Somehow, though, everything is different. I can feel it. The kaleidoscope has shifted a degree. The design is entirely new.

We're all at the dinner table. Charley Bartlett is asking for Jack's opinion on American involvement in Indochina, and I feel a rush of warmth as I listen to Jack talk in his easygoing way about the complexity of the conflict—how it's the French who best understand the politics of that region they occupied for so long. The United States, he contends, can learn by studying the challenges the French have faced. I just listen; I don't have to pretend, he's too interesting not to listen to—those unexpected turns of mind. And somehow simply listening isn't simple at all but throws the whole room off-kilter, the table and candlesticks, the faceless figures of the other guests, the bread plates and the soup bowls—the room is soaked in that casual magic. Light kicks the rim of a wineglass.

He glances up, a little look that, in that moment, is just for me.

You are a piece of eternity, I think. He leans across the asparagus then and asks if he can take me out next week, dancing at the Blue Room in the Shoreham Hotel.

Desire shreds time. Stuns it. A blink later, dinner is done, chairs pushed back, shaking hands and the after-every-dinner-party routine. *A lovely evening. Yes, let's do it again soon. Where are you spending the summer? Oh, fabulous. Thank you so much for coming. Thank you so much for having me.* A Tommy Dorsey record plays in the background and Martha Bartlett is squeezing my arm, everyone chatting and laughing and moving. I remember then what John White said about Jack Kennedy: *a game even you can't win.* I feel a little scowl on my face. I bite my lip to squelch it, then notice Jack watching me across a small free space, three or four others between us, two talking as much to him as to each other, but his eyes are on me, that puzzled look I've seen before when he's met some question he can't immediately solve. Then the moment is cut, the abstracted look gone, and he smiles—a kind of shy and awkward smile; light breaks across his face like a bolt of sunshine that knocks the room down, and there is no sound then, no music, no voices, no laughter, nothing else, no one else. Even the room is gone and there is only him, with me, in a space that belongs to us alone, that smile like some electric bit of loneliness he thinks I'll understand. And I do.

...

For most of that spring, it seems, he's up in Massachusetts campaigning for the Senate. He'll call out of the blue, coins tinkling through a pay phone, to tell me he's coming back into town. He'll invite me to a party or the movies—once a John Wayne Western (his choice), then an art film (mine). He is bored ten minutes in. He has to get up and walk around, he says, stretch his legs. In late May, I invite him last minute to a dance, and I'm surprised when he says yes. In June, we go to the new Gary Cooper movie, *High Noon,* with his brother Bobby and Bobby's wife, Ethel. They met skiing in Mont Tremblant. Then Ethel wrote her college thesis on Jack's book *Why England Slept,* which cemented her into the family.

After the movie, Jack invites me to Martin's for lunch. From his jacket pocket he pulls out a book. John Buchan, *Memory Hold-the-Door.*

"I brought it for you," he says.

A torn piece of paper marks a passage about a young soldier killed on the Somme. *He would destroy some piece of honest sentiment with a jest, and he had no respect for the sacred places of dull men.* I flip a few pages. Another underline. *He disliked emotion, not because he felt lightly, but because he felt deeply.*

"This is your copy," I say.

"You can keep it if you want." That little smile.

"Thank you."

"When I was thirteen," he says, "I was sick in the hospital for a month. Reading kept me sane. This book and others. My father came every afternoon."

"What about your mother?"

He shakes his head. "Always in some fashion house in Paris or on her knees in church." A bitterness in his voice. I can tell he feels ashamed he'd let me see it. He touches the edge of his cuff, folding it back, and I just want to soften his anxiousness.

"The first time I went to England was after the war," I say. "A few of us managed to get an invitation to Buckingham Palace, a garden party. I rounded up the other girls and we all went down the receiving line twice just to shake Churchill's hand."

He laughs.

"Churchill's always been fascinating to me," I say, rearranging my french fries. "Dark angel hurled from power, who maneuvered through failure after failure and rose again. It's a great story."

Jack tells me he was in London in September 1939 when his father was ambassador to Great Britain. The Germans had bombed Polish airfields and Navy ships in the Baltic. Jack sat in the gallery of Parliament when Churchill defended Britain's declaration of war.

"My father disagreed with Churchill completely," he says. "He thought America should keep to its side of the ocean. But I remember what Churchill said that day about how war, in its most noble sense, guards and restores liberty."

"Then you came home, wrote a book, and a few years later became a hero in the war your father didn't want."

He smiles. "I should have stuck with the writing." There are small cracks, I sometimes sense, in the things he tells me. He tries to always be easy, but the shine of his humor hides a sadness. I want to know what that is, that deeper, more vulnerable side. I want to dig past the brilliant surface to what lies underneath.

Leaving Martin's, he says, "So, hey, Fourth of July. Why don't you come to Hyannis Port?"

"On my way to Newport?"

"Come for the weekend. My mother will recite 'Paul Revere's Ride.'"

"Promise?"

As we walk by a Woolworths, he takes my arm and steers me in. "Come on."

"What are we doing?"

"I'm going to buy you some jewelry."

"You are not."

"Earrings? A bracelet? What is it girls like you like?"

"Anything but a ring."

He frowns and I laugh.

"You asked," I say.

He walks past the jewelry counter, the women's apparel with its bony mannequins, all the way to the photo booth at the back of the store. He digs into his pocket.

"Let me guess," I say. "No change?"

He pulls out a nickel, a dime, two quarters.

"That was my change from Martin's," I say.

He puts the coins in the slot, pulls me into the little booth, and draws the curtain closed, his hands on my waist; I'm half in his lap, the seat too narrow. I can tell he likes that I'm close and that it undoes me a bit to be so close. He likes pushing that edge. The light flashes, a countdown, red light blinking, red light, a long solid green.

"Keep still, Jackie. Smile."

His hand around my hip. I feel my body shift toward him. I

want him to touch me, his face near mine, I can smell his skin, his hair. We stare at that little green light, the tiny orb of lens beneath it. He draws me tighter against him as the machine rumbles, gearing up, a funny jolting sound. It goes still. He leaps up. The photo strip starts to thread out. He puts his body between it and me.

"Jack, let me see."

He takes the strip, holding it out of my reach.

"Too bad your eyes are closed."

"In all of them?"

"Yep. No—wait. They're open here, this last one, but it's not too good. You won't like it."

"Jack, let me see."

He smiles, the smile that says, *You want to see? Then come get it.* He starts down the aisle, heading toward the exit. He walks fast, his stride long. I run to catch up. When we reach the street, he shows me the strip.

"My eyes aren't closed. Those are nice. Really nice. Let me see."

He tucks them into his pocket. "You saw."

"Let me keep one."

"Nope, these are mine."

"It was my change from lunch."

We keep walking. That light electric current between us heightens. I can feel it, we both feel it; he takes my hand, his fingers braid loosely through mine. His index finger runs lightly through the center of my palm, intentional, sensual. I let my body brush against him as we walk.

We come to the corner where he will go right and I'll go left.

"I'll call you," he says.

I expect him to turn then and leave—that's what he usually does—but he doesn't.

"So the Fourth," he says. "Okay, Jackie?" He looks down at me. That face. Those eyes. He touches my cheek, a gentle quick gesture, and in that gentleness something new, incendiary.

July 1952

I don't fit in. I feel it the moment I close the car door behind me. Aware—too aware—of my frosted hair, sundress, the sandals with gold straps that wrap my calves. On the lawn, a squall of sun-tanned gods in tennis whites stop their football game to look at me. My fingers tighten on the weekend bag in my hand. Behind them, the rambling white clapboard house, trimmed hedges, a tennis court, a circular drive, and the sweep of a wraparound porch, the lawn giving way to the flat blue calm of the sea.

Jack is walking toward me, that ambling lanky walk; the others watch. Bobby, their brother Teddy, and the sisters, burnished faces and long legs. One stands with a hand on her hip. I met her once. Jean.

"Hey, Jackie," Jack says, "it's you."

My smile feels like cardboard.

Then his mother, Rose, is there, telling him to take my bag into the house and up to the sewing room. She steers me toward the front door, through the hall, the sunroom, and the living room with its recessed window seats, fireplaces, framed photographs, and miles of English chintz.

"The house was quite small at first," she says, a laryngeal scratch to her voice, "but we kept having children, kept adding on rooms, widening the windows and so forth."

Jack has come down; he shuffles behind us, restless, and his mother finally tells him to go out to play with the others since that's clearly what he wants to do.

"I left them short a man," he says.

His mother laughs.

"Come with me, Jackie," says Jack.

"I'll be out soon."

It's Bobby who meets me when I walk outside. A sinking pressure in my chest as I realize they expect me to play. Football. I try. I run where they tell me to run. I drop the ball twice. They bounce me around, team to team, position to position—it's like being swept in a tidal wave. Finally I claim a sore ankle. Only Bobby looks genuinely disappointed.

"I'll just take a short break," I say.

Sitting on the porch steps, I light a cigarette as they tumble over one another on the lawn in their white cartwheeling chaos, flashing sneakers, their rah-rah shouts and grass-stained knees.

Just watching them wore me out, I'll tell Lee later. I lean back into the step to feel the edge of the tread digging into the small of my back, grounding me. The louder they get, the more boisterous and competitive, the quieter I go inside.

"Come back in the game, Jackie," Bobby calls. Teddy grabs the football from him. Bobby knocks him in the chest. The screen door opens behind me. I turn.

"No, please don't get up," Joe Kennedy says, but I'm already on my feet. Here he is—the ambassador, the patriarch, the Judas of Wall Street. The man of legendary ambition who made a fortune selling shares on the eve of the stock-market crash. There's something about him I like, something easy and kind. His eyes dance behind the round wire-rim glasses. He wears golf clothes, the collar loose.

"You're the one Jack brought," he says.

"I drove, actually."

I smile and he smiles back. I sit down on the steps. He sits beside me.

"Did you enjoy your golf?" I ask.

"Damn hot." He looks out at the lawn. "Who's winning?"

"I couldn't begin to tell you." He seems surprised I'd be that frank. "I'd love to hear about the work you did in film," I say. "Jack's told me you have a cinema downstairs, where you screened your movies. Hollywood's a world apart, isn't it? Or is it? Tell me."

He smiles at me, like he knows I might be playing him a bit. But he likes that, as I expected he might, and I can see he's decided, perhaps then and there, that we'll be friends.

The rest of that day is a bustling hotel—other guests arrive, friends and cousins washing in from down the road, football to baseball to tennis to swim. Time slows in the late afternoon. I have an hour alone before dinner. I shut the door of the little guest room and lie down, chaos beading off me, the evening air through the window, the smell of rosewater and starched sheets erasing the staticky rush of the day. My eyes trace the design of wallpaper, a water stain near one eave, a line of dust missed on the bureau. A spider dangles off a silken thread.

There was a night when Lee and I were children. It was winter. I must have been about ten. Our parents were still married. We lived in the apartment on Park Avenue. They'd been fighting all fall, doors slammed, vases thrown. I was learning to read their crazy before it struck and learning to pack my own spiky grief away. That winter, for an interim, things had settled. They seemed almost in love again, in a way that might hold. I wanted to trust that hope nudging in. One night, they were going out to hear Eddy Duchin play at the Central Park Casino, and before they left, my mother came in to kiss me good night. Her fur brushed my face, the scent of perfume, the shimmer of her dress as she swept out into the hall where my father waited. He said something that made her laugh. They were happy, I realized. I remember wanting so desperately for that happiness to last.

I dress carefully for dinner. I walk downstairs as the clock chimes seven. The rest of them are already there. They look up from their drinks, an abrupt silence. They're all in khakis and chino shorts, loafers and slip-ons, twin sets, white oxford shirts.

Jack must see it in my face, the sudden embarrassment; I'm so overdressed. He crosses the room. "Hey, Jackie," he says gently. "You look so nice. Where do you think you're going?" I look at him sharply, but he's smiling, teasing, that conspiratorial smile meant just for me. I laugh then and he takes my hand, and that sharp sense of not fitting in, that hot tiny spark of shame, is brushed away.

Sixteen for dinner that night. Even before the basket of rolls makes one lap around the table, the wild tournament has started, the jokes and comebacks, the stories, the lore. They interrupt, gang up, competing for air and attention—their father's, each other's. Who can top whom. Who can be the quickest, wittiest, fiercest, loudest, and most essentially first.

They talk about the latest movies, the newest books. *What about the new Inge play,* Picnic, *at the Music Box? Everyone's mad about it, haven't you heard?* As the meal continues, more bickering flares. Eunice is still angry about a line call Jean made during tennis, and Teddy and Bobby start arguing: *Who's hoarding the green beans? Save some iced tea for the rest of us, will you?* It's a kind of hazing—whispered glances, barbs exchanged, a bizarre, tenacious bond built as much on loss as love. I've heard pieces— the brain-damaged sister, Rosemary, whom no one ever mentions, the sister Kick whom Jack adored, and Joe, Jr., the golden one, who bore the mantle until his plane was blown apart.

Bobby and Teddy are into it now, over the potato salad. Teddy's mad, red in the face, accusing his older brother of taking more than his share. The whole thing feels so foolish I'm sure it's an act, until Jack intercedes, offering Teddy his potato salad.

"I haven't touched it, really, Teddy." Jack glances at me, nervous. His mouth, I've learned, gives him away. It startles me that he's nervous. Why? Is he afraid—this dawns on me slowly—that I might decide that while they're exceptionally rich and accomplished, they're too Irish, too classless, brash, new?

They're talking now about sailboats and racing. Morton Downey, an old crony of Joe's, leans across the table. "Have you met Jack's best girl?"

"Excuse me," I say.

"The woman he'll always love above any other."

I glance at Jack, then Joe. A joke, I see. They all know the punch line. They're waiting to see how I do.

"Having met Jack's mother and sisters," I say, "I'd love to meet any other woman he holds in esteem."

"*She's* a boat," says Teddy, in a sulk, a trace of something spilled near his breast pocket. Poor Teddy. Bedraggled loser of potato salad. But the rest are borne off on tales of the *Victura*.

"Latin," Jean says. "'About to conquer.'"

It can also mean "to live," I almost say.

Rose and Joe gave Jack the twenty-five-foot Wianno when he turned fifteen. Four years later he sailed it in the Nantucket Sound Star Class Championship and won. It was on the *Victura* that Jack taught Bobby to sail, Bobby taught Teddy, and so on.

"Then you won the East Coast Collegiate," Ethel pipes in.

"No, that was Joe," Jack says.

A tick in the air before the talk moves on.

You don't get past it, do you? That kind of childhood loss. You don't ever really leave it behind.

"A penny for your thoughts," Jack says, his voice near my shoulder.

"But, Jack," I say, "then they wouldn't be mine."

The room falls silent. The ambassador laughs. "Now, there's a girl who belongs at my table."

The next morning, we walk the beach. Thick fog, no wind, just the sound and the dank salt smell of the sea rolling toward us out of the cool white air.

"I love this," I say. "The sea, the fog. How the lines of things smudge out. We could be anywhere."

"Well done at dinner last night. You won my father."

"I wasn't trying to."

"And that's what's nice." A bend in his voice as he says it; I feel something deeper in him shift toward me.

Coming back into the house, we pass the little bedroom on the first floor.

"Can we go in?" I ask. "Your mother told me when you were little, this room was yours."

A child's quilt on the bed, bookshelves, a bureau. I pick up a photograph.

"That's me with my dog Dunker. In the Netherlands."

"You aren't allergic to dogs in the Netherlands?"

"Always allergic, but I'll always have dogs. My friend Lem took that picture. Upstairs, there's another from that same trip. Lem and me at The Hague. I look better in the other one."

I laugh. His vanity surprises me.

Next to Jack with the dog is an older framed photo, faded by the sun. A close-up of his face, the water abstracted behind him, dusty light. There's a focused stillness in his eyes. What was he seeing in that moment? Thinking, dreaming, feeling? I want to ask.

"When was this taken, Jack? Do you remember?"

"No."

He sits on the bed as I kneel by the small bookshelf and run my fingers along the spines. Buchan, Stevenson, Churchill. "Where are your poets?"

"Tennyson's there. Homer and Byron."

"Byron, man of loneliness, brooding mystery. What was that epithet? *The mad, bad, dangerous to know.* Do you think he was?"

"Not as bad as they made him out to be."

"Thirty-six when he died," I say.

"Then I've got one more year." He laughs.

"Byron wasn't one to commit, was he?" I say.

"Why do women always want to pin a man down?"

I feel a heat in my face. "Not all women. Most men are as dull as watching paint dry. Five minutes in, there's nothing left to discover, and a woman has to just stand there nodding, smiling, bored out of her mind."

"Are you bored, Jackie?"

"With you?"

A hesitation in his smile then, like part of him wishes he hadn't asked.

"No," I say. I glance back at the bookshelf. "There's Tenny-son."

"That was Kick's."

The cover's worn, spine frayed. "She loved this one."

"Yes," he says.

I look at him then, and his eyes are on my face, no game in them for once, just an openness I've seen only a few times be-fore, like he might let me in, or even want to.

"When I was growing up," I say, "on Wednesdays after danc-ing class, I went to visit my grandfather Bouvier. I had to bring a memorized poem every time I went. Tennyson's "Ulysses" was one he insisted I learn by heart."

"Recite it," he says. "I want to know what you've learned by heart." He lies back on the bed, his legs dangling off, head propped on the pillow, looking at me, and the expression on his face is one I will always remember—complicated, trenchant, with a naked hunger I feel move through me.

A bell rings. Silence. It rings again.

"That's the lunch bell," he says. "It's how she rounds us up."

"Are we going to go?"

"I think we'll be late. Pick a book. I want you to read aloud to me."

"You should read to me," I say. I pull *The Iliad* from the shelf.

"Why that?" he says.

Because Homer's Troy is the kind of dream that alters us, I could say. *That moves and inspires us. Because it's a vast and tragic myth we can't quite cage—a story of love, rage, devastating loss, which, at its most intimate, is also a form of desire.*

The answer I give is far simpler.

"It's a story I love," I say.

. . .

That night after dinner, we borrow Morton Downey's car to drive to a party in Osterville. A 1950 Plymouth, two-door, light blue.

I recognize the landmarks for a while, the little village, the main street leading through it. We turn onto another road, then another, and it's different. Still the same landscape—shingled houses, beach plum, scrub oak—but at the same time, a place I haven't been.

Earlier that afternoon, we all went swimming. I walked up to the house before the others, changed my clothes, towel-dried my hair, and came downstairs.

"Good swim?" Joe said, sitting down with me in one of the porch chairs.

"I love to swim."

"How far did you go?"

"The second buoy and back."

"You like open ocean."

"Any ocean."

He smiled. Jack and the others were coming up from the shore. I could see them—a laughing, galloping brood.

"And you also like when people underestimate you, don't you, Jackie?"

"Not at all, Mr. Kennedy. Why on earth would you say a thing like that?"

"You want some music?" Jack asks now. He fiddles with the car radio.

"That song, please," I say. "The one you just flipped by, about angels dining at the Ritz." I tuck my legs underneath me. I like the feeling of being away from the house and the chaos, alone with him, heading somewhere, anywhere.

"I think I missed the turn," he says. A car passes, going the opposite way. Headlamps sweep our car, his face. He is beautiful. Not a word a woman would usually use to describe a man. And yet.

When I lived in Paris for that one year, there were late-spring evenings when the light just lasted. I'd leave the Sorbonne and walk the narrow streets, looking into windows to catch fragments of lives playing out there. I'd walk the Seine, the quays and bridges, toward midnight as the sun kept setting in that strange extended day, and I had the sense that if I could just keep walking, I'd outwalk the light, disappear. I want the same thing now, only with him. To just keep driving, with no ending point or destination. Just to stay with him, moving, in this night car.

"Quiet again," he says. That little smile, without looking at me. Another turn in the road. "Here we are."

The clouds are bone-gold shapes passing near the moon. They seem to rush, gauzy, weirdly lit. We head toward the open tent set by the clubhouse; music drifts out, the clink of glasses, laughter. Lanterns are strung along the roof of the tent and woven up the halyards of the boats moored offshore. Paper-bag luminaria mark a path from the tent to the clubhouse stairs.

He drops my hand as a man steps out of the crowd toward us. His cousin Joey.

"Where've you been, Jack?"

We are swept into the tent, then apart, knots of people milling through the space. I recognize some from Virginia and New York. Jack moves away, shaking hands, working the crowd. Here is the younger Hatton, pushing his way through to see me, to say hello. And Lila, whom I know from the horse shows, has my arm and is turning me toward a pretty brunette with a pixie cut, who apparently knows Lee and is asking how Lee is and is it true she's working for Diana Vreeland at *Harper's Bazaar?*

"Right now she's in Rome," I say, "with her new English beau, Michael Canfield."

"How serious is it?"

"Well, nothing's really serious until it is."

Jack is a short distance away, with a fellow in a gray sports coat. Jack is talking to him but looking at me, the way he does, the way I love, with that little fixed look. His eyes pass over my body, slow, more intentional. I feel my flesh burn.

"Jackie—" Lila's saying.

A sudden boom as the sky breaks apart, fireworks; an "Oooohhh" erupts from the crowd; we move in a wave toward the dark at the edge of the tent as raw chains of color and light trail down. Rafts of aftersmoke.

He finds me, his mouth near my cheek. "Are you okay?" he says.

"Yes." I want him near me. I want this.

A Roman candle shoots up, a rising hiss on the ascent. I feel the length of his arm against mine, the touch warm, light.

By the time the fireworks end, a low fog has rolled in, but the high night sky, still, is bright as water. The band starts up, the crowd regathers. A few cars pull away, headlamps stripe the lawn. Jack catches my eye, nods his head to go. We walk in silence toward the car. He takes my hand. The stars are wayward, spinning out there above the fog. I feel like we're on the edge of that night.

In the car, his hand moves over the shift onto my thigh. In the light off the dash, I see him smile; I can feel what it does to me— that smile, his touch—driving fast down that blue night road. We are less than a mile from the house when he pulls off into the grass and kills the lights.

"Come here," he says. He holds my face in his hands as he kisses me, his mouth on mine, that electric touch. I feel my skin rise, his fingers drawing the edge of my blouse open.

August 1952

He doesn't call that week, or the week after. Finally, in August, he calls.

"How are you, Jackie?" he says.

"Just so busy," I lie. "You?"

"Nonstop. The campaign. Say, you haven't had a chance to look at that French book, have you?"

"I started it."

"Well, let me know."

"What exactly do you want translated?"

"I'd love a sense of his take on Indochina."

"Sure." I heard he was in town last week. Some kind of dinner. I don't mention it. The silence on the line feels awkward.

"I'll give you a call when I'm back in D.C.," he says. "It'll be tough, though, from now until the election. We need to hit every town up here."

"Of course."

"I'll call you soon."

He uses it a lot, I've noticed. That word. *Soon.*

I wait, then hate that I'm waiting. I have dates and parties, weekend trips to Newport. During the week, I carry my camera and notebook through the stifling heat up to the Hill to pick off anyone who hasn't skipped town for August. I have dinner one night in Georgetown with my stepbrother Yusha, who remarks, "You seem a little out of sorts, Jackie."

I love Yusha. He is genuine, kind. The only son of my stepfather Hughdie's first marriage to a Russian noblewoman. Of all the steps and half-steps, as Lee and I call them, Yusha's my favorite.

"Sometimes I just think I made a mistake," I say. "Not taking the job at *Vogue*."

"You like working at the paper. You've said that. Having your own column."

"But I lived in France for only that one year. I was just a student. Sometimes I think I made a mistake not going back."

"Then go back," Yusha says. "Just because you made one choice doesn't mean you can't make another."

I hurl myself into work. The season turns, the start of fall. The city begins to hum. Work at the paper picks up. As the days cool, I hear things about Jack Kennedy. He won the Massachusetts primary. No challenge, really, when you basically run unopposed. I dump his book on Indochina into a drawer. I cancel him out of my thoughts. Two days later, he calls, saying he'll be in town the weekend after next.

"You want to get lunch?" he says.

"I'm afraid we're too busy."

"We?"

"The paper."

"Oh. What about Sunday?"

"I am going in to work that day."

"On a Sunday?"

"Yes."

"Leave a little early. Say one o'clock, Martin's?"

"One-thirty."

"Great," he says. "See you then."

I hang up, annoyed I've said yes, then annoyed I would care either way. It's only lunch.

I arrive ten minutes late.

"I thought you might have stood me up," he says, as I slide into the booth, across from him.

I'm happy to see him, excited, and I keep trying to talk myself out of what I feel. I skim the menu, sip my drink, drag my french fries through the ketchup, and I try to push off the butterfly giddiness—that flush of desire I always seem to feel when he's across the table from me. Even when he's just talking about the campaign or politics, no matter how dry the topic is, he seems to make everything interesting. *Foolish, Jackie, stop being so foolish, this is nothing more than a schoolgirl crush on the older, more popular boy. Jack Kennedy's not looking to settle down. He's not that kind of man.* Though I'm not really looking for that either. When I graduated from high school, I wrote in the yearbook, under *Ambition in Life: Not to be a housewife.*

He reaches for the check the waitress brings.

"Thank you," I say.

"I remembered my wallet this time." He looks almost sheepish for a moment, that lonely, sunlit smile. "I'm glad you came."

After lunch, we walk the towpath along the canal and across the little bridge. Children lean against the rail, two boys throwing sticks. We sit down on a bench. It's cool in the shade. He asks about my family. I ask about his. He tells me he read my column last week.

"I love my job," I say.

"Do you think you'll stay with it?"

"I like how it fuels my mind. Every day is a new puzzle I get to build out, then solve."

He laughs and starts to ask something else. Then doesn't. We talk about books. Books, I've come to see, are safe common ground: other people's stories, words, lives.

"Did you read the new Hemingway?" I ask.

"About the Cuban fisherman. Not yet. On my list for November fifth."

"You must have quite a November fifth list."

"How about we go see the movie *Snows of Kilimanjaro*," he says.

"I didn't like it."

"You saw it without me?"

It surprises me he'd put it that way.

"They completely changed the ending," I say. "It was awful. They made it happy, which obscured the whole point of the story. In the film he's a hero, handsome but dull. In the story, he's so much more interesting—you can't tell what he really wants. You can't tell if he loves her."

"That makes him sound weak."

"No, but he's conflicted. That's what makes the story good. He's conflicted about what he's done with his life and if there's meaning. That's why he lashes out at her."

"He's dying," Jack says.

"Which doesn't give him the right to be cruel."

"He knows he can't keep her, so he doesn't try. That wouldn't be fair to her."

"You think that's for him to decide?"

"Who cares," he says sharply, then, "It doesn't matter, Jackie. Christ, it's just a story."

I'm angry. It hits in a wave. Tired of him wanting only as much as he wants when he wants it. I keep falling for him, believing he'll let me in, then out of nowhere he'll shut down, take off.

"Funny you should put it that way, Jack, saying it doesn't matter. I was thinking the other day about those words you told me your father lives by, how it doesn't matter what you are, it only matters what people think you are."

I don't look up. The air has tightened. I stare at the ground ahead of us. Two men walk by. Two pairs of trousers and brown shoes. "I've decided I disagree," I say. "I like your father very much, but when you're his age, Jack, I don't think you'll be looking back wishing you'd been a little more of what other people thought you ought to be."

His hand closes on my wrist, so fast it startles me. The grip isn't tight. By contrast, it's loose in a way that feels like a threat. Then he lets go and looks away. A stony pressure in the silence. I've pushed too far, and I feel sad but at the same time a sense of closure. Things between us were always too close to the edge. Now it's done. I won't have to wait anymore for the phone to ring.

The noises nearby seem suddenly loud. Two girls skipping down the path, a mother scolding her child, those boys still throwing sticks into the rage of water flowing under the bridge. I hate how raw it feels to me—that night in the car on the way back to the house on the Fourth of July, his smile in the light off the dash as he slowed to pull off the road, his mouth on mine. I could tell him now how I've wanted to be back in that car, that moment, that simple and intimate passion. I want the way he looked at me that night as he pulled the car to the side of the road and drew me toward him, the way he touched me. I want it all, all over again, that night, that hour, that sense of my body under his.

I could tell him this. I could soften now, apologize.

I push the thought off. I look at my watch without seeing it and stand.

JACK

It picks at him for days after. That stupid exchange about Hemingway. That argument over nothing that suddenly escalated into something. He should have kept things light.

She's not like other women. She's read just about everything and remarked once, like she was commenting on the weather, how a story told the right way could blow time apart.

She'll come out with things like that, things he'll find himself mulling over weeks later in ways that make him want to see her again. At the same time, there's something too smart, almost maddening about her, and in that conversation on the bench, he felt her push, and he fell right into it, let his cool break down, grabbing her wrist like that. Like some pawn in a dime-store romance who'd just been played.

One afternoon when he's out with Lem Billings, digging around in his jacket pocket for a spare dollar, he finds the photo strip from Woolworths.

"You want to see what she looks like, Lem?"

"Who?"

"Jackie Bouvier. She had this thing about her."

"Past tense," Lem says, studying the strip. "Not your type, pal."

"That's what I'm saying. Not my type at all."

She's skinny. Angular. Narrow hips. Breasts too small. A little bow-legged. Large feet. Nicotine-stained fingers, bitten nails, wide-spaced eyes. She told him once it took three weeks to get a pair of glasses made with a wide enough bridge to fit, but when her eyes get lit over some idea, there's a feral bright core of her he can feel.

You only think you want her because she's not after you, *he tells himself. She's not calling or pestering. She's different. She smacks of wealth but doesn't have it. Catholic, but with all the trappings of WASP. Her sense of humor is cool and dry. Not just smart, she's quick. She gets his jokes and will come back with some stealth reply, enough to show she got what everyone else just missed. She claims politics bore her ("maybe I'm allergic, Jack, like you are to horses"). She just says a thing like that and leaves the comment there. Whether he answers or not, she pretends not to care. She loves to spar, then acts like she doesn't. There's an aloof dimension of her. Like a cat on a leash.*

Months ago, at a party, he watched her put on her gloves. An evening back in May. She asked him to the Dancing Class. Her date had fallen through. "I'm sure you're not free," she'd said, and maybe because she said it like that, he canceled something else and went. She and her sister hosted a small party beforehand at Merry-wood.

"An Auchincloss tradition," she said, handing him a daiquiri. "Boozy cocktails by a pinewood fire. What's the secret, Yusha?"

"Three kinds of rum," her stepbrother said.

"That's right. Dark Bacardi, light Bacardi, and the last?"

"Mount Gay. Plus lemon juice, lime, sugar, and a splash of orange—after the shake."

"Look how it drenches the ice, Jack, like a sunset."

That evening, before they left for the dance, she drew him away from the others to a table by the window.

"Are you looking forward to tonight?" she asked.

"I don't love formal dances."

"But the dowagers, Jack! They'll be perched like owls on the big *mauve sofa at the top of the stairs, looking down on us. Dowagers like Olympian gods."*

"I'm game to skip," he said. "We can tell the others we'll meet them there and go tear around in your car."

She glanced at him then, a quick smile.

"You really don't like dances, Jack, do you?"

"Sort of a waste of time."

"They don't have to be." She picked up her gloves. There was green tint on her fingernails.

"Did you pick that green for me?"

"No. I had a run-in with developing fluid in the darkroom."

"How much does Frank Waldrop pay you?"

For a moment she looked uncertain. "Forty-two dollars and fifty cents a week," she said.

"You tell him I said you deserve a raise."

She glanced at him again, then started to pull on her gloves, nothing eager or self-conscious in the gesture, nothing seductive, but it was strangely erotic because she wasn't trying.

"Button them," she said, holding out her wrists. "I hate these new buttons."

"Then why wear the gloves?"

"If you had green fingernails, you'd wear gloves to the Dancing Class."

He worked on the buttons. They were pattern-cut and snagged at the loop. She went on chatting about gloves and dowager owls, that catty wit she had that made him want her.

When the gloves were buttoned, she was silent. He glanced up then. She was looking away, her eyes fixed on a tree branch brushed with the last of the light through the window.

"Look how beautiful, Jack," she said, and in that moment, her voice was hushed and gentle and soft, no game in it, no edge, no play. He wanted to be inside it, inside her, right up against that wonder of her voice.

Fall 1952

He calls me from a pay phone near an oyster bar in Boston. He's campaigning up there. He asks me to come.

I smile but don't answer right away. I'm standing in the hall at Merrywood. I'd just come in from riding when the phone rang and I picked it up, his voice on the other end. *Hey, Jackie*, he'd said, *it's me*—like it couldn't be anyone else. I felt my heart skip.

"I've missed seeing you," he's saying now, and a part of me wants to ask him then why didn't he call, but I'm just happy, and the front door is open, and the grass and the drive beyond blaze with autumn sunlight.

"You still there?" he says.

There's a hum on the line—static—then the operator's voice is asking for more coins.

"I don't seem to have another dime," he says. "Will you come up, though, to Boston?"

"In all those pockets, Jack, not one dime?"

He laughs.

"That's a yes, then," he says, "isn't it?"

He's on crutches when I meet him in Boston. He mutters something about the hazards of weekend tennis with his sister Eunice. But I can tell the pain is no small thing. He has a folder under his arm.

"Let me take that," I say.

"I've got it. But thanks." A few steps on, the folder slips. An aide runs after two flyaway sheets. I take the folder and sort the papers back in. We keep walking.

"I'm glad you came," he says. "I'm sorry. My back hurts like hell."

We pass through a police barricade. Two men step forward to welcome him, introducing two others. Jack shakes their hands, then pushes the crutches toward an aide and climbs the steps to the dais. He straightens his jacket as he walks to the podium. It's like he's stepping through clouds—golden, magnetic. He welcomes the crowd and starts to talk about the duty of a senator to look after his own, to make time for the affairs of his state and the interests of his constituents. He talks as if he knows them all: the textile worker in Lawrence, the Brockton shoemakers, the men who work the Gloucester piers. I can't take my eyes off him.

Once, as a child in Central Park, I sat with my father on a bench by the water; it was a lovely day, the air warm and soft. I leaned against him and fell asleep, and when I woke up, it was like opening my eyes for the first time. It all felt cogent in that moment—grass, trees, rocks, sky, the still drift of swans on the surface of the pond, the world alive in ways we forget to allow it to be—beautiful, heartrending, impermanent. I closed my eyes again to brace myself against the loss of it. *Jacks.* My father pushed gently on my shoulder. *Wake up, Jacks. Don't sleep right through this day.*

The crowd erupts into a roar.

"Well, I guess I'm a Democrat now," I say as he steps down. An aide comes forward with the crutches. Jack waves him off.

"You can pretend to hold my arm," he tells me.

"Don't lean too much, we'll both fall over."

"That's for another time." He smiles. I feel the rush of heat to my face. I glance away.

"In exchange for being your cane," I say, "when you win your Senate seat, I want an interview."

"We can pretend we've never met."

"We've already done that."

"We can do it again. You can prep me with the questions, so I have good answers."

"I'll draft your answers."

He laughs, but laughing makes him wince. "I hate this kind of pain," he says.

"The answer to the first question will be something like: *And I'm always being taken for a tourist by the cops because I look too young.*"

"What's the question?"

"I don't know yet."

"*If* I win."

"Oh, you will, Jack. Think of all those ladies' teas you've suffered through."

"You have to stop," he says. "Laughing hurts."

. . .

He wins the Senate seat on the fourth of November. By a narrow margin, he defeats the incumbent, Republican Henry Cabot Lodge, Jr.

"My first front page in the *Times*," he says.

Frank Waldrop sends me off to interview the new senator-elect.

"Well, hello," Jack says as his secretary walks me in. Others are in the room, but no one I recognize.

"It's so nice to meet you at last, Senator-Elect," I say. "Congratulations on your win."

His eyes are laughing.

"And what can I do for you?" he says. "Miss Bouvier, is it?"

John White drops by the paper the following week.

"I hear things are getting serious between you and Jack Kennedy," he says.

"John, I could never be serious with someone who's hardly around but always expects me to be."

Those words, though, are harder to stand by when news gets

out that Jack has asked me to be his date at Eisenhower's inaugural ball. John White teases me about it in front of Waldrop.

"Not exactly a trip to the movies, Jackie."

"Jack knows I'm a safe bet," I say. "I'll be polite and wear a nice dress."

But Waldrop doesn't laugh. "Now, don't come back next week and tell me you're engaged."

"Oh, Mr. Waldrop, didn't I just go through the work of getting un-engaged?"

John White laughs, but Waldrop studies me. A pen on his desk is out of place by half an inch. I move it back in line.

In the car on our way to Eisenhower's ball, Jack tells me about a quick weekend trip he took to Palm Beach. Then he asks again if I'll translate a few French books on Southeast Asian politics for his first Senate speech.

"How many is a few?"

"Six or eight."

"That's a few more than a few."

He laughs, and I look out the window of the car, the glow of cold winter air through the glass. I feel him shift closer to me on the seat, his arm around my shoulder. His breath is warm near my cheek. "At least now," he says quietly, "I know better than to offer a penny for your thoughts."

That winter, when he comes back into town, he calls and asks if I'll bring him a lunch. On my way into work at the paper, I'll drop off a brown paper bag at his office—sandwiches, chips with a drink, clam chowder in a thermos. He asks me to go with him to pick out some new suits. He's awkward at the fittings. He always wants the hems too short, and I tell him so. I say it gently, but it still makes him flush, then he smiles, that careless radiant smile. "You're good for me," he says.

But there are still long stretches with no phone call at all.

"He may be dating you," my mother says, "but you're not the only one he's carrying on with."

I sigh, recounting this remark to John White over hamburgers at the Hot Shoppe.

"Go on, John," I say. "Tell me I'm wasting my time."

"You're wasting your time. Does that help?"

"No."

"What do you like so much about him, Jackie?"

He's the most interesting man I've ever met, I could say. *That ferocious mind, the way he's always asking questions. He's at once curious and bold and sometimes vulnerable in just that certain way.* I don't say any of this.

"I thought you'd be smarter than to chase a lost cause," White says.

"That's an awful thing to say."

"You told me to talk you out of it. You're dead set against letting me." Then he adds, "I should at least tell you, a friend of mine saw him out with Audrey Hepburn in New York last week."

There is a crack in the Formica of the table, bits of dirt collected inside. I slide my napkin over it. White pushes away what's left of his hamburger.

"I get it, Jackie," he says. "I loved Kick, and there were dimensions of her so like Jack. We laughed and argued constantly. Every moment with her was alive. When I heard about the plane crash, my brain couldn't conceive of a world without her. I was assigned her obituary. I thought I wanted it. But I couldn't squeeze one decent sentence out. I sat at her old desk, that desk where you sit now, and all I could do was type the word *goodbye. Goodbye.*"

"I'm sorry, John."

"You're set on him, aren't you?"

"I'm not saying that."

He leans back in the booth and smiles.

"If this is what you want," he says, "I'll give you a hint. When it comes to women, Jack Kennedy likes to be the one to hunt. You know it already. Try that and see where it goes."

The next time I come home to a message from Jack, I don't return the call. He calls again, twice, the calls less spaced out. Finally, I call him back.

"I'm so sorry it took me so long," I say. "How are you?"

We go out more frequently after that: art galleries, museums, parties. We go for dinner at La Salle du Bois, which he immediately contends is too French-fancy.

"We like some fancy," I say.

"Like what?"

"At Eisenhower's ball, we decided we like inaugurations."

He laughs. "That's different."

"Inaugurations are fancy, Jack." This makes him laugh more, and I love the way he looks at me through the laughter, that mix of collusion and desire. We debate who will win what Pulitzer. I invite him to a Fellini film. "Long-haired crap?" he says. I answer, "You only get to judge if you go." I write him notes on the salient points I've culled from those French books on Vietnam so he can weave them into his Senate speeches, which I offer to proof.

One weekend, we meet in New York for lunch with my father. They talk about the stock market, movie stars, sports. Jack sips his drink while my father throws back four, but they order the same steak, cooked the same way. The room is airy. Sunlight filters through the long windows.

They talk about the changing landscape of New York.

"We were on Park Avenue when Jackie was young," my father says. "Now I'm up in Lenox Hill."

It pinches my heart, that faint shame in his voice, the vanished wealth he tries to be easy with. My father has always been a man of extravagance, but if he had only a penny left, he'd break it in his teeth and give me half. When I was at boarding school, he'd appear on weekends with armfuls of presents, stockings, magazines. Once a bouquet of fresh gardenias he laid in the snow by my dorm window. He conspired to have my horse stabled near the school so I could take my friends for sleigh rides. In spring, when he came to visit, we'd drive around in his little two-seater. I never tired of feeling that sudden jolt of the car, a burst of untame life, as we hit the open strip of highway. I was the keeper of his secrets. He told me details of his affairs.

"What about that one there, Daddy?" I'd ask at a school event, pointing out one of the mothers.

"No, I haven't had her."

"That one, then?"

"That one, yes," he said.

And I'd laugh. It felt like that was what I was supposed to do.

"Keep her on a horse," my father tells Jack that day we're at lunch. "Then you'll have her in a good mood."

It takes me aback—that he'd talk about me that way, like he's giving Jack license to do the same. I almost say something, a cool witty thing to draw a line. But the waiter is there, and their steaks have arrived. My father cuts into his, suave manicured hands deft with the knife, neat thin slices—a more nuanced precision than one might expect. I glance at Jack. He is looking at me. That look. My father pretends not to catch it. I smile and Jack smiles back, that curious incandescent thing about him that makes the edges of the world feel suddenly so bright.

Spring 1953

"I wish it hadn't rained," Lee says. Her wedding day, but she isn't happy. My younger sister, her exquisite body like blown glass, sinks into the vacant seat next to me. "I hate this miserable weather, Jacks. I should have waited until June."

Our father is dancing with our mother. They spin close to us. He lowers her into a dip, then draws her up, a gallant turn. She catches my eye as he sweeps her away.

"She looks like she's ready to die," I say.

"Michael wants to dance," Lee says, "but I can't dance while they're dancing. Daddy acts like he still loves her."

"He acts. But he was determined to cut a dash for you today. He's been getting in shape for months. Jogging around the reservoir in that absurd rubber suit."

She looks at me. "I'm sorry Jack couldn't come."

"Senate life. But he invited me to Eunice's wedding in May."

I don't mention to Lee that the city editor at the *Times Herald* just asked me to cover Queen Elizabeth's coronation. I almost said no. To go would mean I'd miss Jack's sister's wedding. I asked the editor if I could have a few days to think it over.

"It's a good position Michael's been offered at the embassy," Lee says, but her voice is uncertain, like she's trying to convince herself. "I'll miss you when we move to London, Jackie."

"You'll love it there. You'll go out every night with interesting people, and you'll know I feel a splitting envy, bored to tears back here in the swamp."

"You should absolutely go to the coronation," says my mother a few days later. We're down at the barn with the horses. Spring sunlight falls in sheets through the open stable door.

"What about Eunice's wedding?" I say.

"Jack has plenty of time to find another date, if that's what he wants."

"Well, I'm not sure that's what I want."

My mother frowns. She doesn't quite like Jack or trust him. But there are many things my mother doesn't trust. My wit, for example. Or what she calls my stubborn streak. She made her own mistake once—that's how she sees it—when she fell headlong for my father. It broke her, then made her cold.

She shifts the bridle now and runs the flat of her hand down the horse's neck. "Jackie, if you're really in love with this man, he'll be more likely to find out how he feels about you if you're across the ocean doing interesting things rather than trotting back and forth with his lunch." She adds, "Aileen Bowdoin could go with you."

"I don't want to talk about this."

"Just call Jack. Tell him you're sorry but you'll have to miss his sister's wedding. Tell him you'll see him when you get back."

In England, pictures of the young Queen Elizabeth are everywhere, pasted on the windows and doors of every house we pass on the boat train between Southampton and London.

I write one short feature piece every afternoon, longhand, and send it off airmail. I write about the American crowds that fill London, about dancing at the 400 Club, its walls lined with velvet. I write about the clambake ball thrown by Perle Mesta of the National Woman's Party, a highbrow "hostess with the mostest." I write about Lauren Bacall waltzing with General Omar Bradley, then moving on to a foxtrot with the Marquess of Milford Haven.

She is the belle of that ball, her long body poured like water into a strapless lace dress, dancing away with the marquess until her Bogie ambles over in his old white-tie-and-tails, cutting in to steal back his wife.

Aileen Bowdoin and I stay in a friend's flat in Mayfair. The apartment is unheated, and when it's cold at night, we fill the bathtub with scalding water to warm our feet. I drag Aileen to bookstores in search of titles I can't find in the states. Aldous Huxley, books on Churchill, Irish history, two small volumes of British poetry. I've brought along an extra suitcase for the books, but by the time we're packing to leave, it's full.

"Who on earth are all those books for, Jackie?" Aileen asks as I sit on the lid, working to buckle it closed.

"Hughdie, mostly."

A knock on the door. I hop up to answer it.

"Telegram for Miss Bouvier," says the messenger.

I thank him and, closing the door with my hip, open the telegram. I can feel Aileen's eyes, the quickened silence in the room.

ARTICLES EXCELLENT . . . BUT YOU ARE MISSED.

I slip the telegram into my pocket.

"Jack again?" Aileen says.

"Yes."

I stand above that stubborn overfull suitcase. Books, and more books. Books he'll read for pleasure. Books with ideas that might be useful to him. I've started to admit I want to be useful to him, necessary. In that whole suitcase, there's not one book for anyone else. Not my mother or Hughdie. Not even for my stepbrother Yusha. Only Jack.

I meet an old friend, Demi Gates, for dinner at a small restaurant. We ran into each other at the post-coronation reception at the American embassy. He had traveled up from Spain to London. Tomorrow he'll leave for Paris. We order our food and catch each other up on other people's news. We talk about one summer years ago when we all met in the south of France. Yusha was there, and my friend Solange. There was a nightclub where we used to go dancing.

"Do you remember the violin music?" Demi asks. "Everything was right that summer."

"It's Paris I miss," I say. "Strolling down the Champs-Élysées at midnight. Drinking grasshoppers and getting swanky at the Ritz."

"Then come with me for a few days, Jackie. Before you go back. We'll hit all the places we used to go: Chez Allard, L'Elephant Blanc."

"I want to hear about Madrid and your new life," I say.

He's started a publishing company, he says, that does comic strips and some advertising. But then he says something else.

"So the talk about you and Jack Kennedy?"

My fork stops.

"He's a gutter fighter, Jackie. You're a class act." He proceeds to drench me in tales of Jack's womanizing, trying to talk me out of what I keep telling myself I'm not yet even in. I just sit there, peeling back the skin on my fish to separate flesh from the bone.

"You don't want to be married to a politician, Jackie. You don't even like politics. It's a brutal world. Not your kind. There's no poetry in it, no beauty, no art. Is it the money?"

They will say this forever, I realize. Jack Kennedy has money, so it must be the money I'm after. I could tell them he never carries cash. I'm usually the one who pays for movies, taxis, lunch. I could explain I'm never bored with Jack Kennedy. Never bored of listening to him or wondering what's turning in that bold, intricate mind. I never get tired of how he looks at me or touches me, how his lips graze my cheek, my neck, the quickening of his breath mixed with mine, those more private and intimate moments of heat, skin, fire.

They will never say this.

I remember that day in the little bedroom when I knelt by the bookshelf and those worn spines: Byron, Tennyson, King Arthur and his knights. Jack just sat on the bed, talking about how those were the books that formed him. Stories of war, persistence, and failure, the getting up again and forging on when he was so ill as a child that he could barely make it from bed to bookshelf and back. Books about freedom and faith and the courage it took to fight on the right side of history.

"What makes that kind of courage, Jackie?" he'd asked me that day.

He is more than what they see. More than his father's son or heir to his dead brother's legacy. He wants more. Believes in more.

I can't tell Demi this now. He won't hear it.

Through the restaurant window, it is dusk, the sky steeped blue, city lights on the wet streets.

The day I told Jack I was going to London and would miss his sister's wedding, I ignored my mother's advice. I didn't call. I met him at Martin's and told him there. We sat at the table he'd begun to call "our table."

"I understand," he said. "You should go." But he glanced at me, like he was going to say something else. Then he shrugged. "You'll be missed."

"You mean you'll miss me?" I said gently, almost teasing, and he looked away, pushed a hand through his hair, glanced back at me, his eyes nervous for a moment, uncertain. He smiled.

"Yeah," he said, "that." I felt a bolt of warmth shoot through me, always, at that smile.

. . .

He is waiting for me when my plane touches down in Boston.

"You again," he says.

"And you," I say.

Silence falls between us, shy, a tide of other passengers streaming quickly past, heading to whatever lives they've come home to, or on to wherever else they are going, maybe a connecting flight they're hoping to catch, all these other people, strangers, bound for other destinations.

For us, though, in that moment, everything feels very still and sharp and new.

"Come on, then, Jackie. Let's go."

He picks up my bag, takes my hand, and starts striding through the concourse, drawing me along with him, moving smooth and fast as he does sometimes, like his body just needs to keep up with his mind, which has already crossed into some future I'm not yet aware of, and we are like water, moving through all the other bodies in that airport, disparate faces, voices, lives. We reach the door that leads outside. He pauses and turns to me suddenly, an expression on his face I haven't seen before—a kind of bewilderment, almost fear, but with a tinge of wonder, like a child's fear.

"Are you okay with that, Jackie? You are, aren't you?"

So sweet and unexpected—the vulnerability in his voice.

"Okay with what, Jack?"

"Going with me."

I smile. "You're where I want to be."

. . .

On June 25, we are in *The New York Times*.

Senator Kennedy to Marry in Fall
Son of Former Envoy is Fiancé of
Miss Jacqueline Bouvier, Newport Society Girl

I have to resign from the *Times Herald*. I knew it was coming; perhaps I'd known all along. Jack doesn't ask me to, which I appreciate, but I bring it up so he won't have to. We're at Martin's. Brunch. Our table. The leaves are full and green on the trees. We order root beer floats. I ask for extra whipped cream.

"I know Eleanor Roosevelt had her own column," I say, "but that was different, the focus was different, and she was the president's wife. I'm sure there were strict orders on what she could and could not say. I can't imagine the ambassador would appreciate having his, or your, ambitions at odds with anything the Inquiring Camera Girl might want to ask."

He laughs, then, "Dad did ask if you were going to keep working. But I don't want you to feel you have to stop."

"I know," I say.

. . .

Joe summons us to Hyannis Port. A family weekend, he calls it. Once we're there, he mentions he's invited a few people from *Life* magazine to stop by. He says it like he's explaining why there will be green beans instead of broccoli for dinner.

"They want to do a story on the engagement," he says.

I say, "You mean *you* want them to do a story."

He grins. "Well, there might be a little of that."

The crew from *Life* is there the next day. Jack and I are arranged, made up, our clothes styled casual, collars unbuttoned, sneakers barely tied, hair windblown, just enough. They snap photographs of me swinging a baseball bat and running with a football. Someone suggests the sailboat.

"I'm not really dressed for a sail," I say to the editor.

"We only need you in there for the shot."

"Of course," I say, wondering if I'll ever fit in the corners of this life I play so well. We climb into the boat and set off, Jack at the tiller. I'm beside him, the photographer crammed in the bow, asking me to move closer to Jack and asking Jack to tack, please, so it will look like we're out in open water. The boat starts to heel; the photographer slides.

"That'll cockeye the horizon," I say quietly to Jack.

"Just look happy," he says. "Almost done."

An hour later, back on land, they ask him to hold my hand for a series of shots on the lawn.

"Put your arm around her," the editor says, and he does, but we're awkward, his arm like a metal hanger draped over my shoulders.

"It feels so fake," he says under his breath. "I never stand like this. I hate being fake."

"It's all fake, Jack."

He starts to laugh. They snap the picture then.

At the end of the day, after the crew has packed up their tripods and cameras and left, as I'm walking from the kitchen with my book and a glass of water, I overhear Bobby, Jack, and Joe in the sunroom. I hear my name. They're talking about me like I'm some kind of asset, like I'm the state of Rhode Island. I feel a sharp chill and sit down.

There's still a chance to get out.

But he's brilliant. A maverick thinker, and when I am with him, I can feel my edges burn. He's almost died three times. He is by turns impatient and nonchalant. He has Addison's disease, recurrent malaria, and a spinal condition. The left side of his body is smaller than the right, shoulder lower, left leg shorter. He's a clumsy dresser, lanky, that unruly shock of hair. He's known, too well, for his sexual exploits, every woman smoothing her skirt when he enters a room like the room belongs to him, and—poof!—in seconds, it does.

By twenty-three, he'd published a bestselling book, *Why England Slept,* about how democracy can fail to perceive fascism rising in its midst; by twenty-six, he was a national war hero; thirty-six now and a senator. He told me once he feels like every minute is a race against the fast-circling arms of a clock. Edna St. Vincent Millay's candle burning bright: *It will not last the night.* He's a chary romantic. A fatalist. Who sees too clearly that fortune, health, and luck can all be erased in an instant.

And he needs me, which he won't want to admit, but I can feel it when out of nowhere he'll take my arm, or when he leans in to whisper, *I'll see you soon.* In the warmth of his breath, I feel it. Or when we're in a crowded room and his eyes search me out and he'll fix me with that little look—the kind of burning extravagant hunger that makes you want to throw your soul right down.

And I love him.

The voices have stopped, I realize, just before Bobby and Jack walk out of the sunroom with Joe. The boys head to the window, talking about how the wind has come up, could be a good afternoon for a sail. But Joe pauses when he sees me sitting there. In his face, the slight calculation. I close the book and smile. He isn't fooled.

"I've been looking into that house for you, Jackie," he says.

Jack turns around. "What house?"

"There's a little pink villa in Acapulco your girl wants for her honeymoon. That girl of yours who's not so naïve as to give up her thoughts to anyone. She should have what she wants, don't you agree?" Joe laughs when he says it, the laugh that masters a moment and now is meant to master me. His eyes on my face, I can tell he's still wondering how much I might have heard and if it matters.

"I do love that pink villa," I say.

Summer 1953

Early July, we go to Newport, my mother's house at Hammersmith Farm, a Victorian enchantment perched on the hill above the bay. Egyptian-tiled gardens, lily ponds, stone walkways. A guest cottage and boathouse closer to the shore.

Just months from now, we will be married at St. Mary's Church. Afterward, an outdoor reception on the Hammersmith lawn. More than eight hundred guests, it will take two hours to work through the receiving line. We will be photographed. My dress with its fifty yards of ivory silk taffeta, portrait neckline, bouffant skirt. I wanted something sleeker, more ionic-column, and I won't be able to escape the sense that I look like a lampshade. After an alfresco lunch, as the Meyer Davis band plays, Jack and I will have our first dance, to "I Married an Angel." In a toast, Jack will explain he had to marry me to remove me from the fourth estate so I wouldn't write anything to scuttle his career. I will riposte that while, yes, it's true that I gave up my position at the *Times Herald,* I plan to write a novel. As a wife with no job and time on my hands, I see no reason why that can't be done.

That day in July, Jack's mother, Rose, is meeting us at Hammersmith. She and my mother will discuss plans for our wedding.

"They don't really need us for that, do they?" Jack asks. We are in the deck room. I took him over to the stables earlier to see the horses. He got wheezed up, and now we're just lying around in the heat, the windows thrown open, the breeze off the sea fresh and cool.

"Let me guess, Jack," I say. "You want to send the mothers off to lunch while we go tear around in a car."

"Better a car than a horse."

We laugh and, laughing, he starts to cough, as my mother walks in to say that his mother has arrived and it's time to drive over to the beach for lunch and then a swim. We keep laughing, and Jack is coughing, and we try to catch our breath. We're sprawled across each other. My mother stands in the doorway, surveying us, her mouth a stern line.

"Say, Mrs. Auchincloss," Jack says, standing up from the couch, "how about Jackie and I take our swim before lunch?"

"It's almost one already," my mother says. "We should have lunch first."

"Well, I worry we might get cramps if we swim after lunch. But you and my mother could order lunch for us. Jackie and I could take a quick swim and get back before the food comes."

My mother gives a little frown. "I suppose we could do it that way."

Then his mother is there, and we are all walking out to the car. We fall behind them.

"You knew she wouldn't want to switch the order," I say.

"That's why I threw in the bit about cramps."

"I love that she's a little afraid of you, Jack."

"I don't think that's it. I don't think she approves."

"Of us?"

"Of me."

I feel something inside me catch. He might be right. I don't want him to feel that way.

"That's not it," I say. "She can't push you around, and she's not used to that."

We climb into the backseat of the car, the mothers in front. Their heads kerchief-wrapped, a collar of pearls around each pale neck. We're like two bad kids laughing and joking in the back while the mothers talk about plans for the rehearsal dinner, brunches and luncheons and flowers. A tent in case of rain. September, my mother remarks, can be so fickle. Rose asks if my mother has given thought to bridesmaids' dresses. If not, she has an excellent dressmaker she'd recommend.

"I have a girl," my mother says smoothly. The white heat of the sun bores through the glass.

"Jack, open your window, please," I say.

"This window here?"

"Yes." I smile. "Yours."

He gives a push at the handle, glances at me, that puzzled look. "It doesn't seem to work."

"Of course it works."

He tries again.

"That's the wrong way," I say. "Clockwise. No, I mean counterclockwise."

"I've tried both ways. It won't budge."

I lean across him, grip the window handle, and start to crank it down.

"What are you two up to back there?" my mother says.

"I was having trouble with the window, Mrs. Auchincloss."

"Call me Janet."

"Janet. The handle seems tricky. Jackie's helping me figure it out." His hands are underneath me, touching me, the window halfway down; his fingers run along my waist, my ribs, the edge of my breast, and the salt wind blows through the window, that cooler sweet summer air—bright and hard and fast off the sea. The car turns onto Ocean Drive, and we are falling over each other in the backseat, laughing and trying to stifle it but not trying too hard, and there is only silence, tight-lipped and prim, from the front. My mother's cool dagger eyes in the rearview.

At the beach club, we spill out. I grab my bag and towel.

"A hamburger for me, please," I say.

"A club sandwich," says Jack. "Chowder too, if they have it. Thank you, Janet."

We race past the steps that lead up to the veranda and down to the shore. We drop our clothes in a pile. The water is cold.

"Dive in," I say.

"You first."

I look at him for a moment, then ask.

JACK

"Do you love me, Jack?" she said.

"Of course. I'm marrying you."

"That's not what I asked." Her voice with that flip edge, like she might have been testing him. The water was cold and clear. He'd seen that smile before.

It's not that he doesn't love her. Not that at all. The marriage is useful. He knows that, and everyone reminds him. Her breeding, the sheen of wealth. Well read, well traveled, well mannered, well bred. Not malleable, Bobby once remarked. Their father laughed at that, then said, "No, but she knows how it works."

And she's different. From his sisters, from other girls and women, the ones he still goes after. She is curious. A fiery wit. Ruthless insight. She makes him think. And when she's quiet and he can see her thoughts tick, he feels a kind of thrill—the same thrill he felt when he first recognized the magnitude and reach of her mind.

No one else.

The thought strikes him. He knows it's true, and he doesn't quite want it to be.

She is not like anyone else.

"Do you love me, Jack?" she asked, and he felt a momentary impatience.

He knows what she wants when she says a thing like that. Magic. A fairy tale.

And part of him wants to promise her that, and part of him wants to tell her there's no such thing.

He loves the banter between them, but she'd thrown that question out there like a dare. Waited a moment for his answer, then turned away, like she might not wait. He felt a sudden doubt. He hates that feeling. Too much of his life has been built on it. Doubt, charade, illusion. A charlatan's sleight of hand. The glint of what's unreal.

She's waded farther out in the water now. Up to her thighs. The water breaks as she walks. Drops of sunlight shimmer on her skin, her body long, casually erotic. She stops, noticing something through the surface. She reaches down through the water, her arm disappearing past the elbow; she brings up a stone and turns it in her hand. She catches him watching her. Surprise at first, her features still. Her gaze shifts, deliberate, calculating, that little play. Her arm draws back, and she throws that stone. It wings across the surface, heading out, skip after skip. She looks at him then, her face with a faint expression of triumph, as if to say: You want to watch? Then see.

All of this happens. She happens. *Long body, arm reaching, stone in flight, her blazing face, a collision of imperfect features adding up to a cogent enigmatic whole. He just stares back, a sharp desire for her he can feel.*

She dives in. The surface closes. Her dark shape, underwater. He thinks he sees it, then is less sure. She's gone for so long. He waits, eyes scanning, seeing nothing but the pale reflected sky, the water empty, mocking him somehow. She surfaces twenty yards away. She looks back, he goes to wave, but she's already started to swim, straight out, that lean grace of her arm rising, dark head turning to breathe, her cheek against the surface, lips parting for air, the strong loaded rhythm of her body, ocean rolling off her shoulders like she is made of that water.

Ten years from now, he will remember this moment. Everything he would ever need to know about her was right there.

PART II

We are only what we always were, but naked now.

—ARTHUR MILLER, *The Crucible*

If I had known getting married would create such a shift in him, in me, I don't know that I would have gone ahead with it. He loved me. I knew that. I also knew—even then—he needed not to love me, or anyone, too much. We were creatures of distance, Jack and I. He needed his freedom. I needed my solitude. He kept different parts of his life in different compartments. I wanted to understand why. I wanted to know, too, what lay under that magnetic golden front, that mind that could outwit any other, that cool elusive grace. I couldn't resist feeling that if I could just be more independent, more useful, less spiky, he would love me more. Such an easy net to get tangled in, isn't it? That belief a woman sometimes has that she can change herself to change a man.

Fall 1953

Our wedding is compared to the Astor wedding of 1934. (Joe is ecstatic over this, I learn.) On the front page of *The New York Times,* the day after the ceremony in Newport, there's a photograph of us, cutting into the five-tier cake. NOTABLES ATTEND SENATOR'S WEDDING.

There are painstaking details about my dress—tapered bodice, ivory tissue silk, and the lace veil woven with orange blossoms. There are details of my bridesmaids in their pink taffeta. Lee is my matron of honor. Bobby is Jack's best man. There are details of the reception, over eight hundred of our nearest and dearest flung across the Hammersmith lawn, following the ceremony at St. Mary's Church performed by Archbishop Cushing with the assistance of four priests.

I tease Jack: "How many priests does it take to marry a Kennedy?"

There are no details in the papers, though, about the scratches down Jack's cheek from a run-in he had with a rosebush while playing a drunken game of football with his brothers and friends the night before. No details of how my wedding gown was ruined earlier that week when a pipe burst in the dressmaker's studio, and the dress had to be entirely remade. Nothing written about the tears I bit back when I realized my father was not just late but not coming at all. Something small and old walked over my heart as I took my stepfather Hughdie's arm instead and he walked me down the aisle.

The press is told my father was suddenly struck by a very bad cold—not that my mother sent someone to check on my father at his hotel when she couldn't reach him by phone; that someone found him half dressed in his tux and more than half in the bag.

In the car leaving the reception, I brush rice off my lap and pull rose-petal confetti from my hair. The pearl-and-diamond bracelet Jack gave me the night before, my "something new," glints.

"I'm so happy, Jack," I say. He smiles at me. I lean my head against his arm.

"That's not comfortable," he says, something pained in the set of his jaw. "Just my back hurts from standing all day." He shifts in the seat, turning slightly away toward the window.

. . .

On our honeymoon in Acapulco, in the little pink villa, I feel a strange deep joy being with him, near him, that sense of the sun in my body, an ache in my thighs from where his weight pressed down. A timelessness as the hours pass, marked only by heat, skin, desire.

His fingers brush the hair from my neck. I feel him inside me—a wash of light.

"It's hot," he says.
"How about a swim? A cool drink?"
"Let's go inside."
"Again?"
"Don't you want to?" His smile then.

Afterward, we lie on the veranda in the shade. Once, when I get up, he tugs the edge of the towel I've wrapped around me. It slips from my hands; I go to grasp it, but he takes my wrist and pulls me down.

We drive the winding coastal road up through the lush cliffs, then back down the mountainside into the city that borders the bay and miles of white-sugar sand. We wander narrow streets, past small shops and cafés. A cart heaped with oranges, some halved open to lure passersby.

"Cut?" the man asks in Spanish, a gesture with his hands to mimic a knife.

"*Por favor,*" I say.

He runs the blade through the fruit to quarter it and hands it back to me. I suck at the pieces, peeling out the insides with my teeth, my hands sticky and damp. I toss the peel and lick the juice off.

Jack laughs. "You're a mess." He must see the surprise on my face. "Hey, I was just joking. Sorry." He drapes an arm around me as we walk. "You're a Kennedy now," he says, his voice gentle then, close. "You're going to have to learn to take a joke."

From Acapulco we fly to California. I finally write to my father to tell him I love him but how sad I was the day of the wedding when he wasn't there. Through the window, below the terraced eaves, I see Jack sitting by the pool, talking with a young woman on a chaise longue nearby. He pulls his chair closer.

I leave the letter unfinished and head downstairs. As I come up to them, I toss my book and towel onto the end of Jack's chair.

"Hello, sweetheart," I say.

"Hey, Jackie, this is Margaret. We have all sorts of things in common. Friends mostly."

The girl named Margaret laughs.

"Lovely," I say. "Perhaps you'll join us for dinner tonight, Margaret?"

The girl's face shifts, wary now, dark eyes surveying the two of us.

"I think I have plans tonight. Another time, though." She slips on her pool sandals and strides away.

"I hope I didn't interrupt anything."

"Just a girl," Jack says. He picks the newspaper up off the concrete beside his chair.

. . .

That fall, we've agreed, I'll stay with his parents in Hyannis Port until the Georgetown house we've leased is ready. Joe is delighted. "It'll be a relief to have someone smart around here to talk to."

Jack flies to Washington for four days each week and back to the Cape on Friday. As soon as he arrives, he tosses his bag into our bedroom, sits down for a few minutes, then heads off for a swim, a round of golf, a sail.

"It's like being married to a whirlwind," I say to Joe one afternoon. We sit together on the porch watching Jack cross the lawn toward the shore.

"Go with him," Joe says. "Keep a man company."

It feels like too much to explain that if Jack doesn't invite me along, he's saying he might not want me to ask.

On Sundays, there's a makeshift togetherness. We go to church, walk the beach, and stroll into town. Jack reads *The New York Times Book Review* and circles titles he wants to read. As we talk about those books, authors, and ideas, I feel him move closer to me. The night before he flies back to Washington, he'll touch my face, my body in bed. He'll kiss me. We seem to become more visible to each other when he's on the verge of leaving.

"I'll miss you," I say.

"I'll be back soon." That bend in his voice I love.

Monday again. He's gone.

During the week, after dinner with Rose and Joe, I sit on the porch and smoke, watching the dusk soak into the beautiful lawn rushing down to the beautiful sea. The sky is molten, the dark comes fast. Sitting there, I think of France—Grenoble, Paris, the Seine. The dream of an old life—the thrill of freedom, otherness, a place away. The clock inside chimes ten. I stub my cigarette out and empty the ashtray into the hostas. Rose doesn't like that

I smoke. She says it's not good for a young woman's health or the health of a baby.

"There's no baby yet," I say.

"But there will be," Rose says. "You mustn't worry."

"I'm not."

Once upon a time there was a boy who loved heroes and a girl who married him and found herself in a too-small box of a housewife life.

It will be different. I tell myself this. Soon.

. . .

In November we move into 3321 Dent Place, the house we've rented in Georgetown. In the mornings, I make breakfast and coffee. I trim the edges when I burn the toast. Jack blows through the newspaper, skimming headlines. Then he's out the door.

I make lists to anchor the day.

- Dry cleaners—drop off Jack's suits
- Pick up meat from the butcher
- Take a walk
- A longer walk
- Find a new rug

On warmer days, I walk into the city. I miss my job. I've heard rumors the paper is going to be sold to the *Post*.

"I enrolled in a history class today," I tell Jack one night at dinner.

He looks up. "Georgetown?"

"The school of foreign service."

"Why there?"

"The others don't accept women."

His brow wrinkles for a moment. "That's nuts," he says.

I still haven't registered to vote. I'd gone to a charity tea that morning for the Senate wives. I could feel those women stare like I was something of a curiosity, with my unruly hair and big hands, the bitten-down nails. When I left the tea, I walked to Georgetown, found the office of the registrar, and said to the woman in a navy suit behind the desk, "I need a place to put my mind, please." She looked at me, and I explained I was only joking—well, sort of—and did she have a list of classes I could take. A few months ago I might have told Jack the story, and we would have laughed, but the space between us now feels stilted, tentative, like we're playing at this marriage life but still too new to the script and props that seem to be ours.

He asks me to translate two passages for a speech. "Voltaire and Rousseau," he says.

"I'd love that, yes."

We start to eat. I cut off a piece of steak. He reaches for his water glass.

"Is the meat too dry?" I ask.

"It's fine."

A killing word. *Fine.*

Through the kitchen window, night again now. Our reflections in the glass turn back on us.

. . .

Winter rolls into spring. He works later hours. "That time of the year," he says. To soften the loneliness, I hurl myself into readings for my history class and short trips to Merrywood to ride. I find a new rug, a few pieces of furniture, a lamp, and two oil paintings.

He appears in the living room one night with bills in his hand.

"I'm not going to tell you it doesn't grow on trees," he says.

I'm sitting at the table, my notebook open with a paper I'm writing. He is angry, his eyes like wood, waiting for me to respond. And say what? *How has this happened? What exactly has happened?* When I don't say anything, he moves toward the door; the room feels suddenly erased.

This isn't what I want.

At the door, he turns and holds up the bills. "Well?" he says.
"I'm not going to defend a rug," I say, "or a small painting."
"Two."
"Only one rug."
"Two paintings."

I smile. "One's a seascape. That shouldn't count. A seascape is more of a window, and we both need a window or two cut in this stiff airless space we seem to have landed in, don't you think?"

This stops him. Traces of anger in his eyes still, but those few words struck home.

He tells me then that a photo shoot has been arranged. Early next week. Our life in D.C.

"Time to turn up the BP," he says. That's what Joe calls it. Big personality.

The photographer is young. Orlando. I feel odd at first, self-conscious, but he is kind. He seems nervous himself.

Bobby shows up on the second day.

"Jack said you were bringing the Good Humor ice cream bars," I say.

The camera shutter clicks, Orlando asking me to turn slightly to the right, tilt my head a fraction more. As the hours pass, I realize that with the camera trained on us, Jack and I laugh more, play more. It begins to be an idyll the young photographer captures: Jack and this woman named Jackie he has married, leaning on the balcony rail; Jack and Jackie walking in Georgetown; Jack painting a picture as Jackie looks over his shoulder; Jack playing football with Bobby while Jackie sits with Ethel, looking on.

"I'm perfecting the art of looking on," I say to Ethel. Ethel looks at me blankly.

On the third day of Orlando, he photographs Jack at work. Jack, rising political star; Jack the intellectual, reading with his glasses on. The final series of shots, though, are me, the woman named Jackie, dressed in evening clothes, lighting a candle before a small dinner party, a brightness washing over her bare shoulders, intimate; light chisels the side of her face.

She is almost beautiful, I think weeks later when we see the proofs. That woman named Jackie the young photographer has made.

We're invited to a dinner dance at the Shoreham Hotel. "Where we had our first real date," I say, putting on my earrings. Jack sits on the edge of the bed, trying to pull on his sock.

"Damn it. Will my back ever work?"

"We can cancel."

"No."

But he winces reaching for his dinner jacket.

That night, he sits next to Priscilla Johnson. She used to work in his office.

"I never thought I'd get married," I hear him say, "but I was thirty-six and, in politics, if you aren't married by then, people start to think you're queer."

How dare he? Priscilla glances at me. I just smile at her as if, of course, this is the kind of thing my husband would say and I am just fine with it. I turn to the man on my right. I don't look at Jack for the rest of dinner.

Later, we dance, my hand on Jack's shoulder, his hand on my waist. We are like armatures in a figure-drawing class, our little wooden selves with wire joints.

The song ends. "Let's go home soon," I say.

"I'm going to get a drink. You want something?"

"No."

Half an hour later, he's still at the bar, talking to a tall blonde in a silver dress. She starts toward the exit, a glance at him over her shoulder. He puts down his drink and follows her.

I look away. I don't want to see him walk out that door. No one seems to notice. Then they do. A current passing through the room. Priscilla Johnson, who sat with Jack at dinner, steps toward me, dark hair, pretty face, a compassion in her eyes I just want to pinch out. I pick up my clutch and leave. Everyone saw it happen. Everyone saw everything.

After four in the morning, he comes home; I'm awake in bed. He lies down, a column of space between us. Within minutes, he's begun to snore. The emptiness of the room and the dark, moonlight throwing its tricks and promises across that new rug on the floor. I hate that rug now.

I let an hour pass. At dawn, I drive to Merrywood. I tack up the horse. We start at a trot, then a canter. I ride harder, faster. I want to feel the ground shudder through my body; I want that sense of the speed and the rage and the grief—not just for what I don't have in this new life but for what I gave up.

I ride and the sun climbs into the sky, the world a rush of dizzying passionless green.

When I get home, he's at his desk, working. He looks up, concerned.

"Where were you?" he says.

"You can't think they don't notice, Jack."

"What?"

"Last night. You and Silver Dress," I say, a crushing pressure in my chest. "You can't think I don't care, and you can't think people will respect a senator who disrespects his wife."

We barely speak for the next few weeks beyond the courtesies of two people who happen to share the same house. I leave his breakfast on the table. I stop calling to ask if he'll be home for dinner or if his plans have changed. At first it seems to surprise him. But then he adjusts, like he thinks this must be what I want. Maybe he prefers it this way. No extra emotion to manage. He's in his space. I'm in mine. We are two icebergs adrift, floating on, until one evening in June. I've just finished packing for a week with my mother in Newport. I walk into his study. He's by his desk, bent over, his face a mix of fury and pain and despair. So odd, that look. It takes me a moment to realize he's crying. He can't bend down to pick up a jar of paper clips spilled on the floor.

. . .

"The fifth vertebra is entirely collapsed. Surgery—a lumbosacral fusion—will be the best option."

"Will it work?" Jack says.

"There are risks. Because of the Addison's."

"But there's a chance?"

The doctor nods. "Yes." He pauses, then, "Without it, you may lose your ability to walk."

I watch Jack's face as the words hit.

October 1954. In the Hospital for Special Surgery in New York, they prepare his body with medication for ten days. Afterward, they declare the surgery a success. But even before the fever spikes, I know something is wrong. His eyes are different, glassy. A blurred look.

"Are you all right, Jack?"

"Just woozy from the pain meds."

I lie down beside him. Night. The lamp is off. Through the sheets, his skin burns, lips dry. I hold him gently; he seems so vulnerable, frail. He stirs. I should tell the nurse. I should tell them.

"I love you, Jack," I say.

He opens his eyes—a weak smile. "And you'd think that would be enough to fix it."

The nurses press into the room. They soak him in antibiotics, pack him in ice, but the heat in his body keeps rising. I call Joe and Rose. They come. Rose prays, the rosary clicking, prayers under her breath. Joe sits by the bed, talking to Jack as he floats in and out of consciousness. I kneel on the other side of him, my face on his hot open palm, tears sharp. I'm going to lose him. I don't want to lose him.

The doctor comes, another nurse behind him explaining we have to leave.

"He needs a priest," Rose cries. Joe draws her out into the corridor. *Mrs. Kennedy.* That's the doctor. I kiss his forehead, skin like fire. Jack. Stay with me. *Please, Mrs. Kennedy, you have to leave now.* I suddenly realize they're talking to me.

It's days before he's stabilized, another week before he can sit up in the bed. I bring him books, newspapers, magazines. I read aloud to him. Poetry and cartoons in *The New Yorker.* Movie reviews.

"That one sounds good," he says.

"Sure, if you're John Wayne's grandfather."

He laughs. I feed him apple crisp. He refuses to eat the gray slab of beef on the dinner tray. I slip ice chips into his mouth. One day when I come in, someone has taped a poster of Marilyn Monroe on the ceiling over his bed. He smiles at me wanly.

"Lem," he says.

The first time I heard Lem Billings's name was when Joe told the story of how Lem repeated his senior year at Choate so he could graduate with Jack. That Christmas, Lem showed up at Joe's house with his battered suitcase and never quite left.

A few days later, I notice the poster has been turned and re-taped so Marilyn's legs are an upside-down V in the air.

"Lem again?" I say.

Jack rolls his eyes. "I'm bored as hell locked up in here."

He's been in the hospital for a month when he tells me he wants to write an essay. I listen, ask a few questions. After an hour, we decide it won't be an essay but a book.

"Thank you," he says that evening as I get ready to leave.

"That's a funny thing to say."

He shrugs. "This book will be good for me."

I smile at him and sit back down. "Let's start, then."

"Tonight?"

"Why not?"

He's less than 115 pounds. He still can't walk, and I know that this is what he needs—brusque, practical, no sympathy— a task, all intellect and matter-of-fact.

"You tell me what you want to say, Jack. I'll write it down. We'll go from there."

~

JACK

He should be grateful. He knows it. Everyone tells him. He's lucky he isn't dead. They tell him that too. But he's just so sick of being sick. Sometimes it seems he'll never be anything else.

Four days before Christmas, he's released. They get him up on a gurney and wheel him through the hospital corridors, out into the wind and the rush of the light. The seasons have changed.

He's missed weeks, months.

Back in the world of his father's house in Palm Beach, the wide lawn stretching to the seawall, bougainvillea and barrier hedges that separate the house from the road. The sun, the warmth, the pool, the tennis court, a blue-bright sky and lines of palm trees, the brittle rustle of their fronds—those sounds and smells he loves.

Ramps have been installed so he can move from room to room.

"Can I help you do that?" she'll say.
"Do you need an extra pillow on that chair?"
"Would you like to work on the book today?"

He should be grateful. He's lucky he survived. Everyone tells him. Lucky to have her. They remark on how devoted she's been. Collecting research materials, articles, passages, sending drafts of his essays to Sorensen, making notes on the drafts sent back. All for the book he's writing on eight leaders who embody political courage. Reams of yellow-lined paper, his notes she's transcribed—all of it organized, then typewritten into pages, margins filled with her handwritten edits.

He makes it through the Chrismas holidays, but by January, he's ready to crawl out of his skin.

One afternoon by the pool, he overhears her talking to his sister Jean.

"When we decided it was best to spend the winter here in Palm Beach," she says, "we gave up the lease on the house in Georgetown. We've talked about building our own house once we get through this and Jack is well again. Something simple. A one-story high up on a hill, maybe with views of the river."

"Too expensive," he says.

She bites down on her lip, a faintly crushed expression on her face he regrets. Her shoulders are sunburned. He floats near the side of the pool. Pushing off with the ball of his foot, he feels a sharp twang in his back.

There's a Glenn Miller record on the turntable. Strains of music drift.

He can still barely navigate steps. He can't bear weight on his left side. The pain shoots through his leg, even with the new protocol of steroids and a heel lift.

It's only at night when he feels alive. His body no longer crippled but as strong as it was in the sea off Japan. Hauling boys out of the gasoline slick, calling for each. He was their captain. He'd made a fatal miscalculation and driven them into danger. He was determined to set the wrong right. He called their names, swimming toward each voice and the thrash of their arms, their faces lit with fear in that hell-black water.

He needs to get strong again. To be better and back in the swing of things. He needs to need her less.

At the end of May, he returns to the Senate. At the Capitol, he waves off the aides and the wheelchair, hobbles up the steps for a press photograph, and strolls in.

Spring 1955

We are back in Washington. I'd hoped things might be better once he recovered enough to return to work, but the more he regains his strength, the more it seems I am alone again.

"What are you thinking?" I ask one morning at breakfast.

"Thinking I'm going to be late," he says. He picks up his briefcase and limps out the door.

I don't ask that question again.

Lee invites me to London. She and Michael have bought a flat in Belgravia. Lee has styled every inch of it—curtains, rugs, throws, the divan under the window. There's no clutter. Even the short piles of books are staged according to size and hue.

"It's exquisite, Lee," I say. "I'm not sure I should sit down."

She throws a party the night I arrive. "For you, Jacks," she says, that gorgeous pixie smile. Half of London, it seems, swings by to see the wife of the young American senator, son of the former ambassador. I can feel them wonder why I'm alone, and I explain we're meeting Jack in a few weeks, in France, once work lets up and he can get away. We mingle for a while, then whoosh off to another party, then a dinner dance, then late-night drinks. Lee has orchestrated everything. Weekend trips to Hatley Park and a hunt in Northumberland. Parties and dinners and teas.

"You're trying to turn me into a firefly, Pekes."

We're on a train heading back to Victoria Station. Lee sighs. "I drank too much last night."

"You can't swing from party to party forever," I say.

She looks out the window. I remember what Michael remarked to me one day when Lee was out, how he never quite knew whose hat he'd find on the stand in the hall when he got home.

"Did you find a house in Virginia?" she asks.

"We were looking at one I loved, but Jack grumbled about the price. I found another, and he likes it, so we're moving ahead. I've drawn up plans to redo the bathroom and his dressing room, some shoe shelves built so he doesn't have to bend over."

"Are you happy, Jacks?" she asks.

I don't want that question. She is still staring out the train window, her lovely face eclipsed by a worn sadness, and I realize her question isn't directed at me.

"Are you all right, Pekes?"

"Just trying to figure a few things out."

The night before, at a party, I watched my sister come alive, back to her radiant coquette self, when Prince Stanislaw Radziwill dropped by. Stas, as he was called, was a Polish prince with a wild saturnine look. I watched my sister metamorphose under Prince Radziwill's eyes. The Pekes of my childhood, impossibly beautiful, sexy, and spoiled. Radziwill, I learned, fled Poland at the time of the German invasion of his country. He made it over the border to Switzerland and married a Swiss woman. Her money became his, and he poured it in and out of real estate to make more. Within an hour, I realized that what I was watching between my sister and the prince was a practiced dance.

"I love having you here with me," Lee says now. "Everyone wants to meet you, and I get to show you off. It reminds me of the summer you brought me to Europe. I loved that summer." Through the window, the fields rush by. "And now we are married," she says. "Do you miss Jack?"

"He's always away, it seems, working. I wish we had more time together."

Lee nods, her face distorted in the window, tones of yellow

and gray; her earrings glint like minnows. "I don't miss Michael at all. The air is so much more alive as soon as I get free."

We leave for France. Jack arrives—it's almost like meeting a stranger, a tourist in a world where I'm at home. He seems awkward, cardboardish, his Boston twang and rumpled American clothes.

We go to visit his father in Cannes. As the car turns up the drive leading to Joe's villa, Michael says, "I don't know why you want to be in politics, Jack, when you could be living in this."

"What is that?" Lee says, pointing to liveried footmen interspersed among the trees that line the drive. They step forward and bow slightly as we pass.

"Just Dad roughing it again this year," Jack says. I catch the shame in his voice. He hates the display of wealth. He glances at me, a silent plea for me to say something, anything, to lighten it.

"Topiary footmen," I say. He smiles.

The social roundabout continues. Dinner with the Wrightsmans in honor of the empress of Iran. A formal dance in Monte Carlo. A friend of Lee's has lent us his house overlooking the sea. Sitting with Jack at breakfast one morning, I realize we haven't argued once since he arrived. Everything feels easier between us, less coldness, that sweet banter flickering back, and for a moment I want to stay in this world, however rarefied and unreal, that is not ours.

He's across the small wrought-iron table from me, reading the newspaper. A headline on the front page: CHICAGO BOY LYNCHED.

"What's that article, Jack?"

He murmurs something about being done in a moment. I look down at the garden, the ruffled heads of trees. A motorboat moves toward the dock below.

"He's here, Jackie," Lee calls from inside the house.

Jack looks up from the paper.

"Who?"

"Gianni Agnelli," I say. "Lee arranged for him to take us waterskiing."

I don't say: *Would you like to come?* With his back, he can't risk the hard bounce over the wake. I pick up my towel and start down the hill to the dock. I can feel his eyes on me.

That night he stays close to me, his hand a slight pressure at the small of my back as we walk into the room to meet the others for drinks before dinner. On our way upstairs at the end of the night, he slides his hand along the back of my thigh. I almost tease him. *Did you like watching me step onto that motorboat with Agnelli-of-Fiat-fortune and zoom off? What about it did you like?*

In the bedroom, he pulls up my dress and makes love to me against the wall, then pulls me down on the bed. I wrap my legs around his hips and draw him into me, his mouth electric on my body in the dark.

Fall 1955

I'm in the living room in Hyannis Port with Bobby and Jack as they talk about trouble in the South. A Chicago boy, visiting relatives near the Mississippi Delta, was murdered for whistling at a white woman. Two men came by his great-uncle's house, dragged the boy out, beat him, torched him, drowned him in the river. When he was found, a cotton-gin fan laced with barbed wire had been wrapped four times around his neck to weigh him down.

"Fourteen years old," Bobby says.

"It's another country down there," says Jack.

"If it was, it wouldn't be your problem."

"What those men did, it's unthinkable," I say.

They both look at me, and for a moment it's startling—how different they are, their faces, expressions. Jack is cool, surveying, calibrating. Bobby's eyes, though, are just so bright, an icy fire and an uncommon depth in them I'm not expecting to see.

"Story's everywhere now because of the photographs," Bobby says. "A close-up of the boy's face. Mangled. Another of his mother at the funeral home. She chose open casket."

"And the men were acquitted," says Jack.

"Sure. In a Southern trial."

I'll remember this conversation months later, when I read an interview with Rosa Parks where she talks about how the real reason she didn't get up from her bus seat that day was because she couldn't stop thinking about that murdered boy and his mother who insisted on an open casket so the world could see what had been done—that boy named Emmet Till.

"How do you think it will end?" I ask Bobby when Rosa Parks is arrested for a second time, in early 1956.

"This is only the start," Bobby says.

"Do you think Jack sees it that way?"

"He's going to have to."

I don't say anything then. I'm curious what, if anything, he'll add.

But he changes the subject. "How's the ankle?"

I smile. "I'm afraid that sprain was the end of my touch-football career." I don't tell him I'm pregnant. Jack and I agreed not to tell anyone until I see the doctor again, but the secret has forged something new between us, that giddy and tenuous promise—a baby due later this year.

. . .

The tone of the meetings has changed. Less casual. More formal strategizing. Endorsing Adlai Stevenson for president, Jack manages to get Stevenson's top aide, Arthur Schlesinger, Jr., as an ally. The rumor is that Adlai is considering Jack as a possible running mate. By April, the meetings at our house in Georgetown are day in, day out—in our living room, in our kitchen, on the front stoop, on the stairs. Meetings after work and over lunch. The men leave the toilet seats up. Their crumbs litter the rug, and their drinks mold rings on the end tables. Once, after a shower, I walk out of the bathroom into a knot of men leaning against the wall in the upstairs hall, the air thick with the smoke of Havana H. Upmann cigars. Silent, they stare as I pass through them like a gauntlet, my body wrapped in a towel, the little bulge of my belly, a second towel around my hair. I walk into the bedroom and shut the door.

One Saturday in Hyannis Port, Jack and Teddy are down by the shore, messing around with the boat, trying to set the rigging for a sail. I stand with Bobby, watching them as Jack barks orders and Teddy fumbles around, doing it not quite right, or not the way Jack wants.

"Hey, Jackie," Jack calls. "I left my jacket up at the house, can you get that for me? Don't let that line go, Ted."

"I'll get the jacket," Bobby says to me. "You stay here."

I smile. "I'm pregnant, not an invalid."

"Jack's really happy," he says as we walk up. "He talks about that baby all the time."

"He wants me at the convention."

"You should come."

"Chicago in August, with a baby due in October?"

"Ethel will be there."

"Oh, Bobby, your wife is an ace at being pregnant."

He looks embarrassed.

"Do you think Jack really wants the vice presidency?" I say as we reach the porch steps.

Joe is there. "Don't ask for my opinion on *that*," he says.

"I wasn't, Joe."

"I don't know why the hell he'd squander political capital to be runner-up. They'll all lose to Eisenhower anyway."

"We're just getting a jacket, Dad," Bobby says.

Joe follows us into the house. "I can't imagine it's been nice for you, Jackie, having them all underfoot when you're trying to rest up for my grandchild."

I laugh. "If this were a convenient campaign for you, Joe, would you be so concerned?"

"Schlesinger says Stevenson likes what he sees," Bobby says. "We'll let it play out."

"And blow his chances for the real race?" Joe says.

"Jack's being smart about the vice presidency, Dad. He's not bragging like Humphrey or going around puffed up. Just the possibility of being named VP gets him into the center ring."

Joe pretends to consider this, but he's never put much stock in what Bobby brings.

"It's going to be Jack," says Bobby.

"I hope it isn't," I say.

"Why? Jack wants this."

I smile. "To be second?"

At the convention in Chicago in August, heat ripples off the pavement. Over ninety degrees in the shade. I attend a champagne party for the campaign wives and overhear Perle Mesta complain to another woman she can't believe Jack Kennedy's wife would be such a beatnik as to show up without stockings. My feet and legs are swollen from the heat at the session where Jack nominates Adlai Stevenson as the Democratic candidate. I sit at the edge of the crowd. A hush comes over the convention hall as Jack speaks. His voice has begun to exert a new pull. My hands rest on my belly, marking the occasional slight push of the baby under my palm. I've learned to distinguish the turn of the head, the kick of a foot, what's knee, what's shoulder.

Estes Kefauver, not Jack, is selected to be Stevenson's running mate.

"You're disappointed," I say to Jack in the hotel afterward as we pack. "But you didn't really want the vice presidency, did you?"

He shakes his head. "Dad told me I was wasting it. It just burns that he was right."

On the flight back to Hyannis Port, he is brooding, restless. He sits with Bobby and his closest aides, the Irish trio: Larry O'Brien, Kenny O'Donnell, Dave Powers.

"I'm going to get out of town for a while," Jack says. "A quick trip. I'll see if Teddy will come with me." He's talking to them, but this is his way of breaking news to me that I might not want to hear.

"What about the baby?" I ask later, once we're back in the house alone.

"That's October. It's only August."

"I'll miss you," I say.

"It'll be a quick trip."

He's putting me off. He's angry about the convention. I should let it go.

"I don't want you to leave," I say.

He is sifting through papers. His hands stop for a moment, gray eyes cool. "Don't."

A few days later, he's gone. I leave for Newport.

"What was he thinking?" my mother says. "Leaving you alone only weeks before the baby's due."

"The convention was hard for him."

"Well, it's all been hard for you."

I'm looking at a magazine of paint colors and nursery designs. Maybe I shouldn't have chosen yellow. Maybe I should have done things differently.

"I know you think the trouble with me, Mother, is that I don't play bridge with my bridesmaids."

She doesn't answer right away, then, "I don't actually think the trouble is you."

. . .

It's my mother I cry out for that August morning when I wake to shooting pains in my lower belly that radiate down my legs. The pain is unbearable. A rush of water—pinkish, then darker.

Hours later, I surface in the hospital. Bobby sits by my bed. The room is very white, his face cut against that whiteness, concern in his eyes, the blue intensity hazed by something new. I try to pull my mind out of the heavy sleep. I notice he's holding my hand. Something is wrong.

"Where's my baby?"

He shakes his head. "We almost lost you."

"The baby?"

"No," he says. Then I know. I don't want him to say it.

"Where's my mother?"

"She'll be right back."

"Where's Jack?"

"We haven't been able to reach him yet."

It's right there, on the edge of me—the question about the baby, where it is, that tiny body, tiny self, what happened, how it happened—but the sadness in his eyes is too cutting, too awful and intimate. I need a glass of water. That's all.

"We almost lost you," he says again, moving the chair closer to the bed.

"A girl?"

He nods.

"Arabella," I say. "That's the name I wanted. I knew it was a girl."

His eyes fill, and I look away. Outside, starlings in the trees. Clouds and sky in pieces, caught between the branches and the flourish of summer leaves. Everything so bright and violent. Just looking at the green hurts my eyes.

"We haven't been able to reach the senator," I hear Bobby tell the doctor an hour later. I know what he's doing. Trying to establish a story before another takes root. "We've sent messages through his secretary, but the boat he's on has no ship-to-shore."

A lie.

Bobby glances up as if he hears me thinking it.

"I'm sure there's an explanation, Jackie," he says after the doctor has left and we're alone. I'm sitting up in the bed, pillows propped behind my back. The wall feels hard against my skull. I need that sense of hardness, that ground. Bobby is just looking at me. Do I really have to break it down for him? The baby is gone, so in Jack's mind, there's no reason to cut his trip short.

"How is Ethel?" I ask.

"Fine."

It ends there. Ethel is due within a week. And Jack's sister Pat has just given birth to a little girl named Sydney. Bobby is still looking at me, a compassion in his face that swerves too close and makes me feel. I don't want to feel.

"It's just a mistake, Jackie," he finally says.

There's no mistake, I want to say. The affairs are not a mistake. The coolness, the jokes, the flip remarks that shut me down. Not a mistake. Nor is his fickle desire for me, proprietary at times, like a wife is an article he wants, as long as that wife is strong, put-together, sexual, witty in a passionless way, as long as she keeps herself intact and doesn't need him—because when she's wanting or vulnerable or weak, he has to get out, get away. He can't be there when she's breaking.

Bobby's eyes search my face.

You don't stay with someone because they hurt you, I could say. You stay for the slight and mythical promise of a dream that once meant so much you were willing to trade a different future for it. You stay for what you gave up.

"It wasn't supposed to be like this, Bobby." To his credit, he doesn't ask what "it" is—the loss of the baby, the marriage, or some other loss not yet taken into account. He sits with me while I cry. He stays that night, late. He arranges everything. The service, flowers, funeral card. Everything.

"Good night, Jackie," he says as he is leaving. "I'll see you tomorrow."

"Thank you."

"I'll always be here for you," he says, glancing away like he feels foolish for having said it.

I smile. "So now you're the one I'd put my hand in the fire for."

Years later, I will remember that moment between us, and every time I remember, I'll see some different aspect, a look in his eyes I didn't register at the time, something desperately earnest in the silence, a little rushed as he looked away. Years from now, I will understand how much more complex that evening was than I gave it credit for. In the moment, all we see is what we expect to see.

JACK

The sea is calm. He sits on the deck, legs outstretched. There's a woman nearby. Lying on a blue-and-white-striped cushion, half her face in shadow under the brim of her hat. She has pulled the straps of her bathing suit off her shoulders; her skin is tan, dirty-blond hair halfway down her back. The sun is hot. The kind of heat that erases what you'd rather forget.

He can't forget.

An hour ago, he sent the message back: Say there's no signal, you couldn't get through.

Half an hour before that, he took the call on the radio. His brother's voice through the static on the line. They spoke long enough for him to know there was no point in rushing home. He said something to that effect. Bobby landed on him like bricks. Jack hung up.

He needs time. A few more days before he has to go home and meet that crushing loss he knows is waiting in her face. Time to keep it at bay. The loss, the need, hers, his own. He'll deal with it. Get through it. Soon.

The woman on the deck says his name. She asks him something. He doesn't answer. His eyes are half-closed. The sun is a tattoo on his lids and burns.

The day after the baby is buried, Jack calls. They just put into port, he says, in Genoa.

"How are you, Jackie?"

It's hard to believe he's actually asking that question.

"Jackie? Are you there?"

"Yes."

"Well, I'm going to be coming home." He says it like he's reading from a script, or maybe he thinks I'll assure him, *Oh, please don't worry, Jack. Please stay and enjoy your time in the sun.* I can't quite imagine what he thinks. The air in the room feels wildly still.

"See you then," I say.

"All right. Hey, Jackie—"

But I'm already hanging up the phone. The curved shape of the receiver in its cradle. My hand rests there. That smooth, metal-like cool.

He gets home. Everything feels horribly stilted, layers of glass between us.

"We'll try again," he says.

I don't answer.

"Jackie?"

"It will have to be a very different kind of again."

On our third anniversary, I'm still confined to bed. I haven't cried since those days in the hospital with Bobby, but my body is a yawn of dark grief. When Ethel's fifth child is born, I tell Jack to give the house we bought, Hickory Hill, to Bobby and Ethel. Or sell it. However he wants to handle the transaction, they should have that house, for their lovely uncomplicated marriage, its industry and Catholic sweetness and the babies that keep popping out. They should have the nursery curtains, the mobile, the crib.

He tells me his father has offered to rent something else for us in Georgetown.

"Why?" I say. "You'll be at work or off campaigning for Stevenson. When they let me out of bed, I'm going to visit Lee."

"But Lee is in London."

"Yes."

Someone tells someone there's trouble in our marriage. Or someone takes a wild guess and hits a bit of truth. However it happens, a rumor finds its way into the papers that I'm planning to leave him and Joe's offered me a million dollars to stay.

"Did you see that garbage?" Joe says to me.

"I thought it was a fine idea, but why one million? Let's make it ten."

Joe laughs. "I'm on your side, Jackie. Jack needs you."

"For his political career?"

"And a lot more than he seems to realize."

"Well, I hope he figures it out sooner, rather than—you know—later."

Silence then. He waits for me to elaborate. We're sitting in the living room of his house in Hyannis Port. It's late afternoon. Everyone else is somewhere else.

He stretches out his legs. "You and Jack should take a trip," he says. "The two of you, maybe around the New Year. Antigua?"

"Are you trying to placate or bribe me, dear Joe?"

He smiles. "Whichever you'd prefer."

Your son never apologized, I want to say. *He never said to me,*

I'm sorry for leaving when the baby was coming, I'm sorry for not coming home when she died.

"You need this marriage, don't you?" I say. "Particularly now that plans are being laid for Jack to run." I don't have to say which race. There's only one race that matters to Joe.

"This is no joke, Jackie. Divorce, or even the whiff of it, will kill his chances."

"Then we'll have to make this fun," I say, "so I can be sure to survive it." I smile. "I'll need a small house at some point, and Jack will need new suits. He can't get the hems so short. He can't keep wearing those tired scuffed loafers in the evenings."

"Did you hear what I said?" He peers at me through those thin wire-rimmed glasses. His eyes don't dance.

"No unpleasantness, Joe. I've been heartbroken, and I need to climb out of it. Let's think of things we can celebrate: Jack will have new suits, I will have a little house, and it looks like the Supreme Court is going to uphold desegregation."

From then on, I am careful with my heart. I'll stay in this marriage, at least for now. But I'll keep myself slightly apart. Oddly, Jack doesn't seem to notice. In fact, things between us seem lighter, like he's relieved I've split myself and now he only has to reckon with half. How much simpler things become once I withdraw, once I'm less passionate, less present, less open and honest. Less in love. From time to time, it occurs to me with a stab of sadness that it might be precisely the less that makes me more the right kind of wife.

1957

That spring, we learn Jack will be awarded a Pulitzer for *Profiles in Courage,* and we learn that I am pregnant. I want a baby so much. I'm afraid to trust the joy.

We go to the Paris Ball at the Waldorf Astoria. Marilyn Monroe is there on the arm of Arthur Miller, her body like a vase in her black-halter sequined dress.

"That woman is outrageously beautiful," I say to Jack in the car afterward.

"She's a wreck."

I feel a wave of anger. "A wreck brave enough to stand by Miller during his McCarthy inquisition."

"Investigation. Besides, they were already having an affair."

"Does that make her less brave?"

We ride in silence. The car pulls up to a traffic light. Two more blocks to the hotel.

"Lee is leaving Michael," I say.

"What?"

"He's grown too dull for her. I think she's going to run off with a Polish count. My sister, the princess. Does that seem surprising?" I look out the window. The air in the car is altered. The news has thrown him. Divorce. The light turns green.

I take him to see a house I've found on N Street NW in Georgetown. Three stories, Federal style.

"It leans a bit to one side," I say as we walk over. "The stairs
creak."

"Sounds like me," he says.

"It used to belong to Oatsie." He'll like that. Oatsie is Marion
Leiter. She's close friends with the British spy novelist Ian Fleming. Jack loved *Casino Royale*.

In the house on N Street, Jack seems smitten with an old
doorknob. We leave the realtor and her assistant downstairs.

"I think this will be the nursery," I say.

"We haven't agreed to buy it."

"You fell in love with the doorknob."

He reaches for me then. He touches my waist. An unexpected
tenderness. "I like this crooked creaking house you've chosen,
Jackie." He slides his hand around my back and draws me to
him.

. . .

I'm with his parents in Hyannis Port in July when the phone
rings. Yusha. Calling to wish me a happy birthday.

"I'd like a few more days of twenty-seven," I say.

He was in New York the week before, he says. He dropped by
Black Jack's apartment.

"He didn't look right, Jackie. He's lost weight. He can't keep
food down."

"He must have been drinking?"

"No, actually. That's why I'm mentioning it. He wasn't."

I fly to New York and talk my father into going for tests at the
hospital. I hold his hand as the doctor explains it's late-stage liver
cancer. Chemotherapy is the only option.

I call Lee.

"Too much jai alai," I say, "scotch, and Pan Am stewardesses."

Lee sighs. "Should I come home?"

"You should if you want to."

"I want to if I should, Jacks. You'll tell me, won't you? You'll know. Tell me when I should come, and I'll be there."

But I don't know. My father fails so fast that by the time I reach the hospital after getting the doctors' call, he's gone. Only moments ago, they tell me. My name was the last word he spoke. Is that true? Or is that what they tell all the daughters who aren't there in time?

Once, on a carriage ride through Central Park when Lee and I were young, ice cream dripped on our dresses and our Sunday gloves. Lee began to cry, afraid of what our mother would say when Black Jack brought us back, how angry she'd be. Lee sobbed. Our father couldn't understand what she was afraid of. I tried to explain. He just threw back his dark head and laughed, his laughter so bold and free I felt my breath cut, and from then on, I understood that a glove was just a glove and what mattered was the decadent sunshine, the gorgeous midsummer patterns of sky and park and city, the heat and the green. What mattered was the sugar and cream dissolving on my tongue, the sweet sticky aftermath of that pleasure on our lips and wrists.

After the funeral, I tell Lee, "You should take what you want of Daddy's things. All I want is the desk." The desk is mahogany, French Empire style, with ormolu hardware and a slant front. "You can have everything else, Lee."

"I don't want anything," my sister says.

When Jack leaves again for the campaign trail, I drive him to the airport. The air is humid still, and warm, but we are into the fall, and the slant of light has changed.

"Don't overdo exercise while I'm gone," he says.

"Exercise is good for me."

"Just not too much."

"Someone's going to have to run after this baby."

It makes him happy, every time I say that word.

"I feel like I've forgotten something," he says, looking through the battered leather briefcase. He moves some papers into a folder, then snaps the briefcase closed.

"Just don't forget to come home," I say.

He leans in to kiss me at the door that leads out to the airstrip; I can feel his breath faintly cool, the white rush of the sky behind.

I stay in New York while he's gone. I take long walks in the park. Every morning, I read the papers: Eisenhower sends in the 101st Airborne to protect nine Black children at a Little Rock high school; the Russians shock the United States by launching Sputnik, the first satellite, into space. I read *Faith and History* by the philosopher Reinhold Niebuhr. I cut a passage from *The Observer* to give to Jack when he comes home, a quote from the French filmmaker Jean Cocteau:

> . . . *what is history after all?*
> *History is facts which become lies in the end; legends are lies which become history.* . . .

I watch the leaves turn, and I think about my father, how he will never meet my baby. Loving him was like trying to put my arms around the sun—I could never quite keep up with the speed of the loss, even knowing it was coming, too fast, too soon, and no matter what I did or how much I wanted, I would not be ready. There would be loose ends, always, for what I had not said, for what I could not bridge or hold or save.

Lee and I had decided there would be summer flowers strewn across his casket. Black-eyed Susans, cornflowers, lilies, too, for the heartbroken beauty of their scent. Fierce colors, wild blooms. And those summer flowers are what I hold in my mind as I let go to the rising pull of anesthesia the day before Thanksgiving.

"Please, let all be well," I say quietly. "Let my baby be well, whole and safe and beautiful. Let all things be well."

I will always look back on the day, November 27, 1957, as the happiest of my life. Jack bending toward me, our sweet baby girl in his arms, an expression on his face I've never seen—it kicks my heart over.

"How lovely she is, Jackie." Light pours from his face toward the tiny being wrapped in a blanket in his arms, his hand cupped around her skull. He sits on the edge of the bed, flowers he brought on the table behind him, and it is just the three of us, alone—floating on a raft cut loose from the world. He will always look at our daughter just that way, like he needs to map each detail, each feature—the bond between them tensile, change-less, transcendent.

In the hospital room, her tiny face scrunches up. She opens her mouth to cry.

"Shhh," he whispers. She quiets at his voice.

1958

We move into the house on N Street. I hire a housekeeper and a nanny for Caroline. It's a simple, informal life we begin to build. When Jack is home, we go to the movies with our friends Ben and Tony Bradlee. We host small dinner parties, games of charades, and cutthroat Monopoly tournaments. Charley Bartlett will invariably complain, "Pull no punches, Jack. You play like those little hotels are real." Every other month, I drag Jack to the Dancing Class at the Sulgrave Club. He doesn't love it, but he goes. He'll dance a bit, stay near me for a while, then peel off in search of some like-minded political soul to hash over the current state of affairs. If he doesn't find anyone, he'll drift back to ask how long I want to stay. I send him on another lap around the room—glorious and bored, a tiger in a cage.

"A drink, Mrs. Auchincloss?" Jack asks one afternoon that spring. My mother's come to visit.

"I came for a baby," she says.

"Caroline's sleeping."

"Then I'll wait." Her smile is tight and cool. She's liked Jack less since we lost Arabella—the fact that he wasn't there, that we couldn't reach him, and that he didn't rush home when we did. "You've made some lovely changes to this room, Jackie," my mother says.

Jack smiles. "Bunny's helping."

"Adele Astaire introduced me to Bunny Mellon," I tell my mother.

"The Listerine family?"

"She's become a friend," I say. "Her own house is gorgeous. I've told her I even love the stale candy in the antique jars."

"Speaking of antiques," says Jack, "Mrs. Auchincloss, I'd like your opinion on Jackie's new chairs. Louis XVI chairs, she explained when I got the bill. I've told her a chair is a chair. You just need to sit in it."

I laugh. "All those men working on your campaign, Jack, need comfortable chairs to sit in. They're hostage for hours in those meetings."

Jack rolls his eyes. "What do you think, Mrs. Auchincloss?"

"Please call me Janet." Her smile softens a bit.

"Janet, take a look at this," he says, picking up a copy of the April 21 *Life* magazine. On the cover, Caroline is on Jack's lap, a pink dress, her bare plump legs poking out, one hand gripping his suit sleeve.

I take the magazine and flip through to find the article.

"Where are we, Jack?" I keep flipping the pages. "Oh, here. Way back. Page 132, right after a piece about learning to surf in Australia."

"It's the cover that matters," says Jack, a little defensive, which makes me smile.

"I'd like to surf in Australia." I hand the open magazine back to my mother.

"I'd like a baby," says my mother.

"I'll get her for you," Jack says, heading toward the stairs.

"He loves a reason to wake her up," I say.

My mother starts to say something, then doesn't. She looks around. "I like the chairs."

"You don't think it's too much?"

She glances at me. "It's like anything else, Jackie. Live with it for a while, see how you feel."

. . .

Jack asks me to go on a short campaign trip with him through Massachusetts. An out-and-back in May. Three stops in the morning, a break for lunch, more stops in the afternoon. In the car heading west, I sit in the backseat with Kenny O'Donnell. Kenny was Bobby's roommate in college and worked on Jack's first campaign. Jack calls him "our play-only-hardball gatekeeper."

"How long is lunch, Kenny?" I ask.

"Two hours."

"That's a long lunch."

"It's the deal we made with the ambassador to make sure Jack doesn't run out of gas."

I smile. "Nothing like making deals with the ambassador."

"They told me you were fragile," Kenny says.

"Fragile?"

We walk through the restaurant to a back room. There are plenty of open tables up front, but it's clear this has been prearranged.

"No menus?" I ask Kenny.

"Steak and potatoes are already ordered."

"You eat the same thing every day?"

"Pretty much. And everyone gets a glass of milk."

I laugh. "Might one order something in addition to a glass of milk?" The whole thing feels weirdly clandestine—the gangster back room, lunch all planned. I ask the server for a glass of wine and get out a cigarette. Jack shakes his head at me and mouths, *No.* I put the pack away.

"Now, let's get this straight," says Jack. "Kenny, where's your pencil? Start getting this down." He works through a list: who to call first, who to call after, what needs to be prepped. A litany of directives. Kenny's at his shorthand list; the others talk among themselves. Once, before we were married, when I went up to see Jack in Boston, he introduced me to someone nicknamed "Onions" Burke and someone else called "Juicy" Grenara. Then we all went for dinner at the Ritz.

The food arrives. Jack talks and gestures, his pale eyes cool as Kenny takes notes on the back of an envelope. The pencil tip breaks.

"All set, then," says Jack. "Let's eat."

"I have a question, Kenny," I say. "What exactly do you do with all those things Jack tells you? You write them down. Then what? Go down the list and check them off one by one?"

The table falls silent.

"Funny you should ask," Kenny says. "You know what I do? I wait until he calms down, then I do the things that need to get done and throw the envelope out."

"You son of a bitch," Jack says. "I bet that is what you do."

I laugh. "Oh, Jack, I'm sure Kenny would never not do every single task you ask him to do, right, Kenny?"

Jack relaxes then, the easy smile that's hard to read. "Just like my wife, aren't you, Kenny? I say one thing, and you go and do exactly what you want." But he is laughing too.

I recount this for our friend Joe Alsop a few weeks later—an abridged version of my first political trip and the steak-and-potatoes routine.

Joe Alsop has called me "Darling Jackie" ever since he re-neged on his offer to rent us his house in Georgetown. But I like him, and I love his incisive political column, *Matter of Fact,* and his salon-style dinner parties on Dumbarton Ave. Alsop has a sprawling library, Savile Row waistcoats, and exquisite taste in food. He has a cagey wit and a knack for bringing together the right group of people. "An evening is like a room," he told me once, an elegant wave of his cigarette. "You can construct a room so guests feel at once a sense of ease and excitement: formal dress, then toss in a martini and a topic of hard conversation, some thorny national issue launched as a query. Watch the room ignite. Alliances are forged. Deals get made. Everyone thinks it's just a dinner party." He glanced at me to be sure I was following, then added, "Never discount the bore factor. No bores allowed with eight or fewer people. Only half a bore with ten."

Joe Alsop hasn't always liked Jack, I learned recently. Appar-ently Jack did some crass thing once and got himself crossed off the soirée list, until he married me.

That particular spring evening, Alsop introduces us to Kay

and Phil Graham, loyal supporters of Lyndon Johnson. In his introduction, he calls Jack "the antidote to the sclerotic Eisenhower administration we're all so tired of."

Low music in the background—Ella Fitzgerald.

Phil Graham looks at Jack. "You're after the presidency?"

"That's right," Jack says.

"You're young. Why not wait another four?"

"Well, Phil, first, I think I'm as qualified to run as anybody, except for Lyndon. Second, if I don't run, whoever wins will be there for eight years and that will influence his successor. Third, if I don't run, I'll be in the Senate for eight more years, and as a potential future candidate, I'll have to vote politically, which means I'll end up a mediocre senator and a lousy candidate."

Silence, then Graham says, "That makes sense."

Alsop takes my arm. "Jackie, come with me. You must try the terrapin soup."

"That wasn't politics," I say once we're out of earshot, "what you just orchestrated. That was art."

. . .

August. I travel with Jack to Europe for a Senate Foreign Relations Committee trip. It's Gianni Agnelli who tells us that Churchill is a guest on Aristotle Onassis's yacht. It's also Agnelli who procures an invitation for us. Not to dinner. That point is underscored. But for drinks an hour before.

The mind is water.

That's the thought that strikes me as I step onto the deck of the *Christina*. He is there, Onassis, a man I've heard so much about—shipping magnate; Don Juan of the rich; notorious lover of *La Divina*, the famed opera singer Maria Callas. Their sex and fights are legendary. He's a man whose pockets are lined with ruthless wealth and luck and stars.

Onassis, Jack told me, has no fondness for Bobby, who scuppered a deal Onassis was trying to make in Saudi Arabia. That evening, though, he greets us warmly.

"A tour?" he asks. Jack takes my arm as Onassis leads us through the converted warship, deck to deck, stem to stern, through the famous bar and bathrooms of white marble sourced from the same quarry as the Parthenon. There are painted fish and mosaics, lapis-crusted fireplaces—all of it opulent, lavish, shameless.

"What do you think, Mrs. Kennedy?" Onassis asks.

"It's beautiful."

"Many things are beautiful."

"It reminds me of a line in a poem. 'La Vie Antérieure.'"

"The life past."

"A kind of Xanadu."

"Ah. You will tell me the rest sometime."

Jack is a few feet away, studying a nautical oil painting. He's heard our exchange. Such a curious man Onassis is. His stumpy height, rugged face, hair greased with brilliantine.

"Shall we go on?" he asks.

We come into the salon, where the others, including Churchill, are gathered. The master of history slumps in a chair, white cuffs, handkerchief, black suit, and bow tie, the broad famous jowls of that face. Onassis brings Jack over to introduce them. I follow partway, then hang back. Jack sits down beside Churchill, looking awkward, as he tries to engage the old statesman. Churchill's shoulders curl forward. He's already into his cups.

What kind of memory lives in a man like that? A man who has passed through trials and turns of history. Who has failed and risked, lost and achieved, risen and fallen and risen again. What remains?

Churchill turns in his chair toward a dark-haired man on his left and says, in a booming voice, "I knew your father. Hated him. Isolationist and defeatist. He knew nothing of diplomacy. They tell me you're different. How are you different?"

The man's face is blank as Jack leans across to say that he is the one, son of the reviled ambassador. Churchill turns back to Jack. A snap of recognition, putting the face to the story. But it's hard going. Jack stumbles through the titles of Churchill's oeuvre: "I've read every one," I hear him say, and I remember that day in his childhood room in Hyannis Port on the Fourth of July. I remember what I saw in his face as he read aloud to me—the want, the dream, the reach.

It's why I stayed.

Jack keeps talking to Churchill, trying to light the grim silence, and he is again that boy from the little bedroom—this is his childhood hero. The writer, the statesman, the soldier who failed at the battle of Gallipoli, then led the fight against Hitler, no compromise, no appeasement. The old prime minister is at best a shrunken nodding version of his former self, but Jack speaks to him, his face animated, like these are better days. Churchill just looks bored. He drains his glass, pushes it toward Jack, nodding to the bar. Jack stands, wincing slightly—his back. He takes the empty glass and starts across the room. It's then that I notice Onassis standing alone by the wall, a painting behind him that looks like a Goya, watching me with a curious unwavering intensity, watching this tableau play out. The smile on his face jackal-like, his eyes with their rude desire. Jack pauses on his way to me with Churchill's glass. The rest of the room continues to bustle and mill, the tinkling sound of glasses, plates, passed hors d'oeuvres. Lamps and candles flicker as a warm breeze blows the dusk through the open doors, the night like a tide sweeping in. The sunset colors are fragile, and Onassis is still looking at me—he doesn't seem to care that Jack has noticed, or maybe he does, in a way that turns the night into a sport I didn't realize we'd been invited on board to play.

It was a Greek, Heraclitus, who insisted that change is the fundamental impulse of the universe. Our souls are like the stars and moon, turning bowls of fire.

Later that evening, in the car on our way to dinner, Jack asks me, "Well, how did I do?" It takes me a moment to realize he's referring to Churchill.

"I think he thought you were the waiter," I say.

He sighs. I slip my fingers through his.

"It's just too late, Jack," I say. "You met him too late. That's all."

But I remember that night. Even after we are home, back in the blustery chaos of Jack's Senate reelection campaign, I remember the exotic otherworldliness of the *Christina*. The heady sensation I felt watching that evening play out. The contradiction of Onassis. Not attractive. To me, something almost repulsive about him, the base sense of humor, gargoylish features. At the same time, I felt galvanized by him and his world. Not the blatant wealth; it was more than that—something inexorable, visceral, so alive that everyone else, even Churchill, even Jack, seemed colorless. Only he was real.

Years later, when I see Onassis again, he'll allude to that night.

"It was ten years ago this month, the first time I saw you," he says.

"Yes."

"You were aloof. Why aloof?"

"I wasn't sure I liked you."

"You wanted to stay for dinner."

"I was curious."

"You liked the *Christina*."

"It was a little bright."

"You mean gaudy."

"I said bright."

"You liked the story I told."

"I've always loved stories."

"That night we met, I noticed the unusual way you have of making men look at you."

I smile.

"And I noticed that Kennedy had no idea."

Something snaps between us.

"I'm sorry," he says. "I shouldn't have said that."

But the moment is severed, and I don't answer.

Fall 1958

Things begin to shift in the Senate campaign. The same men gather in our living room—cigarette butts in the ashtrays, papers on the table, glasses of juice, and coffee mugs. But this year feels different. This run-of-the-mill reelection race is only a prelude to the real campaign. And Jack is different—his ambition sharper, not just on the surface but melding into the ideals that drive him. I can feel it in how he talks, thinks, listens.

They want me to go with him to Omaha in September, where he'll speak at a gathering for the Democratic Party. They send Bobby to ask me.

"I've always dreamed of spending my fifth wedding anniversary in Nebraska."

"You'll enjoy it, Jackie."

"Maybe for you, I'll go."

The crowd in Omaha is double the size they anticipate.

"Twice as big with Jackie here than if you were alone," Kenny O'Donnell says to Jack on the plane home.

"That true?" Jack says.

"Yep."

"Well, for Pete's sake, don't tell her," Jack says, and when I glance up, he's looking at me, that little look. He smiles.

We've been happy. It startles me to realize this. Some new

brightness has slid between the careful walls I'd constructed to keep my heart safe.

I take a few more trips with him that fall, but I don't like to be away from Caroline. It's a pull in my body, missing her, her voice, smell, those slight hands on my neck, long hours with her in the warm autumn sun on the lawn.

His team asks me to do another campy show for television, *At Home with the Kennedys*. A living room shoot in Hyannis Port. Rose and I sit together. She asks how I've liked campaigning.

"So much," I say brightly, the good wife, my hands in my lap. "Jack and I have been traveling through the state, trying to meet as many people as we can. . . ."

"Well, congratulations, Jackie," says Rose in her dry laryngeal voice, "and congratulations to Jack that he found a wife who has so enjoyed the campaign."

It's hard not to laugh, but I force the right smile as the producer hits the cue and Jack appears out of thin air; he stands behind us in the living room, under the painting of a raging sea. The young shining hero, with that devastating smile, he thanks every woman across the state for joining his family on TV. He reminds them to cast their ballots on November 4.

And they do. Seventy-three percent of the vote in Massachusetts goes for Jack.

"I think we can call that a landslide," I say.

. . .

That winter of 1959, Lee quietly slips out of her marriage to Michael Canfield and marries the Polish count, Stas Radziwill. Three months pregnant, Lee is still so tiny, just the slightest bob in her shape under the simple white dress she wears for her wedding.

As we leave the church, I say to Jack, "Lee told me once she thought it was worth getting married just to have your own house."

"Now she has three."

I laugh. We continue down the steps.

The days turn toward spring. I set up an inflatable pool in our backyard in Georgetown and fill it with the garden hose. Caroline, eighteen months old, splashes for hours, crawling along the rippled plastic bottom, pretending to swim. We have picnic lunches together and afternoon "tea and cakes" in the shade, the small yard drenched in sunlight. I take her for long walks on the towpath and to Rose Park to play on the swings. Sometimes when I check on her under the stroller hood, I notice she is not asleep, her small face alert, watching the edges of the world from her blanket.

"How long have you been awake, little one? Such a wise little watcher, you."

Her small hands reach from inside the carriage, fingertips warm on my face. No matter how many times it happens, I feel that same flood of joy. "You're my heart, soul, sky," I say, unclipping the safety straps from her slight body, lifting her out.

Almost every afternoon, Caroline looks up at me and says, "Daddy?"

"Yes, darling, he'll be home soon."

I've learned to use that word whether *soon* is tomorrow or later that week.

"Soon," Caroline says, turning the word over. Then she looks past me, or out the window, toward the blue plunge of the sky at the top of the trees.

"Soon."

Before I leave with her for Hyannis Port, where we'll spend the summer, I take one more short campaign trip with Jack, to Yakima, Washington. Just before he's due onstage, he leans over to me. "Maybe I'll close with Tennyson, Jackie. What do you think?"

"You should."

"Give me those lines from 'Ulysses,' the ones that begin *Come, my friends. . . .*"

He passes his speech to me and, in the white space at the bottom, I write down the lines from that poem, one I used to recite for my grandfather Bouvier on our Wednesdays as he sat with his cane resting near his chair, wearing his three-piece suit, the twirled waxed ends of the mustache bobbing. I pass the paper back to Jack. He walks to the podium, delivers his speech, and closes with those lines. A surge of applause from the crowd.

"That worked," he says to me as we're led offstage. "I think I missed a few words. I was trying not to look down."

"You missed less than I would have."

A little smile, almost shy, and he says, "You know that's not true."

They're shaping campaign plans for the presidency. The key players of the inner circle: Joe, Jack, Bobby, the Irish trio, Ted Sorensen. Sorensen is funny—whenever he's near Jack, he puffs himself up like a boy, but he has an uncanny gift for channeling Jack's intellect into speeches. Steve Smith, married to Jack's sister Jean, is put in charge of financing and logistics. Journalist Pierre Salinger is hired to deal with the press. They spend hours pre-thinking obstacles: Jack is only forty-two. Too young, many will contend, to deal with the challenges facing the country. Plus, a Catholic has never been elected president.

"Jack's not even a good Catholic," I remark to Joe one afternoon. "And we all know I'm not Bess Truman enough."

"What do you think of the draft of the biography Jack gave you to read?" Joe says.

Jack steps through the screen door. He sits down next to me.

"It doesn't do him justice," I say. "In the first fifty pages, the author describes Jack as *quiet, taut, casual as a cash register.* And he plays to Jack's detractors, implying he's a lightweight, a puppet of his former-ambassador rich daddy." I smile at Joe. "Johnson will love that."

Joe has an expression he sometimes gets when I speak my mind.

"And I don't like that he brings up the Addison's," I say.

"That was our suggestion," Jack says. "It's going to come out. We want to get ahead of it."

"But he writes about it like you might not be up to the job."

Joe laughs. "Why don't you tell me what you really think?"

On the side table next to my chair is a book Jack's been reading on Jefferson and the August *Life* magazine. I'm on the cover: JACKIE KENNEDY: A FRONT RUNNER'S APPEALING WIFE. Jack is there as well but in the background, muted in a way he never is in life. I don't like the photograph. My face looks too polished, almost smug. But there's another in the interior pages that I love, of me in the surf with Caroline. I'm in my clothes, my pants rolled up as I swing her around. We're both soaked. I barely remember the film crew shooting it, but I remember the moment itself—the cold of the sea and my daughter's fierce laughter as she shrieked with joy, the light ballast of her body as she flew.

No one really wants that on a magazine cover, though.

"It's always bad news, Dad," Jack says, "when she gets quiet and just stares off like that."

"I think you can win, Jack," I say. "But we need to focus on what makes you different—your convictions, your vision and ambition, even your youth." I look at Joe. "And you, I'm afraid, need to be just a nice old man we visit at Thanksgiving and Christmas."

"I can do that," he says.

"Overall, though," I say, "things seem to be going well."

"Nothing wrong with better," Joe says.

"Do you really want this, Jack?" I ask after Joe has left and we're alone on the porch. He's watching the clouds bank over the ocean. Strange, almost vertical bands of grated light.

"Jack?"

"What?"

"Do you want this?"

"Don't worry about that biography."

"I'm asking you a question."

"It's the presidency, Jackie. Don't overthink it." In the past, that sudden sharper tone might have stopped me. Now I can feel the uncertainty behind it.

"Actually, Jack, I think you need to spend a little more time thinking about it. Because that isn't in the pages of that manuscript, and it's not in the world yet either. Give them more of what you believe—this writer and that other man who wants to trot along after you on the campaign trail. Let them in. Decide what you want them to know. And when you go stumping around, no matter what little town you're in—blue collar, white collar, factory, mining, East Coast, Midwest, South—set aside those two-sentence profiles everyone uses to prep you, because what you need to know is: What's unique about this town? These people? What do they want, love, care for? What have they lost or sacrificed? What do they grieve, fear, dream?"

JACK

He watches her face as the words leave her. It's fascinating to him, how words coming out of her mouth, the ideas and passion behind them, awaken her face. They are words she's already forming into lines she might write down, a dashed-off memo she'll hand to him. "Just some notes you might want to use for one of your speeches," she'll say.

He's wanted to be there in the midst of that casual alchemy. In the air around her hand and a pencil, her face studying sentences on a page, that short double line between her brows. He can see it as she goes on talking, those lines like a portal. He remembers what he felt once when they were first together, a kind of hunger to track the complex workings of her mind, and when he realized he couldn't— that, like him, she'd always keep some space of herself apart— something in him wanted to tear the whole architecture down.

The memory comes in a rush. He's not proud of it—the coldness he showed her, the arguments and small cruelties. The odd satisfaction he used to feel sometimes when he said something dismissive and the words hit, and he watched that strong light in her eyes fade. He doesn't like remembering this.

"What are you thinking?" she asks.

He smiles at her. "Come on," he says, standing up. "Let's go find Caroline and take a walk before the light is gone."

1960

On the second day of the New Year, a Saturday morning, Jack stands in the Senate Caucus Room and announces his candidacy for president. I buy him a puppy.

"To celebrate," I say.

He laughs.

"You just wanted a dog," he says.

"No, this dog is for you. Welsh terriers are very kind to people with allergies."

"We'll call him Charlie," says Jack, as he picks up the dog and holds him still so Caroline can stroke the silky ears.

I campaign with Jack that winter, crisscrossing the country, climbing out of cars into the wind and slush. I work down one side of the street while he works down the other; hundreds of hands in the morning, hundreds more in the afternoon. Towns start to blend. I read De Gaulle's memoirs and Henry Adams's *Democracy*, marking passages to share with Jack. In the papers, I follow the story of four Black boys who walk into the Woolworths in Greensboro, North Carolina, sit down at the lunch counter, and refuse to get up until they are served.

I ask him about it.

"We can't afford to lose the Southern white vote," he says.

"Then you might have to figure out how to have that and the Black vote too."

Teddy and his young wife, Joan, rent a house two blocks away from ours. They just had their first baby. I do Joan's grocery shopping and help her find a nanny. For over a year, I've watched Teddy and Joan wash around in an unfinished life, no home of their own, schlepping suitcases back and forth from Hyannis Port to Palm Beach and back.

"It's like riding a metronome, isn't it?" I say to Joan one day. We're sitting in her new living room. The baby has just woken up from a nap. "She's beautiful, Joan."

"She looks like Teddy, doesn't she?"

"She'll be a Hollywood beauty like you. We still need to get you curtains for this room."

"It's lovely," Joan says, "just as it is. You've done so much for me."

"Almost, but we'll get there."

She breaks down and talks about the trouble in her marriage.

"It's not that I don't love Teddy," she says. "It's just felt arranged from the start. Jean introduced us, you know, like Bobby and Ethel, but—"

"The rest of us will never be Ethel enough."

She smiles. Only six or seven years younger than I am but she seems so very new to all this. She straightens the baby's cloth on her shoulder, a stain of spit-up near her hair, in her hair.

"Ted had doubts too," she says. "And I still feel unsure."

"I don't know if one is ever sure," I say. "But this summer, let's be different together. The rest of them can sail, football, and Kennedy around, and you can play the piano while I paint. We'll go for walks on the beach. If we don't come back, they can launch a search."

She smiles, a fragile smile. "I know Ted runs around with other girls."

"All Kennedy men are like that," I say. "It means nothing."

She looks uncertain; I feel something swift and dark move through me. I push it off.

"You can't let it mean a thing, Joan," I say.

. . .

Jack is home for three days in the middle of March before the Wisconsin primary. It's the first warm spring day. We walk down to the canal. On our way home, as we're approaching a crosswalk, a car slows. Jack is ahead, carrying Caroline. He's telling her a story he made up about the sea; her hair spills toward his shoulder, that half-fantasy space the two of them disappear into. The car pulls alongside.

"Jack Kennedy." It's Marion Leiter—Oatsie. "Where are you headed?"

"Home, to get ready for you," Jack says. "Rumor is you're coming to dinner."

She laughs, a long hand draped over the steering wheel. "May I bring a guest?"

"Only someone interesting," Jack says.

Oatsie nods to the man in the passenger seat. He tips his hat.

"Ian Fleming, this is Jack Kennedy, and Jackie."

"You're James Bond," Jack says.

Halfway through dinner that night, Jack pauses mid-conversation with Joe Alsop and turns to Fleming. "Say, here's a question for you. If you were writing the perfect climax for a novel, how would you depose Castro?"

"I'd shame him out of office," Fleming says.

"How?"

"Bombard him with inanity."

"Example?"

"Air-drop leaflets over Cuba with fake scientific facts. Claims that beards draw radioactivity and cause impotence."

The table erupts into laughter. Everyone but Jack.

"Ridiculous, and also smart," Jack says. "Castro's power is built on ego. What else?"

"Infuse the currency with fake bills."

Jack nods. "Skew the economy. Throw his authority into chaos. I like it. Go on."

Fleming picks up a dinner roll and tears off a piece. "Just more of that. Target those illusory things he uses to bolster his myth. Disrupt them. Get him to resign or be forced out. Of course, in fiction, it's all possible."

Jack smiles. "Everything is fiction."

When he returns from campaigning in Wisconsin, I tell him I've skipped a period.

"So only one more trip for me," I say. "After that, the doctor says, I should step back."

"You mean stay home."

"For the baby."

He smiles. That word. I'm suddenly afraid.

"I don't want to lose this baby, Jack."

"You won't."

I touch his mouth, gently. He lets me.

He beats Hubert Humphrey in the West Virginia primary for the Democratic nomination. I fly down to meet him in Charleston. Together we walk into the crowded hall of the Hotel Kanawha. Flags, banners, lights, everyone cheering and yelling his name. Moments later, I've lost him. He's drifted away, lifted by the chanting of the crowd. I push through the warm crush of bodies toward the stairs. Tony Bradlee finds me there.

"It's wonderful, isn't it?" she says, but I can see in her eyes she senses something's wrong.

"This is how it will be if he wins." I wish I hadn't said it. I catch sight of Jack across the room. I wait for him to turn and scan the crowd for me. I touch the banister. The air feels close.

"I'm going to step outside for a moment," I tell Tony. I leave through the back entrance and go to the car. I sit there for an hour in the hard warm dark of the backseat, until he gets in.

"Where were you?" he says. "When did you come out here?"

"Just a few minutes ago. It was so hot—"

"Over sixty percent, Jackie," he says. "Humphrey's thinking about bowing out."

"That's wonderful, Jack. I'm just so happy for you."

. . .

"Will you go to the convention?" Joan asks. It's early summer. We're in Hyannis Port with the children.

"You should go for me," I say. "I have to stay home and be pregnant."

"And tape those radio commercials in Spanish and French."

I laugh. "They're finding all sorts of things for me to do."

"You really won't go to the convention?" Joan says.

"No. I need to read up on disarmament and that black-bearded dictator in Cuba."

Cuba, I've learned, is the perfect way to shift a conversation. No matter who I'm talking to, communist angst is so deep, just a passing remark is enough. I don't want to go to the convention. I have no interest in being pregnant in that southern California heat. I don't tell Joan—I haven't told anyone—how leveled I felt that night in Charleston, how easily Jack turned away and I just stood on the stairs watching the night unfold like a future where I'd ceased to exist.

"You aren't nervous?" Joan asks, her voice careful.

"Nervous?"

"About Jack going alone to L.A.?"

I suddenly realize what she's asking.

"It's best this way," I say. "He'll be free to play tag around the bed with Marilyn Monroe."

The sudden crumbling in her face stops me.

"I'm teasing, Joan."

"I know. Well, sort of."

"Sweet Joan," I say, "you'll know things, even things you wish you didn't know, and you'll move on. Besides, it's much more likely that in L.A., Peter and the Rat Pack will drag Jack off in a car and they'll all drive down to Palm Springs to toast the premiere of *Ocean's 11* and pour rum punch into Jack Haley's pool."

"I know that too," Joan says—again that young smile.

"As Joe says: Doesn't matter who you are, it only matters who people think you are."

"You do such a good imitation of him," she says.

I feel something bend inside me, the youth and tinge of wonder in her voice, and again I remember that day last summer holding Caroline's small arms as I spun her through the surf, the driving sense I had that, if I could just keep spinning, my daughter's body weightless, skimming those waves, I could embed that hard, free joy deep in a way that might last.

"I love Joe," I say, "despite all." Gently, I tuck a strand of Joan's hair behind her ear.

On July 13, at the Democratic National Convention, Jack clinches the nomination on the first ballot. The next day, he invites Lyndon Johnson to be his running mate.

"I'll need Texas to win," he says when he calls from L.A. "For that reason alone, Johnson's the choice."

"Bobby agrees?" I say, knowing the answer.

Jack laughs. "Of course not. But I told him if we win, the first thing I'll make Lyndon do is push Bobby through for AG." Bobby and Lyndon Johnson are oil and water. A few months ago, when Johnson called Jack "a little scrawny fellow with rickets," Bobby hit the roof. Jack just let it roll off his back.

On the phone now, he is happy. I can feel it—that sense of high.

My mother and I watch on a rented television set as Jack, flanked by Kennedys, gives his acceptance speech to close the Democratic convention. "We stand today on the edge of a new frontier . . . not a set of promises—it is a set of challenges. . . ."

"They love him," my mother says.

"I know," I say.

The day after Jack gets home from California, Eisenhower's CIA director, Allen Dulles, flies up to Hyannis Port to brief him on the training of Cuban exiles.

"Training for what?" I ask.

He hesitates.

"You can't tell me, can you?"

"It'll be like that sometimes," he says, "until I figure this job out. Not that I've got it yet."

"You will."

"I'm not always sure I'm up for it." He glances at me. "Forget I just said that."

. . .

August.

Norman Mailer is sweating—a wrinkled, poorly tailored suit, pale searing eyes, boot-black hair. I've heard he likes pretty women and he likes to fight—bedrooms, barrooms, streets. He's come to meet Jack for a piece he's writing.

"Can I fix you a drink, Mr. Mailer?" I say as we walk into the living room. His eyes pause on my face. Disconcerting how he looks at me, like he's rummaging around. "A cold drink? It's so hot," I say, as if the smile might bring things back to the surface. A sheen of sweat on his face. He reminds me of Aristotle Onassis, that same carnal insistence in his gaze.

"I would like a drink," he says. "Thank you."

"A daiquiri?"

He smiles. "No one here needs me on rum."

For a moment I like him. "Iced tea, then?"

"Please."

I ask about Provincetown, where he lives. "I've never been," I say.

"It's one of the few coastal towns in America that's still a true fishing village, a Wild West of the East."

"I'd love to go."

"And how will you go?"

A funny question. "In a car, I imagine, like anyone else."

He smiles, a wolfish smile. "What would it be? Three black limousines or a sports car at four A.M. with dark glasses?"

"And a blond wig," I say.

"You just had a birthday, didn't you? Thirty-one."

"Mr. Mailer, your glass is already empty. Would you like another?"

Later, I watch his face brighten—he nearly seems to melt—when Jack tells him he's read *The Deer Park,* along with Mailer's other books. Pierre Salinger prepped Jack for that moment, telling him to specifically mention *The Deer Park* and not *The Naked and the Dead,* which made him a household name.

Mailer asks questions like my stepbrother Gore—half query, half bait. Nothing is innocent. Bobby told me that even before he arrived, Mailer had written most of the article, which struck me as strange. Why come at all? But that day in Hyannis Port, it's clear. He is still gathering more. Breaking down our world, taking notes on us. No paper, no pencil, no pen. But in his hard eyes, I can see notations, calculations being made.

Jack is away for most of the fall, barnstorming the country. He'll come home for a day, stride in, swoop Caroline up, give me a kiss, stay for dinner, then fly off again. He calls on our anniversary but forgets it's our anniversary. A few days later, when a reporter phones, asking for comment on a statement in *Woman's Day* about how last year I spent thirty thousand dollars on clothes, I laugh and say, "I couldn't spend that much if I wore sable underwear."

As soon as it's out of my mouth, I regret it. Jack is furious. The comment's picked up everywhere.

"That's the last thing you'll say on this campaign, Jackie."

"Okay with me," I say, "although I do hope my clothes have nothing to do with your ability to be president."

I'm meeting Jack in New York when Mailer's article in *Esquire* hits newsstands. I brace myself as I start to read. The piece is brilliant—searing, canny, generous. It's about Jack and America. An exquisite endorsement and tribute. I remember how Mailer watched us that day in Hyannis Port—how hot it was, how high the baby pushed against my lungs; I craved ice, craved the cool, I wanted to slip out of the room unnoticed, but I was tied to the pleasantries, even as Mailer watched us in a penetrating way that wasn't pleasant at all. In the *Esquire* piece, he describes Jack as *a prince in the unstated aristocracy of the American dream.* He does justice to Jack's ideas, his vision and intent, his commitment to service. He barely mentions me. I feel a wave of relief.

I ride with Jack in a ticker-tape parade through Manhattan. A thirty-mile route up toward Yonkers for a rally in Larkin Park, then back downtown. Over a million New Yorkers line the streets as the motorcade presses through. Crowds push against the car. I sit close to Jack, perched on the back of the seat, one hand holding on, the other waving, keeping that strong fixed smile. I can feel the pressure of my belly, breathless as the baby kicks, while sheets of confetti and streamers rain from the sky. Jack leans down to shake the hands reaching up. A group of women surges toward him. The sides of the car seem to bend.

At a break for lunch in Rockefeller Center, our friend Bill Walton meets us.

"I'm concerned about the baby, Bill," I say, loud enough for others to hear. "I'm afraid I should skip the rest of the route." I turn to one of Jack's aides. "Could you please let the senator know?" I slip out of my coat and turn it inside out. "Reversible," I say to Bill. I pull on a pair of dark glasses and put my arm through his.

"I'll get you back to the hotel," he says. "You can rest."

"Oh no," I say quietly as we walk away. "I want to see those new paintings at the Tibor de Nagy Gallery. Come on. Let's go."

When I learn, a few days later, that Martin Luther King, Jr., has been arrested for a sit-in at the lunch counter of an Atlanta department store, I pick up the phone and dial.

"Yes," I tell the operator, "this is Mrs. Kennedy. I need to talk to the senator. I am afraid it's urgent. Please put the call through."

It's not King I'm thinking of, sitting with those college boys in the Magnolia Tea Room and refusing to get up. It's his wife and that other woman, Rosa Parks, and it's that dead boy's mother, Mamie Till. I understand it then. It wasn't the brutal details of her son's murder that blew the world apart. It was the choice Mamie Till made to leave the casket lid open that forced the world to see.

Jack's voice clicks in on the line.

"You must work to free King," I say. "You know it's a trumped-up charge."

"Sarge and Wofford just told me the same thing."

"That's why you hired them."

"Not to cost me the election."

Jack had met with King a few weeks earlier. King had told him to do something to prove to the Blacks his commitment to them was real.

"Wofford's prepared a statement," he says, "criticizing the arrest, calling for King's release. But Kenny says if I lift a finger, it'll kill my chances. Even Bobby thinks it'll backfire."

"King's wife is pregnant."

"This isn't personal, Jackie."

"But it could be."

"You want me to do the right thing and lose?" He gives that quick laugh and, for a moment, I let the silence hang. I do what, by then, I've learned how to do.

"All right," he says finally, "what do you think?"

"Kenny thinks of politics as a chess match," I say. "A winner, a loser, and a strategy of moves you can map out and count on. But not every game is zero sum."

"In a campaign, only one person wins."

"But 'How do I win?' can't be the only question you ask."

"If I help King, I'll lose the South."

"And if you win the Black vote?"

That stops him. I knew it would. Then, "That's not why you're asking me to do this."

"No, but that's why you will."

JACK

He'll remember that exchange with her, word for word, the tone in her voice, a few days later, early Wednesday morning, the twenty-sixth of October, when he calls Ernest Vandiver at the governor's mansion in Atlanta. News of King's arrest has spread. A landslide of petitions have come from the Southern Christian Leadership Conference and twenty other civil-rights groups. Eisenhower has done nothing, said nothing. Only silence from the Nixon camp.

The phone rings twice before Vandiver, half-asleep, picks up.

"Governor, this is Senator Kennedy calling. Is there any way you can get Martin Luther King out of jail? It would be of tremendous benefit to me."

A pause, then Vandiver says, "I don't know if we can get him released or not."

Careful words. Noncommittal. The we.

"Would you try and see what you can do and call me back?"

That afternoon, Sargent Shriver comes into his hotel room and tells him that King, shackled and handcuffed, was driven to the state prison in Reidsville.

"We're thinking you should call Coretta King," says Sarge. "Convey to her that you think what's happened is wrong and you'll do what you can."

Jack thinks of her. Not King's wife but his own. What Sarge is suggesting and what she said.

"You know, that's a pretty good idea," he says. "How do I get to her?"

An hour later, on a plane to Detroit, Jack mentions to his press secretary that he made a phone call to King's wife. Pierre Salinger just stares at him.

"I've got to call Bobby," Salinger says. "Three Southern governors said that if you supported Hoffa, Khrushchev, or King, they'd throw their states to Nixon."

"We'll see."

The following morning, they learn King will be released on a two-thousand-dollar bond. That afternoon, King walks out of his cell into the open sky and steps onto a plane at DeKalb–Peachtree Airport to fly home. Thronged by the press, he'll make a brief statement, acknowledging his debt to Senator Kennedy, who supported his release, underscoring his courage and principles. King will add that Eisenhower did nothing, and neither did Nixon.

Bobby fumes, tracking pollsters by the hour. They've learned to hide under their desks when he calls.

"Like the rest of us," Jack says.

"When the press comes at you," says Bobby, "what are you going to say?"

"That I called Mrs. King because it was the right thing to do."

"That'll look like grandstanding."

"Even if I win, there'll be consequences for that call. They'll expect a lot from me."

"And if you lose?"

"I'll go write another book."

When Pierre Salinger hands him a copy of The Chicago Defender with the photo of King reunited with his family, it's the daughter who catches his eye. About six, in a pale dress, black patent-leather shoes, white socks, a cardigan sweater, small bows in her hair. She stands by her mother's elbow, that shining wonder in her face, a little girl staring up at her father like she can't quite believe he's returned to her.

Over the next few days, the press tweaks the story of that phone call to Coretta King, adding more raw emotion, more humanity, softer phrases, words he never used.

"You said that to her, Jack?" Salinger says.

"Can you imagine me saying that?"

"Seems to be working. Even the Times reported today, Kennedy gaining strength in Southern states once meant for Nixon . . ."

"And the Southern whites?"

"Jury's still out," says Salinger.

"That jury's always out."

"I like to think the jury will see things your way on November eighth."

He shakes his head. "That's the day that, if I win, they'll start to love me less."

The final two weeks of the campaign.

Tuesday: Philadelphia to Los Angeles.

Wednesday: San Francisco.

Thursday: Phoenix, New Mexico, Oklahoma.

Friday: Virginia, then a torchlight parade in Chicago, where 1.5 million turn out for a rally at the stadium. Mayor Richard Daley introduces him as "the Irish Prince."

The following night, the plane touches down long after midnight in Bridgeport, Connecticut. From the airport, the motorcade snakes through the Naugatuck Valley, headlights brushing the stubbled green of trees. For twenty-five miles through town after town, crowds flank the route—lanterns, flashlights, flares. Hands wave, faces lit, nightgowns, pajamas, and slippers under winter coats. They've tumbled from their beds to line the road. Thousands. They chant. The cold dark is filled with his name.

November 9, 1960, Hyannis Port

When I wake, it is night still. The light has just begun to rise. Muffled sounds in the yard below. I pull the curtain back and see them. Dark forms. The number seems to have doubled. They move differently, a certain necessary intention and skill. I can hear Jack's light snore from the bed, still in the dark of the room; I want to crawl back under the covers, move close to him, be in that same dark. My throat feels tight. I watch the men below. My fingernails dig into the sill. What will happen now? To our life? The children? My freedom and solitude, the new glow of happiness between us? Everything, from this point on, will change.

The baby kicks. I run my hand over my stomach, find the knob of one small shoulder.

The night before, I had a quiet dinner with Bill Walton. We asked him to stay with us, in the guest bedroom of the small house Jack and I have rented near Joe's. Bill and I sat together in the dining room after we ate, and we talked about painting. We talked about how if Jack won, I'd need a house away.

"What about Camp David?" Walton asked.

"Sometimes I'll need away-away," I said.

"I'll help you find something."

"Thank you. I'm afraid I've only gotten as far as the purple coat I'm wearing tomorrow."

Around nine, Bill Walton and I walked over to Joe's. Jack was there, with Bobby, Teddy, and the rest of the family. Old friends and aides, campaign workers. Jack couldn't sit still. He'd cross the room to talk to one person, then walk back. He'd sit down, stand up, cross the room again, his fingers worrying his trousers pocket, his eyes bright. At half past ten, when early returns looked like the momentum was heading Jack's way, I told them I was tired. The baby, I said. Joe made some absurd proclamation that, if Jack won, he wouldn't attend the celebration at the Armory. He'd keep to the shadows for Jack's sake, he said, as he had all year.

"Assuming Jack wins," I said, "I think he'll want his father there." I plucked at the cuff of Joe's sleeve and whispered, "You might as well just come—if this lifelong dream of yours is a done deal, they can't unelect him."

Assuming Jack wins.

I've practiced saying it, thinking it. Knowing what I'm not fully ready to know. And soon it will be light. The press will sweep in, past the gate, up the drive, onto the lawn, a wave of flashbulbs, pads of paper, pens, shouldering one another out as they push in, trying to get past the Secret Service, a tightening circle around us.

Outside now, the gray of the sky has paled; threads of fog drift over the roofs as the cedar-shake houses begin to emerge. And still those moving men below. How easily I can distinguish them from the police detail of the night before. These men move like the dead. Noiseless. Trained to disappear. One, standing by the break in the hedge, lights a cigarette. A pinprick orange glow as he inhales. The match drops. His toe grinds it out on the lawn.

...

"We won, Jackie."

Jack grips my hand. A stormy morning, the ocean wild. I came down to the beach for a walk. Fifteen minutes later, Jack came to find me. I felt my heart lift when I saw him walking toward me through the rain.

His eyes are shining. "We won," he says again.

"I know, Jack. And I'm so happy."

"Come back up to the house," he says.

The men are near us as we walk, the Secret Service men, moving at the hem of things.

The house is a tumult. The air shifts ten octaves as we walk in, the rip roar of laughter, cheers, loud faces, pumping hands. Bodies teem through all seventeen rooms; they spill onto the porch and the lawn.

It feels like a glare, this new world.

"Jackie, you must be thrilled!" someone says.

"What kind of First Lady do you want to be?" That's Jack's sister Jean.

Half the room turns toward me, and I say I'm not quite sure how I feel about the term *First Lady*. It sounds a bit like a saddle horse.

They all laugh.

That night we have a small dinner with the Bradlees and Bill Walton. Lem Billings wanted to be there, but he and Ben don't get along, so Lem with his rough jokes and battered suitcase was exiled to the main affair still roaring away at Joe's.

At dinner, Ben tells Jack he should think about replacing Allen Dulles, Ike's CIA director.

Walton agrees. "And toss Hoover out of the FBI. Make a clean sweep."

Jack listens, nods. He tells them he's nominating Adlai Stevenson for UN ambassador and Dean Rusk for secretary of state.

"I thought you wanted William Fulbright?" Walton says.

Jack shakes his head. "I don't like his support for segregation." He tells them then he's been thinking about bringing in some Republicans: C. Douglas Dillon as secretary of the Treasury. McGeorge Bundy as national security advisor. Mac Bundy was a friend of Kick's during the war.

"Roosevelt installed Republicans," Jack says. "Truman did too, to bridge the aisle. Bob McNamara is the third GOP I'm considering. For Defense. What do you think?"

"McNamara's barely GOP," says Bill Walton. "He's in the NAACP and the ACLU."

"Jack likes that he's an intrepid mountaineer," I say.

They laugh. Dinner continues, more talk, more debate, candles flicker and burn. Jack doesn't mention Bobby or his intent to nominate him as attorney general. We discussed it earlier, before our friends arrived. "I might float it out to them," he said, "to see how it lands. Or I might just focus on the Republican appointments and, when no one is looking, slip Bobby in."

I smiled then. "Jack, do you really think there will ever be a time again when no one is looking?"

. . .

He is young. My Secret Service detail, Clint Hill.

I've been told he was assigned to Eisenhower's detail for a year. He grew up in North Dakota. He has a wife and child. But no one mentioned he is close to my age, my height. Dark hair, a solemn, neatly shaven face. In my living room in Georgetown, Clint Hill looks around, that quick scan with his eyes, taking in the sofa and chairs, antiques, bookshelves, marking exits and entrances, windows and doors. I wait for a pause, for something to register, but as his eyes shift back to meet mine, they are blank. And I realize then this detail is not what he wants, to be assigned to the wife. He doesn't want it any more than I do, and in that moment I decide we might get along.

"It's a pleasure to meet you, Mr. Hill. Please sit down." I'm always saying something like this to someone—*please sit down, please come in, please don't get up,* and *what can we get you to drink?* I ask him about a drink.

"Nothing, thank you," he says.

My back hurts. I feel the baby move.

Later that day, I'm scheduled to meet the new girl Jack's office has recommended to serve as my press secretary: Pam Turnure. Or is that tomorrow? No, today. And what about the rumor that this Pam might have had a brief affair with Jack once? Is that true? Does it matter?

I have to call Oleg Cassini. I'm going to ask him to design my clothes. Cassini is an old friend of Joe's, the only friend of Joe's who will understand what I mean when I ask for a suit in a "nattier blue." Cassini will also intuitively grasp that, for me, style is not only art but armor.

So here I am—the Wife.

I feel a wave of nausea.

The other agent with Mr. Hill outlines how things will work. Every house will have a perimeter. Anytime I step over that line, Agent Hill will be with me.

"My baby is due in a month," I say. "I'll be primarily in Washington. My concern is keeping a degree of privacy for our children. I don't want them to feel like animals in a zoo."

"We don't trust the press any more than you do, Mrs. Kennedy," says Mr. Hill.

"So every time I take a walk, you'll go with me?"

A slight smile crosses his eyes, brief; his mouth does not shift.

On a brilliant morning later that week, Mr. Hill and I walk down 34th Street toward the Potomac. I am thinking about that little girl, six-year-old Ruby Bridges from New Orleans, who, just a few days ago, walked through a white mob brandishing fists, guns, and little Black dolls in caskets. Ruby, wrapped in a cloud of U.S. marshals, marched up the steps with her lunchbox into first grade at an all-white school. She's three years older than Caroline.

I wonder what Mr. Hill would think about Ruby Bridges and all those white parents who pulled their children out of the school just because she walked into it? I want to ask him, but I don't really know who he is yet, so instead I say, "Mr. Hill, I've heard you have a son who's just about my daughter Caroline's age. What's your little boy's name?"

Bill Walton spends Thanksgiving with us in Georgetown.

I raise my glass. "To one last Thanksgiving in our beloved house that leans to one side."

"With my favorite doorknob," Jack says.

"Here's to caviar and clam chowder with Thanksgiving dinner," Walton says.

"And a December baby," I say.

Bill has come through on his promise to help find a house in the country, a place where we can be just a family. He found a property called Glen Ora.

"Camp David is free," Jack says.

"That's an official house," I say. "Free in only one sense of the word."

"There are stables at Glen Ora," Bill says, "plenty of land, Jackie, where you can ride."

That night, I hemorrhage. Jack has already left to fly down to Palm Beach for meetings. I lie in bed with my nightgown and overcoat on and, when the ambulance team arrives, I tell them, "I lost a baby once, and I'm afraid. Let's please go now." I try to smile, but the pain is just so sharp. I can feel the wet along my leg.

Later I learn that Bill Walton reached Jack just as the plane touched down in Palm Beach. Jack boarded another plane and flew back.

"The baby's system isn't quite developed."

That's what my obstetrician, Dr. Walsh, tells us about our baby boy once I surface from surgery.

"Will he be all right?" Jack asks.

"We think so."

The baby didn't cry right away, Dr. Walsh explains. He didn't cry even when they held him up and gave his little bottom a slap. They fed a tube into his trachea, blew air into his lungs, and he began to breathe. We'll be in the hospital for at least two weeks, possibly more.

As soon as we can hold him, Jack has the baby in his arms. He sits in the chair by my bed, the small head resting in the crook of his elbow, the unskinned surface of our baby's eyes sponging up the world.

Jack says his name. John. The baby shifts at his voice. Caroline is next to Jack, one small hand resting on his shoulder, watching, transfixed, and for a moment it's like the four of us are held in frieze, the four of us imprinted into time, and I feel something new move through me. The light in the room feels altered. Every object in the room touched by that new light.

From the hospital, I begin to prepare. The private rooms first, to create a sense of home for our family. Everything else will follow. I send Clint to get books and periodicals, histories of the White House, its antiques, architecture, and grounds. I study photographs and blueprints, the before and after of Teddy Roosevelt's design for the West Wing. I make notes on how the various public rooms have been used. I draw up lists of things to be packed from our house on N Street, designating what should be moved where. Shortly before I'm released from the hospital, I ask Oleg Cassini to come. I show him pages I've torn out from magazines and sketches I've made.

"Your sketches are very good," he says.

"Not as good as the ones I used to make on the back of my exam books."

He laughs, his hair stiff with pomade, the deep tan. He was born in Paris, he tells me that day. "At three in the morning, the doctor swept into the delivery room straight from a party, in white tie and tails." He glances at the stack of books on the small table by the window, then back at me. "Have you had any rest at all?"

"It's quite stunning, how much there is to do. I'm not even the president-elect."

"Well, the president-elect didn't just give birth."

"Oleg, what do you think about an American Versailles?"

"America is not France," he says.

"I suppose, but don't you think we could have a little magic?"

As the elevator rises to the Residence, I remember the first time I saw the White House as a child—the soaring promise of the building outside, how inside there was nothing, only cavernous dark rooms and a musty smell, windows that hadn't been opened in years.

In the elevator, the chief usher, Mr. West, stands slightly turned away. An almost British sense of propriety and discretion. When he met us at the portico, he showed no surprise that I was sitting in the front seat of the station wagon while Mr. Hill drove. He led us inside and asked Mr. Hill to wait downstairs.

The elevator slows to a halt on the second floor. The door slides open.

In the hall stands Mamie Eisenhower, her crisp smile and shirtwaist, curled bangs pulled forward and flattened, a noose of pearls. I've heard that Mamie calls me "that college girl."

Mr. West steps forward.

"Mrs. Kennedy," he announces. I wait a moment for the older woman to step toward me, but she doesn't. Mamie only extends her hand, forcing me to take the step to bridge the distance between us. Ninety minutes later when the visit ends, I'm exhausted. The pain flares where my stitches are, those muscles still so weak. The wheelchair we requested never appeared. Later, I will learn Mamie instructed Mr. West not to offer it unless I asked.

Stepping out into the sharp cold day where Clint is waiting with the car, I feel the fresh wind against my face as a white pop of flashbulbs bursts in the shadow of the portico.

We are in Palm Beach for Christmas. I tell Jack I've been thinking about a slightly different plan for the White House.

He's reading a briefing packet. He glances up.

"Different how?"

"The executive mansion is only borrowed by the president. It belongs to all Americans. It should be a living museum of the country's past. When I walked through last week, there were rooms painted seasick green. There's no sense of history or beauty."

We are in the bedroom, the French doors open onto the little balcony, the cooler breeze, the sky.

"You'll have fifty thousand dollars to redecorate," Jack says.

"*Redecorate* is a flimsy word," I say. "What I'm thinking about is more of a restoration." I shift in bed, push off the quilt. "This isn't about me, Jack, my tastes or what I want. It's about the country, and what we've never quite had. We have no myths, no heroes."

He sets the briefing packet down. "We do have heroes," he says, "and I am pretty sure we can't afford whatever you're envisioning."

"Well, you don't exactly know that yet."

"I'll make a bet."

I pause, then, "You're going to need me to do *something* with my time, Jack, so I'm not always hanging on you."

"There will be plenty to do."

"I don't mean ninety-nine cups of tea with some other national leader's wife."

He laughs. "We're not buying Jeffersonian antiques." He picks up the briefing packet.

"Jack, don't worry. We can solicit donations or fundraise to pursue things we don't have."

"Pursue as in purchase?"

"Monroe ordered pieces from Paris."

"The White House had burned to the ground."

"Why don't I just give it a try for a month or so," I say. "Maybe the idea will flop, and we can move on."

He looks at me, a flash of uncertainty, but I can see he is intrigued, and for the moment I have won.

I'm the last to leave Palm Beach. It's like watching a season fall away. I spend days alone with the children on the property caged by tall hedges, palms, bougainvillea.

"It's lovely here," I say to Joe one afternoon as we sit by the pool. "And quiet now. The day before Jack left, I walked out of the bathroom to find Pierre Salinger holding a press conference in my bedroom."

Joe laughs.

"It's going to be a fishbowl life," I say, "isn't it?"

"Just stand by Jack."

"I'm afraid I'll have to request an appointment whenever I want to see him."

"Some days it might be like that. But he needs you."

The water in the pool is still. The faintest wind ripples the surface. The children will stay on in Palm Beach when I fly north for the inauguration. Their rooms in the Residence aren't ready, there's still too much chaos. I don't want to bring them into that, at the same time I can't imagine leaving them. John, six weeks old, is so tiny, too fragile, he isn't sleeping well.

Joe looks at me over those wire rims, his blue eyes penetrating.

"This is a great thing, Jackie."

"I know. The long twilight struggle, the new frontier, a new generation of leadership. I've read the inaugural draft. 'Let us never negotiate out of fear, but let us never fear to negotiate.' I love it, Joe. It's thrilling. A great thing."

"I still think that speech is too short," Joe says.

I smile. "Jack doesn't want anyone to think he's a windbag."

Joe laughs again. For him, I know, this is a dream come true. What is it, though, for Jack? For me? And what will I bring to those people we see, who turn out with their shining faces and their hope? I've been asked by Jack's team to gather details of my life into a brief story they can share. I've collected photographs, jotted down notes. I wrote passages about my childhood, my parents, even their divorce. I wrote about meeting Jack, about our marriage, and the words I used imply an intimacy between us that is not exactly there but could be. The facts are intact, but I've washed the truth. People need a story. I understand that. Just as they need something to believe in.

One request intrigued me. A writer I know was assigned a piece for *Look*, "What You Don't Know about Kennedy." He wrote asking for any thoughts I might share. I wrote back, *I'd describe Jack as rather like me, in that his life is an iceberg. The public life is above the water—& the private life—is submerged. . . .* At the close of the letter, I told him he could use the words I wrote, but with no attribution to me. It did strike me as I sealed the letter that I might not have been so honest about that split between our public and private selves if Jack was here. Somehow the distance made it possible to admit the more complicated terrain that still exists between us.

When I leave Palm Beach, a crowd has gathered on Southern Boulevard as we approach the airport. We pull to the curb at the terminal. I empty my face and step out. I turn and wave. I let my focus blur, as I'm learning to do whenever I feel that leveling fear and flood, taming a rush of people into a softer featureless shape, a darker cutout against the pure blinding bright of Florida sky.

They've come this time not for Jack but for me. As I move closer, a face in the crowd catches my eye, a woman roughly my age, light-brown hair pulled sharply back, a dust of freckles. Our eyes meet, and I feel a splitting ache, that wrench of leaving my children behind. I look at that woman in the crowd. She's a mother. I can feel it. Even without seeing a child near her, I know. I smile at her. She smiles back.

I board the plane. My new press secretary, Pam Turnure, is with me, along with the Secret Service men, who call me Lace. My code name. Jack is Lancer; Caroline, Lyric; John, Lark. As those men walk up and down the cabin aisle with their guns, I look through the plane window to the crowd below, scanning the faces, marking the features I can make out from that distance. I am looking for that woman, that mother, her smile, the flash of recognition between us. I look for her knowing I won't find her, or see her, again.

Thursday, January 19, 1961

The day before the inauguration, snow falls. It layers the streets and trees outside. A blistering wind. It is dark by four. I watch from the window of my bedroom in Georgetown as cars snake through the whiteness, snow falling through their headlights.

As a child, I loved to watch snow fall through light, each flake a soul, emerging for that instant into its own brightness, then falling back into the dark. Beyond the bedroom door, the house is full. It is time.

Eerie, haunting. Those are the words that come to me as the limousine flows through the night streets toward Constitution Hall. Bill Walton is with us. "You'll float away," I told Jack. "As soon as we arrive, someone will come and bear you off. Bill can stay with me."

The three of us sit in the back of the car, snow crushed under the tires. The frost a white dust on the windows, the glass blurred with the inside heat, our bodies and breath. Time slows, like we are moving from the past into the future. I can feel an excitement I've not let myself feel—in the dark mystical silence of the car where we sit on this night journey toward the inaugural concert and from there to the inaugural gala. Jack is in his tails. I am in my white gown, a necklace, heavy and cool against my throat, grounding me. And the snow blows everywhere, free in a way I love, as we travel wrapped in the warm isolation of the car, moving through the cold and the dark outside.

I am with Jack, and I can feel him near me, close. Then he turns to Bill Walton and says:

"Turn on the lights so they can see Jackie."

PART III

I am become a name

—Tennyson, "Ulysses"

''

January 20, 1961, Inauguration Day

The old poet steps up to the podium in the piercing wind and falters. His hand brushes his eyes. The winter sun is blinding, light trapped in the edges of ice, air sparkling, so sharp it feels cruel, as he stumbles through the first lines of the poem, trying to read off the paper in his hands.

Lyndon Johnson stands up to help him, moving to shield the sun with his broad shoulders and top hat. The glare still too bright, the poet finally gives up. He sets the paper down, closes his eyes, and starts with new lines, a different poem, one he recites from memory.

I feel the bite of the wind through my coat. Robert Frost's voice is tremulous but strong, and as he comes to the end, Jack steps up. He doesn't wear a coat. He shakes Frost's hand and takes the old man's place on the dais and delivers the address he has worked and reworked. I know the words by heart. *We shall pay any price, bear any burden, meet any hardship, support any friend, oppose any foe, to assure the survival and success of liberty.* The words flow through my ears, and I let myself go into that inspired bolt of Jack's voice. The crowd surges like a wave and I let it sweep into me, the thunder of applause and cheers.

As the ceremony ends, I'm shuttled to a room with other women. Coffee, hot cider, a glass of sherry someone has pressed into my hand. I catch sight of Jack and push through to him. I touch his cheek, and it is just the two of us. I love you, he says. I love you. Tears in his eyes, he looks down at me. We're here, Jackie, he says. Then the cameras flash, and when my eyes adjust, he is gone again, drawn away by someone who has his arm, his ear. I feel it all that day, how he belongs now to something larger than either of us can grasp—a vision, a mission, an ideal. I am part of that, and from now on I will share him with the world. It isn't only him they need; it's the dream he's promised. On that searing-cold day, minutes flash by. Faces, bodies. Everything seems to glisten and shine. I smile, answer questions, shake hands. After a while I am brought to him again, and to see his face there, so beautiful and free, lifts me. He reaches for my hand and holds it tightly as we board an open car and ride through the winter city to the White House and the reviewing stand, where his father waits with his brothers, my mother, my sister. They are all there. As we draw up, Joe tips his hat, and at the same time, Jack stands, doffing his to Joe.

I make it through two of the inaugural balls before I beg off and return to the White House.

The chief usher, Mr. West, meets me at the door. There's nothing I can read in his face, no opinion or disdain for my fatigue or weakness, no compassion either. The complete lack of expression shoots a warmth through me—gratitude as I realize he sees everything, judges nothing. I almost confide in him then that, on the ride back, it struck me I'd never be able to undo the whole length of tiny pearled buttons down the back of my dress, and since Provi, my assistant, has already gone home to her sons, perhaps I will have to sleep in my dress like some beached mermaid, but the joke of it feels like too much to explain, so I just lean a bit on Mr. West's arm and he escorts me in silence. At the Queens' Bedroom, he turns the knob and holds the door open, and I see then that he has asked a young woman to stay, to help me with the dress or anything else I might need.

I turn to thank him, but he's already closing the door behind him.

It's after three when Jack wakes me up and pulls me down the hall in a sort of hobbling waltz to the Lincoln Bedroom. He hurls onto the bed.

"We are sleeping here!" he cries. "Here!"

We stay there for the rest of that night, and in the morning we talk in bed with the extra pillows kicked onto the floor, the blankets drawn up around our chins, sunlight streaming in.

. . .

Boxes of our things fill the rooms.

He carries photographs of me and the children from the Residence to the Oval Office, which begins to assume the design of a captain's quarters: ship models, paintings of rocky coasts, a plaque engraved with the mariner's prayer. His bits of scrimshaw are set around the room.

The day after we move in, I walk into his office and ask Dave Powers to please leave. When we're alone, I ask Jack if it's true what my chief of staff, Tish Baldridge, just told me, that three days before the inauguration someone in Jack's camp called up Sammy Davis, Jr., and disinvited him and May Britt.

"I told you he wasn't going to perform," Jack says.

"You didn't say he was asked *not* to."

"We barely won this election."

"You did win, and he supported you."

There's an uncertain look on his face, and I realize that whether or not he knew in advance it was going to be done, he doesn't feel good about it.

"We still need the South, Jackie."

"That man campaigned for you because you asked him to."

"Then he went and married that woman."

"A woman he loves."

"Who's white when he isn't."

I look at him for a long moment.

Later that afternoon—almost five—I'm in the Residence with Tish and Pam when the folded note arrives.

Jackie,
Let's declare war on the toilet paper.
Where is it?

I smile. His olive branch. He might not apologize for what happened to Sammy Davis, Jr., and May Britt, but the note is his way of saying he heard what I said.

I continue working, going through boxes, unpacking and sorting, until I come across an unframed photograph in a box from the Georgetown house. The two of us at the Hyannis airport. I don't remember the photograph being taken, but I remember the moment. In the picture, my back is to the camera, Jack is leaning in to kiss me goodbye, an awkward unclaimed intimacy between us, captured in those nuanced dark shapes against the white sky behind.

For those first weeks, the halls ring with the sounds of hammering, smells of paint and linseed oil. Though the house isn't ready for them yet, the children are the focus of my days. I miss them desperately, their skin, their smells, Caroline's voice and laughter, John's sweet sleepy face and how his hands grip and uncurl. He's still so fragile.

"I want my children to have a routine," I tell Pam as we unpack Caroline's books and toys, "a sense of an ordinary life outside the spotlight and fairy tale. Do you think that's possible? To construct a normal childhood for them?"

"It seems to me," Pam says quietly, "you can build whatever you want."

"I'd like to keep my station wagon. I don't want to always drive around in one of those long black cars."

She smiles.

"And when Tish is pushing me to do more, I'd love it if you'd help find people who can stand in for me, so I can take the children on small trips to the circus or the theater. I'll tell Tish before I go, so she won't take it out on you."

Pam is unwrapping a lamp when Mr. West walks in with a short list of questions. Some art has arrived, he says, and would I like the paintings hung before dinner?

"Also, Mrs. Kennedy, we are going to order the playground set and the treehouse."

"Thank you, Mr. West. Let's have those placed near the president's office, so he can see the children play."

He makes a note on the list. "You've also added here a trampoline?" he says, not even an eyebrow raised, as if such a request comes with every change in administration.

"Yes, Mr. West. Thank you. Full size, I should have mentioned, and please have that placed a distance from the swing set."

"But it is for the children?"

"Oh no, Mr. West. They can use it if they're supervised, but, no, the trampoline is for me."

I've hired a designer, Sister Parish, to help me with the family quarters. Ideally, I explain, we'll use what we have and buy as little as possible. I want to keep the funds we've been allocated for the restoration of the public rooms. But things don't go as planned and, within weeks, the budget is spent. We scour the boarded-up rooms and the cellar for antiques. Sister Parish always wears a dark dress with a tremendous white spread collar, while I dress in jeans, sneakers, and an old sweater. They nickname me "Queen of the Rummage Sales." We find a bust of George Washington in a bathroom sink. In the unused carpenter's shop, we find some old statuary and a seventeenth-century table that once served as a sawhorse. I crawl under the table. "Get down here with me, Mr. Hill," I say to Clint. "See how this is carved?" I say, running my fingers down the wooden leg. "This level of craftsmanship would never happen today. Imagine the time it took. This detail is by hand."

Organizing things as well as Field Marshal Rommel ever did. That's how I describe it to Bill Walton. I invite him to the Residence for lunch. I tell him I'm doing what Joe Alsop suggested back in August, in a letter he wrote about art and power.

"Speaking of Alsop," Bill says. "At a party last week, I overheard him call Jack 'Mr. Facing Two Ways.'"

I don't want to think it's funny, but when Bill gives me a quizzical look, head slightly cocked, I laugh.

"It can be a vicious little town," I say. "Just another reason to keep my circle small. You, of course. Because I trust you forever. Tony and Ben, and Bunny Mellon, whom I've come to adore. We've asked Bunny to redesign the White House gardens. And I want her to teach me how to make the sort of arrangements she has everywhere in her house—freesia and tulips in baskets that look like Dutch paintings. I love Bunny's house."

"It's not too shabby here," Bill says.

"And the other thing so intriguing about Bunny," I say, "is that, along with design, she's perfected privacy to high art. She minds her own life and walks around with that absolutely lovely smile, saying nothing. I need to learn how to do that."

Jack is restless in those early weeks. He's assembled his cabinet and named Bobby attorney general, which creates a stir. Bobby's only thirty-five, the youngest AG since 1814, and he doesn't have the legal experience one would expect for the role.

"I need him in there with me," Jack says.

In those weeks, he emerges from long classified briefings looking worn out. He paces the West Wing, the executive offices. Someone finds him in the mailroom, I hear, just standing there with a letter opener, opening unsorted mail. I ask him about it when he comes home to the Residence that evening. He shrugs.

"Just trying to figure things out. Hey, let me show you this." He digs into his briefcase and draws out a letter from John Steinbeck.

"You found this in the mail room?" I ask.

He smiles. "No. But it's nice. His response to my inaugural." He hands me the letter, I sit down and read it. Steinbeck has written how a nation might be shaped by its statesmen and military but is often remembered for its artists. He writes how grateful he feels to Jack for capturing it.

"*Excellently written* . . ." I read aloud, "*that magic undertone of truth.*" I set the letter down. "I love this, Jack."

"Let's replace all the generals with artists." He toys with an empty glass on the table, turning it over like there's something in it he is looking for, and I think about how glass isn't brittle at all but solvent, fluid, when it meets the right heat.

"What's wrong?" I ask.

"Communism. Vietnam. The disintegration I've inherited."

"You've known all of that."

"And Cuba. A plan developed by Eisenhower and his CIA. They want me to back a strike against Castro eight weeks from now. Exiled Cuban leaders trained by our military."

"For what?"

"To incite a civilian uprising."

"What about the UN?"

"There's that."

"Your address was about peace and cooperation, global under- standing. Overthrowing another government doesn't quite align."

"The Cubans want this," he says. "They're depending on it."

"What does Adlai think? He's your UN ambassador."

"Adlai doesn't know."

"He doesn't know what he thinks, or he doesn't know?"

He just looks at me. They haven't told Adlai Stevenson.

. . .

By early February, Caroline's room and the nursery are finished. The solarium on the third floor has been turned into a school- room. I've arranged for Caroline's playgroup to move to the White House. Some of the mothers, I tell Jack, are concerned. He's come home for lunch and a rest.

"Their kids will never be safer than when they're here," he says.

"I've told them that, and now I'm trying to woo them with guinea pigs."

"Good," he says.

I look past him to the molding by the bed table, studying it.

"You're going to need to be discreet, Jack. Here. You know that, don't you?"

"Don't mix that up with the children." His voice is sharp.

I look at him then. "That's exactly what I'm saying."

"I've got to get back to work." He reaches for his watch.

John and Caroline are flying in from Palm Beach. As we drive to the airport, Jack tells me the press will expect photographs.

"Of course," I say. "That will be fine. We can get on the plane and get them ready."

He smiles. "You mean you'll wrap the baby in so many blankets they can't see his face?"

"It is winter."

The White House gardeners have built a massive snowman for Caroline—twice her size, with a panama hat, a carrot nose, a red ribbon bow tie. She flies out of the car and pokes at the coal buttons at its portly waist, then looks back at me. Her hair has grown longer in the last weeks, past her shoulders now, stripped lighter by the Florida sun. So beautiful, her shy, thrilled smile.

Jack asks me to go for a walk that afternoon. He throws a stick for the dog. Charlie bounds away from us, tripping on a crust of deep snow.

"There's a lunch on Friday," he says. "I'd like you to be there with me."

"I was planning to take the children to Glen Ora Friday, but that's fine, we can leave afterward."

"Is the house finished?"

"Almost."

"It's just a rental, Jackie. Whatever you do there has to be undone before we move out."

I clap for the dog, who bounds back, the stick in his mouth, muzzle caked in snow.

"What is it, Jack?" I say. "What's bothering you?"

"Cuba." He shakes his head. "And I can't talk about it."

The rambling mansion is just visible in the dusk as we fly in. John is on my lap, Caroline beside me.

"Look," I say, pointing through the helicopter window. "That's Glen Ora."

Stone terraces, stucco walls, old shutters painted white. Our family place away. The helicopter touches down in a cleared field. It's dark by the time we walk into the house. I squeeze Caroline's hand.

High-ceilinged rooms, a library, a large kitchen, five bedrooms upstairs. Most of the furniture is from our home in Georgetown.

"We'll ride every morning we are here," I say.

"Tomorrow?" Caroline asks.

Jack flies in on Saturday, lugging his battered briefcase full of memos, marked URGENT.

It comes up again and again: Cuba. He shares some of the briefs and memos with me. One from Arthur Schlesinger, the tone startling as he argues that, as the president's first major foreign-policy initiative, an engagement in Cuba *could dissipate all the extraordinary good will which has been rising toward the New Administration* . . .

"Surprising, coming from Arthur," I say. "He reveres you."

"Not in this case."

"How will you respond?"

"If it succeeds, I won't have to."

In March, Lee flies from London to New York. I meet her for dinner and a play.

"You must have things in Washington you're supposed to be doing, Jacks," she says.

"There's some delegating. But look on the bright side, Lee— I didn't delegate you."

"Jack doesn't mind you aren't there?"

I feel a light flash of anger. My sister knows better.

"He'd rather have me away and happy than underfoot and not."

I don't tell Lee about the rumors of the naked swimming parties in the pool while I am away for the weekend in Glen Ora or the scent of other women I sometimes notice on his clothes. As long as I don't have to watch it play out right in front of me. He's that kind of man, like my father. I tell myself that. I knew it going in. It means nothing. I am fine.

"When you're back in Europe, Lee, I'd like your help. I've hired a designer for the White House who I have to pretend doesn't exist."

"Why?"

"Because he's French. Stéphane Boudin. We will focus on American history, American design, but Stéphane has a truly unique talent, and if there's an antique on your side of the Atlantic he recommends, I'll need you to go see it for me. You can be my eyes."

It's the kind of project my sister will love. The conversation takes off, away from Jack.

I return to Washington for a state dinner and two other events, then the children and I fly to Palm Beach. Jack joins us for Easter. We stay with Joe, who insists Jack sit at the head of the table. When Jack refuses, his father's fist comes down. "You're the president now. That's where you'll sit."

I almost point out that since Jack is president, he should be able to sit where he likes.

After dinner, when it's just the three of us, Jack talks more openly about Cuba and a new proposed plan. The men, Cuban exiles covertly trained by the American military, will land at a different beach farther up the coast, near an inlet, the Bay of Pigs. The goal is to spark an organized resistance against Castro's regime.

"They want air cover for the landing," Jack says. "A B-52 strike to take out Castro's air force."

"Who is 'they'?" Joe asks.

"CIA, the joint chiefs."

"Then do it."

Jack shakes his head. "Air strikes are noisy. The plan should be strong enough to succeed without them."

"I disagree," says Joe. "If it succeeds, it's a huge win. You show the world, including Khrushchev, what you're made of."

"And if it doesn't?" I say.

Joe looks at me, his eyes cool.

I stand up. "Well, that's my cue to go and be a good mother."

Joe laughs and says, "I'm sure you haven't finished putting in your two cents."

I smile back. "My two cents, Joe, will never equal your ten."

Jack is quiet on the flight back to Washington, but his mind seems lighter, like the sun and the warmth have blown the dust off things. He sits in the row across from me, alone.

"You've decided, haven't you?" I say as we begin our descent.

When we land, he leaves for a meeting in the West Wing, and the children and I go back to the Residence. It's late by the time he comes home for dinner. I don't have to ask what decision he's made. I can read it in his face. Later, as we lie in bed, the air is full with what we don't say. We listen to low strains of music playing on the Victrola. Ella Fitzgerald. When he falls asleep, I slip out of bed; the floor feels strangely cold under my feet as I cross the room, through the open door into the dressing room. As I lift the needle off the record, I know somehow in that silence he is making a mistake.

. . .

The following afternoon, Jack brings the British prime minister, Harold Macmillan, to the Residence to meet me. I've skimmed his briefing papers:

. . . shot through with Victorian languor . . . He walks with a slow, stiff shuffle that might cause some to think him incapable of serious action, but in fact he is masterful, dominating, shrewd— able to spring onto his toes like a ballet dancer.

Macmillan is tall, gray hair swept back, a high forehead, and an unruly mustache. His eyes droop, but he seems aged and wise, with a kind of shattering dignity, like an old tree. I like him immediately. I've heard rumors about his marriage—his wife and a torrid affair she kept up for years with a man named Boothby.

I mix cocktails for Jack and Macmillan as they pick up the conversation they began a few weeks ago when they met in Key West, about Laos, the political crisis there, and whether or not America should intervene.

I notice Jack doesn't mention Cuba. I can feel he wants to. If Macmillan is advising against military intervention in Laos, what would his thoughts be on Cuba?

Before Macmillan leaves, I invite him to visit us at Glen Ora. Jack looks surprised.

On Wednesday, April 12, during a press conference, a reporter asks Jack, "Mr. President, have you reached a decision on how far this country will be willing to go in helping an anti-Castro uprising or invasion of Cuba?"

"There will not, under any conditions, be an intervention in Cuba. This government will do everything it possibly can to make sure there are no Americans involved in any actions in Cuba."

Friday morning, he asks if I'll take another walk with him. A brilliant morning. The lawns stretch away from us—the light sharp, the sky that steep, untampered blue. We walk down to the pond.

"I have to approve or cancel air strikes in Cuba by noon," he says. "An hour from now."

"And?"

"I don't know." He picks up a stone, brushes off the wet dirt, and turns it in his hand.

"Something else," he says. "That Russian's space flight. I've called a meeting later today. Khrushchev's too far ahead. We have to catch up."

It's been all over the news. Cosmonaut Yuri Gagarin—the first human being to orbit the earth—was fired off in a Vostok rocket from the Baikonur Cosmodrome in Kazakhstan. Shortly after Gagarin landed, Khrushchev issued a statement proclaiming Russia's lead in the space race.

"You sent a telegram to Khrushchev, didn't you, Jack? Congratulating him and expressing a desire to share resources, research."

"I sent it." That's all he says. The American space program hadn't been a priority. Three years ago, after Sputnik, Eisenhower established an organization called NASA to map strategies that might close the so-called "missile gap." Until now, though, there'd been no push, no sense of urgency. Gagarin's flight—and the explosion of press around it—has changed that.

"I have to get back," he says. "I need to decide on the air strikes."

"You'll make the right decision."

I feel a heaviness inside him as we cross the lawn. I reach for his hand.

He heads toward the office. I head to the Residence. At the end of the hall, I look back. He isn't there. I knew he would have already turned the corner, but I look for him anyway. I walk upstairs and pack reports I'll read over the weekend to prepare for next week's visit from the Greek prime minister. I throw in a copy of Edith Hamilton's book *The Greek Way*.

Jack flies to us in Glen Ora the next day. The helicopter touches down just before lunch. I walk out to meet him and know from his face things haven't gone well.

It all looked on track at first, he tells me, but by 11, the UN was involved.

"Then Adlai will handle it," I say.

"He still doesn't know. He can't know and, at the same time, deny U.S. involvement."

I stand still for a moment, light currents of air shifting through my skull. Jack has allowed the United States to back a covert military invasion, and his UN ambassador hasn't been told.

"What's for lunch?" he says.

"Hamburgers," I say slowly.

"Good. Let's eat, then we'll take a drive over to the steeplechase races."

"Why did you come here today, Jack? Not that I don't want you here, but it seems like you'd be able to handle things better from Washington." We've almost reached the house.

"It's out of my hands, Jackie." His jaw is set. "I'm not going to stay and oversee something the United States isn't involved with."

He doesn't last at the steeplechase. When I come back to Glen Ora, I find him whacking golf balls in the back pasture. Strong, hard strikes. He aims for the horizon without looking at it; he just sets the next ball down on the tee.

Sunday afternoon, the phone rings.

"I'm not signed onto this," he says harshly into the receiver. He hangs up.

"Who was that?" I ask. He shakes his head and walks to the bureau. He picks up a tie clip, then puts it down and leaves the room. I follow him. He walks into the kitchen and sits at the table. He looks at me for a moment, then away.

"We're in it," he says. "Rusk told me to call off the second round of air strikes. The generals object. How can men land without air cover?" He is asking the empty room, not me. I sit down at the table with him.

"I have to get back early tomorrow," he says ten minutes later, out of nowhere.

"We'll leave first thing," I say.

The phone shatters the dark at half past four Monday morning. It's the secretary of state, Dean Rusk, again. Then the deputy CIA director, General Cabell, is on the phone. He'd gone to Rusk, begging for air cover.

Jack hangs up and just sits there, on the edge of the bed.

By nine o'clock when we reach the White House, two American ships transporting men and supplies have been sunk by Castro's planes. By three that afternoon, Castro's tanks are on the beach. They've surrounded the exiles.

I find a sheet of paper with his notes on his desk.

Only the one word staggered again and again throughout, circled.

Decision.
 Decision.
  Decision.

When he comes home hours later from the Cabinet Room, he barely meets my eyes. He touches Caroline's head; his fingers graze her hair. He kisses John, then slips past them and goes into the bedroom.

"We'll be right back," I tell the children. I follow him into the bedroom, closing the door behind us. He sits with his head in his hands. He is crying. He tells me the air raids failed—too late, it all failed, a devastating rout. The U.S.-trained Cuban exiles were trapped on the beach. Hundreds of them, surrounded by twenty thousand of Castro's troops.

"Those were *men*," he says. "I sent them off with my promise and I knew in my gut it might be the wrong call, but I kept telling myself to trust Eisenhower's plan, trust his generals. The CIA organized this. They said the invasion would spark a coup, but there was nothing. A disaster. You can't half-do a thing like this and have it end well.

"Dulles wore his goddamn bedroom slippers," he tells me. The CIA director just sat there in the Cabinet Room, puffing away on his pipe, as he went through the list of every damn thing that had gone off the rails, quietly blaming the defeat on Jack's refusal to approve the air strikes and on soft-pedal political compromises. All through that long awful day, news filtered in. The brigade of Cuban exiled leaders trapped, support trucks burned, as Castro's tanks spread out, took over the beaches where the men still alive had fled.

I sit down beside him and say his name. In his face, humiliation and a bewildered rage.

"I never wanted this," he says.

"Cuba?"

"Any of it."

That night, I hold his arm as we descend the stairs to the Congressional Reception in the East Room. No one knows yet. He is in white tie and tails, and we dance to "Mr. Wonderful," played by the Marine Corps band. His smile is crisp, his fingers tight against my waist. At the edge of the dance floor, Dean Rusk approaches Lyndon and whispers something. Lyndon's eyes shift to Jack. They're about to summon him. I see it happen a moment before Lyndon steps onto the dance floor.

I attend a tea the next day for three hundred women, the wives of newspaper editors. When it's over, I go to find Bobby. He's down the hall from the Oval Office, standing alone with a cup of coffee.

"Tell me everything," I say.

"The thing turned sour in a way you can't believe, Jackie. Men shot like dogs. Hundreds captured. We only got twenty-six out."

Bobby blames Dulles. He blames the CIA leaders Jack inherited from Eisenhower. The plan Jack got, he says, was full of holes. Doomed to fail. Eisenhower's men claim it wasn't, since air strikes were in the original plan. They're already chirping that the defeat was because politicians pared away too much for the plan to succeed. But they are the ones who bungled it. And now they refuse to acknowledge their part. There was a leak. The Soviets knew about the invasion. The CIA knew the Soviets knew and still gave Jack the green light.

"What choice did he have, Jackie? If he hadn't moved forward, they would have called him a coward." Bobby's face is tight as he tells me about the message from the brigade commander that came in after midnight. *Desperate. Out of ammo. Will you back us or not? Low jet cover. Can you give us just this?* Jack ordered more air support then, opposing Rusk, and, as they waited for the outcome, he went outside at 3:00 A.M. to walk the grounds alone.

"Stay close to him, Jackie," Bobby says.

"He sent a message this morning telling me to take the children to Glen Ora."

Bobby's eyes pause on my face. "Then that's what you do. If that's what he wrote, it means he wants you there so he can leave all this and go to you."

Jack arrives the next day. He's canceled a scheduled trip on a naval aircraft carrier. Half an hour after landing at Glen Ora, he takes his golf clubs and goes out to chip balls. Morose. Chip. Ball after ball to the pasture. Chip.

"Those sons of bitches with all the fruit salad just sat there nodding, saying it would work."

Chip.

"How could I have been so stupid?"

"You couldn't have known, Jack."

He doesn't answer.

Chip.

"How could I have made this mistake?"

Thursday, April 20, the failed mission hits the headlines. Two U.S. citizens are executed in Cuba, over one hundred of the exiles killed. Castro crows the invasion was crushed.

"It's only a matter of time," Jack says to me that morning in the Residence, turning the paper facedown.

"Before what?"

"I'm drawn and quartered."

Even when he smiles, the rage is there. He's furious with his generals, furious with Eisenhower, furious most of all with himself.

"Here's an unfair truth about war," I hear him say to Bobby hours later. "Success has a hundred fathers, defeat's an orphan. Tacitus. This defeat is solely, squarely mine."

"No," Bobby says.

The three of us are walking down the hall, heading toward the press room, where Jack is due to speak.

"I need to own it," Jack says. He stares at the floor as we walk, his stride long.

"Political suicide to take all the heat for this," Bobby says.

Jack stops. "You're wrong." His tone cold. Flushed of emotion. "United States involvement in Cuba is going to be on every front page by the first of next week. I need to take the punch and get this behind me. I need to tell them why this happened and what's at stake. And if I have to spend the next year climbing out of this dark hole of failure, so be it."

He starts walking again; Bobby takes a quick step to catch up. Neither of them speaks until we turn the corner. A knot of reporters waits outside the door of the briefing room.

"I'm with you," Bobby says, his voice quiet. "Make space in that hole for me."

In the press conference, Jack walks a finer tightrope than I anticipate. Not evasive exactly, but he doesn't come out and admit the central part the United States played. His face is grave, the lid on his right eye lower than usual. His fingers tap the podium. He is measured with his words as he talks about how the conflict on that tiny island is another chapter in the fight of liberty against tyranny, democracy against communism. He talks about the threat of Castro, aligned with Russian interests, on an island only ninety miles off the Florida coast. He describes the Cuban exiles as refugees, not mercenaries, as Castro's dubbed them, and he adds, "We face a relentless struggle in every corner of the globe . . . only the courageous, only the visionary," will survive.

It's a good speech, the words clear and strong, and I understand they are words for the long game, but I can feel the rift between those words and his heart.

We're alone briefly that afternoon.

"I'm sorry, Jack," I say.

He looks at me, that burning anger alive again in his eyes.

"This is failure, Jackie." He bites down on the word. "My failure, my fault, and no matter what I have to say publicly, I need to know it was mine."

I understand then what he's after. It's not simply out of guilt.

The guilt is there—men died for his mistake and in the belief that he'd protect them. *Shot like dogs. Doomed to fail.* These words will ring in him for weeks. He let other men force a decision that was his alone to make. He's not trying to forget or dodge that, though. He understands there's power in accepting the blame. There's power and a galvanizing fuel not to make the same mistake again. I recognize that quiet rage. It's what I saw in him early on, when we were first together, before we were married, when I was falling in love. It's a source of his grit, his strength, a true and real dimension of him I believe in without always having the words to capture it. Jack hasn't become who he is because it was easy. Despite the privilege, despite the wealth, despite whatever his father has bought or traded for him and however Faustian those bargains may have been, Jack was first and foremost a disappointment. The sickly one. Weak, injured, bedridden sometimes for months on end. He wasn't the favorite son. Trapped in a broken body, he knows what it is to be left, crippled, alone. He knows as well how to take that wrenching loss and transform it. And the bold spirit infusing his words, his fight, his fierce sense of meaning and ideals—the spirit that sparks his cool, pragmatic mind—is no unearned thing but rather comes from a concentrate of hardened experience, the doubt and shame and leveling pain he's had to work through and endure.

He'll trust none of them now. I know this. He'll trust only Bobby and his own gut. He'll let this failure and the consequent rage breathe in him until every trace of starry-eyed chaff has burned away.

He glances at me then, that little look.

"I have an idea, Jackie."

He sends a memo that afternoon to Lyndon Johnson. Questions.

Do we have a chance of beating the Soviets by putting a laboratory in space, or by a trip around the moon, or by a rocket to go to the moon and back with a man?

Is there any space program which promises dramatic results in which we could win?

He wants to know how much a program like that would cost. What type of rockets could the United States use?

"I know what it'll look like," he tells me. "Like I'm trying to shift focus in a shell game I've already lost." He's getting dressed, choosing between two ties laid on the bed.

"I don't think it matters what it looks like, Jack," I say, "if it matters to you and if you give people something to believe in that you believe in. Some new dream."

He picks up the navy tie with faint diagonal stripes; his eyes meet mine, and in that brief silence I remember words from his inaugural, words he told me he tinkered with until they were his: *Let both sides seek to invoke the wonders of science instead of its terrors. Together let us explore the stars. . . .*

The children are coming. I hear the light beat of Caroline's sweet footsteps running toward us down the hall.

On May 5, NASA puts the first American into space, astronaut Alan Shepard. The twenty-five-meter Mercury Redstone rocket, Freedom 7, lifts off from Cape Canaveral and travels 166 miles into space for a fifteen-minute suborbital flight.

"Ninety-three minutes less than the Russians," Jack remarks when success of the launch floods the headlines, "but at least we're in the game."

A thirty-page report lands on his desk. A team at NASA and Secretary of Defense Bob McNamara have compiled five priorities to overhaul the U.S. space program, including satellites, high-propulsion rockets, and a manned lunar mission before the end of the decade.

Jack doesn't talk about it much at first. When the Bradlees and Bill Walton come for dinner, he asks a few abstract questions. What are their thoughts on U.S. efforts in space? Is the projected cost too steep? What would make it worth the risk?

It's Lyndon Johnson who gives Jack the nudge he needs. I like Lyndon and his wife, Lady Bird. They're Southern and sometimes awkward in our world—Johnson stands out with his six-foot-three lumbering frame and blunt, heavy drawl—but he and

Lady Bird are kind to me. In the days following Shepard's flight, Lyndon tells Jack that the moon landing is what they should focus on. The human face of the program, Lyndon calls it, contending if NASA gets "guts enough" to back the plan, it's not a question of whether but how.

Together, they hammer out a strategy. Lyndon works to gain support of lawmakers on both sides of the aisle, and on May 25, Jack goes before a joint session of Congress in a televised speech to the nation. He argues the case for more spending on an aggressive U.S. space program to surpass the Soviets and land an American on the moon. It's a speech about freedom and the future, about strong decisive action and the impact of the space adventure "on the minds of men everywhere."

As I listen to his clear, measured voice, I can still see traces of that burning anger in his eyes. How much I respect what he's done, how he's taken the embers of failure and transmuted it to this.

I meet him at the portico when the car brings him back that afternoon.

"You did it," I say.

He smiles: "It's a start."

Dave Powers steps up to us. "I'm afraid we need you," he says. "News from the South."

Turning to leave, Jack pulls me in briefly. His lips brush my face. "I'll find you later, Jackie."

. . .

Inept. That's the word De Gaulle reportedly uses to describe the American fiasco in Cuba.

Within days, we're leaving for Europe. First Paris, where Jack will meet with De Gaulle; then Vienna, for a summit with Khrushchev. I was surprised when Jack told me Khrushchev accepted his invitation to discuss a nuclear détente. Then I realized why. Khrushchev scented weakness, prey. He and De Gaulle see Jack as a boy king playing at world leader who can't keep his own house in line.

"De Gaulle may be an ally," Jack tells me, "but he's a bastard."

"French or not," I say, "I promise to like him less for your sake."

Bobby is with us in the Residence. Jack turns to him now.

"While I'm gone, please keep the civil-rights mess off the front page."

It's been unfolding: The Freedom Riders and the unending violence in the South. Buses burned. Bricks and lead pipes hurled at passengers stepping off. On Mother's Day, an all-white mob barricaded a bus carrying Black and white riders in Birmingham. They slashed the tires, smashed windows, threw firebombs in, and blocked the doors so the passengers were trapped.

"Birmingham one day," Bobby says, "Anniston the next."

"The local police?" Jack says.

"Late." Bobby's eyes are flat. "Every time."

"All right, deal with it."

"I need real support. U.S. marshals, the National Guard."

"Too much fuss. Get it done quietly."

"It's not the kind of thing that's going to keep quiet."

We arrive at Orly Airport on the last day of May to a crowd of thousands waving American flags. De Gaulle has arranged a spectacle—tremendous black horses, motorcycles, waves of gold-helmeted troops. He stands, tall and solemn and alone, on the red carpet at the foot of the steps.

"He'll try to one-up you," I say to Jack as we leave the plane. "He likes to traffic in power, even if France doesn't have what they once did."

"Macmillan calls him 'the pinhead.'"

I smile. "And you're the young dashing one. Look at all these people who've come out for you."

"Or you."

We start down the stairs.

"Just remember," I say, "the world wants a Jack. Someone who overturns what's outdated. They want adventure and change."

"We don't know that yet."

"It's true. And now you've gone on national TV and promised to put a man on the moon."

While Jack meets with De Gaulle, André Malraux is my guide through Paris. Months ago I asked my chief of staff, Tish, to tell the French ambassador I hoped to meet Malraux.

"Your intellectual crush," Tish teased me.

"How could one not be a little in love with a French Resistance fighter turned cultural minister who literally scrubbed the soot-black stones of the Louvre?"

But just a week ago, Malraux's two sons were killed in a car wreck. I sent word to him immediately, saying we should cancel. To my surprise, he wrote back, insisting we still meet.

He is an extraordinary man of intellect and grace. We walk together through the Musée du Jeu de Paume, then drive to Empress Josephine's Château de Malmaison outside Paris. I've told him I want to see the restoration work Stéphane Boudin did on Josephine's house. I find it curious, I tell him, the degree of extravagance Napoleon's wife engaged to shape the most beautiful garden in Europe—not just the two hundred varieties of roses and lilies from her native Martinique, but her insistence on three hundred pineapple plants in the orangery, as well as kangaroos, llamas, black swans. The curator walking with us mentions that Josephine was "extremely jealous" of Napoleon.

This makes me laugh. "But she wound up on her feet," I say, "while he was exiled to Saint Helena."

Malraux smiles. "Tonight at Versailles, we'll dine on gold-trimmed china that once belonged to that exiled emperor."

I take his arm as we walk. "I've been thinking, André, that someday you might lend me a French painting. Who knows, perhaps *La Joconde*?"

He laughs, and a bright joy floods through me that my audacious, absurd request for him to send the *Mona Lisa* might dispel, if just for a moment, the dark grief of loss he suffers.

De Gaulle looms, a towering figure at dinner in the Hall of Mirrors at Versailles. I am seated next to him. We talk together in French about art and my love of Paris, my experiences as a student on Boulevard Saint-Michel. I tell him that earlier that day, when I was supposed to be resting, I asked one of the Secret Service agents to drive me around the city, just so I could cross over my favorite bridges and drive down the streets I walked as a college girl.

The candelabras are lit; the mirrored walls catch the bouncing light like stars. The ceiling soars. Through the tall arched windows, I can see the outline of the night gardens, the spangled flow of water from the fountains.

We discuss French history. "Remind me, please," I say, "who did Louis XVI's daughter marry?" As we chat on in French, I can feel that sterner aspect of him soften. We walk from the dining room to a ballet Malraux has arranged, which was first performed for Louis XV. Flaming torches light the theater.

"And from here you travel to Vienna?" De Gaulle says.

"Yes. The president will meet with Chairman Khrushchev."

"Watch out for his wife," De Gaulle says, a dour smile. "She's the craftier of the two."

. . .

The Russian leader compliments my dress and draws his chair closer. We talk about horses and Ukrainian folk dances.

"Remind me, please, Mr. Chairman," I say, "of the name of the dog you sent up into space."

"Strelka."

"Such a lovely name!"

"There are puppies."

"Why don't you send me one?"

He laughs. "Perhaps I'll send you two."

We are at the state dinner at the Schönbrunn Palace in Vienna. We can hear the low drone of crowds outside.

"It's your name they're chanting," Khrushchev tells me.

I smile. "I think it's my husband's." He studies me for a moment, then cocks his bald head, pretending to listen.

"No," he says, "they are for you."

There's something cozy about him, though I remember a line from the briefing papers about how he gets ornery when he's tired. Just last year, he took off his shoe and brandished it at the UN. Now at the Schönbrunn Palace, I ask Khrushchev about a book I read, *The Sabres of Paradise*, the story of a Muslim guerrilla leader who fought for decades against the czar. I tell him how intrigued I was and ask if he can tell me more. He frowns for a moment, then starts to talk about how the quality and number of teachers in the region are far more robust now under the Soviets than they were under the czar. I let him go on for a while, puffing himself up, then I touch his arm and smile.

"Oh, Mr. Chairman, please don't bore me with statistics."

A blunt silence. Several heads turn in our direction, but Khrushchev only laughs.

"You are charming," he says.

He is brutal, though, to Jack, when they meet the next day to discuss Berlin. "That bone in my throat" is how Khrushchev describes the divided city, a Western enclave deep in communist East Germany. He refuses to discuss a nuclear détente between the United States and the Soviet Union. He turns Jack's arguments around, aiming well-placed shots to underscore Jack's inexperience. When Jack says that a nuclear exchange would kill seventy million people in ten minutes, Khrushchev shrugs and coolly remarks that a Soviet treaty with East Germany by year-end is inevitable. He demands that the United States withdraw from West Berlin. If not, he threatens, he'll cut off Allied access to the city.

"I did it all wrong," Jack tells me afterward in our hotel room. "Everything I'd been warned about his tactics flew out of my head."

"Macmillan told you he bluffs," I say.

"There was no bluff. He savaged me and, because of Cuba, he could."

On the flight to London, Jack talks to Rusk, O'Donnell, and Powers. I try to close my mind to the brooding mood on the plane. Soon we'll land in England. I'll fly on to Greece. Jack will stay for a night to confer with Macmillan, then return to the States. I miss the children. I wish I was flying home to them. Through the window, the gray sky floods away underneath.

. . .

Clint is there when I land in Athens.

"It's so good to see you again, Mr. Hill."

He takes his place in my shadow as we walk from the plane. Evening. The air is warm, and I feel my skin release to it.

The prime minister and his wife welcome us. To the side hovers a group of fidgeting boys dressed as Evzones, the elite Greek military guard. I kneel by the smallest boy and say hello in Greek. He smiles shyly, reaching for my hand.

The sea is cyan blue, outstretched below the villa in Kavouri. I swim that first night before dinner. The next morning, the yacht that will take us through the islands is moored offshore. Fishing boats and small craft dart around it. The Greek Navy pushes them off.

We embark for Epidaurus. The town has been whitewashed to greet us, thyme and flowers strewn through the streets. In the amphitheater on the eastern coast, we sit on a two-thousand-year-old bench and watch a rehearsal of Sophocles's *Electra,* that play about the violence of justice and regret, the story of a brother and sister who murder their mother to avenge their father's death. The title role is played by a young actress—dark hair, slight, her face with a curious intensity that seems to magnetize the open space. Watching that familiar play unfold in the ancient, brilliant light on a dirt-stone stage, where it was first performed thousands of years before, feels uncanny, almost transcendent. Who is to say what endures?

"What did you think of the play, Mr. Hill?" I ask afterward as we walk down to the harbor.

"I liked it," he says, "although I'm afraid I didn't understand a word."

I laugh. "I didn't really either. Apparently, there's another Epidaurus. The prime minister's wife told me. A sunken city off the coast, ruins just meters below the surface. It's a short drive from here." We turn a corner and start across an open square. "Mr. Hill, do you think we might shift our itinerary this afternoon?"

He looks at his supervisor, Agent Jefferies, walking ahead of us. Jefferies is a play-by-the-book kind of man. He doesn't like the little schedule changes I try to weave in here and there to keep breathing room in my day.

"What would you like to do, Mrs. Kennedy?" Clint asks.

"I'd love to see that other Epidaurus. And perhaps swim there." I feel him hesitate. I know what I'm asking for, and I know it's too much. There would need to be an advance. "It's all right," I say. "We won't do that."

"I'm sorry, Mrs. Kennedy."

"Maybe, though, could we bend time a bit this afternoon? Enough for a short swim and half an hour to water-ski?"

He smiles. "That I can do."

I ski off the back of a small motorboat. Clint sits in the stern, watching as I cut over the wake, carving long tails of spray that rise and fall through the air. The light is sharp, the space so bright and open it's as if the sky is hurtling away. I drop the line and the boat circles back. Clint helps me in.

"Will you give it a try, Mr. Hill?"

"There wasn't much water where I grew up."

I laugh. "This summer, in Hyannis Port, I want to teach you to water-ski."

As the small boat picks up speed, heading toward the yacht, the thought strikes through me, a hot current. *I don't want to go back.* It startles me. It's not that I don't miss home. I miss the children intensely. Little voices, faces, hands. And Jack. But I love, so much, the rush of freedom I feel here as the boat flies across that wide expanse.

Overnight, we travel to Mykonos. I wake the next morning into a blaze of light. The buildings on the island tumble over each other like dice. We walk up the steep hill through the winding streets of town toward the villa of Helen Vlachos, the only woman in Greece who owns a newspaper.

"The light is different here," I say to her. "It seems to reveal more." We're eating lunch under an arbor of flowering fruit trees. "I want to bring my children to visit."

"Before you leave Athens," she says, "be sure to make the

climb to Cape Sounion and the Temple of Poseidon. Lord Byron carved his name into one of the pillars."

A butterfly lands on the table near a vase of flowers, its wings bluish, sheer, and I think of that day I first came to Hyannis Port, years ago, Jack and I in his childhood bedroom with all those books, the stories of heroes and legends he'd loved as a child. I remember his face as he lay back on the bed and looked at me, that look I've never seen in anyone but him.

"Go late in the day to Cape Sounion," Helen Vlachos says to me now. "It has an unearthly beauty at sunset. One of the most magnificent sites in Greece."

Days later, I take that walk along the cape near the Temple of Poseidon. As the sun collapses into the sea, I step carefully around an archaeological dig, long pits in the ground exposing layers of rock and stratified earth, pottery, bones—levels of what was once a sunlit world layered over other worlds, the dead layered over the dead like leaves.

We never imagine it. That we will be there someday, centuries from now, skulls ground to unnamed and intimate fragments, trampled by new generations who in turn can't imagine their lives will also be broken to dust. Jack would understand this, the nuanced implications; even if he didn't want to, he would—how everything marked *critical, classified, urgent,* eventually turns to this.

He meets me at the airport. Slipping into the car, I kiss him. He thumps on the back of the driver's seat. "Let's go."

His back hurts. I can tell by the set in his jaw. There was a story in the paper while I was away and photographs of him boarding a cherry picker that would lift him from the tarmac to the plane because he couldn't climb the steps. I know how much he hates it—the weakness.

I hold his hand and watch the moving sky through the window. I feel a strange and heady disconnect, like only half of me is home, while the other half still drifts through the whitewash of those islands, the rising daylight six hours ahead, the gorgeous blue waste of the sea.

That sense stays with me for weeks—even as I rework curriculum plans for Caroline's preschool; even as I skim the landslide of clippings that praise my state visits, saying the intractable Khrushchev was smitten; even when two Russians walk into the White House, bearing a gift from him to me, one of the space-dog puppies, which I name Pushinka; even when Jack starts calling me the "sex symbol," because he's read the same news stories and seen photographs of this glamorous woman who took Europe by storm and happens to be the woman he's married to.

"She's a figment," I tell him.

He smiles. "As long as she's what they want."

. . .

I'm with the children for the rest of that summer in Hyannis Port. Long hours with Joe on the porch of the main house. Every morning, I take Caroline to the stables to ride. In the afternoons, I work through memos and folders of correspondence sent up from Washington.

I've begun to rethink the vision for the state rooms at the White House—the Red Room and the Blue Room. I want to shape something in those rooms: a purely American sense of strength, discipline, purpose. National power, or at least the impression of it, even as Jack grows into the thing itself. I want those rooms to become a space where he, as a leader, can emerge into history.

I keep thinking of Greece—that water and sky, how the ancient, brilliant light revealed more, stripped more away, that light a kind of alchemy. I want to do that here. Work elements of a physical space into beauty and significance, infuse a room with a sense of promise and truth. I don't want artifice. Artifice will bleach to nothing in the light of time. That's not what I'm after.

The days pull toward Friday afternoon and the three-o'clock chime of the ice cream truck, shortly followed by a phone call to say that Air Force One has arrived at Otis and Jack is on his way.

Within the hour, he'll blow in. Caroline will race him up the steps so he can change into sneakers and drive her in the golf cart to the candy store in town before it closes.

"Let me say hello to your mother, Buttons."

"But she'll be here all night, and the candy store won't."

He'll pop his head into whatever room I'm in. "Hey, kid," he'll say—that smile. "It's you."

His back pain has improved, and that lightens his mood. Even when he limps, there's a grace in his step. On those long summer weekends, there are blueberries and corn, clam chowder, and lobster rolls. There are swims or a cruise on the *Marlin*. When storms roll in, there's backgammon, Chinese checkers, and late-afternoon daiquiris. In the main house, away from the children and their rough-and-tumble, there are debates and strategy meetings for Jack, Bobby, and their team about how to avoid a nuclear showdown with the Soviets. A crisis has developed in Berlin. On August 12, a barbed-wire fence went up overnight, dividing the eastern and western parts of that city. Nearly two hundred kilometers, the Berlin Wall runs through cemeteries and zigzags along canals, closing the border between communist East Germany and the West. Jack has refused to do what Khrushchev demanded—remove U.S. troops from West Berlin. "We'll defend free Germany," Jack says.

Toward the end of August, Khrushchev sends a private letter to Jack about how a tentative peace, or at least a hold in the conflict, might be approached. The letter is unofficial, but it creates a sense of pause.

That evening Jack and I sit together on the porch. It feels unusual to have that bit of time alone. The sun is down. Tribes of moths beat around the screen. I tell him then about the walk I took along the dig at Cape Sounion, how the sky seemed to stretch and breathe, the raw, haunted sense I felt in that place.

"It reminded me of Homer's epics," I say. "Those ruins infused with the dead—bodies loved or slain, pressed together in passion or war. Even the heroes."

Jack smiles. "Even the heroes."

"I wish you'd been there with me. I want to go sometime to that place with you."

"I'll carve my name on the pillar next to Byron's."

I continue to feel it—that curious sense of dislocation, like I've moved into a separate space, and though Jack and I are closer, when he leaves at the end of each weekend, I don't feel the piercing ache I used to feel.

"Who's in charge of a woman's life?" I asked John White, years ago, when I was working at the paper and he'd made some remark about one of my columns.

Once, I thought I understood what I was willing to give up when I married Jack. My work, the freedom to go where I wanted or see who I wanted whenever I wanted. But the deeper sacrifice, I've come to realize, is about power and the accommodations a woman is called on to make. To shrink enough, to be small enough, to fit into the corners of a man's world, to file down her own edges to be the kind of wife he'll need, that he and others expect her to be.

. . .

Back in Washington that fall, I'm deliberate in how I map my time. There are always things to do. Events to attend or create, lists of tasks I need to address. I work better, with more intention, when there's the pressure of an upcoming trip, even just a weekend with the children to Glen Ora.

"Little trips away keep me light," I tell Jack. "And out of your hair." That makes him laugh, but I can feel it also unsettles him.

I plan a Shakespeare production in the East Room for the president of Sudan and scribble a memo about it to Pam.

Let's please include a scene from Macbeth. *And some half scenes from the comedies, to capture both the light and the dark.*

I invite cellist Pablo Casals to play at a November dinner in honor of the governor of Puerto Rico. Jack and I throw a black-tie dinner dance for Lee and the Agnellis.

"What about Stas?" I ask my sister. "Is he coming too?"

"He might," Lee says, "or not."

I know what that means. "Oh, Lee."

"It's my marriage," she snaps.

"Well, you alone are a beautiful excuse for a party, Pekes."

At that dinner dance, I ask Oleg Cassini to introduce the Twist. As he's out on the floor, trying to teach a man how to use his shoulders to get the right twisting motion in his hips, Pierre Salinger walks up to me and looks pointedly at Oleg and the couple laughing on the dance floor.

"Too risqué," he says.

"Oh, please don't worry, Pierre. You can send a denial to the press tomorrow. Claim we engaged in nothing more suggestive than the foxtrot."

Stas, as expected, does not attend. Jack raises a glass in a toast: "To Stas, wherever you are."

Around eleven, I'm in the Blue Room when my stepbrother Gore wanders in. He comes over to sit with me, but there's no second chair, so he kneels by mine. He's rather drunk and says a few snide remarks about Lyndon Johnson—"the lox," he calls him, as Lyndon tries to do the Twist, nearly knocking the lovely Helen Chavchavadze to the floor.

"A Mad Hatter evening you've made, my dear Jackie," Gore says. "I do admire it. Though Lem went after me for not being at the Arts Council. He is a—"

"Don't say it, Gore," I warn. "You love to pick fights. I don't want it tonight."

"My lovely step-step, don't pretend you're not half charm, half malice, like me."

"Those aren't your percentages tonight, Gore. You're drunk, all malice, and that's just dull."

He seems briefly contrite. He stands up, wavering on his feet; his hand falls on my shoulder. A moment later, his hand is knocked sharply away, and Bobby steps between us.

"Impertinent son of a bitch," Gore says, throws a punch. Bobby catches his fist mid-swing. We get Gore packed into a car, heading home. I tease Bobby for being so protective on my behalf.

"Was it the hand on my shoulder?" I say. It makes him flush.

"He was upsetting you," he says, but glances away as he says it. I touch his hand.

"Thank you," I say.

We're with Joe in Palm Beach in December. Jack has a brief trip to Nassau to meet with Harold Macmillan. The day he leaves, I'm swimming with Caroline in the pool when Joe comes out onto the patio.

"You're back early," I say. "Too much golf?"

"Too much sun."

I swim to the edge of the pool. He sits down on one of the lounge chairs in the shade, his legs stretched out.

"You look tired, Joe," I say.

"I had to quit after the fifth hole," he says with some disgust.

"Sweet Joe, even you are not invincible." I splash at the water just enough so drops strike near his feet without hitting his shoes. "Go take a rest," I say. "Get into your room, where it's cool."

"Don't you dare call a doctor."

"I promise."

He pushes himself up and walks off, the usual long stride at first, but as I watch, he slows, like his body can't quite keep up with the heat. He steps inside. Two hours later, his niece Ann looks into his bedroom to check on him, and he cannot speak or move.

I'm with him at the hospital every day. On Christmas Eve, Jack and I stay with him until midnight. We take Communion in the hospital chapel. Thrombosis to his left cerebral hemisphere—his right side is entirely paralyzed. He's a shell of himself. He can barely speak. I read aloud to him. I feed him and wipe the shine of saliva from the edge of his mouth.

1962

The day after Jack's State of the Union address, I see him in the
colonnade talking to one of the new interns. Dark-haired like
several of the others. She's the one, I remember, who accompa-
nied Jack on his trip to Nassau. As I watch, his hand finds her
backside, she glances up at him from under a swoosh of her hair.

I have trouble working that afternoon. I cancel an appointment. I ask Pam to find someone to stand in for me. I go out to
the garden, then change my mind. I don't want to sit. Even the
grass feels overwhelming. It's all just too much, the whipsaw of
love, then betrayal after betrayal. He doesn't even try to hide it.

The children have gone to a friend's house to play. I'm alone
and the sky is exquisite, that unbridled ache in the light—so
beautiful, that light. I feel something inside me break.

I slip my sunglasses on and walk away from the garden, away
from the Residence, toward the gate, and out to the street. I can
feel the burn of tears. I can sense Clint behind me, trailing. I'm
grateful he knows me well enough to read my mood and keep a
distance, that young man, his shadow self, staying close like
some dark angel.

I know what those women are to Jack. Some habit he has,
events slotted in on his schedule, another appointment to keep.
But now it's not just the women that bother me. It's how the rumors bend the air—hushed talk in the corridors, stilted looks

from the staff; they seem more gentle with me when I return from a weekend trip. That dirty rub of sympathy I hate. They all know. Do they really think I don't? Or that I don't care?

I need to get out from under it, the weight of the shame and the rage—his casual, ruinous lust. The anger rises in me, and the following Tuesday, as I am leading two French reporters through the restoration and the progress we've made, walking them from room to room, we come to where the girl they call Fiddle is working, tapping keys on her typewriter. I wave a hand and say in French, "And this is one of the young pretty women my husband is ostensibly sleeping with." The air drops, a sharp intake of breath from the reporters, then silence. The girl's pretty head with its pretty red mouth looks up. She clearly doesn't speak French.

"Shall we move on?" I say brightly.

Jack hears about it, of course.

"You can't just say things like that, Jackie, no matter how witty you're trying to be."

"Do you think I said it to be witty? Do you think I said something everyone doesn't know?"

"Be reasonable."

"If you didn't do things like that, Jack, I wouldn't have to say things like that, would I?"

"We're just lucky they aren't going to print it."

One named Fiddle, one named Faddle
Mimi
Marilyn
Mary Meyer

It's like a nursery rhyme. Young girls who come back to their desks, hair wet, after a midday topless dip with drinks and cheese puffs in the White House pool.

I know some of their names. Not all. Just recently I learned the lovely Helen Chavchavadze joined the ranks. Her maiden name was Helen Husted. First cousin to my once-upon-a-fiancé Johnny Husted. What upset me about her, in particular, was that

I'd been the one to invite Helen to a dinner party when we still lived in Georgetown. Of all the fish in the sea, couldn't he have the decency to keep his flings out of my history?

The list is absurdly long. Names I've never heard of—women who perhaps had no names. At least to him. It's like working through a crossword puzzle. One woman across. One woman down. Trying to fill the blanks of all those tiny boxes that pick away at me.

On Valentine's Day, my television special airs, *A Tour of the White House*. The restoration isn't done. I have to keep reminding Jack. Just because the show is finished doesn't mean the work is. I'm drafting new plans for the Green Room.

Jack and I watch the special on a small TV set. I look like a doll in a box. My voice sounds odd, tinny, and I can see the tension in my face underneath the practiced calm—how difficult it is sometimes to keep that kind of expressionlessness. It feels eerie, watching that poised plastic version of myself, that tiny woman in the tiny TV with the bouffant sprayed hair and triple collar of pearls around her neck as she talks through one era of American history into the next, walking from the state rooms to the staircase and explaining how the private rooms of the family were, during Lincoln's time, the offices of the president. Lincoln's bedroom once doubled as the Cabinet Room. The woman on the TV climbs the stairs. "I'm so glad it isn't that way now," she says, that hushed voice, that little smile.

Just days ago, we learned that André Malraux was targeted for assassination. A bomb in his apartment. He wasn't killed or even injured, but a four-year-old girl in his building was blinded. Jack wanted to be sure I knew before I read it in the news. Now, as we watch the woman on the small box of the black-and-white TV screen, I think about that blinded little girl, the anonymous collateral horror. I think of the trees, the snow, the faces she will never see again. She might live into old age, but a simple passion has been stripped from her just because one man was convinced he needed to destroy another. Beside me, Jack shifts a cushion behind his back. He's focused on the woman on the screen, the moving likeness of me, as she talks about the People's House and its evolving place in history. He's unusually still, a warmth on his face, a kind of pleasure, and I can tell he is finally grasping the larger, cogent vision I was after, what I'm still working to achieve.

"It's really good, Jackie," he says as the show ends, that spark in his eyes I love.

A week later, after four postponed flights, astronaut John Glenn—one of the Mercury 7—orbits the earth in an Atlas rocket. February 20, 1962. The world stops that morning. Americans at work, at school, and at home pause in their ordinary lives to watch the countdown and the launch off Cape Canaveral. Glenn asked his children to help name the rocket. They chose the name *Friendship*. Jack shows me photographs Glenn took from space looking back toward the curve of the earth, the land masses below, that rim of blue and cloud, the dark of space behind it rising like a new sky.

"Now we're getting somewhere," he says.

. . .

In March I travel with Lee to India and Pakistan. An informal diplomatic trip Jack has asked me to take. For me it's an opportunity to explore the art, customs, and architecture of two countries entirely different from anywhere I've been. John Kenneth Galbraith, the U.S. ambassador to India, is our guide. We land in New Delhi and spend our first evening with Prime Minister Nehru and his daughter, Indira Gandhi. I ask to travel, whenever possible, by rail and car. I want to see where people live beyond the cities and palaces, those smaller villages where older, unmodern traditions can continue outside time. I pick out books on Mughal art to ship home. I let the prime minister's cousin paint a mark of color on my forehead, green paint made of manure to celebrate Holi, the ancient Hindu festival that marks the end of winter, the coming of spring. The focus in the press—to an almost absurd extent—is on my clothes, Lee's clothes, and the fact that we ride on an elephant. Jack makes light jokes about the elephant in more than one of his speeches at home.

When we land in Lahore, Pakistan, eight thousand people have gathered to meet us. We're welcomed by President Khan. A former general and fluent storyteller, he came to Washington once and, in that brief encounter, he and I had an effortless rapport. I've been briefed on U.S. objectives in Pakistan, including access to an airbase outside Peshawar, which would allow our military to spy on the Soviets. I know my visit here is, in part, to serve those interests, but I love the tales Khan tells of his adventures as a young man—he fought for the British Indian Army in World War II, then became the first native-born commander in chief of the Pakistan Army. He has such passion for his country and a commitment to peace with India. I love the bold swagger in his voice as he describes seizing the presidency in Pakistan's coup d'état. He's arranged a dinner for us in the Shalimar Gardens. We travel to the mountain regions of the country that border Afghanistan. Near the Khyber Pass, once a part of the Silk Road, tribal leaders present me with a sheep and a dagger, curved like a crescent moon. As we drive to the garrison city of Rawalpindi, I admire President Khan's Karakul hat.

"Then it's yours," he says. With a flourish, he takes it off, holding it out to me.

Before we leave to fly home, he presents me with an exquisite bay gelding named Sadar.

"You love horses," he says. "This gift is for you to remember the time you spent in our country." The crowds in the streets outside the governor's palace shower us with rose petals.

It's the first time an American First Lady has traveled to this country.

"I loved that trip," I tell Jack on my first night home. "I love how the immersion into an entirely new place changes the way I understand the world and our accountability to it."

And I forget, I could add. *I forget how hard it is to watch that faint wink I just saw you give the new pretty girl in my office. Though I'd been home for less than three hours, I felt you turn away from me, from us, toward her.*

I don't say it that evening, but the hurt feels sharp enough that I could. However short-lived those moments are, it's become harder to let them skim by. The shame of bearing witness to them and knowing that everyone around us pretends not to see what we all do leaves me fractured. It's corrosive. I am not fine.

"You all right, Jackie?" he says, the evening edition of the paper on his lap. He turns a page.

I don't answer.

. . .

André Malraux is coming to Washington in May. After declining two invitations I sent through the French ambassador, he accepted when the invitation came from me. I felt my heart lift when I received his note. I began to plan a running guest list for the dinner: bibliophiles; intellectual mavericks; authors, musicians, artists whose works are well received in France—Mark Rothko, Julie Harris, Aldous Huxley, Thornton Wilder, Elia Kazan, Lee Strasberg.

The night before Malraux arrives, I completely redraw the seating chart. I run an arrow across the room and move Arthur Miller to my table.

What was it like, I want to ask him, being married to Marilyn Monroe, with her mood swings and sybaritic need? She had quietly filed for divorce, I've learned, the day after Jack's inauguration, maybe hoping the world would be too distracted to notice. I don't allude to any of this, of course, sitting next to Arthur Miller that night.

"I've always been haunted by *The Crucible*," I say instead. "There's something timeless about that play. How every age will have its witch hunt. Tell me more, please, about how you see it."

I've put more personal thought into this dinner than any other. I swapped out all the chairs, exchanging the velvet upholstered ones for delicate bamboo seats. I asked Mr. West to have the bulbs in the chandeliers replaced. The light felt too brash. I wanted it softer, an air of mystery. I spent hours on the menu.

Chilled soup, a lobster salad once served to King Louis XV by a French courtesan. After dinner, in the East Room, there will be a concert. Violinist Isaac Stern, cellist Leonard Rose, pianist Eugene Istomin. Performing Schubert's Piano Trio in B Flat Major.

I care deeply what Malraux thinks.

Earlier that day, shortly after his arrival, I met him for a tour of the National Gallery. As we walked through, he told me he was haunted by one of the Rembrandt oils there, *La Balayeuse*. We stood in front of the painting—a young girl with a broom leaning over a wooden fence; she stared directly at us. I asked Malraux to tell me what he saw, and he pointed out the nuanced shadow on her face and hands, the strong bravura brushstrokes on her sleeves. I gave him a gift—two rare nineteenth-century books of political caricatures. I'd inscribed the inside of one, *How strange to give a book to someone whose books—and words—have given so much to me.*

That night at the dinner in Malraux's honor, I can feel a heady magic working through the room. Between the tapered candles on each table are vases of lily of the valley mixed in with tulips, blue iris. I made sure the vases are low enough so the guests can see one another across the table, talk, debate, laugh.

Lamplight, candlelight, strains of music—words tossed in the quick play of light—strung through the space to mark this singular, intimate stretch of time. I want the night to stay with them days later, like silver through their minds.

Tish finds me at one point to say that George Balanchine almost wasn't let in when he pulled up in a taxi and stepped out in a tattered raincoat.

"Bring him to me, please," I say. "Make sure I see him before he leaves."

Jack is a short distance away, that firm pumping handshake, that flash of smile. His face lit, alive. No matter what other turmoil might be moving underneath, there's no trace of it in his face.

We are good like this together.

As if he hears me thinking this, he looks up, that smile, conspiratorial, as if to say, *We've made this, you and I, this night, this world, a fast, luminous mix of art and politics, music and ideas.* I hold his eyes for a moment and feel a quiet thrill pass through me. This evening has been all I'd wanted it to be.

At the same time, even as the night ends, I can't escape the faint sense that something is amiss. But what? It all unfolded according to plan—the food, program, music. Everyone is milling around, laughing, happy. The air rings, and they linger, they don't want to leave. What is it, then, missing?

It's not until later, when the guests are gone, the rooms empty, dishes cleared. The staff left some of the candles lit on tables in one corner of the room, as I'd asked. I wanted to be the one to blow them out, and as I go from light to light, my hand cupped around each, wick after wick extinguished, just as I used to love to do in those quieter simpler evenings after the dinners at our house in Georgetown, I hear a sound in the doorway. I look up. Jack. I smile at him and continue with the candles, realizing then, with a strike of sorrow, that what is missing is my heart.

I want her back—that girl who craved a sense of wonder. That girl who was not always nice, who swore and laughed at dirty jokes and pranks and scorned sentimental earnestness—that girl who loved irreverence, who loved to push that dull line of what a young woman was supposed to want and say and think and be—that girl whose mind was wicked in interesting ways— the kind of girl who imagined how much fun it would be to place a tack on Zeus's chair, any Zeus, just to watch how he'd jump, see his blustery rage. That girl who sometimes felt she was a mass of brooding want and mischief held in by nothing more than skin. That girl whose faith burned—that girl who wanted a life made of future, an edge of horizon she could hurl herself toward.

And then that girl met you.
You

The next day, when Jack and I are at lunch, talking about my ideas for preservation work in Lafayette Square, Nanny Shaw marches in, a stern expression on her face and holding Caroline by the hand. Miss Shaw explains that one of the trainers came to leash Pushinka for a walk, and when Caroline went to pet the dog goodbye, Pushinka growled and bared its teeth. Caroline gave it a kick in the rear end.

"Excellent work, Buttons," Jack says. "That's giving it to those damn Russians."

Miss Shaw looks put out. "But, Mr. President—"

I sit at one end of the table, half a sandwich on my plate. They never quite hit it off, Jack and Miss Shaw. She thinks he's too lenient. Ordinarily I'd intercede, but today I decide to let Jack solve it. I'm thinking about the *Mona Lisa*. At a pause in the concert the night before, André Malraux, sitting beside me, said in a low voice, *Je vais vous envoyer* La Joconde. "I will send you the *Mona Lisa*." I felt a surge of triumph. The *Mona Lisa* has never left France.

. . .

An article by Norman Mailer appears in *Esquire*. "An Evening with Jackie Kennedy." He'd requested an interview months ago, around the New Year. I turned it down. Now, though, I find the article chilling. Not that he chose to write about me: *not only a woman looking for privacy but an institution being put together before our eyes*. I know I am fair game. It's the intimacy of the article that haunts me, the details he brings forward, with visceral precision, of that summer day two years ago when he first came to Hyannis Port. The August before the election. He has recalled it all: the hectic weather, the lawn of chaos—cameramen, aides, journalists, family, friends, tourists peering in for a glimpse of Jack. Then his focus shifts to me. His first impression: *a college girl who was nice*; his second: *a cat, narrow and wild, fur being rubbed all the wrong way*. It's uncanny how he remembers exactly what I said, how I looked, smiled, stood up, left the room, came back. It's not unflattering, but there are elements that feel derogatory, invasive, and his recall is so clear, I feel sick. A day I imagined was behind us—he's conjured it back.

"A violent love letter to you." That's how my friend Diana Vreeland describes it.

There's a phrase toward the end of the piece that I have to read twice: *She had perhaps a touch of that artful madness which suggests future drama.*

I put down the magazine, a ticking pressure in my chest.

JACK

"You're not going to Italy to get back at me, are you?" he says.
"Of course not."
"But it's August."

She hesitates, the surface of her eyes shift. There's something she's not telling him. Some secret.

She is not unlike him. He realized that when they first met. Leaving is something she knows how to do.

Her face is still and smooth, the way it gets when she knows she's being watched.

"You always think there's a game, Jack," she says. "I'm not playing a game. I love you. You know that. I have to live my life and do things I want to do. While I'm gone, you're free to do the things you want to do. Then we will both be back." She stops, but he can infer the rest. We will both be back in our maison blanche. The dinners and candles and music and speeches. It will be the transactional beauty you want, the kind you need to get what you want.

She doesn't need to say any of this. He hears it. The way she is looking at him. Steady, calm, matter-of-fact.

From somewhere down the hall, the children's voices.

"We won't be gone long," she says, that smile with its implacable charm. "What was it you said to me once, Jack? Flights always return."

Passionless. Her voice. No inflection. Then she adds, "Please don't forget, though, before I leave, we have to meet with Bill Walton about the designs for Lafayette Square."

She is taking Caroline with her to Italy. They'll be gone for three weeks.

He reads about her trip in the papers. The landing in Rome, the short flight to Salerno, where she and Caroline meet Lee. As the days unfold, photographs appear in the press of Jackie with Gianni Agnelli. In those photographs, something taut in the chemistry between them.

Salinger mentions it.

"You think it's an issue?" Jack asks.

Salinger nods. "You might want to ask her to cool it."

He misses her. He misses Caroline more. He misses the shape of his daughter resting against him as he reads aloud to her at night, the weight of her small body, half on his lap on the boat as the wet salt wind breaks against his face and strands of her hair blow across his skin, his arm tight around her. John is different, completely of this world, almost two, all boy, rolling on the floor. Caroline, though. He has always felt bound to her in some great, mysterious way, so even when she is right there, with him, she feels like memory. Her sweet voice, her smell, her hands around his neck, her small heart flipping in her chest as she breathes, mouth falling open, eyes closing to sleep as he holds her—those spare moments of their time together alter him in incremental ways, her laughter, her silence, the dimensions of her moods. She has always been the deep of his heart. Like some tiny god. She's the one soul in the world he feels entirely accountable to. Something of who she is, how she looks at him, what she expects, that sudden naked trust that will break across her small face turned up to his, demanding more than greatness. Goodness. How uncomplicated it is, the way he loves her, the way he's always loved her, as straightforward and essential as wind.

August 1962

The night before we leave for Italy, Caroline and I stay in New York. I wake to the headlines on August 6.

MARILYN MONROE KILLS SELF . . . FOUND NUDE IN BED . . . HAND ON PHONE . . . TOOK 40 PILLS

I stare at the paper and feel something inside me cave. *Nude in bed, hand on phone.*

Who was she calling?

. . .

LESS AGNELLI, MORE CAROLINE. That's the telegram Jack sends to me in Italy a week after we arrive. The curtness stings. I know the photographs he means. We were all there, walking together, but the press cropped the image so it looks like I was walking with Gianni Agnelli alone. Caroline, Lee, Gianni's wife, Marella, and of course Clint were cut from the frame.

The cliff below the nine-hundred-year-old villa in Ravello is rocky and steep. There are lemon trees, stone archways, wrought-iron gates. There are evenings when we smoke and talk, go out dancing, get back late. In my room, I sit at the small desk and write to Jack. I tell him how different the sky seems here—pure, almost cloudless. The sunsets seem to last forever though it does seem a little dull compared to the invasive gorgeous mess of clouds and glowing color we get on our New England coast.

I mention the Agnellis once, as in *Lee, the Agnellis, and I* . . .

I don't mention the stories Gianni tells about fighting under Mussolini, then switching sides to join the Allies, or his passion for gambling, skiing, fast cars, which he claims are all incarnations of one instinct. I don't write about the moment I mentioned that my favorite movie last year was *La Dolce Vita* and Gianni cried, "Ah, but that's the title of my life!" and how that made me laugh. How good it feels to laugh like that—some clenched place in me released.

. . .

Home at the end of August. We spend the weekend as a family in Newport. Caroline and I share stories of our trip. Before Jack leaves for Washington, he asks me to go for a walk on the beach. He tells me about simmering tensions with the Soviets in Berlin. Riots along the Wall. There are reports he's seen that contradict other accounts. Things don't add up.

"Other accounts?"

"While you were gone, we learned Khrushchev sent troops to Cuba. We thought it was just defensive, but last week a U-2 plane spotted what looks like missiles in Cuba."

"So you'll respond?"

"Some response. But I can't give him a reason to stir up Berlin."

We continue walking; he shifts topics—a game of golf he played last week, a movie he saw while I was away. He jokes that he managed to sit all the way through it. I tell him about a message I received from the curator at the National Gallery, who's starting to fret about France's loan of the *Mona Lisa* and her transatlantic voyage.

"He's afraid of the risk," I say.

"Life is risk," Jack says. It's a gorgeous day, the air soft and cool; it all feels a little weightless—the anecdotes, the ritual exchange. He tells me about a two-day trip he's taking to Texas in

September. NASA has finished the new spacecraft center of research and development for the Apollo program. The Mercury 7, including John Glenn, will go with him. Jack tells me Lyndon thinks this trip could galvanize national support for the space program.

"We need people to understand this is a choice we're making as a country. It may not always be easy, but that freedom to choose is a distinctly American freedom."

"And in space, there's no Berlin Wall."

He smiles. "Eisenhower's crew are griping about the cost."

"Did you say you'd be away mid-September? What day exactly?"

"September twelfth, I think."

"Our anniversary."

A pause in the air. He hadn't remembered.

. . .

Joe flies to Washington for a visit. A bright October afternoon. When the children wake up from their naps, I bundle them into the car. We drive to meet him at the airport.

I push Joe's wheelchair into the Lincoln Bedroom.

"You'll stay here," I say, kissing him on the cheek. "Tonight we'll have dinner with Jack, and tomorrow I've canceled everything to have the day just with you. I want to show you the designs we've made for Lafayette Square, the buildings we're preserving—they are so old and beautiful, Joe. You will love this project. The architect's nickname is, of all things, Rosebowl. Some ex–football star. He and I were just talking yesterday about how meaningful it is to spruce up the world a bit, if you have the chance, leave it better than you found it. You understand that, dear Joe, don't you?"

He looks at me—his sweet, incomplete smile—an intermingling of grief and gratitude in his eyes.

The next morning, Jack and I are still in bed when Mac Bundy brings in photographs of ballistic missiles armed with nuclear warheads near Cristobal, Cuba. Large enough to reach the United States.

"Khrushchev can't do this to me," Jack says. He pulls on his clothes and strides out. Later, when he comes home, his face is strained.

"Don't ask," he says. "For now, the less you know, the better."

"What do you need from me?"

"Go about your day as planned."

"I'm with your father all day."

"Good. And we've got that dinner in Georgetown tonight."

"Won't you need to be here?"

"Bobby can be me where I need him." I realize it then. He's already slipping Bobby into meetings with his core group of advisors from the National Security Council: the ExComm. Bobby is the only one he trusts.

In Georgetown that night, we play our way through the dinner like nothing's amiss. As soon as we return to the White House, Jack leaves for a debrief. He comes home late, after midnight.

"What's wrong, Jack?"

"Let's go to sleep, kid." He smiles at me, but the smile does not feel true.

The next day, a new clip in the air. I bring the children to see Jack at the Oval Office. I want to ask about Cuba, the missile sites, Soviet ships spotted offshore, what choices he's weighing now. I know there are at least two: air strikes on the missile sites, or a naval quarantine to stop ships carrying weapons bound for Cuba. But if the United States intervenes, will Khrushchev use it as an excuse to move on his longtime threat to take Berlin? What then? Another round of sparring, or war?

We watch the children scramble over the rug. They play hide-and-seek around the desk. John does a somersault. Off-kilter. Caroline just stands there, still for a moment, watching her brother, the perfect slope of her cheek, a lovely smudge of sunlight on the bone.

What will they inherit?

I glance at Jack. His eyes are on me.

"This," he says. "Caroline and John. They're what I bring into that Cabinet Room, to make the right decision, a sane decision, while the whole fucking world's on its ear."

"Tell me what's happening, Jack."

"At this point, there's nothing I can tell you."

I look at him, wait. Then he says, "I knew it would take time to reach a solution. It never struck me there might not be one."

I take the children and Joe to Glen Ora, as planned. Jack flies to Chicago, as planned. But within a day Clint informs me Jack's returning to the White House with a head cold. A pretense. Jack calls to say he wants us home in Washington that afternoon. He wants me to host a small dinner. That evening he acts like his usual self—peppering our friends with questions about Frank Sinatra, Lord Beaverbrook, and that wild photograph of the model lying on a white bearskin, sucking her thumb. He says nothing about Cuba or Khrushchev.

Later, he tells me he's approved a naval quarantine of ships passing into Cuba.

"A blockade?"

"A blockade's an act of war. We can't call it that." The following evening, he says, he'll make an address to the nation, announcing that the United States will not allow Soviet shipment of any offensive military equipment to Cuba. He'll call on Khrushchev publicly to end this. He'll cite the 1930s as a clear example that aggressive conduct, if allowed to go unchecked and unchallenged, will lead to war.

People have begun to leave the city. Growing fears of a nuclear attack. It feels like everything and everyone around us is peeling away. The sense of time resting on a blade.

"It's time for you to go, Jackie," he says. "Move the children closer to the shelter."

"We're going to stay with you."

"You're not afraid?"

"I am afraid, because you are." He won't like me saying it. I say it anyway, and I see the split second of his anger because I've acknowledged what he doesn't want to feel.

"If you're afraid you should go," he says.

"I am going to stay, Jack."

From then on, there is no waking or sleeping. One day flows into the next. When he comes home for a nap or a rest, I lie down with him. When he calls, I go to his office. He'll pull on his coat, and we'll walk. Sometimes he talks, other times we walk in silence. One evening at dinner, he tells me that while taking a swim in the pool he kept thinking of how every decision he'd make in the next twelve hours would set in motion the following twelve, then the twelve after that, and it would just go on that way as long as the threat of the crisis continued. As he floated in the pool, he says, he remembered a painting he made years ago, in Brooklyn during the 1960 campaign. A watercolor of boats in Sheepshead Bay. He remembered the feeling he had working the pigment on the paper as he painted the wind, how he wanted to capture that wind in the landscape so it bled through the abstract shapes of boats and piers, their outlines half dissolved, because the motion of the world did not differentiate, and all we imagine to be permanent, solid, is always on the verge of being swept away.

John wakes up the next day with a fever. By noon, it's over 100 degrees. While Jack is in meetings, I get John into the car and take him to the doctor.

Soviet tankers approach the U.S. quarantine cordon in the waters near Cuba.

A hostile letter arrives from Khrushchev, stating the U.S. blockade is a violation of terms. In the letter, he implies his ships will run it.

Jack comes back late—two, three in the morning.

"What happened?" I ask.

"I told our men to postpone the challenge to Khrushchev's first ship, an oil tanker, the *Bucharest*. I sent word to Khrushchev suggesting we both hold up until we can talk. I'm not sure it was the right thing to do. It puts the ball in his court. Gives him time."

"John's fever is down," I say. He looks startled and I realize he'd forgotten, then he looks relieved.

On Friday two messages come in, private Teletype direct from Khrushchev, appealing to Jack to de-escalate and offering consideration of terms.

Jack sends me to Glen Ora with the children. He promises to join us the following day.

Early on Sunday, the news is announced that the two nations have reached an agreement.

I'm waiting for him when the helicopter touches down. As we walk inside, he tells me he can only stay for a few hours. We go into the bedroom to talk. Yesterday, he says, it all nearly derailed. An American U-2 plane was shot down, the pilot killed, and McNamara contended that war was not just imminent but inevitable. Jack waited, though. No retaliation, he told McNamara. Not yet. He sent another private message back to Khrushchev, promising to withdraw missiles from Turkey if they could reach terms on Cuba, but he also said that if the compromise on Turkey leaked out, the United States would deny it. Khrushchev conceded and agreed to remove Soviet missile sites from Cuba.

"You must feel good about what you've done, Jack," I say.

"Well, it's done."

I smile. "Give yourself half a day to enjoy it."

"Can't get complacent."

Just a month ago we were looking at portraits of Lincoln, the progression of his face during his years in the White House. "Older and older, like what's happening to me," Jack had remarked.

"Something else," he says to me now. "I need you at home to plan some victory dinners."

"You mean home at the White House?"

"Yes."

"I can do that."

"And you should know we've agreed to seize Cuba and make Bobby mayor of Havana."

I smile. I've bitten down one of my nails. I take a nail file from the bureau and start to work on the torn edge.

JACK

A Sunday in November, Glen Ora.

The rim of the tub digs into his shoulder, that spot where the muscle weaves against the collarbone. It's not an unpleasant pain. Dave Powers sits on the toilet, reading off appointments for the upcoming week.

As he sinks deeper into the warm water, he thinks about his life. He's forty-five years old. There's less future loaded into him than past.

His wife walks in.

Her white shirt wrinkled from being tucked into her riding pants, but she's not wearing pants, nothing but the shirt, boots, a riding whip in her hand. It's unexpectedly violent, the whip and that glimpse of her thigh. Intentional. Her head tips toward her shoulder and she looks at Dave Powers, who is trying to keep his eyes focused on her face.

"Thank you, Dave." She smiles, tilting her head toward the door. "Please cancel the next few hours."

Powers gathers papers together and bumbles out, the door closing behind him, and she laughs, that quietly wicked laugh he loves.

She sits down on the edge of the tub. "How's the bath?" She runs her fingers through the water, her fingertips brush him. "Warm enough?"

"For now. How was your ride?"

"Lovely out today." Her voice is like soft rope, her eyes focused on the trees visible through the window.

He moves in the tub. The water shifts.

"So now what shall we do?" she says.

She is just beyond his reach. She doesn't come closer. Or lean in. Only sits there, the horizontal slope of her bare thigh, and the curved white hem of the shirt, the dressage whip in her hand. If he sat up, he could reach out and touch her, but he understands that as long as he doesn't, she'll remain a body, not his but at a remove, and for that reason seductive, unknown, that wild light at the center of her he can feel.

"Come here," he says.

"No, Jack. You come to me."

Through the window of the bedroom, the trees swim.

Silence. Her body, the heat of her breath near his skin.

In the white space, the margins and the gaps, that's where life dwells.

"Via negativa," she will say absently as they lie together, her arms crossed under her head, that bone of her hip, angular, almost defiant, one leg bent, his hand on her body. He could not, would not, stop.

He will realize later:

He'll never want a woman more than he wanted her in those hours.

He does not tell her this.

She gasps as his knuckles move into her, back arched, breasts tight, her finger twisting on herself, he gently bites her shoulder, her legs wrapped around him, pulling him down onto her and her hip against his in a way that will bruise, leaving a blue-black design he will watch on her body for days afterward with a kind of crazy secret pleasure as it grows, the bruise exploding slowly before it starts to fade.

Later, she slips from the bed, steps over the husk of sheets on the floor. She draws the curtain back. The sun fires into the room. He starts to get up, then doesn't. Someone will come. When they need him, they'll find him. There's so little time in his life anymore that belongs to him alone.

Stay with her in this alone for now.

She's walked over to the chair, her shirt draped over the back of it. He watches her body, the naked length of her, angular, the boyish cut of the hips, slim, small breasts.

"Why are you looking at me like that?" she asks. He smiles.

"I'm remembering you."

It is not the kind of thing he'd ordinarily say.

Even the next morning, though, it is still there. Slight, residual. He takes her hand across the breakfast table, turns it barely, and, with no one else seeing, he runs his fingertip down the inside of her wrist.

November 1962

We turn the clocks back. It's dark by four. On nights when we are home and the weather is fair, we take the dogs for a walk.

I call for Clipper, and he claps for Charlie. We slip out and head toward the gates. We laugh together, wondering how long it will take for the Secret Service car to be behind us.

We talk about Steinbeck, who's going to be awarded the Nobel Prize.

"Hardly a shoo-in," Jack says.

"I'm surprised it wasn't Lawrence Durrell."

"Or Robert Graves."

"I wanted Isak Dinesen."

"I heard last summer it would be Dinesen. I think it would have been."

"If a man had died, they would have given it to him anyway," I say.

Clipper stops to sniff a hydrant. I clap softly. She trots back.

We talk about Eleanor Roosevelt's funeral the week before. I mention the piece I read by James Baldwin in *The New Yorker*, "Letter From a Region of My Mind." We talk about Thanksgiving plans, the children's birthday parties, Palm Beach at Christmas. We talk about the opening of the *Mona Lisa* at the National Gallery in January. Jack laughs when I tell him that, every night, I dream of that painting heading toward us across the Atlantic.

The evening air is cool against my face. I've found a piece of land where we can build in Middleburg, Virginia, on Rattlesnake Mountain—acres of rolling hills and fields, a dizzying stretch of expanse looking out toward the Blue Ridge Mountains.

"We have Glen Ora," Jack says.

"We only rent that. This will be ours. The house will be modest, I promise."

He rolls his eyes.

"And when it's finished," I say, "we'll call it Wexford." Wexford is the name of his family's ancestral land in Ireland. I can tell it makes him happy I'd suggest that.

He asks me then to come with him to Miami when he speaks to the men who were taken prisoner at the Bay of Pigs. His voice breaks off. I wait. He throws a stick. Charlie bounds after it.

"Will you come?" he says.

"Yes."

"It will matter to them," he says. We've been closer since the missile crisis. The easy banter between us has deepened, and in that deepening, I can feel the softer edges of his need.

"Here, Clipper," I call softly, and she runs to me.

A week ago, while visiting Lee in New York, I was flipping through the latest issue of *Vogue* and came to a photo essay on Marilyn Monroe. "The Last Sitting." There were big orange X's Monroe herself had drawn through the contact sheet. There were nudes where all she wore was a scarf. Others where she was in a black wig, her hair styled just like mine, a long messy string of pearls.

"What are you thinking?" Jack asks. Surprising. He never asks that question.

I close my mind and smile. "I'll speak to them in Spanish. The Cuban exiles. When we go."

. . .

Days before Christmas, Bobby brings us a piece from *The Village Voice:* "An Open Letter to JFK from Norman Mailer." He gives it to Jack, who skims it, then hands it to me.

Quintessential Mailer—written directly to Jack, with that acerbic, intimate tone like he's whispering to a friend: *Of course, Mr. President, one does not even know whether it pleases you that America is to a degree totalitarian. . . . Your personality has nuances, almost too many nuances.* The letter goes on for paragraphs, without posing the question it purports to ask but deconstructing Jack's motives during the face-off with Khrushchev that fall: *You were like a poker player with a royal flush, a revolver in his hand, unlimited money to raise each bet.* He challenges Jack's conscience, heart, care.

I glance up. "Do I have to finish this?"

"You should," Bobby says, uneasy.

It's there, in the last paragraph of that open letter addressed to Jack, that Mailer has floated a suggestion, as insurance against nuclear war: *Why not send us a hostage? Why not let us have Jacqueline Kennedy?*

I put the paper down.

"Will he ever stop?"

Jack laughs. "Not until he has you. That man's obsessed with my wife."

Earlier that year, in another piece, Mailer trashed my tour of the White House, describing me as *manufactured, a royal phony.* These phrases circle in me now.

"I'm sorry he drags you into it," Bobby says. "It's Jack he's really after."

It is and it isn't, I could say. If it was only Jack, Mailer's insights might be savage, but he wouldn't target me.

"I don't think he's going to let either of us out of this life alive," Jack says. His eyes dance. It amuses him, Mailer's wit, the artful power of his mind, even when it's harnessed to take him apart.

. . .

Elaine de Kooning is slight. An almost pixie look, a quick smile. She wears a dark jumper, a white blouse underneath. I watch her eyes move when she doesn't think anyone's looking, taking in sofas, vases, art, the play of light along the sills. She's been hired to paint a portrait of Jack. She arrives in Palm Beach just before the New Year. An abstract expressionist, she's not as well-known as her artist husband, Willem de Kooning. They're friends with Krasner and Pollock. I had asked Bill Walton about her.

"She's the fastest brush in the East," Bill said.

"Yes, someone told Jack that. I think he agreed for that reason. He can shuffle around, and the thing will still get done."

"Her portraits are interesting," Walton said. "Those seated men she makes out of bright jagged edges."

I read a feature on her in *ARTnews*, where she described how she wanted paint to sweep through like feelings. I remember those words as I watch her set up her easel. We've been told she doesn't like to hang around. She'll stay overnight, make a few sketches, then return to her studio and build a portrait out of those. At one point that first afternoon, she mentions to me, in an offhand way, that she's more interested in character than style.

"Style can be a prison," she says, then glances at me, apologetic. I smile.

"We all know something about that."

She laughs. She's more at ease with me then, but she maintains a remove. She keeps our world at arm's length. I like that about her.

She stays for four days. I set up a small easel for Caroline next to hers with a little box of paint. I watch Elaine de Kooning watch my husband. I watch her fall a little in love with him. One afternoon, she remarks how different Jack seems from the photographs she'd seen in the papers and when she's seen him on TV. She noticed that difference, she says, the first day she came.

"Different how?" I ask.

"He never stops moving. And there's something elusive about him, always changing, like a shimmer. Larger than life." Her eyes are grayish blue, soft and cool.

"How will you capture that?"

"I don't know yet."

She makes dozens of charcoals over those four days. Drawings, watercolors, a few rough sketches in oil. Then she packs her things. I see her on the afternoon she is to leave. Down on the beach, kneeling in the wet sand, sculpting a shape. Later, when she comes up to the house, I walk down. It's Jack's face she's made in the sand. I stand over it. I can see how her fingertips smoothed the bones of his jaw and cheeks, his forehead, and the ridge over his eyes. There's a weirdly finished quality to the face, the likeness eerie, almost alive, even as the tide begins to work down the edge.

1963

January. The elevators at the National Gallery break down the night of the opening of the *Mona Lisa*. Clint carries the train of my dress as I walk up the stairs. I laugh when we reach the second floor.

"I was afraid I'd trip, Mr. Hill, and we'd both roll right down the stairs, me in my chiffon like pink tumbleweed."

I go to find André Malraux. The painting has been mounted in the West Sculpture Hall, against a velvet backdrop. The French and American flags flank it, along with two Marines. Malraux will speak first, then Jack. I read Jack's speech as he was crafting it. It captures what I want to convey: the discipline of creative work; how art can exist at the heart of power; how it can transcend political and national differences and forge a common ground; how Da Vinci was not only an artist but a military engineer, who understood that the world of events and the world of imagination are one.

"*La Joconde* can be your symbol of the Cold War," I told Jack. "Like your moon landing. A symbol of the work you've done to safeguard freedom. So many people will have the chance to see this painting while it's here. That's what art is meant to be."

That night, the loudspeaker fails in the middle of Jack's speech. The microphone gives out, and he has to shout to still the crowd. He shifts gears to what he does so well. He tells a few

jokes and repeats key words of Malraux's, about hope, the friendship between our nations, and a shared commitment to diplomacy and art. Malraux had described America as a young country
entrusted with the future, but he was too soft-spoken to be heard
over the cocktail chatter of two thousand guests. *Maybe a thousand too many,* I think. But I am happy. Despite the mechanical
failures. No elevator, no loudspeaker, speeches that run off
script, and too much chaos. It won't matter. The speeches will be
printed as they were written. There will be photographs in the
papers, with the chaos excised. To the world, the evening will
appear far more elegant than it was. For me, the life is here—in
the night itself, with all its mad flaws. There's magic in that, imperfect, glorious, free.

Days later, when Jack gives his State of the Union address, I sit
in the balcony. The air in the high-ceilinged room is cold. I can
feel the stiff curl of my hair against my cheek. "I always wanted
the helm of Hades," I told Kenneth as he styled it that morning.
"The one that confers invisibility."

Kenneth laughed. "I don't think that's in your cards today."

The floor seats are filled. Lady Bird sits with me as Jack speaks
from the podium about public service and the nation's courage
during the missile crisis. He calls for a commitment to educate
every child and to strengthen fundamental American rights—the
right to counsel, healthcare, and, most essential, "the most precious and powerful right in the world, the right to vote in a free
election."

He lets a beat of silence fall.

To me, it's the most cogent speech he's given since taking office. He weaves disparate issues together in deft ways. He bal-
ances the accomplishments of the past year with his emergent
vision for the next. There's strength in how he stands, how he
talks, in his eyes. His voice cool. The embers of that early rage
have cohered into a new resolution. Jack is fiercely logical. He
always has been. Competitive, but also strategic. Now, though, it
feels that something new has crystallized—not simply raw ambition or political calculation but some new bright grain of belief,

born from ideals as well as failure. Over these last months, that quiet faith has merged into his rhetoric. He's not a man who likes to be sideswiped by feeling, ever. He doesn't trust it. Perhaps because it already runs deep. But as I watch him speak that day, I understand he's begun to grasp how passion, when it comes from a place of integrity, can be leveraged to invoke change.

. . .

Waves of morning nausea. I've felt it every day for the past two weeks. It hits out of nowhere. I skip coffee, eat dry toast or sip ginger ale to take the edge off.

"Good morning, George," I hear Jack say to his valet. I feel his weight shift, legs swing to the floor. I pull the blankets up. He rummages through the papers, I hear the distant rush of water running into a bath.

At eight, Miss Shaw brings in the children. Their little feet and voices, then a splash.

"That was my duck!" John cries.

"There are five more," Jack says. "Here, they're all up. And we'll find that other one. What about you, Buttons, you're not too old for a duck, are you?"

I slip out of bed. In the bathroom, the children have lined plastic ducks along the tub edge. The cables and memos Jack was reading before they came in are soaked. The ink bleeds.

They stay with him in the bedroom as he gets dressed. They lie on the floor, faces propped in their hands, watching cartoons. John rolls from one end of the room to the other until he strikes a hard surface, a bedpost, his father's leg, then he rolls back. I sit in the rocking chair I had repadded for Jack's back, as Caroline pulls him away from breakfast down to their exercise routine on the floor. They climb over him, their bodies wrapping his, until he has to leave for work. I should tell him soon. It's been four weeks. I'm afraid, though. I don't want to tell him, or anyone, yet.

"Mary," I ask my secretary, Mary Gallagher, later that morning, "would you say I've done enough as First Lady?"

"More than enough."

"Then now that the *Mona Lisa* is behind us, I'm taking the veil."

I don't tell her why. I tell Jack the following weekend when we go to New York to see Lee. After Sunday Mass, as we walk up Park Avenue, I tell him my period is five weeks late. For now, I tell him, I don't want anyone else to know. He doesn't break his stride, but he is smiling.

"You'll have to stop riding," he says.

"Luckily it's winter."

He pauses on the corner, catches my arm to keep me on the curb as the traffic flows by.

"And no water-skiing, Jackie."

"Or tightrope-walking."

"I mean it. You have to be careful."

"We can still take walks."

"Nothing too strenuous."

"Fresh air is good."

"You can't get chilled."

"And not too many teas," I say. He laughs.

"What about the March dinner dance for Eugene Black?" he says.

"I'm always up for a good dinner dance."

"And the Emancipation Proclamation fete?"

"Absolutely."

"King isn't coming," he says.

I nod. Pam had told me. But I don't tell him I already knew. "Did they give a reason?"

"King says as long as young Black men are being arrested for sit-ins and protests—"

"He wants you to move forward with a bill," I say quietly, but in the blare and swirl of the city, I feel the air between us tense.

We're down in Palm Beach with Joe for a few days in February when I bring up Mary Meyer. Tony Bradlee had mentioned how pleased her sister, Mary, was to be invited to the dinner dance in March. Which surprised me. Mary wasn't on my list.

Jack and I are out for a drive in the Lincoln, windows rolled halfway down, sunshine moving through the car. Green hedges, manicured lawns, and low stucco houses flow by.

"Jack, I didn't invite Mary."

"Is her name on the list?"

"You didn't put it there?"

He shrugs, and I know then the talk I've heard about Jack and Mary Meyer is true.

"You and I both enjoy Mary's company," he says.

I feel a surge of rage. He makes a turn, heading back toward Palm Beach. Sunlight blinding off the hood. We drive in silence. There was a look I saw exchanged between Jack and Mary the last time we were all together. Mary had come to the Residence with Tony. She was wearing a shirtdress and those hammered-gold earrings she often wore, which seemed too large for her face but always made you look again. A year after we were married, Jack and I moved next door to Mary and her then-husband, Cord Meyer. Jack had known Mary since they were in school together at Choate. Mary and I would sometimes take walks through Georgetown and along the canal path. Then Mary's son was struck by a car and killed. He was nine. Her marriage split up. We'd seen her less after that. Until recently.

I unroll the window farther and close my eyes.

The following day, I strike her name from the guest list.

"I had Pam call her," I tell Jack, "to explain our space constraints. Eugene Black and his wife invited so many of their own friends, but since the dinner is in their honor, we really have no choice. Mary is still coming for the dancing at ten, so you can end it with her face-to-face."

He stares at me. He doesn't say anything.

"It's not that *I* can't handle it, Jack. Don't you see? It becomes unbearable to me when I think about what Caroline and John will have to endure when it gets out, because it will, someday, get out. You know that. And in my mind, I see their faces. The burning disappointment and the shame. I think about that."

He sits down, silent.

"It's not the women I'm afraid of, Jack. For someone as canny as you, you seem blind about this. I find it stunning you don't realize that someday, some writer, like a Mailer, is going to come along and blow the whole house down. And Caroline will come to you, or to me, and she will say, *Is it true?* Or, worse, she will look at you differently and won't say anything at all."

I pick up the seating chart I've been working on, my pen and notebook, and walk out.

JACK

Two days later, he finds the photograph she left on his desk. Under a folder but positioned intentionally with the edge peeking out. She wanted him to find it. A photograph of her father holding hands with another woman while her mother dressed in riding clothes sits on the fence next to them, staring fixedly away.

He'd seen the photograph before. Jackie showed it to him once, years ago. She said that by the time it was taken, her mother had decided it didn't matter what her father did. She'd accepted her marriage for what it was. He can't quite remember the words Jackie used when she told him this. Only that, years later, she came across that photograph and understood everything she thought she'd known as a child in a new and awful light.

Outside the window behind his desk is the Rose Garden. Caroline and John are tramping through the snow near an unfinished snowman; a hat, a pipe, and a carrot, some black pieces of something scattered on the frozen surface. Caroline has gotten distracted. She's standing over an angel she made, studying the outline among the mess of shapes.

Spring 1963

On the night of the dinner dance for Eugene Black, president of the World Bank, the grounds are covered in snow that fell throughout the day. As music drifts through the rooms, I notice Mary Meyer, on the arm of Jack's friend Blair Clark. She wears a layered dress, chiffon, a swish of pastel, too light, like she skipped a season. Tony tells me the dress once belonged to their great-grandmother.

I see Mary and Jack disappear. In less than five minutes, Jack's back. I can tell by how he moves and talks that he drew a line through it. Later, I'll learn that Mary stumbled around in the snow outside for over an hour before she came back inside, that thin dress soaked, her hair tangled, face streaked with the wet and the cold. It's when I see the expression on Mary's face that I know for certain Jack did what I asked him to do.

In early April, I drive out to survey the work on the house we're building in Middleburg. The house we'll call Wexford. It's the fields I love—the view looking out toward the Blue Ridge Mountains, the rolling expanse under a gorgeous sky.

We bought the land in November, and I'd started on the designs. I tore out pages from magazines and sketched out a floor plan: one level, so Jack won't have to climb stairs; a simple kitchen; French doors; a terrace.

"It's going to be perfect," I tell Jack when I show him the architect's plans.

"Not as palatial as I was expecting."

"It has all these little spaces," I say, "separate rooms, so we can get away from one another and do what we need to do. You can have your meetings. I can paint, write letters, read. The children have their play space and a place to nap. And please don't worry, Jack. The dining room will have the Louis XVI chairs. I don't want you to think I've lost my taste for the extravagant, just because I've spent time in the White House bomb shelter."

The day after Easter, Pierre Salinger reads the statement to the press Pam and I crafted:

> . . . *expecting a baby . . . the latter part of August . . . Mrs. Kennedy has maintained her full schedule of the past few months. . . . Her physicians have now advised her to cancel all of her official activities.*

So there it is.

That spring, Jack and I spend weekends with the children at Camp David. From there, we take the convertible out to visit battlefields of the Civil War—Gettysburg, Antietam—the Secret Service car trailing a distance behind. We talk about tensions in the South, demonstrations, pickets and arrests, King's letter from Birmingham jail, and the Children's Crusade in early May.

The footage from that was horrific. Children's skin torn by the pressure of fire hoses, dogs turned on them; they screamed, eyes wide with terror. Jack watched the clips privately, not talking to anyone, just making himself watch them over and over, his fist near his chin, staring at the screen.

"Nudge him," Bobby told me. And on one of those drives to a Civil War cemetery, I do.

"The issues in the South won't be solved tomorrow," Jack says.

"That doesn't mean we can't start taking steps."

"It has to be strategic."

"Right and strategic aren't exclusive."

I meet his eyes, then look back to the moving shoulder of the road.

He arranges a meeting between Bobby and James Baldwin, along with other Black writers and artists.

"How did it go?" I ask Bobby afterward.

"It didn't end well at all," he says. "I couldn't connect."

"You couldn't?"

"Come on, Jackie. You know I'm on your side on this."

"So what happened?"

"They walked out. The woman, Lorraine Hansberry, said to me, 'You and your brother are the best a white America can offer, and if *you* don't understand, we're without hope.' She's the one who walked out first. A woman."

"Does that surprise you?" I say. "A woman has less to start with, so she has less to lose."

I feel Bobby shift away. I've sensed it before, almost a current of guilt that will sometimes cross his face, and I remember that morning, years ago, when I lost the baby and woke up in a daze to those pale hospital walls, the ceiling falling toward me, and he was the one who was there.

It's Bobby who pushes Jack to speak on national TV about civil rights on June 11, the day students show up to register at the University of Alabama. Many on Jack's team are against it, worried about the Southern vote. Even Sorensen warns him not to weigh in unless there's a crisis.

"The governor blocking the door of that school is a crisis," Bobby says.

An hour before airtime, they're scrambling to nail down the points of Jack's Report to the American People on Civil Rights. The speech is unfinished when he sits down for the cameras, but once he's on air, I can tell the words are alive for him. And watching him, I can feel that his conviction—his sense of a moral imperative—has changed.

The next day when he comes home for lunch, he tells me a

Mississippi man, Medgar Evers, was shot in the back in front of his children outside his own house. He got up, staggered thirty feet to his doorstep, gripping his car keys, then collapsed. He was brought by ambulance to an all-white hospital. They refused to treat him.

"So he might have lived," I say. I feel sick.

"The bullet went through his heart, Jackie. He wouldn't have lived."

We're alone at lunch, the children playing outside.

"How long did it take him to die, Jack?"

"He'll receive full military honors."

"They're cowards." He looks at me; I say it again. "Cowards."

Just before he leaves on a two-week trip to Germany and Ireland, he sends legislation to Congress against discrimination, empowering the justice department to order desegregation. He asks Congress to stay in session until a civil-rights bill is enacted. That afternoon, Bobby comes to the Residence to tell Jack a group of civil-rights leaders has asked to meet, to discuss a march on Washington they've planned for August.

"They've been planning a march since FDR," Jack says.

"This is different."

"Try to talk them out of it?"

"Already tried."

"There can't be violence, Bobby."

"I'll do my best."

"What we're talking about is a problem that involves 180 million people."

"You're going to come out and say that?"

Jack glances at me; I am sitting at one end of the sofa, listening.

"If that's where we're headed," he says, "yes."

"Bring Johnson in," I say. "On this one issue you should. When he spoke in the South, he insisted he wanted Blacks on the platform with him and refused to come if they weren't."

"Who told you that?"

"His wife."

"I don't want Johnson in the Rose Garden with me," says Bobby, "when I meet with King and the others."

He can be so scrappy. Fists swinging. He and Lyndon don't get along, but they come down on the same side of civil rights. I've heard that Johnson complains Bobby's just using a pop gun when he could pull out the cannon.

"Use Lyndon with the Southern whites," I say. "He'll make it a Christian issue, a moral issue. They respect that kind of courage."

I use that last word intentionally. Bobby won't notice, but it will register with Jack. Cowards and courage. I know that.

While Jack is in Europe, the children and I will go to Hyannis Port. He'll meet us there in July. The night before I leave Washington, Bob McNamara and I watch a replay of Jack's speech in Berlin, where he talks about the Wall and the perils of division. I rewind that moment when he cries to the crowd, *"Ich bin ein Berliner!"*—*I am a Berliner!*—so we can watch it again.

"He worked hard to become a strong speaker," I say. "He wasn't always, you know."

I draw another tape off the shelf and hand it to Bob. "This is a speech he gave in the fifties, when he was still quite terrible at it. Watch it sometime; you'll see the change for yourself."

It's curious what happens then. McNamara seems almost reluctant to take the tape. Finally, he does. So interesting, though. Jack's men. They don't want to see his flaws, his weakness, or his humanness. They want to imagine he's just sprung into their midst—godlike, fully formed.

...

That summer, we've rented a different house, a short distance away from the family compound, isolated, at the end of Squaw Island. I swim in the mornings with the children and spend afternoons in the sunroom on the second floor, reading Grimal's *The Civilization of Rome* and writing memos to send down to the East Wing staff. I order a dress for the baby's christening in October. I create a scrapbook for Jack. It's our tenth anniversary this fall. I fall asleep to the lash of the surf against the rocks while the moon rips the surface of the sea. Sometimes it feels like a dream, those nights alone in the house with the children, moody and ethereal, like it's only the three of us, the sea, and the sky.

On July 28, I turn thirty-four. Our friend David Ormsby-Gore gives me a book called *The Fox in the Attic*, about Hitler in Munich and the rise of fascism. Averell Harriman arrives with a jar of caviar so large it has to be wheeled in. A birthday gift from Khrushchev. The contrast makes me laugh.

"He's trying to say he might play by the rules," I tell Jack when he arrives that weekend. "Perhaps he'll agree to sign your test-ban treaty."

Jack shakes his head. "Khrushchev's sense of rules is too fungible to be considered rules, but it's a limited treaty, so he'll sign it."

I take John to Caroline's riding lesson one morning in early August. Jack's in Washington for the week. I'm standing by the fence at the ring, holding John's hand, when I feel the world swim, a wave of weakness. I grip the fence and turn to the agent near me, but it isn't Clint—where's Clint? Is it his day off? Mr. Landis. Is that who it is? My head so light, the air blurs.

"Mr. Landis, I'm not feeling well. I need to go back to the house."

The pain shoots through my body as we drive on the bumpy dirt road. *Faster, please, Mr. Landis.* I've begun to sweat. My skin hot and cold at the same time, the fear rising, I can't breathe, my throat tight. *I think I'm going to have that baby. Please, Mr. Landis. The hospital.*

They fly me by helicopter to the hospital at Otis Air Force Base. Dr. Walsh is with me. Clint drives up as we land.

"It's your day off," I say.

"It's going to be okay, Mrs. Kennedy." He stays with me, walking alongside as they rush me into the wing they've prepared.

"You've told the president, Mr. Hill?"

"He's already left Washington. He's on his way."

"Thank you," I say, because I need to say something. I need him to read my mind and reassure me again, even with that fear in his eyes, that everything will be okay.

Jack is there when I wake up. The room very sharp and white. His face.

"Where's the baby?" I say.

"There's a problem with his lungs."

"Like John?"

"Not exactly. They're going to take the baby to Children's Hospital in Boston."

"You'll go with him?"

"Yes." He is looking at me. I can't quite bear the way he is looking at me. "He's beautiful, Jackie."

"I want to hold him."

"You can't yet. They're helping him breathe."

"John's lungs were undeveloped, and he's fine now. Baby Patrick will be fine."

Jack nods but doesn't answer, and I feel the ground underneath me sink away, like the world has lost its edge.

"What is it, Jack? Tell me."

"Patrick has something called hyaline membrane disease. A film around the air sacs in his lungs."

"And what will they do?"

"We have to wait and hope his own body dissolves the film."

"I want to see him, Jack, our baby, before they take him away. Can I see him? Jack, please."

They wheel him into my room. He is so small and so still. He lies on his back in an Isolette, a little clear box Jack tells me is a pressurized incubator. He has a name band around his tiny wrist. His eyes are closed. He has light-brown hair.

Jack flies with him to Boston. It's Dr. Walsh who tells me the baby is gone. He passed away at four in the morning. They removed him from the oxygen chamber and the web of tubes. They laid him in Jack's arms. He was thirty-nine hours, twelve minutes old.

Clint is in the room when Dr. Walsh comes in to tell me these things. Clint's eyes meet mine, and I feel the grief rip through me.

By the time Jack arrives an hour later, I've tried to pull myself together. But he cries telling me what happened, and I cry again with him.

He comes to see me twice a day, often with Caroline, who brings flowers in small lopsided bouquets. Summer flowers—the kind I love—larkspur, trumpet flowers, black-eyed Susans. My daughter's face is solemn as she holds them out to me, her hair neatly parted, held in place with a barrette. It feels almost too neat, too careful. I don't want this for her.

The following Saturday, Cardinal Cushing holds a Mass in Boston. I'm still not strong enough to go. It's Lee who tells me afterward that Jack put his arm around the small white casket, sobbing, like he would not be pulled away from it, like he just couldn't let it go underground.

"Patrick fought," Jack keeps telling me. Again and again, he tells me this—how tiny Patrick was, how brave. At Children's, he'd started to improve, his breathing had stabilized, but then he went into a sudden downward spiral, and they put his tiny body in a hyperbaric chamber and tried to flood oxygen into his lungs. Jack could do nothing. He could only sit there in the corridor on a wooden chair and wait. There was a round window in the chamber, a porthole window, through which he could see our baby. How he fought. How clear it was that he wanted to live, to breathe. And when he began to die, they brought Patrick out to him, and Jack sat on that wooden chair and held him as he fought right to the end.

Jack tells me this over and over; he goes back to those hours, that moment, when he held our baby in his arms and his heart broke. He looks down at his hands as he reaches the end, like he still can't believe how his hands could have let that slight life go.

Night again. He's gone. They need him in Washington, and he's flown back. He has meetings with the Senate about the test-ban treaty vote. Within a few days, he's promised, he'll return. I can't sleep. The air in the room unsettled. Nurses come and go. I ask them to leave me alone.

I want to stanch it, that grief, a hard, fast, raging thing forcing a channel through in its own most terrible way.

Down there in the ground, alone. He is too small to be down there alone, too small to have slipped, so easily, through some slight crack from our world into that dark other.

Jack flies back to Hyannis on Wednesday to bring me to our house on Squaw Island. As we walk out of the hospital and down the front steps, he grips my hand. He opens the door of the car and helps me in.

We spend hours together, lying on the bed, without exchanging a word. His arms wrap around me, my face against his chest. My tears soak his shirt and his soak my hair, that wet leaking in to soften the leftover ice between us. I feel it happen. Through those long silent hours of August, it hollows us, changing the ways we fit into each other—hands, bodies, eyes—even as the rest of the world starts up again.

When he is in Hyannis Port, he is with me almost constantly. When he has to fly down to Washington, he returns within days. So much is the same as it's always been. The children still come running at the sound of the helicopter in its descent. When it lands and he climbs out, he sweeps John and Caroline up in a hug. Then he comes to find me. That is the difference. Not sometimes anymore, but always. And if I'm not right there with the others, he won't get into the golf cart and drive into town with the children; he'll come to find me first. He'll take me in his arms and hold me, the holding so tight, his mouth in my hair, and I will say to him, "Bring them into town now, Jack, they've been waiting all day. Take them for an ice cream. Go now, before the store closes."

"I needed to see you," he'll say.

It feels unfamiliar—that he'll use that word often now—*need.*

He comes every weekend. If he can, he'll fly up midweek as well, something he's never done before. I watch him nap in the afternoons. I see the subtle tremble on his face, like light circulating in water, the softness and uncertainty. It feels new, vulnerable, open. I want to trust that openness. I can't quite. I keep feeling I'll go to reach for him and he'll do that quick cold thing and shift away. I keep waiting for it to happen, to mark it to tell myself, *See, there it is again, the heartbreaking same old routine.* I keep waiting for that to come, but it doesn't, as if this dark singular loss, the baby he held as it died, the horror of being the one who bore witness, who lived it, has thawed something in him all the way through.

One weekend he comes up a day early and brings a cocker spaniel puppy with a gold-shamrock-studded collar; her name is Shannon.

I smile. "Because we aren't already swimming in dogs?"

We're alone in the house. I ask about his week, just an ordinary conversation, the kind we've had a thousand times. He says something about being at the end of his rope with Rusk.

"Who would you replace him with?"

"Bundy. Or McNamara. The press has already dubbed the Pentagon as McNamara's, why not bring him closer in."

I nod.

"And Johnson wants more of a role," he says.

"That could be a good thing."

He talks about an emerging crisis in Vietnam. "We don't take the time to learn how they see us." He tells me about the March on Washington for Jobs, his concerns about violence. "Not dissimilar," he adds, "when the face of racism in the South is something we, in the North, can't fathom because we don't take the time to learn."

"Maybe we don't want to," I say. He starts to answer, then doesn't. I'll bring it up again down the road. I know he suggested to Bobby they try to shut the march down, and Bobby told him that you can't shut this kind of thing down. He's looking at me now, not saying anything. It feels startling—that foreign and intimate sense of him fully present, with me, his mind nowhere else, not moving on to some next thing, an openness in his face like he's saying he has begun to realize these things will work out. One way or another, they'll work out.

That slight life. Patrick, the curious mixture of the two of us— his life a drop of water or a falling star, dissolving into dark.

The phone rings. He takes the call. He's silent for the most part, listening to someone on the other end who is reading a memo draft. From time to time he interjects, questioning a phrase. It's about Vietnam, a response to rumors of a coup led by South Vietnamese Army generals against the autocratic ruler, Ngo Dinh Diem. Diem, I know, is considered a defense against the Vietcong and communism. Ostensibly an American ally, he's also fickle, obdurate, cruel. Jack has told me Diem can't be trusted.

"Choose between two evils," he says now into the phone. "What choice do we have?" He says something about how he'll support a memo as long as McNamara and Rusk sign off.

Last week, there was a story in the papers about a Buddhist monk who soaked himself with gasoline, struck a match, and burned to death in a Saigon Public Square.

I slip out of the room and go to find the children. They're in the kitchen eating diced apples they picked earlier that day.

. . .

I write to Bill Walton.

Dear Baron . . .

I write to him about the things I am looking forward to this fall—our work together on Lafayette Square, the renovation of Blair House, plans for a state dinner for the king of Afghanistan. I tell him it seems odd to look forward to anything after what Jack and I just went through.

I don't write, *I miss Patrick. He was less than two days old. I never held him. I think about that and try not to. I have been so very sad.*

I ask Bill to visit the studio of that artist in New York, Elaine de Kooning, who is painting Jack. I'm curious to know what she's done with him so far. Then I ask for his advice about the White House guard boxes. I tell him I was thinking they should be painted dark green but I'm afraid they'll look too much like outhouses. I write that knowing it will make him laugh. I set down the pen. There's a cable on the desk that arrived yesterday. A message from Lee with an invitation from Aristotle Onassis for a cruise in the Aegean. I mentioned it to Jack. He shook his head. "That man's a pirate."

On Labor Day weekend, Jack tells me he's planning a trip to Cambridge in October to look at a site for the presidential library.

"When this is all over," he says, "I'll have an office there."

"When what is all over?"

"This public life."

I tell him then I'd like to go to Greece with Lee.

"It would be good for me to see her and have some time away."

"Your sister is sleeping with the biggest crook in Europe," he says. "Onassis."

We're outside in the shade of the flagstone patio. The light has come to the edge where I sit. It skirts my bare feet. My shoes are set next to John's little red sneakers.

"You have so much to do," I say. "You'll barely miss me."

"That's not true."

. . .

Almost evening, on Thursday, September 12, Jack arrives in Newport for our anniversary. The helicopter lands at dusk on the lawn at Hammersmith Farm. I step toward him, and his arms slip around me. He holds me for a long moment.

There are twelve of us for dinner that night, including Ben and Tony Bradlee, Claiborne and Nuala Pell, my mother, Hughdie, my stepbrother Yusha. Everyone gathers in the hall downstairs.

"Where's Jackie?" I hear Jack say through the door to the terrace. "Yusha, where'd she go?"

"I think just outside."

Jack comes through the door as I turn. "There you are," he says; he takes my hand and we walk back in. The others have begun to flow into the Deck Room and to the table set near the tall windows that catch the shine of plates and bowls, the unstable reflections of wineglasses. Those windows give way to the dark plunge of lawn into the sea and the deep lasting blue of the twilight over Narragansett Bay.

We exchange gifts. I give Jack a set of brass blazer buttons with the Irish Brigade insignia, a scrapbook of the Rose Garden, and a St. Christopher medal to replace the one he tucked in with Patrick. He gives me a slim gold ring with ten emerald chips, each stone marking a year of our marriage. "An eternity ring," he says, almost in passing.

"And one other thing," he says. On the carved circular table, he's set out an assortment of unwrapped gifts from the Klejman Gallery in New York.

"All of these, Jack?"

"No, you have to choose."

I smile. "But it's a gift. Shouldn't you be the one to choose?"

"You have to pick the one you want."

Etruscan sculptures, drawings by Fragonard and Degas, antique bracelets.

"How can I possibly choose?"

"Only one."

"But who will you give the others to?"

The room laughs. He is standing across the table from me, waiting, and I realize he's already chosen. Without saying it, among these objects, there's one he wants me to pick. I choose two. A drawing and an Alexandrian gold serpent bracelet. A simple bracelet, exquisite. I can tell by a faint light in his eyes it's the one. I slip it on my wrist.

My mother touches my elbow. Dinner is ready, and do I want to call everyone in?

There are toasts that night, one from Yusha, who strikes a spoon lightly on his glass. He stands and recalls the evening years ago when he first met Jack at Merrywood. Yusha tells the story of how I instructed him ahead of time to make especially fine daiquiris and to not argue about Democrat vs. Republican or Harvard vs. Yale. Jack doesn't glance at me. He is listening to Yusha. But I keep feeling he will look my way to let me know he too remembers that time in our life—that evening of the Dancing Class when we talked about fingernails soaked green from the darkroom solvents and I asked him to help button my gloves. I wonder if he remembers. His gaze is fixed on Yusha, who is still speaking. Jack's face looks older, fragile somehow, a faint tension along the jaw, something I haven't noticed for a while. I realize then that he's going out of his way *not* to look at me, so I stare at him until he does. It's quick, his glance, but his eyes are just so soft before he looks away again. I'm aware of the vaulted shape of the room, a room I've sat in a thousand nights before, for dinner parties like this one, the dark beams and cathedral-like pitch of the ceiling that seems all at once steep, like we are falling through a rush of time and space, and we are not significant— not one of the twelve of us sitting around this beautifully arrayed table with its candlelight, silver, and china, our unfinished meal, crumbs scattered, knives and forks set against the plates to signal completion. There's a loose shadowed imprint of water on the tablecloth where the pitcher was sweating, and through the windows there is night now, and I'm unable to distinguish the shapes demarcating sea from land from sky. I feel a chill, like the temperature has dropped, a window open somewhere in the house that pulls the damp night in.

"Mr. President," Yusha says, raising his glass. "I want to congratulate you. You've been a very good president. I'm glad you had your wedding here in Newport. I'm glad you're celebrating your wedding anniversary here tonight with Jackie. And I must remind you: If you hadn't gotten engaged to my stepsister, neither one of you would be in the White House, and I wouldn't have had a chance to stay in the White House. So I have to thank you for that."

Jack laughs and raises his glass.

The sun is cool and bright for the next few days, the sky sharp. We go to Mass on Sunday at St. Mary's Church, where we were married ten years before. There's a crowd on Spring Street as we leave. Jack waves to them, that shining smile, then strides to the convertible and takes the wheel. We drive off. He slows at a corner where a small group of nuns stand.

He calls out to greet them.

"Jackie here always wanted to be a nun," he says. "She went to a convent school and planned to take the orders."

The sisters laugh, we laugh with them, and it all feels so ordinary—human and hallowed and bright, mid-September sunshine bouncing off the curb, and the nuns laughing, and Jack with his collar loose, his hand on the leather-wrapped wheel while passersby dressed in Sunday clothes stroll on the sidewalk, peering into closed shop windows.

"I like Newport," he says that afternoon when we're at the beach with the children. Running back and forth in the shallows, they jump the little waves. "I like how we can drive around, come to this beach and swim, and even if people notice, they don't seem to care. Maybe we'll spend next summer here."

A seagull passes overhead, its shadow across the sand.

"You're leaving tonight," I say.

"I'll be back next weekend."

I nod.

"Golf later this afternoon?" he says.

I smile. "Sure."

"Good for my back."

"That isn't true."

"It loosens it up."

"Until it doesn't."

"Golf's better than football."

"Yes, Jack, I'll give you that."

John's toy plane and sneakers are at the edge of the blanket. He's in the shallows up to his knees, while Caroline splashes in the bigger waves out toward the break.

"They want to pick more tomatoes when we go back to the house," I say.

"You said they picked them all yesterday."

"John thinks more have grown overnight."

He tells me about a speech he's been asked to give in October in memory of Robert Frost. He asks what I think he should focus on.

"The artist in society," I say. "The artist is the one who has a lover's quarrel with the world—talk about how important it is to say what you believe, then let the chips fall."

"Easier said for the artist than the politician."

"Maybe," I say.

"And I've got the UN General Assembly next week. I'm going to propose a joint expedition to the moon."

"Joint?"

"United States and Russia. Countries should work together in the conquest of space."

"Because of the exorbitant cost?"

"That, and why not?"

"Khrushchev's too wary."

"So be it," Jack says. "We're moving ahead. I'll put the offer on the table."

I smile and pick up a piece of shell. "I like that, Jack."

"I told Sorensen I want that UN speech to signal a new approach to the Cold War. I want to talk about how peace isn't just an event. It's not something you achieve, then it's done. You have to work at it—day in, day out."

"Like a marriage." The words are out before I can call them back. He laughs, and I expect him to say something then, but he doesn't, and silence falls again between us.

JACK

She hasn't turned to look at him again. She's looking away, as if focused on something else, her gaze averted, deliberate, toward the distance past his shoulder. Without shifting her eyes, she says:

"Why are you looking at me like that, Jack?"

He doesn't answer. He is remembering that other question she asked years ago, that day in the water the summer before they were married when they were here, on this same beach, wading in.

"Do you love me, Jack?" she'd asked.

How would he answer that now? Of course he loves her. She's his wife. He loves her beauty, her intelligence and charm, her passion for language and art. Her style and her grace. He loves the way she is beloved. But even as he runs down this list in his head, he understands he's running down a list of attributes that add to her value, and part of him wants to explain he's never really had a chance to fall in love with her, in his own way, on his own terms. Everything's moved so fast. There's always something he's already late for, some fire he has to put out, somewhere else he has to be.

Faint lines at the corners of her eyes. He sees them now, the light on a slant. She is here. Flesh, bone, eyes. And in her face he can see traces of the girl she was ten years ago and traces of the older woman she'll become; he can see these different moments of her life, past, future, woven through the living incandescence of her face, turned slightly away from him.

"What is it, Jack?" she asks again. "What are you thinking?"

He just looks at her. He can't, it seems, stop looking at her.

Her skin lightly tan, that splash of freckles across her cheek that comes when she's had too much sun, her eyes focused on something past his shoulder. He could turn to see what, but he finds himself arrested by her face, the face he has taken apart again and again. He sees it differently now. The wholeness of it. Not just her face but, surfacing in it, the face of the woman she will be—those lines at the corners of her eyes that mark what she's wanted, what he's given her, what he's said and done, withheld and left undone. As she ages, this is the face he will see. The dark in her hair will strip, streaks of gray, silver. She will still smoke, her fingers stained with nicotine. She will bite her nails and he will strike her hand away to keep her from doing it, but more gently, maybe, in the future. He'll try to be more gentle, more patient and aware.

It levels him—this odd want he can feel in his body to be more of what she needs. She is close to him now and, at the same time, light-years removed, her eyes still focused on something beyond him—the children in the shallows or someone walking by.

She couldn't know what he questions sometimes, what he hides, that sense of fear and failure, the weakness he loathes, the shame that hits every morning when that back brace snaps into place, the metal click reminding him of what he will never be or be able to do again. He wants to tell her this, take the weight and nuance of it and pour it all into that radiant, ruthless mind. He wants her to know that sometimes he's quite sure there is no such thing as greatness, or if there is, he is so far from it. There is conviction, yes. There is also doubt, a sense that maybe she was wrong, as the world was wrong, to put faith in him. Perhaps this is all just some glittering palace of illusion. Engineered, unreal. He wants to ask how she sees it—this destiny that wasn't his to begin with, this mantle he took up because someone had to and he was the someone next in line. Fate by default. Where's the greatness in that? And can it ever be enough?

*That underneath the machinations of ambition and power and play,
there's a hope that, in spite of all the doubt and charade, he might
make a difference.*

*One day, when he was still a senator, he sat with her in his office,
piles of books on the table between them. Half-finished speeches,
outlines, everything spread out on that surface. She was the one
who found words from a speech that Oliver Wendell Holmes, Jr.,
gave on Memorial Day 1884—a speech about war, grief, and the
dead who wore their wounds like stars. That day in the Senate office, she copied some lines down on a piece of paper that she passed
across the table to him:* In our youth, our hearts were touched by
fire.

*He remembers this now, that day, those words, and it strikes him
how so much of what's deeply essential can drain away. He wants to
ask if she remembers. He wants to ask if she thinks that kind of fire
can burn a hole through history wide enough that some new brighter
world can emerge.*

How would she see it?

*She glances at him.
"Jack, what is it?" Then a smile. That smile.*

*The silence has softened and the world is different. The wind works
against the current on the bay. White sails race toward the point.*

*She moves closer to him, her body lightly grazing his. She smells
of sky, and underneath all other sounds, the squawk of gulls, the
wavebreak, the shriek of the children playing, he can hear her
breathe.*

*Ten years ago, he was with her here at this same beach, not yet
married, but the gears were in place, everything kicking into motion. She wore the ring, and the mothers were up on the porch of
the beach club, conferring about dates, menus, seating plans.*

*"Let's go," he'd said to her, and she did not ask where, just fol-
lowed him down the steps across the sand to the sea. They'd waded
in when she asked that question, "Do you love me, Jack?" and when
he did not answer, she dove. The surface was a blue mirror where*

she disappeared, the dark knife of her body underneath. He thought he saw it, then was less sure. She was gone for so long. The water fell still like she'd never broken through it, and he waited, eyes scanning, seeing only that pale reflected sky, gorgeous, mocking, empty. When she surfaced, far out, she glanced back; he went to wave, but she'd already started to swim. The water was cold that day—he remembers the creep of it up his thighs as he walked in deeper—and she swam straight out, toward nothing, her body long, that slim grace of her arms, driving forward.

That was the moment he first loved her. He sees it now. That sense of love so intense, he shut it right down. It catches up with him, that memory of her, the awareness of her strength, the loaded will of her body as she swam, the light and the wet on her skin, her head turning to breathe like she was made of that water.

He feels it, what he didn't let himself feel in that moment all those years ago.

So odd. How life can do this. You can have every fact right, every logistic, and still miss the point.

He loved her then, the way he will love her, always.

She is looking at him. "Jack, you aren't upset about the bracelet, are you?" she says, teasing. "I love that bracelet, Jack. You must have known I would. I only wondered why you'd give me all those other things too and ask me to choose." She smiles. "Sometimes it's funny, Jack, the things you don't seem to know."

She is looking directly at him now, not anywhere else.

The world is alive to me because of you.

He thinks it. It's nothing he says. Not yet. There are years to say a thing like that.

Agent Foster is walking toward them on the beach, his head down like he's watching his own shoes moving through the sand. Jack knows the news is bad even before Foster tells him that a cable arrived. A Baptist church in Birmingham was bombed. Four young Black girls killed.

"You have to go, Jack," she says.

He waits for a moment before standing up. "Is the car ready, Mr. Foster?"

"Yes, Mr. President." Foster turns and heads back toward the lot, dark pant cuffs rimmed with sand.

"This kind of violence," she says, "this hatred, it never ends, does it? We make a few steps forward, then something like this."

The sound of a jet overhead. He looks up, squinting, shielding his eyes from the sun. He follows it, the liquid mercury streak of that plane bisecting the blue.

"Are you still planning to go?" he asks.

Late September. He is leaving for a five-day trip to eleven Western states. Shortly afterward, I will fly to Athens. It's Patrick. I've told Jack this. I don't want to be away from him and the children, but I am in too many pieces.

"I'm sorry," I say. He looks at me; it's sharp and endless, the sadness in his eyes—soul so blunt it cuts my breath.

"Stay," he says.

His eyes that day were different. I could see them long after the plane lifted off, his eyes on my face when he realized I would go, the feeling in them raw and deep and new—like he finally understood something had happened between us.

It's not that I love you less, I could have explained. *It's not that at all. It's just these waves of burning sorrow I've felt since we lost Patrick. There are whole days when all I am is grief.*

"Stay," he said. Just that one word. The memory moves around my edges as the coast beneath us falls away. I watch the night-limned clouds, and through the sadness and the missing and the doubt, wondering if I should have made a different choice, I feel a trace of something else—the quiet thrill I used to feel every time I left my life behind to go abroad, the thrill of being a woman with no country, no history, no past at all.

...

At the bay in Glyfada, our bags are loaded onto a dark mahogany speedboat. We fly across the water toward the pale mass of the *Christina,* moored farther out.

We come aboard. Onassis steps forward, takes my hand, and kisses me on each cheek. It's polite, customary, but I feel Clint stiffen behind me. Other guests are already there. Sue and Franklin Roosevelt, Jr.; Onassis's sister, Artemis; and Lee. I'm shown to my suite of rooms; in the private bathroom are solid-gold faucets on the sink, dolphin-shaped.

"Where are we going, Mr. Onassis?" I ask on the second day.
"Where would you like to go, Mrs. Kennedy?"
"I'd love to see the blue mosque in Istanbul."
"Excellent," he says. "I've planned that."
"Already?"
He smiles. "As soon as you asked. Anywhere else?"
"I've always wanted to go to Crete, Knossos."
"So it will be."

On the *Christina,* time is elliptical, dreamlike. The bow plows through the swells. We anchor to swim and water-ski. We drink and talk and cruise. With a wide-brimmed hat and dark glasses, I lie under the white-blue heat of the sky and read. It's like waking from a dream of the world into the world. Everything feels perishable, heightened, acute.

"You're not yourself," Lee says one night as we're dressing for dinner. "I know losing Patrick was a terrible loss, and I'm so glad you chose to come." She's looking at her own face in the mirror, lifting an eyebrow with her fingertip until the arch is set. She frowns, fastening an earring. Every afternoon, she disappears to Onassis's cabin. She and Stas are still married. She makes the pretense of being discreet.

"The loss is only part of it," I say.

Her eyes meet mine in the mirror.

It's hard to articulate, the needing to leave Washington for a while—how it's not just the bright, fast pressure of our life there but a desire to reconnect with some invisible core thing I used to crave and be. I won't find the right words, so instead I tell Lee how when summer was over and I came back to the White House, I braced myself to see the room I'd decorated to be Patrick's nursery. I sent the children off with Miss Shaw and walked into that room, only to realize, as the door swung open, that someone had already stripped every trace. No crib, no changing table, none of the blankets or curtains I'd chosen. It was the high-chair room again, just as it had once been.

Lee turns away from the mirror then, her beautiful eyes lit with tears.

"Oh, my Jacks," she says. "You always seem so strong, I forget sometimes."

I told her the story knowing how she'd react, but still it makes me sad—that it's so much easier to be loved when I seem fragile, broken. *Learn this, Jackie,* I think, *once and for all.*

JACK

It bothers him. The way she left. The fact that she needed to. That there was no other choice.

He's at his desk, looking over a memo draft. He scribbles a note in the margin. Dust streams through sunlight. He thinks about Mary Meyer. It's been months since her last visit, since he told her he had to end it.

He pushes the memo aside, pulls out a sheet of paper . . .

Mary,

Why don't you leave suburbia for once—come and see me—either here—or at the Cape next week or in Boston the 19th. I know it is unwise, irrational, and that you may hate it—on the other hand you may not—and I will love it. You say that it is good for me not to get what I want. After all these years—you should give me a more loving answer than that.

Why don't you just say yes.

Halfway down the page, a wave of what feels like nausea hits.

When Jackie went into labor with Patrick, he was in the air. It was the seventh of August, twenty years to the day since he and his crew, marooned in the Pacific, were rescued. Patrick was born six weeks premature, with the film around his tiny lungs and a 50/50 chance of survival. As the plane turned around, heading back to

Otis, to Jackie and Patrick, all he could think was: I'm never there when she needs me.

On his desk now: the black alligator pad, pencil holder, blotter—a gift from De Gaulle on his first state visit to Paris. Next to that, his calendar, the Steuben glass etching of a PT boat, his inaugural medal, and leather-bound copies of Churchill's Marlborough *and Stendhal's* The Red and the Black. *There's a small 1963 congressional directory, the Hercolite lamp, and an ashtray J. Edgar Hoover gave him as a gift. He has to deal with Hoover. Bobby said that. Hoover and his tapes on King. Hoover hates King. "We've got to manage him, Jack," Bobby said. Manage Hoover; finalize the test-ban treaty; deal with Vietnam—the growing storm between Diem and the army generals who want him gone.*

Every hour, some new crisis.

Why not slip Mary in? Take a break.

Years ago, during the Senate campaign, when Jackie was pregnant with Caroline, he was leaving to board a plane. He remembers that day without remembering where he was going. Jackie walked him to the door of the Hyannis airport. She said his name. He turned to her. "What?" His voice impatient. She didn't answer, or if she did, he can only remember how she scanned his face, like she was looking for some way into him. Her eyes dropped, she looked away.

He hates the sense of "without her" in the house. It fills him with an odd dread.

When did she leave? he wonders. When did that door inside her close? When did she vanish, standing right in front of him, the children turning somersaults on the rug as she called them to come brush their teeth, get their shoes tied?

All of this was happening. Years of his life transpired, while part of her, he understands now, was absent all along.

He looks down at the unfinished letter to Mary Meyer. He puts it away in the drawer.

That night, he calls Caroline. She and John are in Newport with Janet.

"I'll be there soon, sweetheart. How's your brother?"

"He misses you."

"And you?"

"I understand." *She says this in her grown-up voice, which makes him smile.*

"Is the water still warm enough to swim?" *he asks.*

"I jumped in, but it might be too cold for you."

"Never. I love you and I'll see you soon."

"When?"

"This weekend."

"Not until then?"

"That's Friday."

"Well, Friday is soon."

On the phone table, there's a homemade pink valentine she made for him, a cardboard backing to keep it upright.

"In your opinion, what will the American press do with this?" Onassis asks.

We are somewhere off the coast of Crete. It's late. Most of the others have peeled off to bed. The three of us sit near the pool. Lee has moved closer to Onassis now that the others are gone, her hand on the edge of his thigh.

"What will the press do with what?" I say.

"Your trip here."

"The usual things, I assume. Where we went, what we ate, who we met, what I wore. They might be kinder this time."

Lee breaks in. "Because of the baby—"

"You're drunk, Lee," Onassis says. Cool and dismissive, the way he says it, and while he might claim it's out of respect for me, I like him less.

We've been on board the *Christina* for almost four days.

There was a photograph I once saw of the *Christina*—the same space where we're sitting tonight, configured differently. In the photograph, the mosaicked deck was lowered to form a swimming pool but there was no water in it. Onassis and Churchill sat in that drained pool in two rattan chairs, Onassis in lightweight slacks and a loose-fitting button-down shirt, Churchill in his black suit. He had his cane and wore his hat, black dress shoes resting on the mosaicked flank of the minotaur.

"Is it going to rain?" I ask Onassis the next morning. A low body of clouds appears to move toward us over the sea.

"No," he says.

"How do you know that?"

"By how the clouds are moving. How the air smells."

"So interesting," I say. "It's interesting, too, the way you're so sure."

"It isn't much good to be otherwise, is it?" The faintest smile then.

After dinner, we move out onto the deck, and he tells stories of Greek history, mythology, and heroes; stories of Odysseus, his wandering and battles; stories of the master craftsman Daedalus, who became a prisoner of the labyrinth he had designed, those massive wings of wax and pinion he built to escape with his son Icarus.

"The old poets say that every evening the sun falls into the sea is a reminder of that story. For them, the gods were not remote at all. They roll our lives like dice."

He looks at me then, like we share a secret. I feel a flash of anger. There is no secret. He's toying with my sister, and now he's begun to tire of her, which only makes Lee cling more tightly.

That night in my cabin, I look through sketches I've made. Watercolors, rough landscapes with the edges unfinished, I'd wanted them that way—fading color toward the margin, the blue sky and a wash of sea, the scrawl of an island, the horizon— a grayish thin taut line, far off.

"Stay," you said as I was leaving.

Painting on deck earlier today, I thought of you. The sun bright on my face, I could feel all the things I wanted to say before I left,

*things I couldn't get out of my body to say aloud. Things about de-
sire and voltas, what you spoke into my neck once, years ago, about
everything and more. And as I felt these things, it was like I walked
through a door in the air, and I was with you, and beginnings were
beginnings again.*

*It's been two years since I came to Greece for the first time. How
different it seems to me now, not the place, but my understanding
of it, my sense of what a hero is, what legends are. As Sophocles
wrote—the good and the evil, the dark and the light, joy pierced
with regret. It's only there—in those intimate fault lines—that what
is larger than life exists.*

*"Stay," you said. Just that one word. How open it was—the look
in your eyes. I'd wanted to fall into that openness. I wanted it to last.
I was afraid it wouldn't. I was afraid that, as soon as I gave myself
over to it, you would leave again.*

In three days, we go to Marrakesh, then London, then home.
Before we disembark, Ari has said he wants to show me Skorpios. His island. I notice sometimes I use his first name in my
head now.

I set the sketches down, take out a sheet of blank paper, pick up
a pen. I write the date in one corner.

I miss you, Jack. . . .
I think that I am lucky to miss you—

The next morning, stepping out of my stateroom into the hot
scattered sunlight on the deck. I'm aware of him suddenly. Onassis. Standing a few yards away.

. . .

When I arrive home on October 17, I've been gone for almost
three weeks. As I start down the steps of the plane, Caroline
rushes up, a flash of white dress and ankle socks, John behind
her, climbing one stair at a time. I wait for them at the top of the

stairs. Caroline flies into my arms. I hold her tightly, the warm beating realness of her cheek against mine. John wraps himself around my leg. Then Jack is there.

"You're back," he says.

We're together for only a night. He's leaving for Cambridge to visit a site for the new library.

"I have a favor," he says at breakfast. "While you were gone, Governor Connally was here."

"I don't like that man."

"He reminded me I promised to visit Texas."

"Not now, though—when they hate the test-ban treaty and the civil-rights bill."

"He's asked if you'd come."

I feel something in me pause. "Texas?"

"I'm only asking you to think it over."

"This isn't for what's on the table, is it? This is for the next campaign."

"Just give it some thought, Jackie. Please."

The last weekend in October, he comes to Wexford. I can feel he is restless the moment he walks through the door—some bright, sharp current running under the skin.

"What's wrong?"

"Nothing. I'm here."

"You seem like you'd rather be somewhere else."

He looks at me. "I'm here."

Vietnam, I realize over the next several hours. I start to piece it together. What's already happened, what might happen next.

When we have a few moments alone, I ask him about it.

"It's all going down," he says. "That memo I agreed to in August, indicating the United States *might* support a coup. But I was clear there were conditions—"

The phone rings. It's rung, it seems, every half hour since he came. Someone picks up. He leaves the room. A door slams. I hear him swear, then, "How can this house have no closets?"

When news comes from Saigon that a coup to overthrow

Diem is imminent, the South Vietnamese military commanders refuse to give Jack the forty-eight hours' notice he asks for.

"Won't? Or can't?" I ask.

He shakes his head. "I've told them I need forty-eight hours to find another way."

Three in the morning on Friday the first of November, the phone rings.

"It's begun," he says when he hangs up. "Four minutes. That's all the notice they gave."

He gets out of bed, snaps the back brace into place. Before he leaves the room, he comes over and kisses me. "I love you," he says.

Diem is dead, he learns the following day.

Jack is shaken. He had been promised Diem would be extracted peacefully, taken into exile. The military who led the coup try to claim it was a suicide, but photographs surface, showing Diem and his brother lying in blood in the back of a truck. Executed. Stabbed and shot, hands tied behind their backs.

"It shouldn't have happened like this," Jack says. "I should have known."

"You couldn't have known."

He glances at me, his eyes so much older now.

"That doesn't mean I shouldn't have."

. . .

Franklin and Sue Roosevelt are the ones who tell me about Adlai Stevenson in Texas. They've come for dinner at the Residence, along with the French ambassador Hervé Alphand and his wife, Nicole. Jack is late. We've had two rounds of cocktails when I decide we'll start dinner without him. As soon as we sit down, Franklin tells me it's not a good idea—our planned trip to Dallas.

"Because of Adlai," he says.

"They threw a placard at his head," says Sue, "and left an awful bruise."

"That's not what happened," Franklin says. "The placard

missed him, but they pelted him with eggs. Called him a communist, a traitor."

I listen, absorbing this.

"We're not saying you shouldn't go, Jackie," Franklin says.

"That's exactly what you're saying," says Alphand.

"Jack has to go," I say.

"But you don't. You could say your doctors have advised against it."

"Hard to say that after three weeks in Greece," I say, my eyes on the curve of the spoon skimming through the soup.

"You needed that trip."

"I'm not sure Texas will be so understanding."

"Well, go, then. But skip Dallas."

Jack is coming. His steps in the hallway.

"They started without me, Mr. West?" I hear him say, teasing the chief usher as they enter the room. I don't look up as Jack sits down. I want to put my face back together, push the fear out—he'll know something is awry. He would be angry with them for telling me about Adlai.

Bill Walton phones. He tells me he went to see Elaine de Kooning in New York. Her studio was filled with images of Jack, over forty oil portraits, raw sketches and charcoal studies of his face pinned to the walls and scattered on the floor—Jack standing, seated, energy in the rough brushstrokes, like he's about to bolt right out of his chair. She had a ladder set up to work on a massive canvas that reached to the ceiling. There was one painting, Bill says, he found particularly stunning. In an abstract sea of color and shadow, only Jack's eyes. De Kooning told Bill that all year she'd painted Jack. Only Jack. She'd finish a portrait, then she'd have to start over. Each time she felt like she'd missed the essence and all she was able to catch was a glimpse.

Caroline gets out of school early. Our things packed, the children and I fly to Wexford. While John marches off in boots and helmet with his toy gun toward an army tent the agents have made for him, I take Caroline to the stables. The afternoon is starched and cool. As we ride, I feel that chill air cut against my neck. Caroline turns her pony off to work in the ring, but I urge Sadar across the open field. The horse's pace quickens, my legs tight against the flank, a sensation I love—that sense of speed and control as the yellow-green trees flood by.

Clint is waiting at the stables. Caroline was hungry, he says; she's gone up to the house.

"Walk with me, please, Mr. Hill." I fold my riding gloves into my jacket pocket. I can feel the burn of the ride still, that sense of alive. "Mr. Hill, I'd like to know what you think."

"Of course, Mrs. Kennedy." He doesn't look up, his face solemn, attentive. He seems almost bodiless sometimes, but he's become a confidant. I trust him. He is always there.

"Mr. Hill, do you think the climate in Dallas is so hostile to the president that the people could mistreat us as they did Adlai?"

A pause, then, "Anything's possible, Mrs. Kennedy. But as far as I know, there are no more threats in Dallas than in any other part of the South right now."

He doesn't look at me when I catch his hand. It's brief—the touch. I hold on for only a moment, then let go.

"Thank you, Mr. Hill. You always know the right thing to say to me."

JACK

Rockefeller's the one he worries about. Goldwater he can beat. The Arizonian might be quick, but he's too extreme to be a threat in the campaign. Rockefeller, though, is a centrist. That mystique of old American money. In early November, five days after the coup in Vietnam, Rockefeller announced his candidacy, slamming Jack's "failures at home and abroad" and citing a Newsweek poll that named him "the most widely disliked Democratic president of this century among white Southerners."

Jack called Bobby, told him to start booking strategy meetings for the reelection campaign. "Let's hit the ground running, knock Rockefeller's feet out from under him before he gets in this race."

Saturday at the house in Virginia, Jack sits on the patio, talking with Ben Bradlee about Texas, how Connally's at it with Senator Yarborough, how even Johnson's lost the power to mend that feud. The mood in Dallas is ugly.

Clipper is at Jackie's feet. Her hand strokes the dog's head. She'd been talking to Tony, but now she's looking out toward the land. Thinking about the horses, he'd bet.

She taps her cigarette into the ashtray. I'll finish this one—that's what she's thinking—then tell them I just need to walk down, check on Sadar. I'll slip in a quick ride.

He can read it in her face.

She turns and smiles at him then—a pure bold strength in her smile, beautiful but with a new look, removed.

She's been different since Greece, or maybe since Patrick. Different.

She draws in on the cigarette, turns away and exhales.

"Come on," he says, standing up. "Before you leave me for your horse, let's take a walk." He brushes off his pants and starts down the steps to the stone path, the green lawn flung on either side. The children fly across the yard, running to catch up. John saunters ahead. Caroline slips her hand into her father's, little fingers weaving through his.

The world is a cage of light, tenuous and sheer, hills rolling away beyond.

Jackie's right, *he thinks*. This will be a good home for a while.

They've begun to talk about "after." After his first term ends. After he runs for another and, assuming he wins, after four more years, which will pass in a week like a dream.

He wants to write. He knows that for sure. He wants to get back to who he was before his brother Joe was killed and this work fell to him. He wants to pick up those older threads and start new. There's so much, though, to do before then. The poverty initiative, the space program, the civil-rights bill. And, next up, the trip to Dallas to smooth the rift that bill has ostensibly caused.

That rift was always there. The country was built on that kind of hatred. Built on slave labor and the racist American violence that runs through the nation like veins. No one likes to admit that, but it's true.

So just do it. Get through the 88th Congress. Get that bill out of the House Judiciary and passed. The tax bill, too, which is stuck in Ways and Means. Get that work done, effect what change you can in the years you have left. Get things on the rails and have some fun along the way.

Enjoy yourself. It's later than you think.
  That old Guy Lombardo song.

She is walking next to him, her long legs keeping stride with his, and as they cross the lawn under that free November sky, an unfamiliar feeling sweeps through him, something sweet and brutal and sad. Not pleasure. He'd recognize that. This is different, clear and strange.

  Happiness. Would that be the word? For this moment, this walk, this life, the echoing sound of his footsteps on the stone under the trees, the shade and the cool autumn air. John is singing some tuneless song he's made up, and the four of them are just walking, listening for birds, or a pattern in the rustle of leaves, or silence, Caroline clutching his hand. He can feel the moist beating warmth of her palm pressed hard to his. His back hurts, his shoulder hurts, and none of that matters; the pain seems almost irrelevant against the looming depth of this new feeling, the ache that comes with this kind of happiness.

  The spaniel bolts across the path, Clipper in pursuit, and the children run after the dogs, the breeze ransacking their hair, and it strikes him that life has never felt as close as this. She is telling him quietly that she's going to peel off soon, walk down to the stables, and, if he doesn't mind, she'd like to take a short ride. Sure, he says, and they keep walking. The light is sharp. Blades of liquid silver on the leaves.

· · ·

Thursday, November 21.
  On his desk, a stack of newspapers and an updated schedule for the next few days: ten hours on the ground, three major cities, five motorcades.

1:30 pm	**Arrive San Antonio**
1:40 pm	**Motorcade through city**
2:25pm	**Arrive Brooks AFB to dedicate Aero Space Medical Health Center**
3:30pm	**Depart for Houston**
4:15 pm	**Arrive Houston**

5:00 pm	**Arrive Rice Hotel**
8:20 pm	**Drop by reception of Latin American Citizens in hotel**
8:35 pm	**Depart Hotel for Coliseum dinner**

He skims halfway down the page to the second day, November 22.

11:35 am	**Arrive Dallas Love Field**
2:35 pm	**Depart Love Field for Austin**

I'm going to need an hour rest somewhere *is what he's thinking* when Evelyn Lincoln appears in the doorway.

"Ambitious schedule, Mrs. Lincoln."

"Time to go, Mr. President."

He's told Jackie to pack her hats. Unless there's rain, the cars will be open.

"What about a bubbletop?" Pam Turnure had asked.

"Hats," he repeated.

The conversation ended there.

Two days ago, before Salinger left for Japan, Jack said to him, almost in passing, "I wish I weren't going to Texas."

Stepping out of his office into the hall, he hears the sound of shredded air as the helicopter nears.

John cries as they are leaving, clutching his father's leg.

"I want to come," John sobs. Jackie kneels beside him.

"Just a few days, darling," she says. "When we get back, it will be your birthday, and we'll have a big party."

John reaches up then; Jack lifts him and, for a moment, buries his face into that sweet boy smell.

"Take care of him, Agent Foster," he says.

"Yes, sir, Mr. President."

Jack turns away. Since Patrick, it's sandpaper on skin now— every leaving.

A heat wave is flooding Texas.

"You're going to be hot," Jack says to me on the plane.

"I'll be fine."

"They're calling for rain in Dallas, so maybe we'll bubbletop it after all."

"You don't want that, though."

"No one comes out to see the president through a layer of glass."

I read over the speech I'm giving tonight in Spanish. Jack's talking now with Kenny O'Donnell about the feud in Texas, about Connally and Yarborough, splintering the Democrats.

"Texas will be hard enough to win without that," Kenny says.

Jack changes the subject. "Any furniture broken last night at the party?"

"Just a Bobby and Ethel party," Dave Powers says.

"Who was more wild?" Jack says. "Ethel or the kids?"

Dave and Kenny laugh.

"And that was only Bobby turning thirty-eight," Jack says. "Imagine when he hits forty."

Before we land, I go into the bedroom to change. White skirt, black belt. I clip my hair under my hat—not a beret, but enough to keep things from being destroyed in a car with no bubbletop.

I finish pinning the hat. The light is blinking. We've begun our descent.

The crowd is a dark sea beneath as we touch down in San Antonio. Jack leans back, shifting in his seat. He turns, looks at me, and grins.

"All right," he says. "Let's do this thing."

The route is lined with people, hands waving, banners, flags.

"Jack, look," I say, pointing to a massive cardboard sign.

Jackie

Come Water-Ski

in

Texas

Dave Powers glances at me, then at Jack. "They're here for her," he says.

That night at the Rice Hotel as we're finishing dinner in our suite, the Johnsons come in. Lady Bird wants to know what she can arrange for our visit to their ranch.

"I'm sure Jackie will want to ride," she says. "But what about you, Mr. President?"

"I'll ride with Jackie," he says, as if riding horses with me is the most natural thing in the world. He asks an aide to have the White House ship his riding pants to the Austin Air Force Base.

"My trousers, Lady Bird, will meet us at your house."

"I like them," I say as the door closes behind the Johnsons.

Jack laughs. "You used to call them Colonel Cornpone and his little Porkchop."

"They're kind," I say.

"Do you think she'll ever call me Jack?"

"On the last day of your presidency. Or maybe the day after."

We're alone, and he tells me then about the oxygen chamber he saw earlier that day at the aerospace center. He's sitting at a small desk, digging a pen into a doodle on the hotel stationery.

"I pulled one of the scientists aside," he says, "to ask if space medicine would have saved Patrick."

Every time he says Patrick's name, I feel a shift in him, like the name is a key that unlocks a door that swings open into a pool of dark. He keeps on with the doodle, silent.

"It's time to get ready, Jack."

"I know."

I cross the room and kiss his cheek. I see it then, the sketch on the hotel stationery. A sailboat.

"I love that, Jack. Look how fast it's going. But no one is in it. Who has the tiller?"

"He's behind the sail."

"Why's that kite up in the corner?"

"That's the sun."

"Shaped like a diamond. Reluctant abstractionist, you. Are you sure it's not a kite?"

He laughs and puts the pen down. "Where's my tie?"

JACK

Later, he'll wish he'd grabbed that little drawing on the way out of the room. Folded it into his pocket to give to her on the plane home.

But he forgets all about it. She is late, and he forgets almost everything but the fact that she's late. He knocks on the door of the room where she's getting dressed. No answer. He knocks again, more sharply.

"Be right out," she calls.

He paces the hall.

When the door opens five minutes later, he looks up and she is there, black velvet dress, long sleeves, her neck roped with pearls. The hotel staff is in a neat line as they walk down the narrow hall together. He greets them as they pass: "Hello." "Good evening." Back in their suite, someone else is packing their belongings, bringing the bags downstairs and loading them into the car for the drive to the Houston Coliseum, the dinner there, then on to the airport.

They cross the mezzanine floor of the Rice Hotel and walk into the ballroom, where Spanish workers from the League of United Latin American Citizens are gathered.

He steps up to the podium and says a few words about the Alliance for Progress. Then he introduces her and steps away, leaving her alone on the stage. She hesitates for a moment, then begins to speak in Spanish, the words slow, the smile almost shy. They quiet for her. He catches a word here, a word there. He can feel her voice resonate, that pale of her face and her long dark shape, and the feeling of her is like water in the rage of the lights shining down, that almost otherworldly calm about her, grace.

Afterward, on the forty-five-minute flight to Fort Worth, he tells her what he overhead Lyndon Johnson say to his aide Valenti. "People just love that gal."

This makes her laugh.

He does not tell her that when Lyndon said that, Valenti almost didn't hear him at first, because he was staring at Jack's right hand and the involuntary shake of the fingers.

It's worse, more intense, when he's tired. He'd shoved his hand into his pocket, and Valenti's head snapped up, embarrassed to have been caught staring.

Thirty minutes into the flight, she's worked through nearly half a pack of Newport menthols. Eight stubs in the ashtray. One smolders. She notices him watching her. She picks up the one still lit and softly grinds it out.

. . .

George wakes him at 7:30 A.M. Gray rain beats against the window. "Let's hope it lets up, George," he says.

The Connally vs. Yarborough conflict is in the headline news.

STORM OF CONTROVERSY SURROUNDS KENNEDY'S VISIT.
WIDENING DEMOCRATIC SPLIT.

Half an hour later, he walks out of the hotel into the drizzle and crosses the red-bricked street. The crowd thickens. Chants of his name mix in with the rain. A woman runs up to him, aiming something black at his face. A flash goes off, then someone gets hold of her and she is borne away. "Just a camera, sir. Sorry about that."

The crowd is chanting her name now: "Jack-ie! Jack-ie!"

Her schedule had been on the table; he'd glanced at it before walking out of the room. Next to breakfast in the grand ballroom, *her handwriting in red script.* JBK won't attend, *she'd written.*

"Tell Clint to get her down," he says now to the agent with him. "I know she didn't plan on it, but tell Clint to explain I need her down here. Now."

They've set up a makeshift stage on a flatbed truck. He's offered a raincoat. He shakes his head and steps up, turning to the crowd. They cheer, he raises a hand, and they still.

Play it right. Just get this day right.

Stepping back inside, he glances at his watch, then at the agent. "Well?"

"Clint says Mrs. Kennedy will be right down." The agent tries to sound reassuring.

"What else did she say?"

"She asked us to remind you that you told her to make sure she out-belled the belles."

Walking toward the ballroom, he runs into Yarborough.

"Mr. President," Yarborough says, all smiles.

"Stick to Johnson like Duco, will you, Ralph," he says. "For Christ's sake, just cut it out."

He strides toward the kitchen, glancing back once to make sure his team is there, behind him, in place. They duck through the kettles and around the counters to keep up. He comes to the double doors that open into the ballroom.

"Everybody set?" he says. "All right, let's go."

Twenty minutes into the breakfast, the door to the kitchen opens again.

Clint is with her as she pauses for a moment, copper and stainless steel through the open kitchen door behind her, and in the ballroom two thousand conservatively dressed conservative Texans are rising from their chairs to catch a glimpse. She steps into the room and the chaos of klieg lights. They call her name, clapping their hands. She smiles, her eyes deer-like, bright, finding his, looking nowhere else, only at him. She threads the gauntlet of long tables toward the dais. Clint's eyes dart, sweeping left, right, always shifting, watchful. Jack has witnessed it, the precise formal dance between them. He has watched them arriving at the White House from Virginia, Clint driving, Jackie stepping out of the passenger seat, her hair windblown, face flushed, the scent of cigarette smoke on her clothes. She trusts Clint completely. She'll ride down a highway with him, windows open, her feet on the dash, smoking, listening to the radio. Some casual interval of ordinary life.

She has reached the dais. She takes the few steps and passes Jack on her way to her seat. Her hand, for an instant, brushes his. Then she sits down and smiles, the sweet warmth in her face so sudden and uncertain, he feels a sharp ache. He turns back to the crowd.

The cheers roar like fire.

November 22, 1963

We have an hour before the flight to Dallas. Walking back to our suite, I hold his arm.

"I couldn't decide, Jack, between the long gloves or the short gloves, and then once we came outside, Clint explained I was going to a breakfast in a ballroom."

"Now we're back, and we can have breakfast."

"I want to look at the art," I say. "Did you see what they did in the room—the art they hung for us? They must have stripped their whole museum. I was too tired to really see it last night, then I woke up to Van Gogh, Picasso, and that sculpture of the girl."

There's a catalog of the art on the coffee table. Jack flips through it.

"Does it say who put this together?" I ask.

"A Mrs. J. Lee Johnson III. Why don't we call her?"

"Did you know they were doing this?"

"I know everything."

I laugh. "How dim of me not to remember."

"It was in the papers. Kenny saw it and told me."

"I don't trust Texas, Jack. Connally—I hate his big soft mouth."

"You mustn't use that word."

"Mouth?"

"Hate." He looks at me. "Let's give Mrs. J. Lee Johnson a call."

"She's probably a Republican."

"I'm sure she's a Republican."

"Do we have time?"

"Always."

"If that was true, you wouldn't need to rush me to get here and there, would you?"

"The faster you get down to things like ballroom breakfasts, the more time you have with me." He smiles as he says it. It's not the kind of thing he'd usually say, and he's only half serious. That's how he talks around things he cares about—he floats them out in a teasing way, making a joke, testing the air or the heart.

He picks up the phone and asks the operator to help hunt up this Mrs. Johnson III. I study the Van Gogh on the wall. The paint does not seem dry.

"Well, Mrs. Johnson," Jack says into the receiver, "Mrs. Kennedy would like to express her thanks to you as well. Let me get her for you."

He holds out the receiver, and I take it.

"That was nice," I say, hanging up.

"Come to California with me."

"Is that the next trip?"

"In two weeks."

There's a knock on the door.

"Open," he shouts. He's still looking at me, waiting for my answer.

"I guess I'll go anywhere with you, Jack."

The papers Kenny O'Donnell brings in include *The Dallas Morning News* turned to a black-bordered full page and a large headline that reads: WELCOME MR. KENNEDY TO DALLAS.

"It isn't good," Kenny says. "This either." He tosses another paper on the table, with a half-page article about how Jack has failed to recognize the needs of the South.

"I was looking forward to the treason leaflets myself," Jack says. "Got one of those for me?"

Kenny digs into his jacket pocket and tosses one down. I pick it up. Two photographs of Jack—mug-shot style, one face forward, one at profile. Underneath in large type:

Wanted

For

Treason

I skim the numbered list.

1. *Betraying the Constitution*
2. *Turning the sovereignty of the U.S. over to the communist controlled United Nations.*
3. *WRONG on innumerable issues affecting the security of the U.S.*

Farther down:

He has given support and encouragement to the Communist-inspired racial riots. . . . Aliens and known Communists abound. . . .

I set down the leaflet.

"How can they even think this, let alone print it?"

"Texas," Kenny says.

"I don't like it here, Jack," I say. "They don't like you at all."

"They don't like change," Jack says. He taps the leaflet. "Keep one to frame."

. . .

12:20 Main Street, Dallas.

Clint Hill jogs alongside the car. Every few blocks, he hops up on the running board to catch his breath, until Jack throws him a look; then Clint hops off and starts jogging again in the street. The sun strikes off the dark waxed surface of the car. We pass the looming stretch of a department store.

One intersection, then another. A turn.

The crowd swells and ebbs. It's like any other crowd, a tide of faces, waving hands, bunting, loud cheers in the hot white glare of the sun. Behind them, the expressionless blank windows of factory buildings flank the street.

Another turn.

Up ahead, a tract of green where the space opens—trees, blue free sky.

"You can't say Dallas doesn't love you, Mr. President," Nellie Connally says, twisting around in her seat, a wide smile, bright-pink cheeks.

Jack smiles back at her. "No, you can't."

An underpass ahead.

~

JACK

12:31 P.M. CST

*"Take off your glasses, Jackie," he tells her. He sees her squint—
the sun hot, bright.*

You can't say Dallas doesn't love you, Mr. President. . . .

*A boy standing on the curb with his father stares as they pass by, a
newsboy cap, scrubbed face; slowly moving, a tentative smile surfaces through the freckles and pale skin, a small hand creeping up,
starting to wave.*

*A motorcycle backfires, scorched air, the light blinding, that
sound and its echo, the world contracts. The boy on the curb is
gone. He turns to find her, his wife, the turning a reflex to anchor
the sound; she is facing away from him, toward the crowd on her
side of the car, her hand raised, sunlight bright off the bracelet on
her wrist, her gloved hand moving back and forth like a tiny flag.
He starts to turn back, his eye skimming hers as she turns in his
direction even as he is turning away, his hand raised now, waving at the people cheering from the curb. The air cracks again,
the backfire from somewhere behind them. He jerks forward.
Arms twitch. Hands lurching up. Someone is shouting. He goes*

to answer; a sea fills his throat, the pain searing. He turns again to her, his mouth open to ask, and her face is near his face, her eyes dark, wide, the strangest expression, terror, her hands grip his arm, her body lifting, as she tries to force his arms down—the sound again—

Night blooms in his head.

The sound deafening, now only silence. As he watches, the world picks up speed, the sky above them on a tilt, clouds, a hem of buildings, trees, the edge of what might be a park floods by, the rush of the car underneath, and she is there.

Jack.
　He reaches for her—

Jack,
　her voice a tether
　Can you hear me, Jack?
　I love you.

Reach

The echo of that sound still, her face gone to pieces right before his eyes.

. . .

At the border was light.
　A photograph. She is with him, standing in the doorway of an airport. He is a senator, and it is June 1957. The year of the Pulitzer, the year of the Famous Five. He is boarding a plane and leans in to kiss her goodbye. Her skirt is full of wind, his face half in shadow, only the edge of his jaw lit. That soft knock of sun. Behind them there is brightness, the blurred nose of the plane, tarmac, the fatal and glorious sky. Her back is to the cam-

era, but he remembers her face, her searching eyes; she had wanted something from him in that moment, in the rush of hot wind, a yearning he closed himself to, and the soft dusk of her voice. Jack. She was asking him something. He tries to remember now and cannot. What was it in that moment she had wanted?

Why can't he remember?

I'll be home soon, he must have said, something easy, bland, his mind already ticking off lists for the days ahead.

He was always saying words like that to keep her calm, to put her off.

Later
Soon

It passes through him now like some strange and awful bolt to light the life he will not live.

. . .

Now it is later.
Time is gone.

Parkland ER. Clint has pulled out a chair. Always with her, and now in the hall he pulls out a metal folding chair for her, then a second chair, empty, beside it. Someone hands her a towel. She starts to wipe her face, then puts it down. She says something to another man, who takes a pack of cigarettes from his trousers pocket and lights one for her.

"Thank you," she says, but does not smile. She sits and smokes and stares at the wall.

There are things he will miss. Tiny nothing things:

His feet following his own shadow across the lawn
The scent of the Rose Garden
A bracing wind on the water, that cold salt soak, the mainsheet in
his grip
His daughter's hands

In Caroline's eyes he could see the future, a searing infinite blue.
He could feel that future as she hurled herself across the room
toward him, flew fast and hard like she'd fly straight through his
open arms through the window behind him into the great tall
world.

His wife's mind—sly, brilliant, not always kind—that meditative
way she'd run her finger absently along the edge of a page she was
reading in bed.

These throwaway details of a life.

"Look how beautiful, Jack," she'd whispered to him once, her
hand on his wrist, eyes fixed on a lit branch through a window, her
face with no play in it then, just open and gentle and soft, and he
fell in.

Once
Later
Soon

Her stare now in the hospital corridor, boring through him—
mystical, vacant, relentless—looking off into some middle distance
caught in the grain of the wall. Her lips tighten around the ciga-
rette, the pull of smoke into her lungs and out again, yet under-
neath that stone remove, he sees her still: the girl he fell in love with
all those years ago.

Admit it. Can you?

This is a love story.
Always was.
A love story.

He moves toward her, brushes through, and moves on.

PART IV

*One day in a whirl of winged horses, the sun changed course
And turned his holy face away.*

—EURIPIDES (trans. Anne Carson)

November 22, 1963, 12:47 P.M. CST

They tell me they found no heartbeat, no breathing, no pulse.

In the hallway where I sit, a glacial coolness—white tiles along the wall, black linoleum floor. Clint is near me. Others cluster, voices anxious, hushed, someone walks away, someone else comes back. A nurse pushes through.

Three and a half seconds—that's all it was—between the first shot, which missed, and the second, which did not.

If I'd been looking to the right.
If I'd recognized the sound for what it was.
If I had not been complaining in my head about the heat, or how close their hands and blurred faces came as the car took a turn, if I hadn't been so focused on all that or wondering how I could slip off, with you, away from that grueling, unbearable sunlight to the cool dark of the tunnel ahead.

Take off your glasses so they can see you, Jackie. Let them see you.

A hypnotic burst of light off my bracelet as I waved.

And the roses were there, on the seat between us, spilling toward the floor, petals soaked, his blood, stems broken, the dark, wet iridescence of those roses crushed in the white-hot glare as I leapt to grasp a piece of his skull flying away.

I do not quite remember that last part. What happened after.

They killed you over that bill.
I know it.
The civil-rights bill.
That's what they killed you for.

. . .

In the Parkland Hospital corridor, I sit in the folding metal chair and smoke, very still. They scuttle around—feet, voices, that awful hospital smell.

I look down at my lap, my skirt—then wish I hadn't. I look back up, through the moving stream of them to the opposite wall.

"Mrs. Kennedy, shall we go into the restroom and get cleaned up?"

"We've brought you a new set of clothes."

They keep saying things like that.

When the doors to Trauma Room 1 open, the corridor goes silent, and a doctor steps out, his face telling me what I already know. I stand up, stripped to nothing now, just a woman in the shape of a blade. I walk past them through the operating-theater doors to the body laid out that is mine, my lips to his feet, my face to his beautiful face, his lovely shattered head, no less beautiful, eyes open still. Not blank yet.

The world is shadowless. Time bent. No before or after. Just that hard brutal sound when everything slowed and your head jerked back, hands to your throat, that puzzled look. I remember thinking you looked like you had a slight headache.

We are made of stars, and I loved you from the first moment I saw you.

"Mrs. Kennedy, Vice President Johnson is going back to Washington and he would like you to go with him." Clint is saying this. They have sent him to tell me. I look at him, then can't.

We are back in the hospital corridor. Outside the closed doors of Trauma Room 1. The doctors are doing something else in there—I can't remember what. We are waiting again, and Clint's eyes are as young and raw and dark as I have ever seen them.

"Mr. Hill, please explain to Vice President Johnson that I am not going anywhere without the president."

"Yes, Mrs. Kennedy," he says, and steps away.

They wheel an empty casket in from outside. Bronze. Up on a metal dolly with small rubber wheels. O'Donnell and Powers step in front of me. *What are you doing?* I almost ask, then realize they're trying to shield me, to block my view as it goes by. Another doctor comes and urges me to leave.

"Do you think seeing a coffin could possibly upset me?" I say. "My husband was shot in my arms."

The doctor gets small in his white coat when I say this. Down the hall, Dave Powers is raising his voice to someone—the medical examiner, who is saying the autopsy must be held here according to Texas law. Their voices bounce off the linoleum, Dave yelling now, saying the vice president is waiting at Love Field for Mrs. Kennedy, and Mrs. Kennedy is waiting for the president, and the autopsy can be held in Washington no matter what the stupid Texas law says about homicide and jurisdiction. None of it matters. They argue, then figure it out. It is almost time to go. Jack is leaving soon, and I will leave with him. At a certain point, the casket with the large handles glides out of Trauma Room 1, and I know he is in it. I stand, and the casket is cool to the touch, and we walk outside to the white hearse. When Clint asks me to ride in the car behind, I have to explain, "No, Mr. Hill, I'm going to ride with the president." I climb into the back of the hearse with Jack. Clint climbs in too, and we ride with our knees scrunched up to our chests.

Crusts of blood on my stockings. My left glove is missing. For a moment I wonder where I left it.

I should not have allowed you to come here.

I should have listened, seen it, known ahead of time or in the instant.

I should have pulled you down.

The casket won't fit through the door of the plane. They try to wedge it in on an angle. I watch from the bottom of the steps; heat rising off the tarmac prickles my skin. I could tell them this won't work. It will never fit. The men at the top with the casket exchange a few words, but from the base of the steps I can't hear. Clint is with them. He glances back at me—a warning look, I realize, a moment before they break the handles off, that awful sound of metal ripped from wood. They jam the coffin through the door of the plane. I walk slowly up the stairs and follow it inside.

In the Presidential Cabin, someone has laid out a dress for me, a new jacket.

A light knock on the door. Lady Bird comes in.

"What if I hadn't been there?" I say.

"Let's get you changed," Lady Bird says gently.

"No. I want them to see what they have done to Jack."

She doesn't seem to quite know how to answer that.

"Could you please send in Mr. Hill," I say. "I need to give him a message for my mother and Miss Shaw. About the children."

On the flight, I sit with Jack and the Irish in the rear of the plane. The crew has taken out the seats to make room for us. I do not take my hand off the coffin. Someone somewhere is eating soup. The smell makes me feel sick. They grumble about Johnson. Did he really need to take the oath of office in Dallas? Couldn't he have waited? Johnson told them he talked to Bobby and that's what Bobby told him to do, which Bobby never would have said. At one point, they break off, realizing I am watching them. There is blood on Dave Powers's suit. For a moment I stare at it. I tell them about Abraham Lincoln's funeral and the book in the White House library. I ask if one of them could please make sure Pam remembered to message J. B. West to find that book so we can use it to plan.

"We are going to have a funeral like Lincoln's," I say. "A riderless horse. I need to read again exactly what they did with that horse—the tack, how it was led. We will do that."

The flight continues. They tell stories about Jack. They drink whiskey. They've insisted on pouring me a glass like I'm one of them now. They go on talking. I remember a late afternoon last summer. I was with the children, driving, just the three of us alone in the car. Up ahead was a bend in the road, and as the car took that turn, a slant of evening light shot through the green, the light like a portal; my heart kicked over, and I felt a sense of hurtling wind and speed, the future rushing through.

. . .

Moments after we touch down at Andrews Air Force Base and come to a stop, there's a commotion at the front of the plane. Bobby. Pushing down the aisle, he blows right past Lyndon, Lady Bird, everyone, until he reaches me.

"Hey, Jackie. I'm here."

His face is strange. Bright. Like someone who's come through a desert. I just look at him, trying to catch up with that weird, ravaged distance in his face. He puts his arms around me, and I feel something deep inside dissolve.

There's a helicopter, he says, waiting to take me to the children.

"Oh no," I have to explain. "I am staying with Jack."

Someone somewhere starts to cry.

God, I wish they wouldn't.

I say this quietly, so only Bobby hears it. He takes my hand and we walk to the door and step off the plane into a deafening silence. At first I think the airstrip is empty, but as my eyes adjust, I can make out a dark mass where crowds of people stand. As I move forward, they appear. Bobby keeps hold of my hand; we walk together down the stairs, and something pure and irrevocable moves between us, and, from that moment on, there is no one else.

It is evening. But that sense of evening is no longer anchored in time.

He rides with me and Jack in the back of the ambulance to the Navy hospital at Bethesda.

"Do you want to hear what happened?" I ask.

"Yes."

I tell him.

Afterward there is silence. He draws the curtain back and looks out the window.

"This is a long ride," I say.

"We're almost there."

He is still looking out the window.

"What are you looking at?"

"Just outside." He drops the curtain.

"I didn't read the Skybolt report," I say. "Before we left for Dallas, Jack asked me to read it and I didn't."

"It doesn't matter, Jackie."

"Do you know what he said when he gave it to me? He said, 'If you want to know what my life is like, read this.'"

Again, Bobby looks out the window, like he can't look at me for any length of time. He keeps reaching for the curtain and drawing it back.

"I could have stopped it," I say, "if I'd understood sooner what was happening."

"There's nothing you could have done."

You weren't there, I want to say, then I realize he already knows this and it's killing him.

"I held his brains in my hand," I say. My fingers rest on the lid of the casket. Bobby is still looking out the window.

"What is out there, Bobby?"

He looks at me then. "It wasn't about the civil-rights bill."

"What?"

"They found the man who did it. Oswald. That's his name. We think he acted alone."

"No. It was that bill. That's what they hated Jack for."

"Oswald is a communist."

"What does that have to do with anything?"

"Nothing."

I let it sink in.

"So he died for nothing. That's what you're saying."

He reaches for my hand, but I can't feel it, I can't feel or hear or see anything, only Jack—that puzzled look, his beautiful mind, and the life flooding out of it.

"We're going to have to make some decisions," Bobby says. "You don't have to. I can take care of it."

"It's all in the book on Lincoln," I say. "The lying-in-state, the rotunda, the riderless horse. I asked Pam to call Mr. West to ask him to find the book. Everything is there." The force and clarity in my voice is surprising. Not the soft voice, but the voice I used to have.

Bobby tells me then he was eating lunch when Hoover called.

"I could have done something," I say.

"No, Jackie. There was nothing."

He shifts, and I push into him like he is ground that will keep me from falling.

"Please," I say. "Cut it out of me."

. . .

My mother and Hughdie are waiting for us on the seventeenth floor at Bethesda. The Bradlees are there, Mary Gallagher, Pam,

Ethel, the McNamaras. Bob McNamara is arranging a house where I can live with the children in Georgetown. We can move in anytime. I murmur my thanks. Dave Powers is mixing drinks. One appears in my hand. A smoky liquid like amber. I take a sip, taste nothing. I put the glass down and pull Kenny O'Donnell aside to explain that, at the hospital in Dallas, I made a mistake. The ring I tried to put on Jack's finger didn't fit; it wasn't meant to be there, I know this now. I'd like it back. Can he take care of this for me? He nods and heads toward the door. He seems grateful to have something to do.

I learn the children were taken to my mother's house at Merrywood.

"No," I say. "Their lives shouldn't be disrupted, now of all times. Tell Miss Shaw to bring them home so they can sleep in their own beds."

Someone will have to tell them. I should be the one to do it. I want to be with them. I want to get them from my mother's house and bring them home. But then I'd have to leave Jack, and I can't do that.

I start to cry. My mother holds me until I've pulled myself together. The grief is a brick in my throat.

They are all so careful. They handle me like I'm a bit of glass. Ethel touches my arm. Her sincere, pretty face, telling me Jack went right to heaven, no stopovers.

The little blue pill I'm given doesn't work, so Dr. Walsh gives me a shot. Shortly after midnight, Dr. Walsh has fallen asleep in the chair, and I'm wide awake, hunting around for a cigarette.

They've learned things about Oswald. Bob McNamara tells me this, not because he offers it but because I ask. He seems surprised I'd want to know.

These are the things they've learned:

The kind of gun he used.

That he spent thirty-two months in the Soviet Union.

That he was married to a woman named Marina.

McNamara sits with me while the rest of the room buzzes on, more slowly now because everyone is tired, but Bob, like me, is awake. As he talks, I feel like he's holding me up with his eyes. The soft rectangle of his face, the neat circle of his glasses. Everything about him is ordered, calm.

"Do you want me to tell you again what happened?" I say.

"Yes."

I glance around the room—my mother, Hughdie, Ethel.

"When I start to tell them," I say, "they shrink. It's too much, I think."

"To hell with them," McNamara says. That makes me smile.

"Dr. Walsh says I should say it as often as I need to and try to get rid of it."

He nods.

"You see, the whole front of his head jumped out. He went to reach for it, but it wasn't there. Are you sure you want to hear this?"

"Yes," he says.

So I tell him the story. I tell it again, second by second, the way it happened, and McNamara just sits there listening, until I come to the end.

"I don't think he should be buried in Brookline," I say, "even though Patrick is there. What do you think?"

"We can work it all out," he says.

"You'll help me?"

"I will."

He is sitting on the floor near my feet. I am on a low stool. Eight times since I came into this room, someone has asked if I would like to change my clothes. But Bob is not asking me this. He is just looking up at me with those clean wire-rim glasses, that arrow-neat part in his hair, and his eyes with their strength, their understanding of violence, decisions, consequence.

"Can I tell you again what happened?" I say.

Late now, after 1:00 A.M. Already Saturday. Everything is taking so long. Mr. West and Bill Walton have sent a message from the White House. They've found the Lincoln book. It wasn't in the library, but they've found it and they have begun. And Bunny Mellon has arrived at the White House, Pam tells me. Lovely, generous Bunny. She flew through a tremendous thunderstorm, but she is there now, and she will do the flowers.

"Pam, please tell Bunny to use the blue vases."

"Yes, that's what you said."

"Those large blue urns France gave us."

"Yes."

"Bunny will know what to do. Nothing too melancholy. It should be like spring."

Pam looks down at her notebook and starts to cry, like these details have gotten the best of her. I put an arm around her. "Oh, Pam," I say. "I'm so sorry. This is such a terrible thing for you."

They keep telling me to rest.

I keep wishing you were here to tell them to shut the hell up.

They want me to rest, because they think that when I wake up, I will be like them again. I will see the world as they do. I will be able to fathom tomorrow. They do not understand that if I lie down, the dark will devour me.

"You should go home, Jackie," Ethel says.

"I'm not leaving until Jack does," I say.

At least they have finally stopped asking me to change my clothes.

After two in the morning, I think of it again. I'd thought of it earlier, then pushed the thought away. It was harder than any other thought. I go to find Bobby.

"What about your father?" I say.

"Teddy and Eunice have flown to Hyannis Port."

I nod. I feel suddenly very cold, very still, like a hinge has snapped.

"Is there anything you need, Jackie? Anything I can get you?"

I shake my head. There's a chair nearby. I suddenly have to sit down.

Blank, I want to say. *What I need is to be empty, unbroken, blank.*

Like the ceiling or the sky.

. . .

Four A.M. The motorcade winds through the wet city night. A light rain has begun. Bobby and I are with Jack again in the back of the ambulance. *We should take a different turn,* I almost say. The three of us. Take a turn and drive off.

"How much do you think they've done so far on the East Room?" I say instead.

"I'm sure they're taking care of it," Bobby says.

A pressure in my chest. I'm on the verge of starting to tell him again what happened, but I don't. And I don't explain that when I am not thinking about what happened, I am thinking about how an asymptote is a line that continually approaches an axis but never meets it.

The word *asymptote* comes from the Greek, *not falling together.*

In the back of the ambulance, Bobby pulls me to him. It is sudden and clumsy, his grief. My mouth faces into his jacket, my cheek near his chest; I can feel the thud of his heart, the rise and fall of his breath.

"I'm planning to walk," I say.

"That might not work," he says. "But we can talk about it later." He is trying to calm me. His voice is kind and soft, and I wish I could let go and lie down in it.

In my head, I've begun to make a list of readings. No dull sermon. No Twenty-third Psalm. Jack never liked that. I want to find words he would love. I remember a coda he once made up to the chapter in Ecclesiastes: "There's a time to fish and a time to cut bait." We'd all laughed. "And now it's time for a swim," he'd said, standing up, strolling out the door.

In the car now, I want to keep driving. I don't want the car to turn into the northwest gate.

The honor guard is there to meet us, young Marines in formation, their faces rinsed with rain. Beyond them, the drive is lit with flaming pots.

"We'd just begun to figure everything out," I say to Bobby.

Inside, the staff is lined up. I cannot look at them as I walk by. I start to, then it's too much.

Mr. West steps forward.

"Where are the children?" I say.

"Safe in their rooms, Mrs. Kennedy."

What an odd word to use. *Safe.*

They carry Jack into the East Room. Swags of black crepe. The catafalque identical to the one used for Lincoln. Just as I asked.

It is only a few steps from the doorway to where they've set him down. I kneel, my forehead pressed against the wood. I kiss the edge of the flag and pray to a god that has ceased to exist, and when I stand up again, I am like light rising; I've left everything behind—hope, faith, rage, sorrow, even fear. My body is smoke. Beyond the doorway is the hall that leads upstairs to the bedroom where I will not sleep and the desk in the West Sitting Hall where I will sit and write thousands of words over the next few days. Lists of names to be invited. Lists of readings and music and hymns. There will be cross-outs and carets, the tip of my pen working into the page.

There is only one way this can be done, and that is how it will be done. I will walk next to Jack. It will not be Holyhood Cemetery in Brookline, where Patrick is buried. It will be Arlington.

Later someone will write: *She bore the grief of a nation.*

I didn't do it for them. I was never that good or that generous. I did it so the children would have something noble to hold on to. I did it for you.

In the doorway of the East Room, I pause. Jack is on the catafalque behind us. Bobby is beside me. *What will happen to you?*

I start to ask him. That same thing I've been asking each of them in turn. It bursts then, the wall in my heart giving way. I don't realize I'm falling until he steps in to catch me. He pulls me against him, an arm around my waist, his face filled with a pain I don't want to see. Somewhere in the room, someone is crying again, then someone else starts. Together, Bobby and I walk past the crying and out of the room.

Provi is waiting upstairs. I take off my clothes and lay the suit on the bed.

"Fold it, please, Provi," I say. "Put it in a bag, the shoes and hat as well, even the stockings. Find the box Chez Ninon sent with it. Don't let anything be cleaned. Just put it in the bag and put the bag in the box. Make sure my mother gets it."

Provi takes a white towel and lays the stockings carefully into it. Bits of dark stuff flake out onto the white.

I run a bath. When the tub is full, I step into it.

. . .

I lie down on Jack's side of the bed, that awful mattress like concrete. I do not sleep. It grows light outside. Raining. The wet shines on the windowpane.

I get up and write out a list of names to be invited.

The Bartletts
The Bradlees
Bill Walton
Aristotle Socrates Onassis
The Ormsby-Gores

On a separate sheet of paper, another list:

- Caparisoned horse
- Cadets from Ireland
- Black Watch Highlander regiment

Because you loved it when they came to play, you sat with me and the children on the South Portico to listen. There is a photograph of the four of us there, our backs to the camera, four heads, two light, two dark—Caroline's small white gloved hand resting on your shoulder.

Take off your glasses, Jackie.

Yesterday, in the rooms on the seventeenth floor of Bethesda, Arthur Schlesinger told me I was your "full and inseparable partner in the most brilliant and gay and passionate adventure" he has ever known.

You would have smiled. You might have made a joke, rolled your eyes. You hated sentiment like that.

On a new sheet of paper, a list of things to put in the coffin:

- Inlaid cuff links
- Scrimshaw with the presidential seal

There's a terrible noise from down the hall. Someone is sobbing. Shouting. Bobby, I realize. From the Lincoln Bedroom.

The first night we spent in this house, you slept in that bedroom where your brother is crying now. You threw yourself on Lincoln's bed and yelled with joy that you had won and this was ours. You cried out at the ceiling like the joy would explode from inside you, like you were shrieking across time to the ghosts of all the men before you who had lived and led and died and worked and aged in this terrible house.

To think I almost didn't go with you to Dallas.

What if I had been here or out riding in Virginia, or somewhere else. Not with you.

Raining now. Miss Shaw brought the children to me this morning after their breakfast. John climbed into the bed, cried for a bit, then asked about his birthday and when the party would be. Caro-

line came in pushing that huge toy giraffe you gave her. Jack, she
was so quiet, like a clock gone still. Her face is not the same. I can
feel it. A distance in her eyes, the incandescent wreckage of her
face, like she knows something now about the word forever. *In less*
than a week, our daughter will be six. This morning she wrapped
her arms around me, pressing close, like she could dig all the way
in. Miss Shaw told her last night before bed, and Caroline asked
Miss Shaw if God would give you a job, since you always had so
much to do here. Miss Shaw told her God had already made you an
angel to watch over us and that you would look after Patrick, who
is lonely up there in heaven.

Do you remember what I told you, Jack, when we lost Patrick?
Do you remember how I said losing you would be the one thing I
could not bear—

. . .

"He's dead, isn't he?" Caroline whispers. At the private Mass
in the East Room, she kneels with me on the pew by the coffin.
When I bow my head, Caroline bows hers. When my lips move,
she half-follows, trying to keep up with the words. I stand, and
my daughter takes my hand. She looks up at me. I see Jack's face
in her face. Someone is sobbing. Pam. Bill Walton puts an arm
around her. The others try to manage their grief. If they can't,
they recuse themselves to the Green Room. I look for Clint.

"Mr. Hill, would you arrange for the children to be taken out
this afternoon? To lunch with my mother, then for a drive."

"Yes, Mrs. Kennedy."

"Oh, and, Mr. Hill?"

"Yes?"

"Please tell Mr. West I want to go to the president's office."

I wait while Clint speaks to the other agents. Then he walks
with me in silence to the Oval Office, where Mr. West is waiting.
The new carpet I'd ordered was installed while we were in Dallas. Jack's things are being packed up. I make a mental inventory:
photographs, a small clock, scrimshaw.

"Do you remember how much he loved this desk, Mr. Hill? How excited he was when the children played hide-and-seek with the little trapdoor?"

I rest my hand on the rocking chair, and I'm startled when it moves.

Out the window, I can see the trampoline, the sandbox, the treehouse.

"Mr. West."

"Yes, Mrs. Kennedy."

"I need you to be honest with me."

"Of course."

"My children—they are good children, aren't they?"

"Certainly."

"They're not spoiled."

"No, indeed."

"The president loved the Green Room most. It was his favorite room. I want to do something in that room for him that he would love."

Mr. West's eyes fall. That he would *have* loved, I realize. That's how I should have put it.

"Also, I'd like to give small gifts, things of Jack's, to members of the staff. They've been so good to us. Will you help me?"

"Yes, Mrs. Kennedy."

"Oh, Mr. West—" My voice starts to break then, and I can't let it. So I thank him and leave, Clint beside me; we walk along the colonnade. I look out to the saucer magnolias planted in the four corners of the Rose Garden. They came from a tidal basin, their branches silvered pale. In the rain, they glow. I remember a day in August 1961, when Jack and I came ashore from the boat to Bunny Mellon's house on Cape Cod. We'd come for a picnic and, as we walked toward the low dune, Jack said to me, "I'm going to ask Bunny to design a garden like the ones we saw in France."

"You should do that, Jack," I said.

"I'll tell her I've read Jefferson's gardening notes and I want the same flowers he would have had in his time."

"And you'll tell her you won't take no for an answer."

"That's the easy part," he said. "I never do." He reached for me then and pulled me close, his arm around me, as the house came into view. Then his arm dropped, he drew slightly away, and it was there again, that thin layer of remove that only really broke down in those last few months, after Patrick.

Had we really begun to figure everything out?

I turn away from the Rose Garden. Clint and I continue walking.

. . .

"We'll have to keep certain things," I tell my mother. "I've drafted a list. Documents, letters, everything on his desk—notes, doodles, even things that seem like trash."

My mother nods. "Yes."

"And the suit," I say. I see her face shift. "Have it stored just as it is."

Because when these four days are over, the world will churn on. The world will forget, and I can't let that happen.

I go to my room and lie down in that place on the bed where he will not be. I lie there and do not sleep. My mind is fire.

Saturday afternoon.

"I am going to walk with the caisson," I tell Clint. "I'm letting you know now because you are the one Bobby will send to talk me out of it."

"It might not be safe, Mrs. Kennedy."

"Well, we can't all be rushed around in fat black Cadillacs."

I look for the smile, some lightness again between us.

"If you walk, there will be concern for others as well," he says.

"Oh, Mr. Hill. They can do what they want. I am going to walk with the president." A sudden tightness in my throat. It takes me a moment to register it as anger. "I'm going to walk with the president to the church. I've told Bobby once already, but he either thinks I don't mean it or that I'll forget. I'll tell him again later today, and he will send you to talk me out of it."

He almost smiles then. How kind he has been. His cigarettes, my hair loose as we talked and smoked and laughed and drove with the windows unrolled out toward Wexford and the horses waiting in the fields, the chilled air in sheets of mist across the ridge.

They've begun to tell me things I do not remember:

That I climbed out of the seat and onto the back of the moving car.

That Clint ran forward, leapt, and pushed me back like some dark angel.

That when we reached Parkland Hospital, I wouldn't let go of Jack, even as they kept pleading with me, until Clint read my face and understood. He took off his coat and wrapped Jack's head and torso carefully, and only then was I willing to let go.

I don't remember any of this.

I remember the roses, the hospital corridor, the folding metal chair.

. . .

Sunday, November 24

I wake with a start and call out. His name in the echo. My eyes adjust. The room feels tight and empty. A room like a fist. I turn on the lamp so the light can push the dark out of my mind.

A soft knock. Bobby. He comes in and closes the door. He sits on the edge of the bed, holding my hand. He is drunk. It's after midnight. He starts to tell me about dinner—the jokes they made, how they were all laughing, then crying, how Ethel's wig got tossed like a Frisbee and landed on Pierre Salinger's head. I tell him about the conversation I had with Bunny earlier that evening, when Mr. West couldn't find the veil I wanted. Bunny found him frantic in the basement, almost in tears. She told him not to worry, she'd have one of the girls make a new veil for the morning.

"We call them girls," I say. "Why do we do that? They're women." Bobby nods, and I realize how drunk he is. He looks at me blankly and the blankness feels like someone stepping on my heart.

I fall asleep in his arms. When I open my eyes again, he's still awake. Hours have passed. Raw light has begun to sneak in. I wonder if he slept at all or if he's just been waiting that way, staring at the wall, that set in his jaw that makes him look old.

"You slept," he says.

I can't not see it. The crowd and the sun and the dark of the tunnel. That piece of your skull snapping away.

I've looked for scars on Clint's hands. I keep thinking that if it happened as they say it did, that he leapt up and pushed me back into the car, there would be scars from when he held me down and torched bits of me flew like embers through the air.

I don't tell Bobby this. He'd worry. I don't tell him how that day is a fractured collage on a screen in my mind.

"I'm going to walk," I say.

"You can't do that, Jackie. They'll all feel they have to walk with you."

"I don't care what they do."

He looks at me, like he's about to say something else.

"I need to see Jack again, Bobby, before they take him away. Will you go with me?"

"Yes."

"You'll come in time so we can do that?"

"Yes."

There is the sound of someone walking down the hall outside. We wait until the sound is gone. Then he gets up and leaves.

...

From the doorway of the East Room, I watch as they shift the flag partway down and raise the lid.

I take Bobby's hand. We walk up and look in.

"Mr. Hill?" I say without turning to look. I know he's there.

"Yes, Mrs. Kennedy."

"Will you bring me scissors?"

I put the cuff links into the casket, and the scrimshaw. Bobby puts in his PT 109 tiepin and a silver rosary. I tuck in the letter I wrote, Caroline's letter, and John's (Caroline had guided John's hand). Clint gives me the scissors, then steps back and quietly signals the guards to turn away as I bring the blade against Jack's cheekbone, above his brow, and cut a lock of hair.

In less than an hour, the children and I will walk down the steps of the North Portico. The guards will bring you out to a caisson drawn by gray horses. We will get into a car with Bobby, Lyndon, and Lady Bird, to follow you to the Capitol, down a gauntlet of people along the cold avenue. The crowd will be silent. No cries, no calls, no ringing of your name, just the rhythmic strike of hooves against pavement, sticks against drums. I will whisper to Caroline, "We're going to say goodbye now, tell Daddy how much we love him and how much we will miss him, always. . . ." She'll kneel with me, her little face glancing toward mine. "You just kiss like this," I will whisper as we lean to kiss the flag that covers you, my eyes half-closed more for her sake than anyone else's, my lips moving in a prayer that feels weightless. Always. How that word lingers. I can just see her small hand reaching like she wants to lift the flag to peek underneath, to touch you one last time.

...

Riding back from the Capitol, Bobby tells me Oswald was shot that morning, coming out of the police station basement garage.

"They were moving him to a jail," Bobby says. "Some man, a

nightclub owner, stepped out of the crowd and fired. Point-blank range."

"He'll survive?"

Bobby shakes his head.

I feel a chill then, deep, settle in me. I don't speak for the rest of the ride.

I am aware Jack is gone as soon as I get back to the Residence. His body nowhere near me now.

That afternoon, I step out of the elevator. Onassis is there, waiting, as if materialized out of thin air.

"Thank you for coming," I say.

"Of course."

"When did you arrive?"

"An hour ago."

"You spoke with Lee?"

He nods. "I was in Hamburg when she called. She told me to come, but I waited until I received your note. You were kind to think of me."

I take his arm, and we walk through the Center Hall.

"I want you to let me know if you need anything," he says.

"Thank you."

"Anything."

"They say it was a silly little communist who did it," I say. "But I don't believe that."

"They will say many things."

"And now Oswald's been shot, so we'll never know for sure."

"There's very little we know for sure."

"That's true, I suppose."

"You are a strong woman. Noble and wise and brave. You'll survive this, as awful as it is."

I tell him then that I am determined to build something transcendent to outdo this awful thing they did to Jack. I am aware that I use the word *they*. I don't correct it. Someone has lied. I'm not quite sure who. Talking to Onassis, I feel more grounded than I've felt since it happened. Maybe because he's a stranger. Not of our world. He knows what it is to be outside.

"How has Johnson been?" he asks. I'm grateful he does not say President Johnson. Onassis will do this, I've noticed. Intuit these tiny things that matter.

"He's been good to me. Though Bobby doesn't agree."

"Why?"

"He says Lyndon shouldn't have forced me to take part in the swearing in. I don't see it that way. I wasn't forced. These last few days, Lyndon's been only generous. 'Little Lady,' he said to me yesterday, 'anything you want in these rooms is yours.'"

Onassis laughs. "Always the wonderful mimic."

"I've told Johnson all I want is his promise that the work Jack started will be finished. The civil-rights bill passed and, at least for now, no turnover. Everyone who wants to stay in their jobs should be able to stay."

"And what about you?" Onassis says. An open-ended question. I am careful as I answer.

"The children and I will live in Georgetown for now, in a loaned house, until I find my own. It is disconcerting watching our life being boxed up, trying to keep track of what will go where."

He nods. He's about to ask something else, then his eye is caught, a slight hardness. I turn. Bobby's walking toward us from the stairs.

"We need you for a few decisions, Jackie," Bobby says. "We're in the West Sitting Hall." He doesn't say who the *we* are, but the implication is that Onassis is not.

"Thank you for being here, Ari," I say.

Onassis holds my hand for a moment, then lets go.

. . .

That night, Bobby brings me the Mass card with Jack's picture. At the rotunda, he says, hundreds of thousands are in line to pay their respects. At a certain point they'll have to turn people away.

When I wake up, he is gone, the sun rising, curtains rinsed in flame. Today is John's birthday. He's turning three.

Getting dressed, I tell Provi, "I can't let John's birthday get entirely lost in this day."

As Kenneth is setting the veil to my hair, Pam comes in to remind me I need to be ready by 9:45. The car will be waiting.

I look at my face in the mirror—swollen eyes, swollen cheeks, like I've spent the night underwater. I draw the veil down.

"I'd like you to come, Jackie." That's what you said a few weeks before Dallas. Then you added, "You'd be a great help."

"That's why you want me to come?" I teased you. "So I can be useful?"

"I want you with me." It was strangely direct, the way you said it. Then you did that little awkward thing with your hair you used to do when we first met, pushing it back from your face, and I suddenly realized you were nervous. Even after ten years of marriage, it made you nervous to admit you needed me.

"I've changed my mind," I tell Miss Shaw. "The children should stay here this morning. They don't need to go to the Capitol. They can meet us at St. Matthew's."

I take the elevator down with Bobby and Teddy. The car comes around to the North Portico. We drive down Pennsylvania Avenue. I'm between Jack's brothers as we enter the rotunda. We walk to the casket, kneel, rise, and walk back out the same door. A blaze of daylight. I reach for Bobby's hand. At the base of the steps, we wait as Jack is carried down to us. We wait until he's lifted onto the gun carriage. Then we climb back into the car.

"Unroll the window, please," I say. Strains of the Marine Corps band drift as we flow down the road to the White House and a milling sea of world leaders. My mind starts to work through them, cataloging, like I used to do at a state dinner or event. De Gaulle, Prince Philip, the king of Belgium, the mayor of Berlin, Eamon de Valera, Queen Frederica, Haile Selassie.

All morning, Bobby says, there've been assassination threats. Dean Rusk has tried to talk Lyndon out of walking. They've tried to persuade De Gaulle to take a car, citing the nine attempts on his life so far. Just before we get out of the car, Bobby asks again if I really think it's wise to walk.

"What does *wise* mean at this point?"

I take my place with Bobby and Teddy as the procession assembles. The cadets; the Marines; the Scottish Black Watch in their white spats, plumed headdresses, tartan kilts. The bagpipes begin; notes rend the air. I reach for Bobby, but after several steps I drop his hand and walk alone. Rows of people everywhere, along the sidewalk and gathered on the balconies above, children standing with solemn faces on the curb. I keep my eyes fixed on the riderless horse, the sheathed sword, empty saddle, boots reversed in the stirrups. It's a huge gelding and the young soldier leading him is tall, but he can't manage that horse. He can't make it behave. Everything else is in such perfect order, not a beat off—all but that mad, lovely horse and the dissonant tattoo of its hooves on the street, the bright defiant glint of tack.

For you, history was never something bitter old men wrote. History, you told me once, makes us what we are. As we walk, I watch that horse and think of you as a boy in that small bedroom, reading stories of kings and warriors, the Knights of the Round Table, your Buchan and your Marlborough. For you, history was full of heroes. Human, flawed, dazzling.

At St. Matthew's, I wait for the children. The car pulls up, and they scramble out in their pale-blue coats. I take them by the hand, and together we walk up the steps. I feel stronger when they're with me. As I bend to kiss Cardinal Cushing's ring, John starts to cry.

"Where is Daddy?"

"Shhh, darling," I say, and he bites down gently on his lip, trying to be good, and for a moment I regret it.

During the service, I lose my composure only once, when Luigi Vena sings *Ave Maria*. Clint Hill leans forward to hand me a handkerchief, and I realize I'm crying. Caroline has edged her small body right up against mine, like she could hold me there, in place. John squirms on his seat, and I feel a stab of panic. I just need to get out, sweep them up in my arms, away from all this.

Mr. Foster picks up John and carries him away as Cardinal Cushing says, "May the angels, dear Jack . . ." His voice breaks. Caroline is still pressed right against me, and I can feel the riderless horse outside, waiting, the buck of that horse, its dark mad revolt, the weight of absence on its back.

Afterward, on the steps, Mr. Foster brings John to me.

They secure the casket to the caisson. The men salute. I lean down to John and whisper. He raises his hand to his brow.

I tell Clint I've changed my mind again. The children will not go to Arlington. He and Agent Foster work to find a car for the children. They're taking someone's car, asking the man and his wife to get out of it. They bundle the children in, and I am suddenly alone.

"Mrs. Kennedy," Clint says. "It's time to go."

At the close of the ceremony at Arlington, following the gun salute, "Taps" is played. I take Bobby's hand. The hill is awash in flowers.

. . .

Before heading upstairs to the children, I meet with De Gaulle, Selassie, and others at a reception in the Yellow Oval Room. I spend a few moments with De Gaulle. I show him the chest he'd sent as a gift after our visit to Paris. Daisies in a vase on top of it. I take one and give it to him.

"*Souvenez-vous*," I say. Remember.

He puts the flower carefully in his jacket pocket. When he raises his eyes, the expression is not what I expect. Depth, a true sorrow.

He inclines toward me, a slight bow. "You have taught us how to grieve," he says.

"Jack wanted very much to be a friend of France," I say, "but it didn't quite work, did it?" I'm on the verge of adding, *You didn't let him,* but Jack would not have wanted me to be bitter, and now it's too late. De Gaulle knows what he did, and he knows what I wanted to say even without my saying it.

"I am sorry," he says, and in his eyes, there is shame.

"I have to leave now. You see, it's my son's birthday. We are going to try to have a little party upstairs. This is what I have left to do."

Upstairs is chaos. Children hopping around, paper hats and streamers, balloons and noisemaker horns. I watch little John go from kneeling to standing, then balance on one foot like a pelican on a chair. I take my mother aside.

"Will you do something for me?" I say.

"Of course."

"Find Pam and have her send a message. I want the tack of the riderless horse. Have it saved for me—saddle, bridle, blanket, boots, sword. Instruct them not to clean it."

My mother nods, and the party continues. The adults look tired, but the children plunder on. John, with bits of cake and frosting ground into his shirt, is tearing through his gifts. My heart quickens, watching him.

They will say I was calculating, dispassionate, an actress. They will say I kept that tack for show. They will say that day was theater, as if my grief were some kind of charade. They will not know how much I craved it—that sweet stink of horse mixed in with oiled leather, that trace of the dance and the fight. How much I wanted to sink my face into that smell and remember.

. . .

Midnight again. Everyone is gone, asleep, or they've left, flown off. The day is done. Bobby and I are alone in Jack's office. The lights are off. The curtains open. I asked for them to be left open. I wanted to look out at the night, the stars in bloom.

Bobby stands with me by the long windows. Neither of us can

sit for any length of time. The sky so clear. Moonlight rakes the floor.

"Well," he finally says. "Shall we go?"

I pick up the phone. "I'd like to speak to Mr. Hill, please."

The flame is visible as we cross the bridge, the rows of stones bright against the hill. At the grave, Bobby stands beside me, his hand woven through mine.

"What are you thinking?" he asks when we're in the car again, driving back.

A day, years ago. Jack and I were out sailing. I'd caught sight of a bird—some kind of hawk. The light was in my eyes and the bird was a distant shape. I tried to identify the lines of its wings and flight. I shielded the light from my eyes and tracked the bird as it shifted course, heading toward the coast behind us. The boat tacked, and a sea rushed under the hull. The bow rose, then dipped. "Hang on, Jackie," Jack said. I turned. He was just sitting there, open water behind him, managing the lines, one hand on the mainsheet, one on the tiller, his face bright, that casual beauty of him so brisk and alive, like he was cut right out of the wind, the salt air, and the light.

"What are you thinking?" Bobby asks again as the car turns onto the avenue. I don't answer. The memory fades. His asking dimmed it. I lean my forehead against the window glass to close my mind.

I can't sleep. I can't even lie down without seeing his head destroyed in my lap. I wander around, sit in a chair, smoke. The room has a terrible wrongness. I take one of the little blue pills. I still can't sleep. The stars drift.

Later that night, I hear Bobby cry out again from a bedroom down the hall.

I should go to him, I think.

. . .

At the desk in the West Sitting Hall, I write to Lyndon.

> *Thank you for walking yesterday—behind Jack. You did not have to do that—I am sure many people forbid you to take such a risk—but you did it anyway.*
> *Thank you for your letters to my children. . . .*

I pause. Bobby still doesn't trust him. Just yesterday he called Johnson "the usurper."

"You've never liked him," I said. "But we weren't always fair. We ridiculed him."

"He never knew."

"It was still awful."

Bobby looked at me, his eyes level. "I won't let him take credit for what Jack did."

"He and Lady Bird have been kind to me, and I am grateful. They're going to let the White House school stay open so Caroline and her friends can finish the year."

"He wants your support. Ask him to rename Cape Canaveral after Jack. Jack would've wanted that."

"Jack wouldn't want me to ask."

"He dreamed of putting an American on the moon. Renaming Canaveral is a way to say that."

Then, because it is Bobby, I agree.

I learn that the caparisoned horse is called Black Jack. The night after Caroline's birthday, I write to the secretary of the Army to inform him I'd like to buy that horse when it is retired.

. . .

Thanksgiving Day. We go to visit Jack at Arlington, then fly to Hyannis Port.

Rose meets us downstairs. "I have to keep busy," she says. "I can't stop praying."

I go to find Joe. He is in his room, waiting for me. This man who cannot move or walk, can barely speak. The ambassador. The king. The maker of legends. We were all so certain then. His face brightens when I come in. I sit in a chair by his bed, hold his hand, and I tell him the story of his son's death. I talk around the gap of time where my mind is still scrubbed out.

I tell him that Bobby and I will make good decisions about Jack's library. I tell him they want me to tell the story, not just of Jack's death but his life, because if we don't tell it, others will, and those others might tear him apart and try to dismantle his legacy. So they're asking me to do this. We've chosen a writer named William Manchester to create an official account. I ask Joe if he remembers Manchester and that other book he wrote, *Portrait of a President,* the one Jack liked.

I stare at the bureau as I tell Joe these things, tracing the knobs and inlay, whorls of wood through the lacquered finish.

Joe makes a little sound. Tears flood his face.

"I'm so sorry," I say. "I've said too much, haven't I? You see, there is just so much in me right now, and I feel you should know everything. I want to make sure this all makes sense to you."

His eyes search mine and, in his eyes, I can see that for him, as for me, everything is meaningless now.

...

The morning after Thanksgiving, I call Theodore White and arrange an interview.

"I will do this," I tell Bobby. "I'll do all these things you're asking me to do, because that's what Jack would want. But when it's over, I need to disappear."

Theodore White arrives that night in a heavy rain. I sit on the low sofa. He sits across from me.

"How can I help you?" I say.

He reminds me we spoke in the morning on the phone. I called and asked him to come.

"I will tell you the story," I say.

The biggest motorcade from the airport.
        It was hot. Wild. Like Mexico or Vienna.
    The sun was so strong on our faces. . . .

I tell him about the gap of seconds between seconds.

I do not cry. I keep my hands folded, everything in me very still except the words. They are bright and molten, flowing out of my mouth. I see it like it's still happening. A perfectly clean piece of skull detaching itself from his head, rising away as I reached.

It was not repulsive to me for one moment. Nothing was. Your head was so beautiful. I was just trying to keep it in. That wonderful expression on your face you'd get when you were asked a question, just before you answered.

"I would have done things differently," I explain to White. "Turned sooner—after the first shot—and pulled him down, but I was so taken by that expression on his face, that abstracted, puzzled look I've always loved. *What is it, Jack?* I went to say, and then the next shot came."

I go on talking. White goes on writing. There are others in the room. They listen like trees, and the rain strikes the window, and bits of my words and his questions float, parsed smaller, splintered to powerless dust, rings of smoke shot through with sickening yellow lamplight.

"Jack was magic." I use that word, then stop.

We never pay attention, do we? To what we should.

In the downstairs room that night with Theodore White, his notepad, pages wrapped thick around the top edge, pencil flying fast across, and the darker shadows of Bobby and the others, silent at the hem of things, faces half lit, ghostly, obscure, a quiet word exchanged, they watch and wait, the occasional bright orange glow of a cigarette.

The children are asleep upstairs.

We imagine time will clarify our intention. Who we were, how we lived, what we achieved. We want to believe we will be treated with integrity, with fairness and compassion. But history is not so forgiving, is it?

"When did farewell really come?" White is asking me now.

Turn on the lights so they can see Jackie—

Take off your glasses, Jackie, so they can see you.

These moments, I could explain, these little things Jack used to say when he was asking me to be more visible, to play my part—these are the lean, sharp cliffs of my mind where I walk.

"When did farewell really come?" White asks again.

How dark in the room it's grown.

"It's become almost an obsession with me," I say. "This one small thing I want to tell you. At night, before going to sleep, Jack loved to listen to music. He loved the record from the musical *Camelot*. I'd play it for him on the old Victrola. His favorite lines, near the end: *Don't let it be forgot, that once there was a spot, for one brief shining moment, that was known as Camelot.*" I pause. "You imagine I'm making things up."

I inhale, and the cigarette brings back a little of my mind.

White has stopped writing. "I think I have enough."

"There's more," I say. I suddenly find I don't want this to be done.

"Let me start with what I have." He smiles then. A strange sad smile.

I show him to a small room, a typewriter on the desk.

When he returns with typewritten pages, I've sharpened two pencils. I read on the sofa. He's written eloquently. Beautifully. Nothing graphic. No blood, brains, gore. On the one hand, I'm grateful. At the same time, there's a great deal missing. I work over each line, the pencil marking up the text.

At two in the morning, White stands by the wall phone in the kitchen and dictates his story to the *Life* offices in New York.

"The *Camelot* bit?" he says into the receiver but glancing at me. "You're saying you want to strike that? Or tone it down?" He catches my eye. I shake my head.

"No," he says into the phone. "That stays."

Then he is gone. They are all gone, and the house is empty again. Just me and the children. A glass of water on the nightstand. I lie on the bed and sleep without sleeping.

It is almost tomorrow, I think.

December 1963

At the White House, they've laid out Jack's clothes on the bed. For me to decide what to keep.

Trunks and boxes, lids flung open. Such a disarray.

I put the Lincoln book back. Not where it belongs. Just flat on a shelf. Mr. West will find it. He will set it in its place, and all will continue.

The day before the children and I leave, I walk through the house with Mr. West. In the doorway of the state dining room, I pause.

"Mr. West."

"Mrs. Kennedy."

"I love this portrait of Lincoln."

"As do I, Mrs. Kennedy."

"I love that it was at first rejected for not being enough, but then his son bought it, because he saw his father in it, and his wife sent it to Roosevelt, and now it is here. Things don't always happen in a straight line, do they, Mr. West?"

I told you once I wanted the children to understand it would be temporary, living here. But in the end, it was ours, wasn't it, Jack? This house I never loved. It grew up with us. Became beautiful with us. Restored to something it never was before but was always meant to be.

"Mr. West, do you think you could do something for me?"

"Of course, Mrs. Kennedy."

The sun is low. Afternoon rays shoot like arrows through the windows as we make our way upstairs. We come to the bedroom.

"I'd like a mantel carving for this room," I say. "Do you think that would be possible?"

"Yes, Mrs. Kennedy." A gentleness in his voice I almost can't bear.

From my pocket, I draw out a folded piece of paper.

In this room lived John Fitzgerald Kennedy with his wife, Jacqueline—during the two years ten months and three days he was president of the United States, January 20, 1961–November 22, 1963.

"Thank you, Mr. West."

I hand it to him. How many lists I've made on yellow lined paper just like this. Lists of names and plans.

The next day is Friday, the sixth of December. It's the slightest thing, the sadness I feel, the children's small hands in mine as the three of us walk out the door. Fresh cold air snaps my face.

No photographs of him. Not yet. I still can't bear to see his face.

I lie upstairs in the house in Georgetown with books, cigarettes, magazines. Everyday sounds unfold around me. Provi and Nanny Shaw getting the children dressed, my children, their little sweaters and coats, Caroline's bag packed for school. I want to be with them. But I'm still too far off to the side.

I regret that flimsy trope of Camelot already. So desperate. Saccharine. You would have hated it. Even if you did like the song. I should have chosen something heroic, about greatness, strength, risk— something to do with the Greeks.

In the afternoons, I let the room grow dark. I watch how the last of the daylight retreats and the dusk begins to rise, the room by increments destroyed.

. . .

At first there's a constant stream of visitors. I keep thinking I'll be happy to see them.

Joe Alsop, Betty Spaulding, Ben and Tony Bradlee. I tell them the story.

I should have done it differently, I say. Turned sooner, after the first shot.

I've said the same words so many times, and each time, I feel closer to saying it for the last time. Each time I feel something lighten inside me. But an hour later, the dark of it is back.

If only I'd looked right instead of left
If only I had pulled him down, the second shot would not have hit
If I'd been paying more attention
If I had not been complaining in my head about the sun
If I hadn't been wanting so much, the cool promise of the tunnel ahead, the green of the park beyond.

And why red roses in Dallas? Everywhere else they were yellow. I should have known then.

. . .

Bobby comes. He has breakfast with the children and brings Caroline to school. He comes again at the end of the day. He reads to the children and puts them to bed. He tucks them in and teaches them prayers they did not learn. Then he comes to find me.

"How are you?" he asks.

Everything hangs by a thread. The world, I could explain, is split. Terrifying. Simplified. Every night I lie down with fear and a clarity so sharp it cuts behind my eyes. Jack was killed by American violence, he called it that once, the hatred that built this country.

"We're soaked in it, Bobby," I say, "this violence we pretend we've outrun."

I tell him again, detail by detail, the story of what happened. Like Scheherazade. Each night extending into morning. Only each night, here, the story is the same.

"I have to tell it until it is out of me," I say.

We lie on the bed, fully clothed. He has taken off his tie. We are close, his hand on my face, fingertips moving lightly. He does this sometimes, touches me without seeming to realize. It is not sexual or intimate but like he's trying to remember what touch feels like.

Through the window, the moon.

We talk about the library and about some papers I need to sign. I ask about Ethel and his children. I tell him how I want a Christmas in Palm Beach with lights and stockings, like every Christmas, where John and Caroline can ask the questions they always ask: *How big is my present? How many will there be?* At the same time, I don't want Christmas at all. Then he leaves and everyone is gone. Even the room is gone. The bureau. The bookshelves. The bed. All that remains is the window.

Sometimes after midnight, in the blue dark with my cigarette smoke, I will say Jack's name. The one hard syllable carries. I call to him quietly as though he might come back to me.

...

Bob McNamara sends over two portraits of Jack, with a message saying he'd like me to keep one as a gift and he will keep the other. He's asking me to choose. As I look at the two paintings, it gets harder to remember Jack in my mind, to see, for example, his face as it was that day I walked in on his bath a year ago wearing only my boots and the long riding shirt. How intimate it was—the surprise in his face—one of those small nothing moments in a marriage where everything happens.

I leave the portraits propped outside my bedroom door. I'll ring McNamara tomorrow, thank him, and explain that for now I need to return them both.

That night, John comes into my room with a lollipop, looking for his toy train.

"In the basket in your closet, darling?"

"Not there."

"Downstairs in the kitchen?"

"No."

There's a stain of lollipop around his mouth. I am suddenly exhausted.

"Time to brush your teeth, my love. Go do that, then come kiss me good night."

"My train."

"I'll help you look in the morning."

He studies me for a moment.

"I promise," I say.

Satisfied, he trots out but stops in the doorway, looking at something around the door. The paintings, I realize, as he takes the lollipop out of his mouth and leans to kiss the canvas.

"Good night, Daddy," he says.

. . .

Days slip by. The sunlight tidal. It creeps in, floods the room, recedes.

It feels bizarre, even cruel, how the world continues.

What did you know, before it happened?

You didn't want to go to Dallas. You could feel it, couldn't you? The hatred lying in wait. They talked you into going. They said everything would be fine.

How much has been lost for the sake of that word—fine?

Someone is home. John and Nanny Shaw. I hear his small voice. Footsteps below. I should get up and go downstairs. It's cold—the *should*.

Nighttime again. The children stand at the foot of my bed. They want to kiss me good night. Sweet, pinched faces, miles away.

...

Still Bobby comes.
Beloved.
Familiar.

"How are you?" he says, just like always.

The world is hardly there.

"What can I do for you, Jackie? What do you need?"

I need Jack.
I need everything back the way it was. Even the things that infuriated me, the things we had not yet dealt with. I miss them now, desperately. What else could I possibly need?

January 1964

Outside this interim house that is not mine (lent to me, as much of my life, it seems, has been lent), crowds linger on the sidewalk. They call my name and leave bouquets of flowers and gifts, offerings that get trampled, stolen, knocked over.

"They want to eat me alive," I tell Bobby.

"No," he says, "they worship you."

"Only because I'm obliterated."

I hate how bitter it sounds. I know it bothers him—that tone in my voice. Like I'm accusing him too. Which isn't what I mean.

We talk about the writer Manchester, who's anxious to get started on the book he's been contracted to write. Not yet, I say. I'm not ready. There are other interviews as well that have to be done with Arthur Schlesinger about Jack's presidency.

"To set the historical record," Bobby says. "We need to start in a few weeks."

Too soon.

He tells me about the Warren Commission investigation of the assassination, to confirm there was no conspiracy.

"How could there not have been a conspiracy?" I say.

I've gone back to the Edith Hamilton book, *The Greek Way*. I've reread, twice, the chapter on Euripides, who wrote about war with a modern eye, peeling away the sham glory of violence to the evil underneath. He was the one who wrote about the women. Hecuba, Andromache, Cassandra. The ones who were left.

"I won't be able to stay here," I tell Bobby. "In Washington."

"Where do you want to go?"

"France."

"I mean where here?"

"Not here."

"New York?"

"I love New York."

"Good," he says. "We'll move to New York."

I smile. "We? That'll cause a stir."

"I'll run for senator from New York. We'll move there."

"Won't we have to stagger things a bit? People will begin to think the unimaginable."

He doesn't answer, and I suddenly realize he's already considered this.

"No one will think anything," he says, "because there's nothing to think."

"You must try to like Lyndon a little more," I say lightly, "if you want to run for Senate."

Still Bobby comes, every morning, every evening. And still there's the burnout design of that day in November between us—the memory I have and he does not.

Sometimes we talk. Sometimes hours pass without us exchanging a word. Sometimes I cry, and he holds me until I sleep. Sometimes when I wake up, he's gone, but more often he's sitting by my bed in a funnel of light with my book *The Greek Way,* underlining passages, dog-earing a page.

"That book will be ruined, Bobby, if you keep going at it like that."

He glances up, like he'd forgotten I was there.

"Read to me, please," I say, taking the book from him, turning pages until I come to a passage I want. "Here."

His voice is awkward at first—the funny harsh twang that reminds me of Jack, though his voice is rougher. I settle against the pillow, close my eyes. The words feel soft and cool.

He comes to the end of a section.

"Do you want me to go on?" he says.

"I love the stories of the Greeks," I say, "how they believed in tragedy as transformation, that out of horrific pain you could construct a way forward."

He doesn't say anything.

"It wasn't a perfect marriage, Bobby."

"That doesn't matter."

"I shouldn't have left him last fall to go to Greece with Lee. I was devastated over Patrick. That was most of it, but I was angry too."

I don't elaborate. Even to say it feels like a betrayal.

"Jack loved you, Jackie, more than he ever loved anyone—"

"Don't. Just lie down with me for a while."

He is looking at the wall across the room. I touch that part of his cheekbone, not with love or sympathy, not with anything really beyond an abstract macabre fascination. I can see how grief has done its work, shifting the structure of his face under the skin, darker hollows below his eyes. Scoured. The line of his mouth is thin and dry.

The sky is clear. I've left the curtains pulled back, and the moon shines through the divided window sash.

That night I cry for hours, my body like some vague streak of lightning in his arms.

He is gone when I wake up again. The overhead is off, but he left a lamp on. The room is empty. Just that pool of lamplight and the burning strangeness of being the one who remains.

. . .

I agree to meet with Arthur Schlesinger for the oral history he's building about Jack's presidency.

"I won't talk to him about Dallas," I tell Bobby the morning Arthur is due to arrive.

"You don't have to."

"And these tapes will be sealed, for as long as I decide they should be?"

"Yes."

"And I'll keep the right to strike anything I wish I hadn't said?"

"It's all up to you."

"What about the writer, Manchester—is that also up to me?"

"If that's what you want."

"Good."

As the tapes begin to spin, it's like I can't talk. Arthur's voice is familiar, kind, but the words slip over the surface of things.

"Jack would read," I say, "waking, at the table, at meals, after dinner, in the bathtub, a book propped open on his bureau as he was doing his tie. It's funny, the things you remember that surface out of nowhere."

I talk about General de Gaulle, Khrushchev's wife, and the missile crisis—how hard it was, tense and strained, those thirteen days.

"When Jack came home for a nap, I'd lie down with him. When he went for a walk, he'd take me with him. And do you know what he said when the crisis was over? 'Well, if anybody's going to shoot me, today's the day they should do it. I'll never top this.' He was the most unselfconscious person I ever met. In America, we have a great civilization—and so many don't realize it. He and I used to talk about that."

I stop there.

I don't say anything about how *Once upon a time there was a girl who wanted to disappear, but instead she grew up to be an artist whose medium was fame.*

I don't talk about how every relationship requires its own set of strategies.

I don't say anything about mad young hearts or how once, before we were married, I was reading a poem to him, he leaned over and kissed me, and the words and the heat mixed between our mouths.

I do not, of course, tell about that day of the tub and the whip at Glen Ora, or how I told Jack it wasn't the women—it was never the women—it was the writer who'd come along someday to dig the dirt up and blow the house down.

I don't talk about how after Patrick slipped out of the world, I left and went to Greece, even when Jack asked me to stay. I turned away from his face and the longing in it I had waited years for because I'd finally given up waiting, and I didn't want to risk my heart, and now I deeply regret that. I don't talk about Dallas: the blazing sun, the sound, the sudden dark of his blood—hypnotic, mystical, iridescent.

You don't get time back. Any of it. You don't get to make a different choice in a moment you think will be just another moment in a span of years you assume you have.

You don't get the chance, for example, to turn around and choose instead to stay.

Sometimes, oddly, I see him throwing a football in Georgetown, that free, beautiful strength of his body, even when his back would twist and he would be in pain.

I don't talk about the countless times he'd look at me across a room, at a political event, a dinner, or a party. He'd search a sea of people to find me, his eyes on my face, and I became transparent, rootless, a balloon, belonging nowhere and to no one else when he looked at me that way.

I say none of this.

Life, when it happens, is more full of silence than words. I give Arthur only the words he came for.

The tapes spin. One reel flows to the next. I tong ice into a glass, sip my drink, and I tell him how sometimes, at night, Jack and I would read together and sometimes he'd ask for a record, the floor cool under my feet as I crossed the room to set one on the turntable; the notes would rise, and when the songs ended, every night before bed, he would say a prayer.

I glance at Bobby. Another match, another cigarette; it all continues on until we get to the part about happiness.

"I was happy," I say, "for Jack, that he could be proud of me. Because you know it made him so happy, and that made me happy. So those were our happiest years."

The words catch in my throat. I glance at the tape. Arthur looks at me. I nod. He shuts it off.

There was nothing rarefied about it. It was simple. A boy and a girl. A man and a woman. A marriage. With all the tiny thorns and joys that reside in that word.

"Sometimes I feel it's wrong," I say. I don't look at Bobby, because I know he won't want me to say this. "We talk like there is only one history."

"People believed in Jack," Arthur says. "I think if there's something the world will need a year from now, or fifty years from now, it will be to know there was once a man worth believing in."

The tape is still off. My throat so dry, like all that's real are those things left unsaid.

A few weeks ago I was out with the children, dirty snow plowed up on either side of the street. We ducked into a drugstore. I'd promised them hot chocolate. As I walked up to the counter to order, John saw the magazine cover with the blurred photograph of us in the car.

Mummy, close your eyes.

. . .

"You have to get stronger," Bobby says to me after Arthur leaves. "Get past this. Move on."
"That's Ethel talking."
"There's a priest we'd like you to meet."
"Ethel thinks I need some God."
"He's a great tennis player."
"Ethel thinks I need a better forehand."
"Please, Jackie, just try."
I look at him, the dizzying rush of alone.

He thinks he understands. Your brother. He thinks we are in this together, but he was eating lunch when he heard. A tuna fish sandwich. Ethel answered the ringing phone and told him to pick up the patio extension. It was Hoover. Calling to say you'd been shot. That's how Bobby learned. Through the words of a man he did not trust.

He knows nothing of bone and blood.

I am suddenly angry. Ethel is moving on, the rest of the country is moving on, and your brother is telling me to move on, even as he is still falling apart. He's lost weight. He barely sleeps. He's been wearing your clothes—your old blue topcoat, your leather bomber jacket that hangs all wrong on him, your kid brother, his frame too small. I should be more forgiving. He is sleepless, as I am sleepless. Tormented by the possibility that actions he took in Cuba and how he cracked down on the mob, those choices he made as attorney general, could have led to your death and maybe did. In that sense, perhaps, he is no further away from the awful dark of it than I am.

"I'm sorry, Jackie," Bobby says.

We take the children to ski in Sun Valley in March, then to Antigua for Easter. We stay at Bunny Mellon's house in Half Moon Bay.

Every evening before dinner, I swim from the edge of the cliff to the forked palm tree and back. Bobby doesn't like it. Too close to dusk, he says.

I smile. "What are you afraid of? Sharks?"

He waits for me on the beach. When I turn my head to breathe, I can see his small dark figure, knees tucked up to his chest as he waits for the sun to go down and for me to come out. He meets me in the shallows with a towel.

"Thank you," I say. He takes a step back. There are new faint splits in the bond between us, moments when his hand brushes mine. Or he'll reach for my face without thinking. Then his fingers will pause, retract.

We don't talk about it. It means nothing.

A few nights before we leave for Washington, he and I sit out on the porch after the others have drifted off to bed.

"You shouldn't smoke," he says. I keep smoking. He won't say it again. Then it is just the silence and the two of us alone, awkward again, under the weight of the hot night and the terrible stars.

I'd kissed him earlier that evening. After my swim. I'd gone past the palm tree. He followed along the shore, carrying the towel. I got out at the end of the beach. We were far down, out of sight of the house. As he put the towel over my shoulders, I turned and kissed him. It startled him at first. Then not. I moved closer. No one else was there. His hands touched me, and it felt almost familiar—the touch—not awkward at all. No shock in it. Only his hands on my body, my neck, my face. I felt like I was no one. Like we were two people who had ceased to exist. In the dusk, his eyes were empty, pale as glass, apart from that cool hunger. Then his hand dropped, and I pulled the towel around me. We walked in silence back to the house.

"I used to love the night," I say to him now on the porch.

"What did you love?"

"Walking around in it. In the summers, in Newport, I'd go down to the edge of the lawn and watch the boats and lightships on the bay. It felt magical, that glow of night water and lights in the distance. Sometimes I would just lie out there in my night-gown in the grass and watch the stars in their massive Van Gogh pinwheels."

The porch ceiling fan spins, a low creaking sound through the heat.

"That's a nice memory," he says.

"It's only memory," I say. "You can't expect too much of it."

. . .

A week after I come home, a letter arrives from William Man-chester, requesting a meeting to talk about the book he's been contracted to write. About the death of the president. The few days before it happened, the few days after, the map of decisions and events.

"I need more time, Bobby. There must be others he can talk to."

"He's already started."

"Writing? How can he have started?"

"The agreement—"

"I don't want a book about that day."

"There will be books," Bobby says, his voice calm, pragmatic, like he's talking to a child. "You need to meet with Manchester, then the Warren Commission. Then the record will be there."

"And I can stop?"

"Yes."

"And it will be over?"

"Yes."

Yesterday, at Hickory Hill, I played tennis with Father McSorley, Ethel's priest. As we played, I asked Father McSorley if God would separate me from Jack if I killed myself.

"What about John and Caroline?" the priest asked.

I explained I feel like I'm no good to my children as I am right now.

"They'd be better off with Bobby and Ethel. They could have a normal life."

"I don't agree," the priest said.

The score, I remember, was deuce. I served. The ball nicked the edge of the service box and flew out of his reach. My point.

"I need all of this behind me," I say to Bobby now.

It's spring again. Buds on the trees. How can it be spring?

. . .

The writer, William Manchester, is edgy, red-faced. Faint stains of sweat when he takes off his jacket. Nails bitten down to the quick.

He's arrived with his tape recorder, his notebook. He has a kind of unkempt intensity. Feral. He was a Marine, I remember, as Bobby walks him into the living room.

"Please sit down, Mr. Manchester," I say. "Would you like a cigarette?"

"Quit two years ago."

I strike a match. "Are you sure?"

He hesitates, then accepts, and I relax. He is not a Mailer. He's one I can manage.

"Are you going to put down all the facts," I ask, "like who ate what for breakfast? Are you going to put yourself in the book too?"

He looks at me for a moment. "I'm not part of the story."

"I think you know what I mean. How will you create an objective account?"

He places the tape recorder behind the plant on a side table.

"Have you started the tape?" I ask.

"Do you hear it?"

"No."

He nods, a little smile.

As his questions begin, I realize he's already lived through that day. He is asking the questions that matter.

Manchester is different.

"You seem to know most of the details," I say. "What do you really need from me?"

"Everything you remember."

He's nervous. I can feel it. He is also looking for something in me no one else has wanted to see. I remember Bobby telling me that Manchester was in the ground war at Okinawa, the island battlefields of Tarawa in 1943, from November 20 to November 23. Twenty years before Dallas, he was in the middle of death. Men next to him were killed. He's been spattered by blood. Like me, he knows what it is to be the one who survives.

"Mr. Manchester."

"William."

"Yes," I say, but I won't use his first name. "You were in World War II, like my husband."

A veil across his eyes draws closed.

"Did that change you?" I ask.

He shrugs. "You see things differently. Afterward."

"You mean you can't stop seeing it."

"Yes."

"That day in Dallas, Mr. Manchester, I see it over and over in my mind. Every night."

"Tell me."

It's fascinating and also repellent—how he wants to get right inside that day, into the backseat of the car, those eight seconds. He wants me to take him into that gap of time when time blew apart. He wants to feel every moment of slow-motion horror, the shock of the sound that threw me right out of the world, the metallic wash in my mouth I could taste for days after.

"What about the film stills?" he says. He pulls out the photographs of the woman crawling over the back of the car. The Zapruder images. I can't look at those pictures. He spreads them on the coffee table. I pretend to look. I know I'm the woman in the photographs, but I have no recollection of doing the things they claim I did.

I shake my head. "I stayed right with Jack. That's what I remember."

"There must be more underneath," he says.

He's gaining confidence, his tone more aggressive. He pours another drink and sets it in front of me. *Don't drink it,* I think, watching the sprawl of color over the ice cubes as they melt. He is more like Mailer than I thought.

- Then you climbed onto the back of the car.
- I don't remember that.
- What happened next?
- That's all I remember.
- You don't remember climbing onto the back of the car?
- Is that what happened? They keep telling me I did that.
- Yes.
- I don't think I did that.
- You were asked "why" shortly after, and you said you were going after a piece of the president's skull.
- I don't think I said that.
- Or were you trying to get out of the car?

I feel myself shake my head. White sunlight. Heat. The sound of the sky blown apart. The writer stares at me, ruddy cheeks, relentless eyes, focused to the point of being cruel.

Once upon a time, there was a woman in the backseat and a man beside her she was trying to pull down.

If she had been stronger. If only she'd been able to.

"What else do you want, Mr. Manchester?"

I could tell him that, recently, I've begun to wonder if those are in fact the details that matter or if what really matters is how the dog, for example, is still waiting for Jack to come home. Circling the rug by the door, the dog has paced one edge of that rug bare. What matters is the smell of the tack of that riderless horse, the buck and the fight. What matters is how Jack looked at me once, on a street corner in Georgetown, a year before we were married. He looked at me and I felt my soul wash open.

If I trusted this man, I'd explain the danger in the hours of night silence—not only the grief but what might have happened differently and who might have killed Jack. Was it really Oswald? Only Oswald? Killed now too, so we can't ask him. What about the rumblings I catch sometimes, about Johnson, the CIA, more than one shooter? Sometimes I wonder what Bobby really knows. Does he tell me everything? Why would he keep things from me? What is he afraid I would do?

This all pushes up in me at once. I look from Bobby to the writer, then back again. My mind unspools. Like a film cut and spliced. I look again at the creep of sweat on the writer's shirt. I should stop this now, stand up, ask him to leave.

"What else do you want, Mr. Manchester?"

"The truth," he says—that smile not awkward now but hard, predatory, in this theater of a living room where we've been thrown together.

I give him everything then, the underside of those days in November, every limbic and intimate detail. The story I've told a hundred times since it happened, but never this way. I have never given away so much, to anyone.

That day it was the coolness of the tunnel I wanted—I wanted to whisper to you—in the blinding white heat of Dallas, I wanted to tell you how much I craved the dark of that tunnel ahead. I wanted those shadows to wrap my face, my hands, to wrap you in with me.

I wanted to tell you that this is where forever lives—in the wanting. This is where life turns godlike.

I wanted to whisper to you that day in the open sweltering car that the dark ahead was what I was waiting for. Your hands and your mouth in that dark. I would steal across the seat and surprise you with a kiss.

Then the sky cracked. How fast it can happen. Like chalk off a slate. The sound again. No blood at first. Then it's everywhere. The roses on the seat are the wrong color. And a woman in the car, his head blown apart in her lap, pieces she's trying to keep held together, his beautiful mind all over her.

One mind unlike any other.

You are like no other.

When I surface again, the living room is filled with smoke. My drink is empty, the pitcher of daiquiri nearly empty as well. We've been at this for hours, and the writer is looking at me, his madman eyes not darting anymore, not uncertain or restless, but fixed, exultant.

"Who helped you into the car?" he asks. "Who was seated where? Do you have a recollection of the speed?"

He knows these things. Why does he need me to say them?

"What about Mr. Hill?" he asks.

"Clint?"

"Where was he?"

It's a strange power the dead have—not to cross over or enter the physical sphere but to step down on the heart.

"What were the last words he said to you, Mrs. Kennedy— your husband, the president, do you remember what he said?"

Take off your sunglasses, Jackie, so they can see you.

Turn on the lights. I want them to see you.

Say, maybe I can take you for a drink someplace?

Don't tell me you're a romantic, Jack, I teased you once.

You shook your head and grinned. Nope. An idealist without illusions.

"You're not going to answer?" the writer says, almost sneers. He seems annoyed.

"No," I say.

"Let's go back. Once more. Tell me again what you remember as the car was moving toward the tunnel."

Over a year ago, your last winter, I watched you walk out on the South Lawn with Charlie. The snow was up to your knees. You'd throw a stick, and the dog would fly after it, dig that stick from the snow, then rush back to drop it at your feet. It went on for half an hour. Just this. You throwing the stick, Charlie fetching it back, the stark and gentle winter lawn, bare trees, and the dog moving through the snow. That chromatic light. I watched you from the window, wanting only to stay there, watching you, in that forever of an ordinary moment.

"The tunnel, Mrs. Kennedy?"
My mind snaps back.

Everything and nothing. The shade of the tunnel, how much I craved that dark—it was so hot—but we've already been over that, I've already told them all how it felt like the sun was stripping our faces. I had my sunglasses on. You told me to take them off. Then there was that sound, and the sky tore.

"Mrs. Kennedy, is there anything else you'd like to tell me?"

The smell of salt, your hair blown around in the wind, sunlight on your skin.

"Is that all?"

The way you said my name.

"Thank you, Mr. Manchester," I say as I see him out.
"Never again," I tell Bobby after the door is closed.

I take Caroline and John to Hyannis Port for a long weekend. I bring them to the beach. They run into the water up to their knees, then back to me, shrieking with the cold. I put my arms around them, and they push into me, shivering. John wants me to dry him off; I wrap him in the towel, dusting off bits of the sea. His small shoulder blades like wings.

"Come on, John," Caroline says. Grasping her brother's hand, she pulls him off, and they run back into the surf, his little legs churning to keep up. I feel a sudden fear in my throat. I want to cry out, *Come back.*

I spend June and July on Squaw Island. In a sense it's like every other summer, only Jack doesn't come on weekends. Bobby tells me there's going to be a short film about Jack at the Democratic National Convention. It was supposed to be on the first night, but he's learned it's been moved to day 4. He blames Johnson.

"You don't know it was Lyndon," I say.

"Who else would think they had a right to move it?"

The two of them are still at it. Trying to catch me up in their tug of war. It's Jack they're fighting for, each trying to pick up his legacy, because they don't understand—they've never quite understood—that politics and power are palaces of breath and want and air. Only as real as we believe them to be.

"One more thing," Bobby says.

I smile. "You always say that."

"*Look* wants to do a memorial issue."

No is my answer. But he needs me.

"All right," I say. "For you."

"For Jack."

"Yes, but you're the one running for Senate, and I want you with me in New York. So we each get a something."

He starts to laugh, then stops.

"Will you always look after me, Bobby?"

"Always."

"It's a thankless job."

"Not to me."

I pose with the children for the *Look* photographer. Carefully designed shots, where I pretend to be serene, coming back to life.

I tell the editor I hope this piece might capture the way Jack loved words, how even while he was working through the challenges of nuclear disarmament, he'd lie on the boat, reading poetry.

"I want people to understand there was a man behind it all," I say.

"Why don't you write a tribute we can include?"

"I can't even write a letter to a friend."

"It doesn't have to be long. And it will be your words. You'll have complete control."

After they're gone, I walk inside with Bobby. The children still play on the lawn. It's almost dusk.

"Will you hurl yourself into Tennyson with me?" I ask.

"Sure."

"Or Shakespeare?"

"Whatever you want, Jackie."

I look at him and he doesn't look away. It happens then, something stopped in the air between us, and through the awkwardness and the silence, I can hear the waves, the laughter of the children, still with that raw and terrible magic.

I pull out a book, find a page, and hand it to him. He reads. The lamplight plays its tricks, and his face looking down at the page is lovely and hungry and doomed. He glances up.

"What?" he says.

"I was thinking about a letter your father wrote to me once about Jack. How he was a child of fate. If he fell into a puddle of mud in a white suit, he'd come up ready for a Newport Ball."

His eyes close to me then.

"Yes," he says. "That's one of those things my father would say."

It isn't about Bobby, is it? It never was. It's about some other deeper thing inside me he ignites. Some deep, lost burning that reminds me of you.

That night, I sit at my desk. A stack of books, a pad of paper, a pen.

I start from memory. Incomplete passages, fragments. Not my words but the words of authors Jack loved. The writing calms me. I copy lines from Tennyson, lines from *Richard III,* lines from Buchan's *Pilgrim's Way.*

I spend hours writing it out. Then I go back and make cuts and margin notes, my own words this time, which I weave into the rest. I tear up most of what I've done and start again. Each time I rewrite it, I know it's not what I want and it isn't enough, but it's more than I had before.

I put the pen away.

In the dark you come to me. You cross the room from the window. You've just come in from sailing. Your clothes damp, hair raked with salt. But you are there, reaching toward me through the moon.

There was an evening once, years ago, when we were walking back to our house from dinner at your parents'. Caroline was with us. She danced on ahead, her white dress flitting. "Like an angel," you said, then you stopped walking for a moment, your head tilted back, and the dark poured over your throat, your skin so pale, looking up toward the stars, those bits of radiance we barely noticed that fell like tiny bright knives through levels of distance and time.

How does it happen?
    I want to ask you this.
    How can I wonder something like this with anyone other than you?

. . .

I spend September with my mother and the children in Newport.

On September 12, I come downstairs early. The light is ragged, the morning overcast and cool. Alone in the dining room, I skim the headlines. Hurricane Dora, school bussing, Vietnam. In two days, the children and I will move to New York. The apartment I bought at 1040 Fifth Avenue is nearly finished. I've chosen what furniture to keep. The Louis XVI bureau where Jack signed the test-ban treaty; my collection of miniature paintings from India; my father's Empire desk. I find it easier to inverse edit, choose what I want and let go of the rest. Caroline will start school, and the new agent assigned to John will bring him to the zoo and the park. He reminds me of Agent Foster. I'll have to tell him not to spoil John, not to throw him up in the air every time he asks.

A year ago today, it was our tenth anniversary. We were here, in Newport, and you set out those gifts, including the snake bracelet, and asked me to choose.

The memory cuts.

Later that afternoon, when the children and I are driving home from the beach, I take the longer route. The speed is a visceral comfort, the road pulling under the car as the wheel twists lightly in my hands. Behind me on the long vinyl backseat, they are asleep, a sprawl of legs and arms, sweet lips sticky from ice cream, Caroline's fair head, John's dark one. I tilt the mirror to catch them in the rearview, and a sudden warmth floods my body. There's a dirt turnoff up ahead. I pull in and park on a lip of packed gravel that washes out with every storm, the car idling, windows unrolled halfway, the scent of beach rose, sweet pepperbush, the salt smell off the marsh. I can hear the light sound of the children's breathing. I don't want it to end. I cut off the engine. There is nothing else I need to do, nowhere else I need to be. Only with them. Only here.

. . .

Onassis writes to me. I wait a few days before I answer.

> *Dear Ari,*
>   *I received your note, and yes, I would enjoy dinner sometime. Let me know when you'll be here, and we will see. . . .*

Lee told me months ago that things between them had cooled, then ended. It was short-lived, their affair, as my sister's flings often are. The children and I have moved to Manhattan—it has felt uncanny, being here, in this city, like time has folded back on itself. The week we arrived, I took them rowing in Central Park. As we walked toward the boathouse, it struck me how alive the city is. No one noticed us, or if they did, they paused only for a moment, then moved on. The children were happy, and it felt like just a week ago I was their age. Lee and I used to go for walks in Central Park with our nurse. One day I wandered off. I was careful to let it appear unintentional; I didn't want the nurse to notice I was gone. I looked back once, walking backward until she and Lee fell out of sight. A curious sensation, I remember how I loved it even then—that sheer sudden thrill of being unseen, unaccounted for.

I am going to the new Broadway show about the Jewish immigrants, which just opened, *Fiddler on the Roof*.

One day in October, I stop with the children at the news shop on the corner for two chocolate milks, and it's there: *Time* magazine, with a photograph of Oswald. A banner of text: THE WARREN COMMISSION: NO CONSPIRACY, DOMESTIC OR FOREIGN.

John is tugging at my hand. "Mummy." I look up, over him, to the wall lined with chips and cans. My eyes drop. Caroline is watching me. She picks up a travel magazine and places it squarely on the rack to cover Oswald's face. Then she takes the lollipop from John's hand, puts it on the counter, and says to the cashier in her grown-up voice, "We will take this, please. How much will it be?"

The spell snaps. I fish through my coat pocket for a quarter. I hand it to Caroline, who pays the man and doesn't wait for change, and the three of us walk outside. Bells on the shop door ring as it shuts behind us.

I remember what I said to Bobby that last day of the interviews— the day the writer Manchester left.

"I need to get out." That's what I said.

I'll never get out. I realize that now.

. . .

One day bleeds into the next.

- rise after not sleeping
- smoke
- coffee
- wonder if the newspaper is safe to open
- wake the children

Bobby comes when I ask him to. He'll leave early from the office or come after dinner. He'll say good night to the children and sit with me.

"Tell me this will end, Bobby. If not this year, then someday. I've always loved the ritual of reading the paper with my coffee in the morning. Now I can't even do that."

"It's only temporary," he says. "Until the anniversary. The day after, they'll start talking about other things."

In a photograph of Oswald, he is holding a gun in the backyard of a house. A notch in the stock.

The ballistics matched, supposedly. Bullet fragments found in the car matched bullets from that gun. Bits of fabric caught in the rifle were the same colors as the shirt he was wearing when he was apprehended.

How did we not grasp ahead of time the shape of what would come? That you would be killed. That it would be violent. There was too much rage in the world for it to be otherwise.

How did we not understand it was inevitable—the way love or war is inevitable, the way art and truth eventually rise? How could we not have seen it? Maybe you did. Maybe that's why you'd make those chilling morbid jokes. Maybe you understood that if not Oswald (if it even was Oswald), someone would have done it.

There were too many who hated what you stood for. Too many who didn't want the seismic change you brought, that toppling of an order, a way of life with its implicit injustice that served some and destroyed others.

You were too easy to scapegoat. You were incandescent. That was the word.

You were the walking, breathing incarnation of the youth that would ultimately upend them.

You were adored and, because of that, you were dangerous.

Bold, brilliant, extraordinary. You burned, it was just so bright— that future you were after. The America we saw.

A small knock on the door. Caroline.

"You're crying, Mommy."

"I'm not. Just waking up."

"You're crying about Daddy, aren't you?"

"I'm just waking up."

"It's okay," Caroline says solemnly. "I'll take care of you. It's time for you to come."

"I love you, sweetheart. I'm coming."

I meet with Dorothy Schiff from the *New York Post* because Bobby has asked me to. He wants her endorsement.

"Bobby's not what people think," I tell her. "They call him ruthless. But he's the opposite. He's been so good to my children and me. He is kind, and the thing about Bobby is that he can't *not* tell the truth. So he might seem ruthless. Because the truth is exactly that."

When the phone rings that afternoon, and it's Bobby, I assume he wants to know about the meeting with Dorothy. A bright day. The leaves on the turn, the light with that longer slant in it I love. Miss Shaw has taken John out, and Caroline will be home from school in an hour. But Bobby is not calling to ask about the meeting with Dorothy. He is calling because he wants me to know what's happened. It will be in the papers tomorrow, and he wants me to hear it from him.

"Just tell me," I say.

"Mary Meyer was shot and killed walking the towpath beside the canal."

The walls peel; the ceiling is an eggshell.

"They have the man who did it. They're sure."

"If they're saying they're sure, they must not be."

"Jackie—"

"I'm glad you let me know."

Hanging up, I remember, of all things, the dress. The bedraggled mess of layered chiffon Mary wore that night she went out in the snow and came back soaking wet.

Mary used to love to walk the towpath in the middle of the day. She'd work on a painting in the morning, then go down to the canal before lunch. Remembering this, I don't see Mary in an oversize shirt streaked with paint, walking along the canal. I see her in that dress, a little tipsy, her face smeared with mascara and tears, that woman who wouldn't stay on the course the world had laid out.

A week later, more details are released. We learn that the murderer was a Black man. He claimed he was fishing when the police came after him for something he didn't even know had taken place.

"He didn't do it," I say to Bobby the next time he stops by.

"He shot her twice."

"Someone shot her twice."

"Jackie, don't. There's nothing behind this. They found him wandering in the woods, the fly of his pants unzipped."

"He claimed the police did that to him."

"He shot her twice," he says again, as if that somehow proves it.

"Don't be a fool, Bobby, or imagine I am. Mary knew too much, and they killed her for it."

He stares at me, and for a moment I regret being so direct. But I'm right and he knows it. That man didn't kill Mary, but Mary is dead, and somehow we all played a part in that.

It will get brushed under the rug. There's too much at stake right now. The election is coming. Martin Luther King, Jr., just won the Nobel Peace Prize. Rumors are bubbling up that Khrushchev will be deposed. Mary and the Black man will be lost to all that. The man will sit in prison, go to trial. More than likely he'll be convicted, and the layers of what really happened will just drift away.

. . .

On November 3, Bobby is elected to the Senate and Lyndon Johnson wins the presidency.

The *Look* magazine commemorating Jack is coming out on November 17. They send over proofs with photographs and the words I wrote. Those passages from literature Jack loved that I compiled. It is beautiful, and it is heartbreaking.

I spend November 22 with John and Caroline. I've canceled the *Times* subscription until November 24. I don't read the tributes in the newspapers or magazines. There are requiem Masses I don't attend. Television documentaries I don't watch.

I eat a quiet dinner with the children. I put them to bed. I stay up late and write letters.

A flash as that piece of your head shot away, and I saw it flood out—vision, brilliant spirit, light.

Then the day is over. It is midnight. The next day. And I have gotten through it.

On November 25, John turns four. He wakes up early and hurls himself into my arms, asking when are the presents, when is the cake, when is the party. Breakfast first, I tell him. We walk into the dining room together. I sit down with my coffee and unfold the newspaper. On the front page are excerpts of my testimony to the Warren Commission—my "what ifs" and "if onlys."

1965

The sun rises, then sets. The last of the leaves fall. The trees are bare, waiting for snow. Smoke from a chimney, fires snap, lights turned down at bedtime, then snuffed out. The windows darken and the sky is bright with stars—their disordered burning without design, stars flung around like dice.

Christmas in Aspen. Skiing with Bobby and the children in Vermont. In February, I go to Puerto Marques, then rent a house in Hobe Sound. I read the papers. The assassination of Malcolm X; the attacks on King and flights of protesters marching from Selma to Montgomery. They are met by police, tear gas, and nightsticks; they're beaten at the bridge.

"This isn't someone else's country," I tell Bobby.

In New York that spring, I go out with a string of escorts—intellectual, witty, gentlemanly gentlemen. I sleep with one or two of them once or twice. Even if it were more than that, it would mean nothing. These men are friends. I talk and laugh with them. I trust them. Only one feels more serious—the architect Jack Warnecke. Bobby warns me it's too soon.

"Too soon?"

He doesn't answer.

"Are you jealous?" I say, teasing. "You, with your nine children, and your lovely live-wire wife, with her cheery faith in you and God and all things Kennedy. Bobby, you couldn't be jealous."

He's been moody recently, brooding over Johnson, who's taken the high road on civil rights that Bobby had staked for his own. On national TV, Johnson pledged support to King and the marchers at Selma. He called for the passage of a new voting-rights bill. All things Bobby would have done.

"It's good Lyndon's taking a stand," I tell him. "What matters is that the bills get passed."

He doesn't answer.

Dropping ice into a glass, I say, "Ethel doesn't need people going around saying you've been seen leaving my apartment in the early morning."

"Ethel's fine."

But it comes out hard. The *fine.*

David Ormsby-Gore calls from England to ask if I'll attend a memorial ceremony in May. The queen wants to dedicate a tract of land at Runnymede in Jack's name. I tell David I'll think about it, but only because he's the one asking.

"Harold Macmillan could speak in my stead," I say.

"I don't know," David says. A pause. I remember then: the Profumo affair. Macmillan's secretary of state, John Profumo, lied about a scandal and was caught in the lie, and though Macmillan had done nothing wrong, the incident drove him to resign. There was a young model involved and a Soviet attaché.

"Harold wrote me a wonderful letter last February," I tell David on the phone. "Fifteen pages about his time in the war. I tried to write back, but nothing I wrote made sense."

"Will you say just a few words at the ceremony?" he asks again.

"Will you have Macmillan speak as well?"

"I'll have to see what I can do," he says.

"Oh, David, please do a little more than that."

"So you'll come, Jackie?"

I smile. "I'll have to see what I can do."

Soon it will be summer again. When I can bike and walk and swim and drop my mind. I want to watch our children in the waves, limbs baking brown, legs longer this year, running down the beach. This summer, as they wade farther out, I will watch the light shift across that line of sea and sky, that taut edge of the horizon you live behind now.

Lee throws a party for me.

"But there's no occasion, Pekes," I say.

"A party is the occasion," Lee says. "Just a teeny tiny dinner dance for less than a hundred. I've picked out a dress for you. You can't wear that old yellow thing you've worn for every single dinner since you moved to New York."

"I didn't wear it for every single one."

"You did."

"I didn't."

"People are starting to notice, Jackie."

It feels like a slap.

"We have to be forgiven," I say, "for things we've done since Jack died."

Lee looks at me. "We?"

She thinks I mean Bobby. That he is always with me or near me. People have talked.

"Things like wearing the same dress, Lee. That's all I meant."

I don't tell her that when Aristotle Onassis was in town two weeks ago, he invited me for dinner. Very last minute. But I went. I didn't wear that old yellow dress. I wore a different dress.

Averell Harriman is my escort the night of Lee's party. Stas welcomes us at the door. He and Lee seem to be patching things up. Bobby is there. He catches my eye, then looks away. It's a beautiful party. That's what Lee does—she traffics in beautiful things. Everyone is kind. They mean well, I know, even as part of me has gone off to sit in the corner, a casual absence. We move from course to course, cycle through predictable topics of conversation. My practiced smile. I laugh when cued. The evening is like water rushing by.

Someone mentions how well I look.

You don't get past it, I almost say. You don't even really move on. The world moves on. But the wrenching loss remains. With no logic and no lexicon. You live that loss again and again.

. . .

I fly with Bobby, Teddy, and the children to England for the dedication at Runnymede. On the plane, Bobby asks about the speech I wrote. It's not long, I tell him. Just some remarks about how English literature influenced Jack as no other dimension of his education did. How he loved history. He believed that history was alive in the present, continually shaping the course of events.

Bobby nods, his face reflected in the plane window. A palpable remove between us now, cool. I don't bring it up. I miss him. I miss the closeness, though I have no right to.

By the makeshift stage in the field at Runnymede, thousands have gathered in the bright-soaked meadow where the Magna Carta was signed, that first written document that sought to balance power with law. Justice, fairness, the rights of the people. Tree-blossom stuff is adrift on the air.

Macmillan speaks first. His calm voice floats over the field. He wrote to me soon after Jack died about being wounded in the Battle of the Somme. Shot, he fell and lay for hours among the dead. When his comrades came for him, they found him alive and took him from that place, but he was never able to escape the sense that it was wrong for him to live and leave the dead behind. He could not escape the sense that he had failed them.

"*But this,*" he had written, "*what has happened to you and (in its way) to all of us. How can we accept it? How can we explain it? Why did God allow it? . . . Can there really be a God?*"

Those words rise in me now, and I suddenly understand I cannot get up and say the brief remarks I'd planned. I cannot stand on that platform overlooking the field where King John met the barons and signed the Magna Carta. Neither side kept to the terms. Less than a year later, they met again in war, and King John was killed by those same men. Because violence is tidal. Violence does not end. It spills over and soaks, one generation into the next.

I lean over to Bobby. "I can't do this."

"You can."

"No."

It's not that I'm too weak, I could explain. If anything, it's the opposite. There is simply too much of me now. This jagged, unbridled intensity.

"Maybe that intensity is what you always were," Onassis remarks when I tell him about that day at Runnymede. Early June. He's come to New York. He's invited me for dinner again, and here we are.

"I couldn't bear to stand in that field and say beautiful things when all I can see now is how hate, and the violence it creates, is always there."

"That isn't all that's there."

I tell him about an argument I recently had with Bob McNamara over Vietnam. McNamara's been quietly pushing me to align with Johnson.

"Of course they want your support," Onassis says.

"Johnson takes credit for work Jack did on civil rights. It enrages Bobby. Then they ship more troops to Vietnam and blame Jack for his part. Which is unfair. Jack always felt that conflict could only end badly."

Onassis nods, listening.

"There's not a civilized nation in the world," I say, "that talks about its civilizing mission as grandly as America does."

The first-course plates have been cleared. McNamara and I did not leave on good terms after that argument. Two days later, he sent over a stuffed tiger as a gift for John. I'm making a watercolor of a tiger now to thank him but feeling somehow sick about it. Like I'm back on that stage, playing a role.

I dust a few crumbs off the tablecloth.

More and more often, Onassis seems to have reasons to be in the city. He stays at The Pierre. He'll phone me a few weeks before. Mention he's coming to New York on business. He'll ask if there's a night I might be free.

"I've brought something for you," he says now.

"You shouldn't do that."

"It's small."

He withdraws a slim book from his jacket pocket. A collection of poems by the Greek poet Cavafy. "You've read him?" he asks.

"Only a few things," I say. "Thank you." I open the book. He tells me that much of Cavafy's work has roots in the historical and mythological past, and while Cavafy believed in art for art's sake, he often worked politics into his poems. Then, almost as an afterthought, Onassis remarks that pre-Socratic philosophers believed that the soul was born out of the sea, and the sea's mist was the link between the earth and sun.

"I love that," I say.

"I thought you would."

"I'm planning to read Kazantzakis this summer."

"Which book?"

"*Report to Greco.*"

He smiles. It says everything, the smile.

I put the Cavafy book into my bag as our entrées arrive.

"Are you happy in New York?" he asks.

"I can almost disappear."

He laughs. A quick laugh. Alpha teeth. White and strong.

"You should come back to Greece," he says.

Such a curious man. With his overtures. Presumptuous at times. But when he tells his stories, the room slips over my head.

Over crème brûlée, I mention the ongoing battle with the biographers, even Schlesinger and Sorensen. "Jack would hate what Sorensen's done," I say. "Too hagiographic."

"Better than the alternative."

"I suppose. Schlesinger has portrayed Jack as a Roman senator, cool, unemotional. I told him that was all wrong. Jack was more like the Greeks. He brought light to the dark. He made decisions with an eye to the long throw of time."

And an eye to glory, I almost add. Like Achilles. That's the comparison Jack would have wanted. Achilles or Odysseus. Neither, though, has ever felt quite right to me. I tell Onassis then that I sometimes think of the scene in *The Iliad* when Achilles murders Hector, the Trojan prince. For twelve days, out of grief and rage, Achilles drags the body around the walled city, and every night, after each desecration, the gods quietly restore Hector's body. Heal his cuts, the broken bones and wounds. They rinse the dust from his skin.

"It's how myth is made," I say. "Destroyed, resurrected, destroyed, retold."

Later I will feel like I talked too much, too freely. Why? Because he's an outsider? Is that why?

"In the American papers," he says, "everyone seems quite concerned about which invitations you accept and which you decline. They talk about you like you are their queen."

"I do have to consider what Widow Kennedy can or should do."

"Because there are other Kennedys with ambitions?"

"Bobby's good to me," I say. "And he is so good to John and Caroline."

"He's a noble man."

A lie, I know. He doesn't like Bobby. He never has.

"Are you going to Hyannis Port soon?" he asks.

"Yes."

"Give him my best, please." A slight smile around his mouth. Not kind.

"We were having such a nice time," I say.

"I meant it in a perfectly nice way."

"Please, Mr. Onassis, don't be like everyone else and pretend."

There was more we spoke about that night, but that, for me, was the note on which it ended.

. . .

The first night I spend at the Cape that spring, the house has the cold damp smell of winter trapped in wood. I throw the windows open.

Last night I dreamed of you, and in my dream, I was with you again, and you washed through my body like a wave.

Lessons I've learned since you died:

How to pack certain things away with precision—heartbreak, of course, grief and regret, but also anger—the kind you always told me I should bite back.

The rituals of summer. Cooking fires on the beach, lobster, corn, blueberries, and peaches. Early-morning swims and being barefoot all day long.

I read the book of Cavafy's poetry.

On my birthday, I call Ted Sorensen.

"I miss Jack," I say. "Even the stupid things that used to irritate me, like when he'd track sand into the house in the cuffs of his pants."

"Can I take a ride over?" Sorensen asks.

"Please."

He brings doodles Jack made during the missile crisis. Sheets of yellow lined paper with little pictures and words staggered among the drawings—*Khrushchev, Soviet Submarines.* On one page, the word *Missile* circled over and over.

"Before, we would've just thrown them away," he says.

You loved him, I almost say, but it's so obvious, I feel ashamed.

Sometimes I can feel those layers of other summers when you were here. Collateral moments—the warm green shadows and how the sunlight fell across your shoulders and your face. I could see you aging, but I'd still catch that unmistakable careless grace I always loved. Sometimes I see it still, even with you gone, even as the seasons change and new rituals begin to rewrite the hours, erasing you, as summer moves toward fall.

When I feel you close to me—your presence and the loss—I just wish I'd given more, said and trusted more. It's like breathing in lightning, the want and the regret.

The man accused of shooting Mary Meyer is acquitted. It's in the papers that August. A Black female lawyer took his case and argued that the man accused wasn't the size of the suspect a witness had seen. Mary Meyer was shot twice, once in the head, once in the shoulder, by someone who knew how to push a bullet straight to the aorta; her mind went dark in an instant. Both shots were mortal. This detail, more than any other, haunts me.

I swim in the ocean, and my mind turns: Mary Meyer, two shots, a Black man fishing, the chiffon dress, its hem soaked with snow, drunk lovesick Mary wandering the White House lawn.

One evening, when the sky is bright, I take the children for a walk. The street is empty. John pulls at my hand while Caroline skips ahead. John stops, squatting down beside a puddle in the road.

"John, that's dirty," I say as he starts to reach for the water.

"No, Mummy, I want it. The moon."

It strikes me then—a sudden feeling I almost don't recognize. I am happy. That's what it is, the feeling.

"You're crying again," says Caroline.

I pull my daughter to me, and John as well. I hold them both. John's hands wrap my neck, but Caroline's arms stay tucked by her side, her body like wood, that rigid sorrow. She's holding her breath, holding everything in.

"It's okay, sweetheart. Caroline, my love, it's okay." I feel her body give, a tiny sob in her throat. "He was our world, my love. That's why we cry."

...

That fall, I rent a house in Far Hills, New Jersey. Simple, clapboard, down a dirt road. Almost every weekend I drive out with the children to ride. Coming back into Manhattan late one Sunday, we get stuck in traffic. It's after eleven when we finally reach 1040. John's asleep in my arms, and as I walk in and turn on the hall light, I'm startled to notice how the apartment has become home. The old-world curtains, blue-and-white lamps, long shelves of books, the cherry-blossom screens. Near the window, my easel with a canvas. My eyes sweep the photographs: horses, dogs, the children, Jack.

On November 2, a young man named Norman Morrison sets himself on fire to protest Vietnam. I read about it in the papers the next day. I've had a fever, and I am still in bed. Morrison was a Quaker, the secretary of a Friends Meeting, and he set himself on fire by the river entrance to the Pentagon, forty feet below McNamara's office. Not yet thirty-two years old. Three children. His baby daughter in his arms as he doused himself in gasoline and struck a match. As the flames caught his clothes, he set the baby on the wall behind him. A bystander swept her out of reach.

Below the article is an advertisement for a sofa and the caption *Have your Danish with a martini*, and there, what I don't expect, a tiny news story: *Mrs. John F. Kennedy ill with the flu.*

Good Lord.

I think about Bob McNamara. I should call him about that man Morrison. In my gut, I know he was in his office when it happened. He would have stayed by the window and made himself see it.

The phone rings. It's Bobby. A first draft of the Manchester book will be finished next month. They're going to send a copy for me to read.

"I don't want to read it," I say. "It's been two years, Bobby. I am just starting to breathe."

Silence then.

"You read it," I say. "You'll know what we should cut."

John's birthday falls on Thanksgiving Day that year. I drive with the children out to New Jersey on Wednesday morning. The next day is Thanksgiving, then a dinner celebration for John's birthday, gifts, cake, a song. Two days later, we celebrate Caroline's. Driving back into the city, I decide that every year from now on, it will be this: the long Thanksgiving weekend, the three of us together, each of their birthdays celebrated on its actual day. Just this way.

1966

The world begins to spin again.

In June, I take the children to Hawaii. Jack Warnecke is living on Oahu. He's designing the new state capitol—an open courtyard, columns, a reflecting pool. I fall in love with Hawaii. I can go to a beach or a luau, I can walk into town, eat at an open-air restaurant, paint watercolors, or wear a bikini. No one seems to see me, or if they do, they don't care.

"I'd forgotten what it was like," I tell Warnecke, "to explore a new place and be unnoticed."

The children and I come home to the Cape in July. The day after we arrive, Bobby walks over to tell me about the sale of excerpts from Manchester's book to *Look*. They're going to publish in the fall.

"That can't be on every newsstand," I say. "Tell them no."

"You said you wanted me to handle it."

"Just remind them that publication can only take place once we've given our permission. We haven't done that yet."

"Jackie."

It's how he says my name. I realize then. He's already given permission.

"What exactly did you tell them, Bobby?"

"The Kennedy family will place no obstacle."

I sit down on the sofa, my head in my hands. Rage, heat, fury, tears. It all pours into my hands.

"You told me to handle it, Jackie," he says.

"I can't do this," I say. "I'm just getting out from under it." I don't look at him. I know I'm being unfair. "Please tell them you misunderstood."

"But I didn't."

The room feels airless.

"Tell the writer to come," I say.

I serve iced tea on the porch.

"Do you water-ski, Mr. Manchester?"

He shakes his head and for a moment looks uncomfortable.

"We'll just go for an hour," I say. "Then we'll have some lunch and talk things through."

I ski off the back of the boat, carving back and forth; I cross the wake, then cut the opposite way. After twenty minutes, I drop the tow. The boat circles back.

"Do you want a turn, Mr. Manchester? I'm sure you'll have fun."

"No."

"All right, then. We can just swim."

"I'm afraid I'm not much of a swimmer."

"Oh, don't be modest, Mr. Manchester."

He follows me reluctantly over the side. I wave the boat off and start in. Within fifteen strokes, I've left him behind. He straggles onto shore half an hour later, still out of breath when he reaches the porch. I hand him a towel. A puddle on the floor where his trunks drip.

"Why have you asked me to come here?" he says.

"You can't do this, I'm afraid."

"You're talking about the serialization."

"I'm talking about all of it."

"We have an agreement."

There's a pitcher of iced tea on the table and a plate of sandwiches. I unwrap the sandwiches and refill his glass.

I want to ask about things I've heard: how, as he wrote that book, he worked all day and night, gripping his pen so tightly, it forced blood from under the nail; how he was hospitalized for weeks from nervous exhaustion, didn't eat, didn't sleep; how, in Dallas, he crawled across the roof of the book depository to put himself into Oswald's sixth-floor view; how he asked to see the clothes I wore that day. He unfolded the white towel my stockings were in, blood flaked off in grains.

When Bobby told me this last detail, I'd pushed for more. In some terrible way, Manchester wanted something no one else really did.

"Please read the book, Mrs. Kennedy," he is saying now. "Then you can tell me what you object to, and we can make changes."

I glance at Bobby—I'd almost forgotten he was there, and has been since we came in. His chin rests on one hand. He stares at the porch rail. A wave of rage hits me. These men. Moving me around like a piece on a game board, with their egos and ambitions. They want to take my private grief and torque it for their own ends. I've let them. Bobby glances up.

"I am going to fight this," I say, looking at Bobby.

"That's a mistake," Manchester says.

I turn to him. "It's all a mistake, Mr. Manchester."

He doesn't leave. He stays sitting where he is, half a sandwich on his plate, mayonnaise squeezing from the corner. His eyes dark and angry, rims with scattered bits of red fatigue.

"The only thing you want," he says, "is the one thing you can't have. One blank page for November twenty-second, 1963."

"We're going to sue," I tell Bobby a month later back in New York.

He shakes his head. "That would be a disaster."

"For whom?"

I know the question will hurt him and it does, but even through the hurt, he can't look away, and there's a part of me that wants to reach across the deep rift between us, run my fingertips along his cheek. Cutting and bizarre, the unique desire I felt for him, that sometimes I still feel, a desire I once thought might be enough.

"You failed me," I say, because I just need to end it.

1967

As soon as the news of the suit is public, they go after me. An avalanche of headlines.

MRS. KENNEDY "IRKED"
UNEASY RESTS THE CROWN OF JKF'S JACKIE

FROM MOURNER TO SWINGER

JACKIE COMES OFF HER PEDESTAL

They describe the conflict with Manchester as *undignified* and *pointless*.

Just after the New Year, I visit Bunny Mellon in Antigua. As I'm coming out of the water one day, brushing the sea from my eyes, a shadow falls in front of me. I look up. I'm surrounded by reporters; two photographers are wading toward me, cameras held like snapping Cyclops eyes, legs chopped at the shins by the waves.

"In Skorpios, there are no reporters," Ari says when I tell him about it on the phone.
"And Cyclops?"
"That I can't promise. Did you yell at them?"

I smile. "No. Though I think a little blasphemy is good for the soul."

"But your people don't see it that way."

"I'm afraid my scuffle with Manchester isn't good for their politics."

"Just say the word, I'll be there."

"An ocean and six time zones away?"

"You must realize that, to me, that's no distance at all."

"Bobby's very upset," I say. "But the world wasn't going to love me forever."

"What does he want you to do?"

"To settle with the writer."

"I see," Onassis says. "And will you? Settle." The emphasis he places on that last word isn't lost on me.

"It might be better to have them despise me so much, they wipe me right out of the world."

"The world would miss you."

"That's okay."

"You'd be bored."

"I would be mystery."

This makes him laugh. "Lorca once said only mystery allows us to live."

"Exactly."

"I was in Buenos Aires with Lorca."

"You mean with him there or there at the same time?"

"I drank with him. He was a refugee. I was a young man working at the telephone company with a wild scheme to produce a new type of cigarette. Back home in Greece, I'd seen my uncle shot in the head in the village square. In Buenos Aires, I decided I wanted to be rich, because I believed that with wealth, I could undo what had been done."

"What did you learn from drinking with Lorca?" I ask.

"*To burn with desire and keep quiet about it is the greatest punishment we can bring upon ourselves.*"

"He wrote that for Dalí."

"It applies to any desire." He says this casually, like it's only abstract.

"You know what I like about you, Ari? You never fail to surprise me."

"Good," he says. "So will you settle? As Bobby wants you to?"

"I might drag things out a bit. If I'm going to be yanked off the pedestal, I want to be sure they get all the screws."

"When are you coming to Greece?" he asks.

"Are you going to ask me that every time you call?"

"Only until you say yes."

I agree to settle. I ask for a proof of the Manchester book and, on a rainy day that winter, I read it. I find it fascinating—how he got right into Jack's shoes, Oswald's shoes, even mine; he traced every event, from every angle and point of view; he got right under the skin of that day.

He relives it as I do. He could never have written it like this otherwise.

The next time I see Ari Onassis, it is May. A ceremony in Newport News to christen the aircraft carrier named for Jack, two days before he would have turned fifty.

I'm sitting with Bob McNamara. My eyes sweep the faces in the crowd. Some familiar, many not. I tell McNamara, "I'd like to leave directly afterward, please. Is that all right?" He nods. My eyes shift across the space, and he is there. Onassis. What is he doing here? My eyes snap away.

The ceremony ends. McNamara sends Lyndon on ahead and walks me to the helicopter. Upon landing at the airstrip in Hyannis Port, I take a car along the familiar road, which looks as it does every spring, to the house and the upstairs room where the old man waits.

I sit with him, like always, and I tell him about the ceremony in honor of his son. I kiss his papery speckled hand. His flaccid face. In his eyes I can see he understands. He can read me as easily now as he did when we were whole.

I stay with him until he nods off.

There's a rim of caked sand and salt along the window sash.

That night, after the children are asleep, I walk down to the beach. I know the agent is behind me in the dark, near enough if I should need him. I stand at the edge of the sea and the night and the stars, their distant fugitive selves, and I am alone. Only the future ahead.

High summer. Greece.

A craft appears on the horizon. He recognizes it.

"Gianni Agnelli," he says.

"You can tell from here?"

"Lines of the boat."

We're at the house on the island. He steps to the edge of the terrace. "It's Agnelli." He is annoyed. "I'll go down."

"Are you going to tell him I'm here?" I say as he starts toward the car.

He looks back. "Is that what you want?" I don't answer. He smiles. "I didn't think so. I'll manage it."

I wait on the unfinished terrace. Everything about these last days has felt that way—half composed, surreal. The island, Skorpios, is like nothing I've seen. Seventy-four acres. He had utilities laid in, two hundred varieties of trees planted, a villa built, an airstrip, a dock. He bought a second island nearby with a mountain on it to pipe fresh water to Skorpios. Sand shipped from Salamis to make a sandy beach. He has told me these things since I've been his guest here. He doesn't ever spend the night on the island. The rooms in the house were built for visitors. He only sleeps on the *Christina,* moored in the bay off the coast.

From the terrace, I can see them below. Ari leaves the car

running, the door open to signal he has no intent to socialize. He strides up to the boat as two men disembark. He was right. One is Agnelli. I recognize him now, the lean posture, that ease in how he stands. They look small from where I sit on the cliff above the trees. I shift my chair, so even if they were to look up, I'd fall into the shadow of the umbrella. Their voices rise. Ari's telling them to leave. Agnelli and the other man get back into the boat and cast off. Agnelli looks up at the house. His eyes scan the terrace like he knows someone is there, but from that distance he can't pick me out from the lines of the house. I am wood, stone, fabric, tile.

I've been in Greece for four days. I don't want to go back. Not yet.

At home, Bobby is cementing his intent to run for the presidential nomination on an anti-war, social-justice platform. All summer, he's spoken out in support of Blacks, even as waves of unrest sweep up from the South. News of unemployment and fall-apart housing. Riots erupt, leaving a wake of the dead. In Newark, a Black cabdriver is beaten by police, a neighborhood burned to the ground. It's felt like the end of the world. At the Cape, the Kennedy machine is revving up again—meetings, campaign strategy sessions, rings left by their drinks on coffee tables, cigarette butts in the ashtrays. I found myself in the crush of it—nowhere I wanted to be. I've begun to plan a longer trip for this fall, to visit the ruins in Angkor Wat. The kind of trip I used to take, before I met Jack, the kind of adventure I dreamed about when I was young. I've wanted that lately—to find my way back into who I was then, those things that once brought me alive.

It was a July afternoon in Hyannis Port when Onassis called. He was coming to New York for two days. He asked if I'd be in town.

"There's a dinner that weekend up here," I said.

A pause, then, "So I won't see you?"

"Not that weekend."

"When are you coming to Greece?"

He always asked that question. This time I answered it differently.

"Three weeks from now," I said. "Would that work for you?"

I told no one, not even Bobby. Definitely not Bobby.

I sleep with Onassis on the *Christina*. He makes love to me until my body aches, my mind split apart, gone. Everything is ended in those hours. I am only a body, a woman with no past.

Afterward, we lie on the bed in the cooler air through the open window. The dark gathers. The stars burn through. We stay up past midnight and he tells me stories of his childhood, about his adored mother, Penelope, who died, and his grandmother, who taught him that men have to forge their own destiny. He tells me how, as a boy before the occupation, he loved the port of Smyrna—the smells of coffee, fresh baked bread, pine tar, jasmine, the sounds of ship engines and folk music in the streets. He tells me how forty years ago, in August 1927, Pascia's troops moved into the region. His father was arrested and thrown into a camp. Ari was captured and lied to the military about his age, pretending to be only sixteen. The soldiers let him go, and he devised a simple plan to free his father. It was only after he'd helped his father escape that Ari, with two hundred dollars sewn into a hidden pocket in his coat, left Greece for Argentina. A third-class ticket belowdecks in the ship's hold, packed with other immigrants. In Buenos Aires, he worked as a telephone operator and fell in love with a woman who opened the doors of the city, then broke his heart and left him for another man.

"So curious," he says, "the immigrant's sense of always being split between two homes, two lands, two languages. It never leaves you. The country you came from and the feeling of being divided. You're half past, half future. And when you leave the place you're from, as I did, young, in the midst of war, for what might be forever, you know that, even if you return, the home you go back to will never be the same as what you knew."

It's unexpected—the vulnerable mix in his voice of passion and loss, grit, failure, hardscrabble dream. He smiles at me.

"This surprises you. You thought I was someone else. Is that it? Someone who just goes after what he wants until he gets it, who feels nothing, then moves on."

"I never said that."

"You don't have to."

My body is half under the sheet. He runs his hand along the edge of my breast. Silence then.

"You're going to leave?" he says.

"I'll come back."

"When?"

"In a few months."

"Or next year."

"Before that."

"Or the year after. Or seven years from now. It doesn't matter. I'll be here."

His mouth is on me again. His hands everywhere. I lie back on the pillow, breathless, the inside of my left thigh sore from where his body did not mold easily to mine. It will ache in the morning. That weird aftermath of pleasure mixed with pain. I will be exhausted. The sun will wake me. I'll have coffee and toast. I'll swim, then sleep on the little beach, or on deck, somewhere in the sun.

I tell him that when I came to Greece before, I found it almost too beautiful, dangerous somehow, and when I left, a part of me was secretly relieved. Isn't that odd?

"And now?" he says.

"It feels different to me now."

He tells me his assistant Kiki describes me as a cat.

I laugh. "What did you say?"

"I told her someday you'll bring John and Caroline to visit, and I will take them fishing."

"Anything else?"

"No," he says. "But I'd like that."

I smile.

"Come back in October," he says.

"I'm planning a trip to Cambodia. Apart from that, I'll be with the children."

"Stop in Greece on your way back from Cambodia."

"I'll have to see."

"Are you going alone?"

"David Ormsby-Gore is going with me."

He nods. "Safe."

"Kind."

"Is that a front? Or is he the real life behind the front?"

"David is a good friend, a front, and real life as well."

"Three for three," he says.

"All true."

"No. Truth is what we eat and sleep and want and fuck and dream."

I swim in the rain the day before I leave. A sudden storm. He told me it would come. Rain was rare in summer; the sky had been so clear and I did not believe him. We almost argued about it that morning. Then the wind changed. Vertical bands of clouds blew in off the sea, wrapping the island. I knew then he was right. The storm would come. It would not clear. The rain would last all day.

I swim in it. Heavy drops strike the surface, bounce, shot through with air and daylight. I feel a curious delight watching them and a strange splitting grief for what I can't yet name.

1968

"There's too much risk," I tell Bobby. "Just come out against the war. That's all you really want. You can do that and not run. You don't need to run."

He's distanced himself from me. Maybe Ethel, maybe the rumors about Onassis, maybe I haven't behaved as a Kennedy widow should. He still comes to see us. He is good with the children, always. He tells them stories of Jack.

There are fewer instances when we're alone. But in a crowded room, at a party or event, he'll draw close to me. Almost like he can't help it.

He's told me he's been tracking the breakdown of American support for Vietnam. In October, one hundred thousand protesters marched on the Pentagon. They descended on the mall, chanting songs, waving banners. They desecrated draft cards, threatened to dye the Potomac red and burn the cherry trees. By February, after the Tet Offensive and the Battle of Saigon, a Gallup poll showed that more than 50 percent of the country disapproved of Johnson's handling of the war. Johnson was nearly beaten by Eugene McCarthy in the New Hampshire primary. He won by less than three hundred votes.

Four days later, on March 16, Bobby stands in the Caucus Room of the Old Senate Office Building to announce he is entering the race. For president.

At a party at Diana Vreeland's brilliant red "garden in hell" apartment, I take Arthur Schlesinger aside.

"I know this is what everyone wants," I say. "But do you know what I think will happen to Bobby if he wins? The same thing that happened to Jack. There's too much hate in this country. Bobby doesn't believe it. He isn't cynical or fatalistic like I am. He imagines he can change their minds."

When I hear the news that Martin Luther King has been shot in Memphis, I'm on my way out the door to a concert. I cancel.

Bobby calls the next day.

"It could have been you," I tell him.

He'd been boarding a plane on his way to a campaign rally in Indianapolis when he heard. By the time they landed in Indiana, King was dead. His team told him to cancel the rally. There would be riots, they said. It was too dangerous to go out and speak to a Black crowd. Bobby went anyway. From the back of a flatbed truck, he spoke to them, about King, about nonviolence, about the need for compassion, justice, and love.

"It could have been you, Bobby," I say again.

He comes to see me that evening, and I ask him to tell me more about that night King was shot. He tells me his team gave him a speech they'd written, but he didn't use it. He just stood up there in the back of that truck, the crowd of faces around him, wet with tears of mourning and rage, and he told them about his own grief, the feeling he'd lived with since Jack died. It was the first time he'd spoken publicly about Jack.

"I know it's not the same, Jackie. The world is white and what I know of suffering will never be the same as what they know, but I needed to give them something that was real, at least to me. I didn't do it to win their vote."

Watching his face as he tells me this, the brutal earnestness, I understand this is what makes him different. Why he's always been different. Even from Jack.

He tells me that when he spoke to them that night, he quoted from the book I'd given him, *The Greek Way*. Lines from Aeschylus, but he got them wrong.

"Even in our sleep, pain which cannot forget falls drop by drop upon the heart, until in our own despair—"

"It's *despite*," I say, "not *despair*."

"I know. I didn't mean to change it. I've always felt it should have been *despair*."

I love him very much in that moment. The way he is with me right now, the way he was that day years ago when I woke up to his face in the hospital. I'd just lost my baby, Arabella, and I woke up to the pale walls of the hospital room and his face so strangely bright, his eyes harsh and torn and blue when he told me the baby was gone, and he sat with me while I cried, holding my hand like he'd never let go. Everything was simple then between us. He was with me in that devastation, the loss of the baby, Jack's absence. He was there, holding my anger and my sorrow. It was uncomplicated, pure. Everyone knew their place, their role.

"Coretta Scott King reached out," he says now. I feel my breath tighten. I know what's coming. "They're asking if you and I will attend the funeral."

"What did you say?"

"That it might be hard for you."

"Yes."

"Will you go?" he says.

"I don't want to."

"That's what I thought."

This has drawn us together. Of course. The thought bitter. It would have to be this kind of price. I'll go with him to Atlanta, but I'm afraid some terrible thing will happen.

"King was a tricky man," I say.

"He fought for what was right."

"You told me he was drunk the day of Jack's funeral—"

"Hoover fed that to us. We've all learned since then, Hoover had his reasons."

I don't answer.

"So you'll go," he says, "for King's widow's sake?"
"And yours."

. . .

I do not belong here.

The words rise in my mind as we walk through the narrow front
entrance of the Ebenezer Baptist Church. The heat is stifling
that April day in Atlanta. Two hundred thousand people have
streamed into the city.

I clutch Bobby's hand. He drives a path through the crowd.
We find space in a pew. I barely hear the words. Even King's
voice playing over the loudspeaker—the last message he gave—is
distorted, like it's coming across a great distance. I can't stop
looking at the faces—devastated, oddly silent, no shock, just an
awful resignation. They've seen this too many times before. This
kind of violence has already taken husbands, fathers, sons.

When the service ends, I grip Bobby's hand again, and we
pass back through the sea of bodies toward the shaved rectangle
of light that marks the exit. We're adrift, just the two of us again,
our lives and actions untethered from everyone else.

"People will be outraged for a while," I say on the plane heading home. "They'll feel sad, and guilty, but they hate feeling that
way. It won't last. Then they'll turn."

I know how harsh it sounds, but I can't get out from under it.

"I don't believe that," Bobby says.

"I know."

. . .

I do not belong here.

Those same words rising in me again, days later in Hyannis Port,
as a stream of young men arrive in their dark-blue suits, their
light-gray suits, loosening their ties. Some I know. Others seem
familiar. I've seen these young men, or men like them, a thou-

sand times before—fresh-faced aides pulling into the drive, stepping out of cars, hauling weekend bags to rooms upstairs,
reappearing in loafers, polos, khaki shorts, golf sweaters. There's
iced tea, lemonade, sometimes an early daiquiri. There are cigarettes and ashtrays, and they sit around the room and talk about
the challenges and opportunities created by King's death, what
needs to be considered, what can be capitalized on, shaped into
rhetoric, and no matter how moral the cause is, the parsing of it
into strategy feels predatory.

I sit in my corner and listen. Bobby asked me to come, so I'm
here. When he speaks, his eyes blaze, more impassioned than
the others. This is, after all, what drives him, this desire to set
the world on a better, more just course, to lift those who've been
pushed down, to give them voice in the world. This is what makes
him more. This is what I believe in and will always love.

Sandwiches and more drinks are brought in. The talk shifts. A
lightness restored to the room. So easy it makes my skin crawl.

I see it then—what I've known for too long. This is what those
Black men and women in the Baptist Church will never have:
the choice to turn away.

I stand up. Bobby glances at me. He must see something new
on my face, because he stops talking, he's on his feet, heading
toward me as I head for the door.

"Jackie," he says; he is close to me, that sweet, crushed hunger in his voice. I avert my eyes from him toward a photograph of
Jack on the console, one I have not been able to look at head-on
for over four years. I look at it squarely now as I walk out of that
room. It is all distilled in a moment—intimate and beloved—
a different time, a different life.

When I see Onassis again, I understand that he has simply been there. Waiting. The sense of him emerging. He's been a shadow in my life—an outline, mythical.

I remember something Lee said once. "For Ari, everything is a chess game. His patience is enduring."

He's offered his plane to fly me and the children to Palm Beach for Easter. I wonder how he knew our plans. Does it matter? He's on his way to meet his daughter in Nassau. He talks to the children as the plane heads south. John, seven now, loves anything in flight. Ari brings him up to the cockpit to sit with the captain and work the controls.

Ari comes to sit with me. "How is Bobby?" he asks.

"Running for president. I don't see him often."

"He'll win, I think."

"If that's what he wants, I want that for him."

"So Bobby will win. And then what?"

There are gifts. He calls them *little nothings*. "Just trinkets that made me think of you," he says. A diamond-and-ruby bracelet, a sapphire pin, a string of pearls.

In May, he invites me for a short cruise through the Virgin Islands.

Bobby has won Indiana and Nebraska, but the numbers aren't conclusive enough to throw McCarthy out of the race. Bobby and a raft of other Kennedys fly to campaign for Oregon and California. I don't go with them. Instead, I fly to St. Thomas and the *Christina*. After dinner, we sit on deck, our voices mixing with the smells and sounds of the dark, the play of the waves, the distant chain of lights that mark the islands.

"It's like cruising through stars," I say.

Ari laughs. "But not as beautiful as Greece."

He's smoking one of his Montecristo cigars. The gangster-style glasses that storm his face rest on the table between us.

"So when are you coming back to my island?" he asks.

"After the election."

A momentary blind comes over his eyes. Then he smiles, and that hardness just as suddenly is gone.

The day I fly home to New York, Bobby loses the Oregon primary. I call him.

"If I lose California," he says, "I'm out."

"That's silly. You're not close to out."

"I'm out if I don't win California."

"It'll work," I say. "I didn't want you to do this, but I can see now it's the right thing."

"I don't trust Onassis," he says abruptly.

"He's not a bad man, Bobby."

"Tell that to the European press."

"You're saying I should make my decisions according to the press?"

"I'm saying Greece, since the coup, is a military dictatorship and Onassis has no convictions."

"His convictions may not be political. That doesn't mean they don't exist."

"He's a danger, Jackie."

The word stops me for a moment. Then I say, "You don't mean he's a danger to me, do you, Bobby?"

"That is what I mean."

"You mean he's a danger for you."

"No," he says. "It's more than that." But I struck a nerve. I can hear it in his voice. Does he really believe he's protecting me? That he still needs to? I feel a rush of tenderness toward him, then it tightens.

. . .

He wins California. I stay up late on the night of June 4 to watch the final results come in. Then I go to bed. I'm tired, and he won't give his speech until midnight West Coast time.

When the phone rings, I'm sure it's him. The sound is sudden. I feel across the nightstand for the phone, lift the receiver.

"Hello," I say.

"How's Bobby?" a voice asks.

"Stas, is that you?"

"How is he?"

"He won!"

Good Lord, it's four in the morning—couldn't he have just flipped on the TV?

"No, I mean how is he?"

"He won California, Stas. Isn't it wonderful?"

I'm still half asleep, shaken by the jolt of the ringing phone. I'm not quite caught up. Loud noises still tear into me. Stas knows this, and I wonder again why he's calling when he could have just switched on the TV.

I can feel the silence on the line. Like something has been disconnected. The receiver is cool in my hand, the mouthpiece against my cheek. I watch the city lights play down the edge of the curtain. Like mercury falling. I wish I'd turned on the lamp before picking up. I wish there was no sign of that beautiful dancing light—its promise and its heart.

Don't say anything. Don't ask. Keep holding the receiver and the silence.

"Stas," I say finally.

He tells me then.

...

Later, I'll piece the details together—how that night, walking through the kitchen of the Ambassador Hotel, Bobby was shot, once in the head, twice in the back; he just kind of slipped to the floor, the ground pulled out underneath him. Shouts, screaming, cries. Blood pooled from his head. Ethel fought through the crowd to reach him and, when she did, she pushed them all back to give him space and air.

Learning this particular detail, I do not want to imagine Ethel's face.

I fly to L.A.

Chuck Spalding and Richard Goodwin meet me at the airport.

"I want it straight," I say.

Bobby is in a tangle of medical equipment. Ethel lies over the bed, crying, her face across his legs. She is pregnant with their eleventh child. Teddy prays by the bed, on his knees. Other faces stand at the edges, ravaged. The same faces. It's too familiar. Crushing, airless, the bright hospital light. I just want to stop, to drop to my knees next to Teddy, not to pray, just to feel my knees against that implacable linoleum floor, like the sense of hardness meeting hardness might be enough to push the dark down.

I stay for a while in the room, then step out into the corridor.

Richard Goodwin tells me that he and Ted Sorensen had been upstairs in the suite, watching the speech on TV. They turned it off and were about to head down to meet Bobby when they heard screaming from the hall, the sound of running. They turned the TV back on and watched it unfold on the screen.

I want to hear it, detail by detail, from every point of view. I want to feel it, know it, as if I'm waking up. I want to be there in the horrible glare. I want the full weight of it to cut me loose. The grief is immeasurable. A vastness I'll never come to terms with or have the words to explain. I stand in the corridor outside the room where Bobby lies, hooked to machines that keep his chest rising and falling, his heart beating, though his brain is gone. No doctor will dare give the word to let him go. Ethel is stretched over him, Teddy still on his knees, with his bowed head and prayers.

At one point during the course of that day that goes on forever, Ethel glances at me across Bobby's body that is no longer Bobby, and there's an expression on her face—some question mixed in with the grief—that until the end of my life I will not know how to interpret. Then she stands up, touches Teddy on the shoulder, and draws him out of the room. For ten minutes, I am alone with him.

Then it's midnight again, then half past, then one. His chest still moving up and down, machines whirring away. We are gathered around him—in our places, a tableau.

It's time. No one says it. We all know. There's a pressure, faint, like heat on my skin. Ethel is looking at me. I meet her eyes. It's time. She nods, turning away, that impossible mix of agony and sorrow in her face as it caves.

1:44 A.M.

You have been the last dream of my soul.

Machines stop, his chest falls,
And it is done.
Mind, words, body, knowledge, dream.

Done.

When he died, you understand, that was the end, your beloved brother's death the final stroke of yours. There was no incentive then. No legacy. No passing of the torch. All we sacrificed and fought for and believed in. What was left of my heart broke and that was it. We stayed there gathered around his bed. It was like living your death all over again, and I was one of them and at the same time already fading from their view, passing out of their reach, alone. I saw the fabric of it all—how carefully we'd tried to build it, tried to keep it, and now the dissolution—Ethel with her lovely faithful head bowed, the rest of them, their eyes cast down, tears paving their faces, and I was there and not there, I did not cry, not then, and they did not notice. We all just stood there, without seeing. Watching our lives turn into history.

PART V

The heart of a woman who waits, her mind like a man's

—AESCHYLUS, translated by Chappell

After war, after any act of inconceivable violence, the world is neatly divided between those who are dead and those who remain. Troy was no different. When that ten-year siege was done—the walls of the glittering city razed, pillaged, burned—when the Greeks set off from the shores, when the old Trojan king was murdered along with his sons and the baby Astyanax hurled from a parapet, his tiny skull smashed—past and future leveled in an instant—afterward, who remains?

The mothers, the daughters, the wives. And sometimes, that's when the play begins.

I am someone who did not die when I should have died.

Hecuba said that. The Trojan king's widow. She'd watched her husband, sons, and daughters killed. She was destined to be exiled, enslaved.

Yes, I remember thinking when I read those words, I do know that feeling.

One day took a world away.

Yes, that too.

But the dream of the story continues. In some gorgeous zone of the imagination, told and retold, as if some new incarnation might shape a keener sense of meaning out of what was broken, burned, slain.

I have already decided by the time the children and I walk down the aisle of St. Patrick's for Bobby's funeral. The organist playing Mahler's symphony, Teddy standing up there alone to speak, holding such a mantle of weight on his shoulders. His voice shakes and I feel his mind veer.

I have already decided as we leave the church and a woman turns to me, extending a hand in sympathy—Lady Bird? Is that who it is? I've already begun to recede from this world with such speed and distance that in that moment I'm not sure I know her.

After nine that night, Teddy and I kneel beside the coffin on the hill at Arlington, the same hill. Candles light that same dark, the night like a hand on my shoulder, the smooth chill of the coffin, the reflection of the moon on wood, slipping over the surface. I stand up and it startles me—that fallstreak hole of the actual moon perfectly round in the sky, the rush of air on my face like I'm hurtling away from the rest of them toward it.

Back in New York, I write to Ethel. Crumple up a first draft, a second, then finally I get down what I want to say, about her children. I want her to know that *I'll take them around the world + to the moon + back.* I want her to know that if she needs me,

I'll be there, now and always. Then it's finished, the envelope sealed. I look up. It is my apartment—chairs, sofa, curtains, desk—but everything seems a shadow of what it was before. Even the view from the window. The maze of streets and park and city. The books on the shelves. Spines flat. Closed.

I've told no one what I've decided when I'm sitting with Rose in Hyannis Port and she says to me out of the blue, "You deserve happiness."

Late June. The day lilies in bloom.

I tell Rose I've asked Teddy to go to Greece with me in August. Ari wants to host a party for him, to show his support for the family. "Teddy and I will go together," I say. "We'll stay at Ari's house in Athens." I haven't said anything about what I've decided to Ari either.

The chintz in Rose's living room is essentially the same as when I first came that Fourth of July sixteen years ago. Rose is asking if I'd like another cup of tea. Her hands are veined, with a grace in them I've never really grasped. Those hands lift the teapot and start to pour as John rushes into the room, clutching three toy planes—a jumble of wings, noses, tails—long-boned contraptions of paper and tin. He holds one out to me but won't let go of the others. There's something he needs me to see, a wheel that has loosened and a place where the wing is bent. What kind of tool to fix it, he wants to know, and where would he find such a tool?

I study the plane, turning it over. "I think I know, John," I say. "I'll help you in a moment."

I take the planes from his hands, set them on the table, and draw him to me. I can feel his little body squirm to get loose. *You are my joy*, I say, breathing in his skin, his softness, his smell, which will be mine for only a while.

And the next time Ari asks me, I say yes.

Away.

Is why I did it.

Away is what he gave me, and for that first year after Bobby died, away was what I needed most. Hours, weeks, a season alone, with only beach, water, sky, a vagrant blue, the small house on the cliff, the steep fall into the green, the scent of jasmine, olive, and the wind like the breath of the god I no longer believe in.

Here on Skorpios I am free of the cult, the icon, the legend. I can design the life I want, the life I want for the children. Trips to museums, archaeological sites, plays, concerts, the movies in Athens, flights home to New York. Time to read, paint, swim. Ari's money keeps them safe. My children. No one understands that. Why should I have to explain? Their approval means nothing.

Sometimes he is here with me, but after the first few weeks, more often he is not.

"You are marrying Greece," he told me. "Now you will be a Greek wife. My Greek wife."

I remember very little of that day in October 1968. Twenty guests in the tiny chapel. I wore a simple white dress, ribbons woven through my hair. There was the exchange of rings and dark wine from a silver goblet. John and Caroline stood beside me, white lit tapers in their hands, their faces brave and somber as the priest intoned the Greek prayers I had learned. Outside, it began to rain.

"Rain at a wedding is a sign of luck," Ari's sister, Artemis, whispered to me.

. . .

AMERICA HAS LOST ITS SAINT, runs a headline in the *Bild Zeitung*.
SAD AND SHAMEFUL, claims *France-Soir*.
And in *The New York Times*: THE REACTION HERE IS ANGER, SHOCK, AND DISMAY

"The *Times* gave us a whole page," I tell Ari.
"How will you respond?"
"Do I have to?"
He looks . . . amused?
"If you had to, what would you say?"
I realize he's testing me.
"The honest thing would be to say I'm going to do this because it's what I want."
A faint wicked spark in his eyes. "My dear, you've already done it."

The papers say it's the jet-set life. They say he's ugly but irresistibly powerful. They call me desperate, hysterical, fearful—palatable things for a woman to be. They say I married him to outdo my sister. Poor Lee. Lee was upset at first but not that I was with him, only that I'd kept it from her.

It's Artemis who tells me what Fellini's wife, the actress Giulietta Masina, says: "Myths, when they are human, are fatally subject to wear and tear. Why marvel if a woman at a certain point tears off the veils that cover her like a monument—a thirty-nine-year-old monument, still beautiful, extremely alive, obligated to a role that does not belong to her?"

. . .

That fall on Skorpios, I learn Greek and how to dance the sirtaki. I ask Ari's friend Yiannis for lists of books on ancient Greek history, archaeology, art. I visit Artemis in Athens and wander the streets of the old quarter. I start to change things in the house— curtains, rugs. I move the furniture around and relandscape the gardens. One afternoon, reading Cavafy on the terrace, I overhear two of the older workmen grumble, "Winston Churchill's feet touched these stones, but they're not good enough for her. Soon, not even Mr. Onassis will be good enough for her."

When I know Ari is flying in from Athens, I pull things into order. Declutter the house—books neatly closed, magazines in neat piles off to the side, flowers in every vase. When he is with me, we spend each night on the *Christina*. He sings to me and tells me stories. I read poetry aloud, and as his cigar smoke falls in delicate ropes around us, he tells me about the new business he has brokered with the junta, a factory he'll build, a new oil refinery. He says it's the largest investment ever made in Greece.

"The colonels love my new spectacular American wife."

"I thought I was your Greek wife."

When I reach for my cigarettes, he swipes the pack from my hand. I swipe it back. No malice. Just a running joke between us. After dinner, we dance on the mosaic deck of the swimming pool. I'm drunk on the ouzo from dinner; I can feel the night roll off me as I take it all in, the warmth, the heady rush of his hands slipping the edge of my blouse off my shoulder as we dance, like he will undress me right there. "My boat," he would say, "my wife, why shouldn't I?"

I fly to the children in New York; both in school now, it's harder to peel them away. I come back to Skorpios in early November. I'm alone there. Ari is in Paris. Artemis stays with me.

"After Jack died," I tell her, "the air was different. I could feel him in it."

That day is still fire in my head. Molten. Unfinished. And there's a pain that comes in my neck out of nowhere, then throbs for hours.

I do not tell Artemis this.

For the fifth anniversary of Jack's death, I am with the children. We spend that week at a house I've rented in New Jersey. I ride with Caroline. We celebrate John's eighth birthday on November 25. Caroline turns eleven two days later. Thanksgiving falls late that year, and I feel an aching loss—not just for Jack and Bobby, but for those years gone and all that's changed.

. . .

The following summer, the children come to Skorpios for July. One afternoon on the deck of the *Christina,* Ari tells them the story of Icarus. Caroline's heard it before but listens politely, keeping her silky distance. John's face is rapt as Ari tells them about the boy whose father made him wings, and for the first time I wonder, *What kind of young man was Icarus?* That day in the labyrinth when his father came with his harebrained scheme and drew the route of their flight in the dirt—two bodies like matchsticks with those huge makeshift wings, woven quill, osier, wax. What did Icarus think as his father mapped it all out? Did he feel it then? The need to risk the sky?

More than once you said, almost in passing, that my mind was the thing that drew you to me. It was different, you said, it made me different from any other girl.

"Time for a swim?" Ari says. I glance up. "Yes or no?" His eyes are fixed on me.

"Sure," I say.

"You weren't listening."

"I was."

"You should have been. The story of an arrogant young man who aimed too high."

I don't want him to see me react, not in front of the children.

"Icarus reached," I say. "And there's meaning in that."

"Don't rewrite the myth."

"I'd love a swim." I stand up, brushing off my shorts. I turn to the children. John jumps to his feet, but Caroline waits, listening, absorbing the harder underside of everything not said.

. . .

Days before I turn forty, the spacecraft Apollo is launched—an answer to Jack's pledge to put a man on the moon before the decade's end. As Neil Armstrong, Buzz Aldrin, and Michael Collins head toward lunar orbit and the Sea of Tranquility, Teddy drives an Oldsmobile Delmont 88 off the Dike Bridge into Poucha Pond with a girl named Mary Jo in the passenger seat. He gets out of the car and walks away. The girl doesn't. He waits ten hours before reporting it, for reasons that will never quite be clear. The car is found in the water, upside down, by a boy who's come to the bridge to fish that Saturday morning. The story is on the front page of the paper the day those astronauts take their first steps.

CAR PLUNGES INTO VINEYARD POND

MAN WALKS ON THE MOON

I feel something inside me tear. Tattered dynasty, that spent dream. It was always going to end with something like this.

Ari throws a party for my birthday at his favorite *bouzoukia* in Athens. I wear a short Pucci dress with a long string of pearls and flip-flops. He gives me a gold belt with a lion-head clasp and a second gift he calls "a sentimental trifle": a pair of diamond, ruby, and sapphire earrings to mark the Apollo moon landing.

"Is this your way of asking me to forgive you for the Icarus remark?" I say lightly.

"Why would I ask forgiveness from a wife who doesn't know that a myth is just that?"

"The earrings are thoughtful, Ari." He looks at me, wary. "I mean it," I say. "A beautiful gift. That moon landing is what Jack"—I'm about to say *reached for*—"believed in," I say instead. A brief smile, then I turn away, because the tears burn, and I just need to push them back; those tears aren't for Ari but for the sudden rush of grief for all that Jack believed in and did not live to see.

"Those earrings are exquisite," my friend Katina remarks later that night.

I smile at her. "And Ari has told me that, if I'm good, next year he'll give me the moon itself." I take out a cigarette and go to light it. Ari knocks it from my hand.

"Dirty," he says.

. . .

The children fly home. They'll spend two weeks with their cousins in Hyannis Port, then they'll go to my mother's in Newport. I'll meet them there. The first night they're gone, things revert. Fine bands of tension between us—an angry word, a tone of voice. An occasional insult under his breath that's never quiet enough for me to miss. He's begun to call me names. Circe, after the beautiful witch who ensnared Odysseus with her spells, turning men to pigs. Mummy is the name I hate. He swears it's an endearment, but every time he says it, I feel something in me shrink.

"I fly out tomorrow," he says one evening at dinner.

"So soon?" I say, picking a piece of octopus from a film of oil on my plate.

"Why bother to stay?" he says. "Your nose is always in a book, why should I be here?"

He leaves, and the house is empty. The island empty, except for the housekeeper, the workmen, the guards. We've been married for almost a year—apart for 141 days.

. . .

Joe dies that fall. On a small table in the bedroom is a photograph from his seventy-fifth-birthday celebration. September 1963. Joe has always loved that photograph. Every time I came to see him, he'd have me pick it up and bring it over to the bed. In the photograph, everything is as it was: Jack was alive, as was Bobby, everyone joking, laughing, only a few looking at the camera. Teddy was young, in a crisp blue shirt, his face unlined and tan, unmarked by his brothers' deaths and the more recent disaster of the car and the girl Mary Jo and what he didn't do to save her. In that photograph, Rose's sweater echoes the chintz, and Joe is in his silk loungewear in the green upholstered chair. I kneel beside him, my younger self, sheathed in white, dark hair a cloud around my face. I never quite recognized myself in that photograph, apart from the slightly crooked smile. We'd lost Patrick only a month before, and you could see it in my face, a sadness that felt nearly timeless, even prescient. When I asked Joe why he loved that photograph so much, he would point to me in it, kneeling beside him, looking off to the side.

It is Teddy who calls to tell me Joe is dying. I leave Athens that night and fly to him.

Sitting by his bed, I talk with him and hold his hand, watch his wandering eyes. He cannot speak, and now he does not try. I stay with him as he sleeps, Teddy curled in a sleeping bag on the floor. I stay until Joe slips off, on November 18, 1969—two nights before Bobby would have turned forty-four.

. . .

I go on mapping each season—my life in New York, the interludes in Greece—weaving a sense of order for myself and John and Caroline. There are birthday parties and boarding schools. I work with children at a shelter in Spanish Harlem and volunteer with wounded veterans. In their eyes I see the familiar dismantling of the ordinary. Some have endured things so much more severe than what I witnessed.

One evening in late spring, in the kitchen of my apartment in New York, as I'm taking down a glass from the shelf, something trips inside me, and I remember a warm night on one long weekend, as Jack and I walked home from his parents' house in Hyannis Port. He took me by the waist and twirled me slowly around. He spun me out, away from him, then drew me back; his lips brushed my neck, and he kept on walking. I wanted to stop, to stand with him in the middle of that soft evening, to stave off the night and make everything stand still, but Jack never stopped, and so we kept walking, though he held my hand a moment longer than I'd expected he would.

I've forgotten to breathe, standing in the kitchen of my apartment, the cool glass in my hand, my mind light. How does it happen? Those slight rogue details one forgets that lie stored in some quiet dark of the underself and burst forth like angels— magnificent, bold—remembered only years later, radiant only then.

I'm holding the glass and then not. It slips from my hand and hits the floor. I expect it to shatter. It just rolls away.

. . .

The arguments escalate. Ari's business dealings have begun to slip. The junta has not been the ally he'd hoped for. His influence has faltered. His archrival, Stavros Niarchos, has plans to marry Ari's ex-wife, Tina. Their daughter, Christina, elopes to Las Vegas with a California real estate dealer.

He turns his rage on me because I am the one who is there. Slight things set him off. He complains I am cold, too quiet, too fey. I smoke too much, read too much, spend too much. I baby my children. I'm always in New York. I am not a dutiful-Penelope wife, patiently waiting at home.

Once, in a restaurant, when I point out that he's mixed up the capitals of two African nations, his rage erupts. He calls me a cunt. The heads of the diners at the surrounding tables swivel toward us, the room stunned. I look down at my hands in my lap. I say nothing else for the rest of the evening. But I find slight ways to rebel. He hates a mess, so I find excuses to make one. I'll leave pools of dripping water in the wrong spot on the deck of the *Christina* after jumping off and climbing back on board. I give the children haircuts in the bathroom; Ari explodes when he finds little hairs in the drain. He yells at me. I tune him out—a cool smile, a docile "Yes, Ari," which infuriates him.

I know the night it ends.

We are at the house in Athens. A rainy evening. His friends Miltos and Yiannis have come for dinner. After we eat, I sit at one end of the sofa, reading, while the men talk. It feels awkward. As I slip a torn piece of paper into my book to mark my place, I notice the conversation has lulled. They seem to have come to a stopping place. I look up then and ask Yiannis what he thinks: Did Socrates really exist, or was he just an invention of Plato, a kind of paragon stand-in for the ideal Athenian philosopher?

There's a pause as Yiannis considers the question. He opens his mouth to answer, but Ari stands up and takes an odd, deliberate step into the space between us. He turns on me. "What is the matter with you? Why do you have to ask about stupid things? Have you never noticed the statue of a man with a mustache in the center of Athens? Are you too stupid to recognize that is a statue of Socrates?"

I don't think or hear or see or feel anything—only the faint stain of leftover rage in the air.

Even in the bigger houses, the walls were thin enough that Lee and I could hear our parents fight. Their voices broke like plates against the walls. I'd hear my sister crying. I'd go into her room, crawl into her bed, and hold her, her silky face against my chest, hands woven through my hair. We'd float that way together, an island of just the two of us. Lee would ask me to turn on the light, and I'd have to explain that, no, I could not do that, a light would bring them in, their whirling rage in tow. "It's much nicer in the dark, Pekes," I'd say instead.

I stand up from the sofa, Ari's mouth still moving, loud words directed toward me coming out, which mean nothing, are nothing, because he is cruel. For the first time in so long, it seems, I have no fear. Beyond him, there is rain on the roof, light notes of beautiful rain. Rain for luck, Artemis told me once, but luck is worthless against the choices that we make. Still, that beautiful rain. That's what I listen for—that sense of the world that remains. Ari takes another step toward me, the great maw of his mouth open. I hold my book tight against my body and thread my way between the chairs where the other men sit, unhappily looking on. I go upstairs, find my raincoat, and walk outside to where the floodlights sever the trees. As I cross the lawn, the wind hits me. Rain strikes my face, and the world is dark, the salt smell of the sea driven in on the rain, the smell of jasmine, the fainter smell of orange trees. The night on my skin is like fire. After a quarter of an hour, Ari sends Miltos out to find me. I don't come right away, and by the time I do, it is over. The guests are still there, Ari still fuming. I come back into the hallway, passing by a vase of flowers on the side table. I walk into the room where the men still sit, an uncomfortable silence as I enter that I don't try to fill. I sit down on the sofa next to Yiannis. My clothes are damp, and I watch the stain of the wet spread like a faint dark continent away from me. I see Ari notice it. "You're making a mess," he says with contempt. I just look back at him without saying a word, waiting for the explosion. It doesn't come, and I understand that I have won. I am not Circe and he is not Odysseus. It was never that magnificent or noble. We are a man and a woman in a marriage that has failed.

. . .

Months later, another terrible call.

The plane was an old Piaggio. Alexander, Ari's only son, told his father the plane was a death trap. They arranged for it to be sold in Miami. Alexander took it up on a test ride with the young pilot he'd hired to fly it across the Atlantic. They left the runway. Moments later, the controls failed, and they crashed.

I am in New York when the news comes. I fly to Athens. Alexander is in a coma, the right side of his face destroyed, his skull crushed.

In the weeks after, Ari won't let me out of his sight. I hold him for hours when he cries. Decimated, he refuses to have his son buried; he refuses to accept that the death was an accident. He's convinced it was the junta or the CIA. He has enemies, and their names twitch like rats in his brain.

He does not sleep. He paces the deck of the *Christina*, murmuring to himself. I find bottles of ouzo knocked over, rolling under a chair. He wants to deep-freeze his son's body in a cryonic state until science has advanced enough that his shattered head can be restored. It's Yiannis, always the good friend, who gently tells him that a father has no right to impede the journey of a child's soul. So the body is flown to Skorpios, and Ari allows his son to be laid to rest in the white marble vault. He sets a makeshift bed beside the grave. When anyone talks to him about God or heaven, he answers: "My son is dead, I'll never see him, I don't believe in anything you say."

One morning, he tells me to bring Artemis to the chapel for lunch. We arrive to a table set with four places, pressed napkins, silver, wineglasses, a linen tablecloth. Ari is already there, in one of the chairs turned toward the vault. He speaks in Greek to the fourth chair set beside it, raises the glass in his hand. The ouzo spills as his hand trembles, and he toasts his dead son.

By spring, his moods grow darker. Artemis tells me that since Alexander's death, there is gossip that I—"the American Woman"—am the reason his son was killed. Before I came, people say, the Onassis family was strong. Now Alexander is dead. Olympic Airways is failing. Ari's business deals have begun to sour. The black widow, they call me. The curse.

Artemis tells me that at first when Ari heard such things, he dismissed them as rubbish.

"At first?" I ask.

We spend Easter that year on the *Christina* in the Bahamas. The islands rise like sleight-of-hand coins as we cruise. The children are with us, a few friends, and Stas and Lee. Also on board is Lee's young lover, photographer Peter Beard. Another headlong affair my sister is in right under Stas's nose. It won't last. Lee is too sulky, then contrite. She needs too much, and Peter is too strong to put up with it for long. He will love her until one day he wakes up and doesn't.

Four hundred meters off the shore of Harbor Island, we anchor. The water is shallow. We can't get closer in. I tell Ari that Lee and I want to go ashore.

"You don't need to go shopping."

"We want to explore the town."

"We're not going ashore."

"Come on, Ari."

"We need a good lunch."

"So you can tell a string of nasty jokes? No one wants that kind of lunch."

I knew it would set him off. He hates having anyone think he's being run by a wife. I see the fury brewing in his eyes, the anger of a cornered man who wants more control of life than life will give to him again.

"You're not going ashore," he says. He turns to the others. "Lunch—who will join me?"

My clothes are noiseless as they strike the deck—the linen shirt, tank top, shorts, and hat. They fall in a pile, and I am over the side, swimming away toward land.

. . .

In the fall of 1974, I buy a two-story converted barn on ten acres in New Jersey. Ari comes to see me in New York. A few days later, he falls ill with the flu. His vision doubles. His speech begins to slur. He is hospitalized, diagnosed with progressive myasthenia gravis and a compromised heart.

Stress, alcohol, fatigue, the doctors explain. I sit beside him and listen. The cortisol they've injected makes his face swell. His eyelids droop. They prop them up with plaster.

He leans on me heavily as we leave the hospital, his eyes shielded by dark glasses.

"I've lost my touch," he says sadly that night as I fix him a plate of bland food.

"You need to rest," I say, "take better care of yourself. You'll come back from this."

"There are some voyages, Mummy, a man does not return from."

My hand pauses, pouring a glass of water for him. "Don't call me that again."

I don't return with him when he flies back to Athens. He falls ill again. I go to him then. I help Artemis and his daughter move him to Paris, where his doctors are. He refuses to go to the hospital, insisting he is fine, he will be fine. He'll stay in his apartment, he says. His doctors will come to him. He'll take whatever pills or infusion they force his way. He'll rally.

I'm in New York, getting ready for a party to celebrate the premiere of an NBC documentary Caroline helped produce. She's only seventeen. It's late morning when the phone rings.

"Just Christina was there," Artemis tells me. When Christina knew her father's fever was rising, she never left his side. She told his doctors not to call anyone else. She wanted his last hours to be solely hers. An hour after he was gone, she tried to slash her wrists.

I set the phone back into the cradle and walk into the guest room, where my friend Karen has spent the night.

"Ari's dead," I say. "Please stay here and stand in for me as hostess. For Caroline. This is her night."

As I pack, I try to close my mind against the unvoiced disappointment that my daughter—with her astute grace—will try to hide. She'll understand my leaving. She will say it's okay. This is what she's learned to do. I consider staying the few extra hours, through the day, the party, the evening. But the world will watch. I know that. The world will be quick to judge the fact that hasn't broken in the news yet, the one I can't undo—that I wasn't there when he died.

I close the suitcase, shift the lock.

Teddy flies with me through time zones. The Atlantic streams underneath as we gain on the night. I wear a black trench coat, a black leather skirt.

"They're going to crucify me because I wasn't there," I say.

"They would've either way."

He tilts his glass. Dark wine swirls. We fly in silence.

"I have to make a statement when we land," I say.

"No, you don't."

"What will the press say if I say nothing?"

"We'll explain you're grieving."

"I'm not."

He looks at me sharply. He never particularly liked Ari. None of them did. But they want me to play my part.

"Ari rescued me at a time when my life was very dark," I say. "I can say something like that and still be telling the truth. It's almost a cliché, Teddy, but I'm forty-five, and the older I get, the more important it feels to live the truth."

Teddy, like so many others, never understood how I could have let myself be pinioned into that Greek-wife life. That's how he'll claim to see it, though I know that he, of anyone, grasps the complex weight of what it is to be a Kennedy. The summer after Bobby died, Teddy would take the boys out to sail—Bobby's sons and my John. Teddy was drinking so much then, wine settled in the cracked seams of his lips. He looked blasted all that summer.

"No one wants to be a myth," I say. "We're taught it's what

we're supposed to want. No one tells you ahead of time the cost. They cry for you, jeer at you, cheer you on, hold you up, and, when that gets dull, they tear you down. It takes work, Teddy, in that charade, to piece together who you really are—what you think and want and believe. Jack and I used to talk about that."

Silence then. Through the window, sheaves of cloud fall away.

Why is it, I want to ask, *that every loss brings up every other?*

The plane strikes the runway with a jolt. As the wheels find the ground, Teddy asks about the will.

"We'll settle that later," I say.

"This might be your chance."

"Christina just lost the father she never had. That's enough for now."

"Then I'll ask," he says.

"Please don't," I say. "Not yet. But it's nice, Teddy, that you look after me the way Jack would have wanted you to."

He bites the edge of his lip, a boy again, the youngest, the scapegrace who was always trying to pull himself together enough to catch up.

Ari is buried in the chapel on Skorpios where we were married seven years ago. White lilies fill the courtyard. Red velvet drapes the stones. Cherry trees bloom on the terraced hill. The day is gray and overcast. Christina sobs, her eyes swollen. Artemis quietly weeps.

I do not cry. I can hear the word move like it's coming alive out of the stones, *curse,* a lean, distinct black thread through the rustling grief and keening of the women. *Curse.* I grasp it then, standing in the damp chill of that small chapel. I could have stayed with Caroline that night. No matter what, they will hate me. Even if I'd been at his side when he died, they would hate me. At the same time, I understand that their hatred is a gift. I am the curse, black widow, outcast. Because of that, every last tie will be cut. I owe his memory nothing. I am free.

When I return to New York, I recognize it for the first time in years—the exquisite chaos of the city at night below my window. Above the moving lights of cars and the scrawl of trees in the park, the stars are faint, but they are there—what I can see and what I know exists beyond the range of sight—those irreverent solitary burnings yoked into constellated lines we imagine will hold them, lines that let us think, mistakenly, they do not belong to their own lexicon but to ours.

I am home, and my home, for the first time in my life, is solely mine.

What will I make of this now?

PART VI

Through corridors of light,
where the hours are suns . . .
their lips, still touched with fire

—STEPHEN SPENDER

Mornings, I linger over newspapers. Drink my coffee. Jog around the reservoir. One day, a blond baseball-capped reporter steps in front of me on the sidewalk. There's been an article in the *Times*, he says, about Ari's daughter, Christina, and "bitter hostilities" between us.

"Would you care to comment, Mrs. Onassis?"

"I've just received an invitation to her wedding in July," I say. It's essentially true. The invitation was Artemis-extracted. I go to step around him; he blocks the path.

"So, for the record, you deny the claim that Christina Onassis is 'hostile' toward you?"

"For the record," I say, "my life is very dull right now. I shop at the local A&P. Excuse me, please. I need to go. My son is on his way home from school."

I tell Tish about this over lunch a few days later.

She laughs, then says, "But how are you, Jackie?"

"Oh, Tish, you always ask the tricky questions."

How would I explain it? It's not the loss of Ari. It's not the children growing up and into their own lives. I wouldn't want that any other way. It's not that I'm lonely or bored. I have plenty of dates and events, theater and concerts and readings. What then?

I study the menu. When the waiter returns with our drinks, I order a hamburger.

"Tish, I've decided that as long as you do your push-ups and jog around the reservoir, you can never go wrong with a hamburger."

"*You* can never go wrong with a hamburger."

I laugh, but I'm thinking about an article I read in the paper this morning about the fall of Saigon. Communist tanks rolling up to the palace, the boulevard strewn with burning cars. U.S. troops were picking up Vietnamese who fled in boats. Former soldiers blended in to lose themselves in crowds. One soldier walked up to an army memorial and shot himself. That stopped me. I read those lines twice. The war was over, to the extent that something that never should have been started can be over. *More complex than any dark hell Shakespeare looked into.* That's how Bob McNamara described it once. But isn't there something after every end?

"I want to work, Tish," I say, "but I haven't had a paying job since I married Jack."

"What about Viking? You love books."

"Loving books and being qualified for a publishing job aren't the same."

"You know Tom Guinzburg. Wasn't he a friend of Yusha's in college and part of your *Paris Review* circle?"

"I only wish it were mine," I say.

When Lee married Michael Canfield, I'd felt a twinge of envy, not because my younger sister was racing ahead to the altar but because Lee was marrying into a publishing family. I couldn't imagine anything more thrilling than spending breakfast, lunch, and dinner talking about what books were being acquired, critiqued, reviewed. Funny. A twinge like that, so easily dismissed.

"You were a reporter," Tish says as she picks up her fork and starts on her salad.

"A quarter of a century ago."

"You've lived through an important part of history."

"I suppose."

"Just call him, Jackie. Call Tom and talk to him. See what happens."

Years ago, there was a letter in a book you showed me, written by Einstein to the grieving family of his closest friend:

> Now he has departed from this strange world a little ahead of me. That means nothing. People like us, who believe in physics, know that the distinction between past, present, and future is only a stubbornly persistent illusion.

Which is the equivalent of saying that the dividing line that marks "what happened" from "what will happen" is no more substantial than the fog of a child's breath on glass.

. . .

I don't call Tom Guinzburg. Not that I wouldn't want the work. I'd love it. But what if I can't handle being out in the world that way? How would I act? How would the world act toward me?

A few weeks ago, my friend Peter and I went to the opera, and Peter remarked that taking me anywhere was like taking King Kong to the beach.

I drive out to New Jersey to ride. When I get back to New York, I realize there are no eggs in the refrigerator. I walk to the store. On my way home, I run into Jimmy Breslin. He takes the bag of groceries and walks with me for a few blocks.

"Jimmy, do you remember how you told me once there have been so many of you in the course of your life, so many Jimmy Breslins, because you kept turning into the people you wrote about and they turned into you? You said that at a certain point it became impossible to pin down any one Jimmy Breslin."

"So this is a serious conversation?" he asks.

"I'm thinking about going back to work."

He stops walking. "You?"

"Yes, but which me?"

He laughs. "Do you really think you're just going to attend openings for the rest of your life?"

The morning Tom Guinzburg is coming over, I dress carefully, and when I can't choose between two tops, I realize I'm nervous. Silly. I've known Tom for a long time. He's too kind to laugh at me, even if he thinks it's absurd that I'd just show up at his office, dragging the circus behind me.

Whatever I do, the world will say what it says. I can't live fighting or running or hiding from that. I can't spend the rest of my life watching raindrops sliding down the windowpane.

Black top, I finally decide. White pants. Straightforward. Low-key. I put on my earrings in the mirror.

"There will be a fair amount of learning the ropes at first," Tom Guinzburg tells me.

"I don't have to convince you?"

He laughs. "If things don't work out, I'll just fire you."

"That would be a story. Though I've been through worse."

"There's no glamour in publishing, Jackie."

"I want to learn."

"There will be plenty of that."

"And I want to start where anyone else would start. Agreed?"

"You can take notes for a while. You don't have the background, really, to be an editor. It's not that you don't have the talent or skill. You just don't have the training. But you can sit in on meetings, and eventually we can work toward acquisitions."

"Perfect."

"How are the children?" he asks.

"Caroline's going to work in London this fall."

"Exciting."

"I wish it wasn't so far."

Silence then. The quiet rush of sunlight down the curtains into layered maps across the floor.

"Listen, Tom. You're not doing this just as a favor, a handout?"

"Not at all. You must realize this has advantages for me."

"I don't want to be anyone's pity case."

He starts to smile.

"If you're going to say something," I say, "please say it. Otherwise I'll think all sorts of things." I say this easily, with warmth, the way I've learned, but he gives me that look I've seen before when someone is surprised I've read the nuance of a moment they were trying to hide.

"I'm just not clear yet what your title would be," he says.

"Aren't you supposed to tell me my title?"

"This is an unusual case."

"Well, what's the lowest title in publishing?"

He hesitates. "Consulting editor."

"There it is."

Fall 1975

There's a crowd gathered outside the Viking offices at 625 Madison. I slip out of the taxi a block away, into the side entrance.

Tom introduces me to the staff. They're polite, of course, but skeptical. Why wouldn't they be? I try to connect. It all feels awkward. Tom shows me the office that will be mine. It's small, so simple my heart leaps. Just a desk, file cabinets, a swivel chair.

"I love it," I say. "Now I can work my way up to a room with a view."

The crowd is there, outside every morning when I arrive and every afternoon when I leave. When I dash across the street to the diner for lunch, I steel myself just inside the door. I close my face into the empty face and push out into the flash of camera bulbs.

Weeks pass. I begin to get a handle on my days. I bring my lunch in a paper bag and eat in my office. I get my own coffee. I draft my own memos. I wait in line with everyone else to use the Xerox machines. And there's a certain electrifying magic to the ordinary. I feel like this is something I've waited my whole life to know. Most evenings, I have a quiet dinner with John at home. After we eat, while he does his homework, I read manuscripts. I work only part-time. I call into the office every Monday and Friday to check in.

Some of the crazy continues. One day a bomb threat. Often, uninvited strangers arrive at reception, insisting I'll want to see them. There's a heavy stream of interview requests and canvas sacks full of what Tom calls "Jackie mail." Once, among the letters and manuscripts, a .38 caliber arrives in a manila envelope addressed to me with a note.

I'm stepping into my office when Tom tells me about the gun. I stop, my fingers on the knob. It will never end. The mail and the threats will come. The crowds will wait.

"Are you all right?" Tom says.

"Oh yes," I say. I step into my office, take out a blank sheet of paper, and I start a list for twenty potential book projects—why they might work, ways I can help make them work, why they are stories that need to be told.

That weekend, Caroline is home from London for five days. When John gets out of school on Friday afternoon, we pile into my jelly-bean-green BMW and drive out to the house in New Jersey. There was a storm the week before. The leaves had turned, and that storm took them down. Now they're strewn across the road and the fields, gorgeous streams of burnished reds, coppers, golds. The children are bickering—not an argument—just that playful banter of *you're wrong and I'm right*. John tells his sister that he's planning to raise a python in her bathtub while she's away. "Noooooo," Caroline says. "You won't let him, Mom, will you?" The road is awash with leaves; the beauty of them catches in my throat.

...

Just after Christmas, at a dinner at my apartment, the Schlesingers, the Mudds, and the Duchins raise a glass to my new adventure.

"Say a few words," Arthur says. "Tell us. What's it like to be a working woman again?"

"I love books. It's that simple. I love how they expand my mind. Like travel, books let you explore other cultures, perspectives, histories—worlds markedly different from your own."

"Hear, hear!" Arthur lifts his glass. The others join in. The candles are burning down into castled piles of wax. No one mentions the rumblings in the news—allegations of Jack's affair with Judith Exner, a woman linked with mob boss Sam Giacana. The unraveling has only begun. In my gut I know this, and I hate what I know.

A few days later, an outline of Exner's half-finished memoir appears in the *Times*, along with the claim that our marriage was in poor shape. In early March, news about Mary Meyer hits the papers. *Two-year White House affair with D.C. artist . . . J.F.K. smoked grass.* Laced through the smut are details of Mary's murder.

That familiar awful heat under my skin.

It will burn for a while. Every detail—true and not—will catch like tinder. It's our children I think about. And I think about walking into work tomorrow. The meetings I have next week. The ballet I was planning to attend. It'll be everywhere by then, and I'll relive it every time I meet someone's eyes and see that complex web of pity, disbelief, and parasitic wonder. I told you this would happen.

I grab my coat and take a taxi to my friend Karen's apartment. I walk in and sit down.

"You've read it," Karen says.

"As much as I'll read."

Karen sits down next to me, and I want to explain that as long as it was secret, I could handle it. The rules of marriage were different back then. I knew what I'd signed up for. I don't say that. I don't try to justify it.

"Learn to let things go," you told me once. "Be like a horse flicking away flies in summer."

The edges of my eyes burn now for how ironic it is—that your wisdom should intercede to help me through the awful consequence of your foolishness and your hubris, your belief that the world would never turn against you.

As I leave Karen's that day, a woman in the elevator turns around and stares. There's no one else in the elevator. I slip on my sunglasses and look straight ahead, hoping all that woman can see is her own reflection in the mirrored lens.

. . .

I hurl myself into work. A book of Abraham Lincoln daguerreotypes. *The Firebird,* a collection of Russian fairy tales. Lawrence Durrell's new novel, *Sicilian Carousel.* I take on a project with Diana Vreeland, who, over lunch one day, leans across the table to me with that Kabuki face and jet-black hair and says:

"There's nothing duller, Jackie, than a smooth, perfect-skinned woman. A woman is beautiful by her scars."

One afternoon, soon after Jack's birthday—he would have turned fifty-nine—as I am walking up to the reservoir for my run, I notice that my sneaker lace is loose. I stop to retie it. There's a couple nearby on a blanket, young, graceless, fumbling with each other like they can't keep up with their own desire. A few yards away, a baby carriage in the shade. It is a Sunday. Services are over. The bells are ringing. I turn away and start up the path, the sound of those bells melding with the dappled shadows and the trees.

The landslide of tell-alls continues. Thirdhand gossip, anonymous interviews, insider secrets "newly revealed." Jack's affairs, our alleged unhappiness—it all gets dredged up. Juicy bits, nasty bits—some true, most conclusively not. It's heartbreaking, humiliating, but after a while it just becomes too much to brace myself or try to anticipate what someone might say to John at school, what someone at work might have seen in a tabloid magazine while standing in line at the drugstore. Headline after headline. Jack and I, Jack and the women, Bobby and I, those nights after Jack died, the drink and the grief and those little blue pills—what might have happened that shouldn't have, and in the end did it? God, there's just so much. That glittering trash.

At a certain point it begins to feel like it's the mirage of a woman they've conjured. She and I only happen to share the same name. She's a caricature cobbled out of smear and myth, a cartoon life that runs alongside mine. Maybe it was always this way. I slip out from under it. I go on living my life—a woman in a trench coat, a scarf, and a pair of sunglasses, walking to work, so ordinary and visible I disappear.

"There's nothing more important than books," I say to John one evening after dinner at home. "When people are reading, they're thinking. That's how change takes place."

John nods—his earnest dark eyes, patient with me always. At the same time, I know there's no easy combination of words I can come up with to express the thrill of living in the world of books. I love to read the early drafts of a manuscript, to feel the work of a mind unfinished, then read it through again and mark it up, pencil carving the text so it comes alive on the page.

Cut it back, I'll write in the margin. *Be ruthless. Hold to what you want to say and how you choose to tell it. Everything is story.*

. . .

August 1977. Hammersmith Farm will be sold. I go to walk the rooms of the house where I grew up. Then my mother and I drive to Bailey's Beach. We sit on the porch at the beach club and order lunch, and I remember the swim Jack and I took the summer before we were married.

"Do you love me?" I asked you that day. It was the first time I felt bold enough to ask. And our mothers were calling us from up on the porch. We pretended not to hear. We swam and we did not get out;

they kept calling, waving, two figures with their dresses and stock-
ings, their hats and pearls, like tiny paper dolls, and I understood
then that the mothers belonged to the formal machinations of that
world while you and I belonged to the sea.

"Are you going to order?" my mother is asking now, glancing over
the menu.

"What?"

"For lunch, what are you having for lunch?"

Once, on Air Force One, I was changing between events. I'd started
to unbutton my blouse; it was half off my shoulder when you came
up behind me and touched me. It surprised me—that you'd come so
near without my realizing, and that you had touched me that way.
You ran one finger down my body, from the edge of my breast to my
waist, and then you looked at me and you did not say it, because it
wasn't the kind of thing you would say, but your eyes did. They said,
You are mine.

Some sand has blown in under the clubhouse door. I stand up
and drop my napkin on the chair.

"Where are you going?" my mother says as I slip off my shoes.
Tucking them under the table, I step toward the door with the
crack underneath, then through it, to the porch and the bands of
sun beyond the veranda, steps leading down to the beach.

"Jackie, where are you going?"

"Don't worry," I say. "I'll be right back."

. . .

I leave Viking and go to work at Doubleday. The following year, I
find a stretch of coast on Martha's Vineyard. I buy the land to
build a house near the cliffs of Aquinnah, where the sea is woven
into the sky. That spring, I walk the land with Bunny Mellon. We
talk about the long gravel drive I love that winds over a creek
with an old wooden gate. We draft the details of the house—
saltbox, cedar shingle, white trim. I tell Bunny I want a home the

children will want to return to, years from now, with their children.

"I want it to be happy," I say, "with comfortable places to sit and flowers in every room."

On the ground we lay the house out with string.

Caroline is finishing her junior year of college. John will be a freshman in the fall. There's a girl he's begun to bring around. Shy, dark hair, a glowing smile. They stop by the apartment one night on their way to the movies. They have an hour to kill. We talk for a while. John, restless, checks his watch, pushes a hand through his hair, and walks to the stereo. He sets a record on the player. As the song begins, he asks the girl, "Good for you?" She nods. She glances from John to me, then back to him, as he walks around the room, that caged gorgeous energy he has. *Don't lose your heart,* I want to tell her. But how beautiful it is, that shining hopefulness of love before it learns. He comes back and sits down, leg still jiggling, and the air is filled with music, a sweetness to the night that reminds me of a life I lived before; for a moment I let it rush in—the joy of what I loved and dreamed and lost.

When they leave, I walk them out. They're heading downtown. I'm going the other way, meeting my friend Maurice for dinner. The doorman offers to hail a taxi. "We're all going to walk tonight," I say, "but thank you." I hug my son goodbye. His arms come around me, quick and strong and tight, then he lets me go. Half a block up, I look back. His arm around the girl, they've crossed the street toward the park, the wall and the dark and the shapes of the green. Light off the streetlamps rains down on them like blessings.

The presidential library is nearly finished. A tower of glass at Columbia Point that overlooks Boston Harbor. When the work is done, there will be a dedication. Teddy has told me he intends to run against Jimmy Carter. He won't win. I know this. I left the last family meeting in Hyannis Port knowing it. A vague misguidedness hangs like a shadow over his campaign. But I'll stand by him if this is what he wants. Or what he thinks he has to want. At the dedication of the library, Teddy will speak, as will Caroline, and John will read a Stephen Spender poem. One evening, when I am with Maurice, I read the poem aloud to him. My eyes ache as I near the last stanza.

Born of the sun, they traveled a short while toward the sun . . .

Maurice's hand slips over mine. He doesn't say anything, but I can feel he understands. Poetry is not a luxury. Not to me. It cuts to the quick like any other tool of survival.

"In the days after that day," I say, "I realized my only chance at life was with the children. They are my home." I look at him when I say this.

"Of course," he says. "How could it be otherwise?"

I feel something in me settle.

It's unique, the friendship between us. I can tell him things I can't share with anyone else. I can talk about Jack—not only Jack in the past but how he still burns through my present, and how I've come to understand that desire for what is irretrievable can be a sort of prayer. I've told him how Jack devoured life in a way that both fascinated and terrified me, like a man sucking the meat out of a lobster claw—the books he read, the food he ate, the boats he sailed, and, yes, the women. While the library is about his legacy, his ideals, and his call to service, for me it's also a way to keep alive the catalytic hunger that defined him.

With Maurice, I can also share the harder things that even now, years later, I can't bear to look at head-on, how Jack and I seemed to be finally figuring things out in those last few months before he died. I can still feel the sharp, heartbroken beauty of that time, that fall of 1963, at once so brief and endless, and the rage when he was taken from me. Maurice just listens, and something in how he listens softens the bitterness.

He is kind to me. He helps manage my finances, and he un-

derstands that the money I have is not simply money but freedom to live on my own terms. I love the nimble reach of his
mind. Erudite, curious. We read poetry together and speak
French. We go to concerts, museums, and for walks in the park.
I first met him when Jack was a senator and Maurice was a diamond merchant in Africa. Part of me loves that he has that window into my past, though we rarely speak of it. He's the kind of
person who grasps that memory is wreckage touched in sunlight,
and the soul isn't something whole inside us. Rather, it comes to
us in fragments, and it's for us to build a sense of order out of
shards and meaning where there's none. He is still married. He's
moved out of the home he shared with his wife into rooms at the
Stanhope Hotel, a few blocks from 1040 Fifth Avenue.

. . .

I turn fifty at the end of July 1979. There's a flurry of articles.
One I actually like comes out of an interview I agreed to do with
Gloria Steinem about what it means for a woman to work, which
women of my generation were not supposed to want to do.
There's a scathing piece in *The Washington Post* I decide to read.
I pick up a few errors, typos, *Skorpios* spelled incorrectly, and
punctuation where there shouldn't be. I'm halfway through
when I realize I'm bored. It doesn't *say* anything, and it strikes
me then how often it's just this way with a woman's story. No
one wants to know the real story—the private story—the evolu-
tion of a woman's interior life. They want events on a linear
string. Some twists and turns, a little joy, a little danger, tragedy,
of course, and, if there's some transgression, comeuppance. When
they tell the story of a woman, they never get right up against
what she might have felt and thought and seen and feared and
wondered. Rather, they tell the story of what happened to her,
and in the world's eyes, usually what happens to a woman is
men.

Until at a certain point, perhaps, she decides that's not what
the story will be.

I fold the newspaper, put it aside, and pick up the manuscript I was working on.

Because the world will just keep at it, poking around, digging, turning over the dirt. The world will never stop trying to see past the drawn curtains of a room I stepped out of years ago.

PART VII

L'histoire de ma vie n'existe pas. Ça n'existe pas. Il n'y a
jamais de centre. Pas de chemin, pas de ligne. Il y a de
vastes endroits où l'on fait croire qu'il y avait quelqu'un,
ce n'est pas vrai il n'y avait personne.

The story of my life does not exist. Does not exist.
There is no center to it. No path, no line. There are
great spaces where you pretend there used to be
someone, but it is not true, there was no one.

—MARGUERITE DURAS

There is a dream I have—often—of you. I dream that you come for me, but I hold up my hand.

Once, not really thinking about it, I mention the dream to John. It's morning; he's home from college for the weekend. We are in the kitchen. I tell him about the dream, how it recurs, how it haunts me, how abstract it is and how real it seems, how I keep dreaming it, month after month, year after year, and how it makes me wonder, if you came for me now, would I go with you?

John listens, and only later do I realize I inadvertently upset him. He misinterpreted what I said. I wasn't saying I don't or didn't love you. I was reflecting on how far I've come from the girl you knew. Perhaps I should try to explain that to John. Perhaps it is cruel not to. In the end, though, I decide to let it lie. He should be able to live with the ambiguity—that raw uncertainty our hearts are made of.

. . .

In the summer of 1993, I turn to Maurice. We are in the caves in the south of France. "I am not quite well," I say—a strange fever, the walls spin, rock pouring into rock, suddenly liquid, and those lines of a cave painting someone made thousands of years ago. I feel a flush of heat, my body suddenly weak. Maurice reaches for me and takes my arm. He has always been that kind of man, prescient, gentle. He guides me, step by rising step, out of the cave into the sunlight of Arles, the rocks and the ground and the wild swirl of cypress trees, the gorgeous blazing world.

A summer flu, a doctor tells us.

That August on the Vineyard, preparing the house for a party, I sit at the dining table, writing out place cards. Something strikes past the window. A shadow, a bird perhaps. Farther down, past the lawn and the scrub, is the sea. The surface shifts, the distant bulk of Nomans Land under a translucent sky.

My head is light.

Marta, folding the napkins, glances up.

"Are you all right?" she says.

"Oh yes," I say. "I'm fine."

I feel it, though—that odd and haunting loneliness that sometimes comes in high summer, even in the midst of life, when the house is filled with children, family, friends. Every morning a swim or a bike ride along Moshup Trail, then long afternoons reading books and manuscripts on the bricked corner of the patio behind the library.

I force the loneliness down. I finish the place cards. The menu was set days ago. The shopping is done. Maurice offered to do these things—"It's a party for you," he said. Caroline and John offered as well. They had wanted it to be more of a surprise, but I prefer it this way. I know who should be seated near whom to feel at ease. It feels important—still—to build a room, a night suspended from time, with laughter, conversation, shine.

You'd appreciate it, wouldn't you? Some of my younger friends—the ones you never met. What would you say to them? How would you size them up? What would you ask? I've wondered this.

Your face, still, wherever I go.

I am tired. That drained sense I've felt since the trip to France.
There's a manuscript I want to finish before the guests arrive. I
tell Marta I'll be on the patio, working. I sit in the chair, a blanket
over my knees, a wide-brimmed hat. The breeze is light on my
face. A few chapters in, I close my eyes.

When Caroline was getting married, I said to Carolina Herrera,
"I'm going to let Caroline decide with you what she wants. I'm
not going to interfere, because I had a very bad experience with
my wedding dress. It was the dress my mother wanted me to
wear, and I hated it. Caroline told me the boys want blazers and
white pants. No morning suits. If they're happy, let's do it. Just
call me from time to time and let me know how it's going."

As promised, Carolina Herrera would call after each fitting.

"Is Caroline happy?" I'd ask.

"Yes, she's very happy."

"Perfect. That's the only important thing."

Caroline's reception was in Hyannis Port. There was a dance
floor, a tent, Japanese lanterns, and a thousand flowers, like the
world had come into bloom. That night, Teddy raised a glass and
called me "that extraordinary gallant woman—Jack's only love."

As Carly Simon sang, the fog rolled in off the sea. The fireworks were suffused in that fog, muted flashes of light and color
like summer lightning, tethered to the earth.

I wanted you to see it. So many things I've wanted you to see.

*Earlier that day, Teddy had walked Caroline down the aisle and
given her away. Afterward, on the church steps, I stood with your
brother and watched our daughter in a cloud of white organza, as a
sea of people flooded in around her. I could not escape the sense that
she was being lifted off, wrapped in the hands of an unseen future
already woven through the summer air. The bouquet of orchids in
her hand, the glint of pearl and diamond earrings, once a gift from
you to me. I watched our son blow his sister a kiss as she glanced
back to smile at me, before lowering her head into the waiting car.*

I was still standing with Teddy at the top of those steps. He waved to the crowd, and I let him carry the moment for us, as the car with Caroline in it slowly pulled away. I let my head rest on Teddy's shoulder, and I looked through my tears to the stone at our feet, just to hold that image of our daughter—the bold, shining strength she had become—heading into her own life. I wanted it fast in my mind.

I told you once, Jack: These are the pieces we're made of—births, marriages, deaths—these things that happen to anyone, these ordinary moments of a life.

I wake after three, Marta shaking me to say my friend Joe Armstrong has just arrived.

"I brought you a present," Joe says.

"No gifts!"

"It's just a cassette. The recording of a Beatles song, 'When I'm Sixty-Four.'"

"I don't know that one." I take the cassette, walk over to the stereo, and plunk it in.

"It's from 1967," Joe says.

"Well, sixty-four was old age then."

We lean on the edge of the sofa together and listen until the song has played through. Then I take his hand and pretend to be earnest.

"I'll always feed you, Joe, and I'll always need you. Even when I'm eighty-four. Now, come and meet my house."

I introduce him to the kitchen, the sixteen-burner Vulcan stove.

"Perfect for someone who barely cooks," I say. The fridge is covered with photographs of the children, the grandchildren, and there is one of me with Maurice. We walk through the dining room. In the library, I gesture toward the long shelves of books. "These are my other best friends."

He inclines his head, a mock bow.

"I've been rereading Vasari's *Lives of the Artists*," I say. "There's a wonderful chapter on how Da Vinci would walk through city streets where caged birds were sold. He'd buy the birds, just to set them free."

"You and I need a street like that," Joe says, "and a new project, since we've finished saving the ballet."

"You love ballet now, don't you?" I say. "Almost as much as I love my new favorite Beatles song." I smile at him. "I want to show you the orchard. John says the trees get shorter every year."

The house is set on a rise overlooking Squibnocket Pond and a sweep of woods and fields strung through with old stone walls. As we walk the path to the beach, I tell him I love how tough things have to be in order to grow in this kind of soil—the pitch pine, the bayberry, the scrub oak—their maze of gnarled roots that snake down through the sand as it blows up around them. The salt rose too, which blooms through storms and cold, throwing its scent deep into the fall.

We stop at the rowboat pulled up to the dunes, its hull splintered. I take off my sneakers and leave them on the thwart.

"Have you named it?" Joe asks.

"The boat?"

"Yes."

"*Beauty School Dropout*," I say.

"That's good!"

I love that Joe's first job was as a busboy at the Dixie Pig in Abilene, Texas, and that he wears Justin cowboy boots with a three-piece suit. I love, too, the story of how when he was at *Rolling Stone* magazine and employee morale was down, he'd blast "Drop Kick Me, Jesus (Through the Goalposts of Life)" over the loudspeakers. The first time I heard that story, I called Joe up and invited him to lunch. We talked for four hours that day. We've been friends since.

As we walk along the beach, I tuck my arm through his. He asks about the books I'm working on. He asks about Caroline and her children. She has three now: Rose, who just turned five in June; Tatiana, three; and little Jack, six months old.

"And how is John?" Joe asks.

"He's been very busy getting written up for hundreds of dollars in parking tickets and for eating apple pancakes with Daryl, biking with Daryl, dancing half naked on a roof deck with Daryl."

Joe laughs. "Do you like her?"

For a moment I'm grateful he'd ask the question any mother should be asked.

"I do," I say, aware the inflection in my tone makes it less clear. "He's thinking about leaving the D.A.'s office to start a magazine. Maybe you could talk to him tonight, get a sense of what he's thinking."

"Then try to talk him out of it?"

I laugh. We keep walking. He asks about my trip to France. I tell him about the caves in Arles and our visit to La Camargue, the ritual of the horses running into the sea. I mention the summer flu that took weeks to shake. I don't tell him that just this morning, I woke up, my sheets drenched, my body still so tired. I drank an extra cup of coffee with breakfast, which seemed to do the trick.

He is asking me now why I never wrote a book.

"I don't even let them put my name in the acknowledgments, Joe."

"You don't even think about it?"

"I only want to look ahead."

That last fall before you died, there was a day with the children at the house in Virginia, the stone path marked in sunlight; John was not quite three, running down the path ahead of us. He leapt to hit each stone and the dogs bounded alongside him, and the grass was trimmed short, a clean, open stretch of green on either side, that flagstone path laid out as bright and clear as anything I could have wanted for their lives. Caroline walked slowly by your side, her hand in yours, her blond head turning every so often to check her own small shadow trailing behind.

Thirty years since then. How could time have moved so fast that it feels at once like yesterday and like an entirely separate life?

"Jackie?"

"Oh, Joe," I say, putting my mind into place. "I'm so happy you are here."

...

After dinner that night, they gather around to sing me "Happy Birthday."

I forget to make a wish. I eat a skinny piece of cake, then pull on my jacket and slip out for a quick walk and a smoke. The night is velvet on my skin. From the edge of the lawn, I can see them through the window. Caroline, her hair burnished in the lamplight, seems to glow, laughing with her brother and her uncle, with her husband, Edwin, as always, nearby. How different she seems since she married. She's always been very much her own person. But it's more noticeable now. At the window, Maurice glances out. He does not see me. I'm too far in the shadows. Then he turns and moves back across the room, that quiet, lumbering grace. They are all there, in that house I laid out in string, inspired by a vision of nights just like this one. Their voices drift through the open window across the lawn, mixing with the play of the waves and the distant toll of a channel bell near the lightships farther out.

I drop my cigarette, the hiss of it extinguished in the wet grass. Night dew has begun to bleed through my shoes.

As a child, I used to wonder who I was before I was a child. I used to imagine an egg living under the snow or a star pinned in the high dark, waiting to fall. I was convinced there was a definitive place I came from—a room of the world, a place of trees and rocks and sky, outside time.

I should go back in. I know this. I should go back and rejoin these people I've gathered here—the living that I love—but there's a certain pleasure in being unseen, simply bearing witness to how they continue, in that house, those rooms, this hour, without me.

...

I wake early the next morning. I have coffee, rub cold cream over my face, and drive down to the pond to meet Carly Simon for our swim. By the time I come back, the house is awake. Caroline's little girls have dragged the dollhouse into the hallway and are zooming tiny cars at breakneck speed across the floor. Through the trees and past the garden streams the light, a pendulum at play.

At an afternoon beach picnic, the girls swim with Caroline, while Carly and I sing "Itsy Bitsy Spider" to baby Jack, who's crawling around a blanket on the sand. I take him for a walk, just the two of us. The wind is soft and warm, and he turns his face into it, his little eyes half-closed. We walk and I tell him how smart he is, how kind he will be, and the extraordinary things he will do in this life. His head tucks into that hollow place at the curve of my neck, where it just fits. "Next summer, you'll be in my kayak," I say. "I'll put you in a life jacket, and we'll go off on a paddle."

The house begins to empty—first the guests, who need to get back to their lives, then the children, with kisses and promises to return soon. When they're gone, I go through the house, looking for toys or books left behind a cushion or under a chair. There's a sadness that comes when the oak floors are empty, no mess strewn about, everything in its place. Maurice stays for a few days, then returns to the city. The days flow by. There are dinners with the Styrons, Carly, and the Clintons—Hillary, whom I like very much. One Sunday, Lady Bird comes for lunch. It's a lovely day and we sit under the arbor. Shadows stripe the table and the silver and our hands. We talk about our children and our present lives. We do not talk about the past.

I've wondered this: Would you have wanted to know that severe daylight in Dallas would be the last you'd see?

...

Every Monday I drive to Oak Bluffs to see Dorothy West.

"Do you know I lose my way almost every time I come here?" I say.

We're drinking tea in Dorothy's kitchen in the house on Myrtle Avenue. A small plate of egg salad sandwiches, a bowl of carrot sticks, and manuscript pages on the table in short piles arranged by section and chapter.

"I'll tell you what, Dorothy. You get this book finished for us, and I promise not to get lost anymore between my house and yours."

"By next summer?"

"Yes. Next summer."

Dorothy likes to talk, to tell stories. Someone once remarked that Dorothy didn't know when to set a period, but I love Dorothy's voice—that hard, open Bostonian *A*—and her stories. She tells me about living in New York with Zora Neale Hurston and starting a magazine with Richard Wright. She has a column now in the *Vineyard Gazette,* and on our Monday visits, she always insists on serving tea.

"Does it ever strike you," I say, "that here we are, the two of us. You never married. I've been married twice and am quite finished with it. And here we are working on a book called *The Wedding.*"

Dorothy laughs.

"Look at these pages." I pull out a section of the manuscript and point to a passage I've marked. "This. What's happening here—it's brilliant. The voice in this passage."

"That's a voice from forty years ago," Dorothy says.

"I know. Don't lose it."

Driving home, past the moors and the tumble of brush and stone wall, I think about how solitude is the stuff the self is made of. When I am here, on the island alone, I remember who I was before I met you—half a life before. Sometimes what I remember is clearly, definitively true. Other times I feel like it's only a loosely glued collage of what took place, what I witnessed, did, and felt.

Who would I have been if I'd stayed in France or moved to New York for that job at Vogue? *If I'd pursued more, risked more, let myself want more. What would have happened if I had made—all those years ago—a different choice? And why does it seem like such a radical thing? The idea of a woman in love with her own life?*

The days stream by, one after the next, into fall. Storms come, fronts building far out on the water. From the house, I watch the iron-dark walls of rain move over the surface, the bright strike of lightning. The gaps in time between those flashes and the thunder shrink as the storm nears. Since I was a child, I've loved storms, the reminder that what is wild and unpredictable is always there.

From that time
all his angels

have the one
same
face.

I am reading something intimate and unexpected. A young poet, Anne Carson, I haven't read before, who blends Sappho and Euripides with modern slang and syntax. I'm curious to know what you'd make of it—these disparate elements merged. But it can happen this way, can't it? Things meld, and that larger order we call history changes as we age. And yet—does that make what we once believed in less?

I pull my mind back. I'm treading water in the cove with Carly, the salty taste of ocean on my mouth. We've taken the Jeep down for a swim. In a few days, I'll return to New York. As we float in the still-warm water, she tells me about her childhood, how hard it was, like a Tennessee Williams play, she says; she wonders if she could write about it. A buzzing sound overhead. A helicopter circling. At first I think it's the Coast Guard, then realize it isn't.

Carly hasn't figured it out yet. She will. She stares at the sky, curious—how lovely she is, long rectangular face, expressive mouth, her hair plastered dark and wet over her broad shoulders. She has that exquisite, almost violent strength glimpsed from time to time in younger women, a strength not yet fully owned.

"The press," she says.

We start to swim.

. . .

When do I know?

It's almost imperceptible. The slight changes in a body that occur as some new dark thing takes root. A cold that lasts longer than it should. A funny lingering chill that a second sweater can't stave off. I close the windows earlier in the evenings, even though I hate them closed. That sign of another summer done. I don't want that funny chill. I tell myself there's always next year. I pack up the house—manuscripts to bring back to the city, summer clothes I'll send to be cleaned and stored. The light has changed, and it is beautiful, a sharper angle of it on the marshes as they turn.

Forty years ago in September we walked into St. Mary's Church, then went back to Hammersmith for the reception. After the cake was cut, I stood and told the eight hundred guests that my mother had always contended you could judge a man by his correspondence. Then I held up the postcard of a passionflower you'd sent to me when you were in Bermuda.

Wish you were here, *you'd written.* Cheers. Jack.

"And this," I said, waving the postcard, "is my entire correspondence with Jack."

I glanced at you then, and you met my eyes and laughed, a faint blush—a little sheepish—rising through your skin that filled me with a sharp, exquisite joy.

. . .

It's a glorious autumn in New York. That dull feeling in my body, though, still. Like the bones are drenched.

"I'm tired," I tell Maurice. "I've just been so tired."

He is the only one I tell.

Breakfast, coffee, the paper each morning. A children's dance performance at the Brooklyn Academy of Music. A dinner for the Municipal Art Society.

I do yoga and take my runs around the reservoir. I watch the grandchildren once a week. I go into the Doubleday office on Tuesdays, Wednesdays, and Thursdays. I no longer wear the sunglasses and scarf every time I walk in the streets. What a thrill it was, the first time I did it, to find that only a few heads turned, one or two whispers, then they looked away, and I realized that just as there was a switch I could turn on to draw a room toward me, there was another I could turn off to disappear. I could step out into the street and vanish, just a middle-aged woman in slacks and sneakers, a tote on her shoulder, ballet shoes tucked in with the books and manuscript pages, walking north toward Central Park.

I tell Tillie, my yoga teacher, that when I think about old-ladydom, the one thing I want to always be able to do is ride.

. . .

November again.

Thirty years this month. You come near me, as you do, every November. A momentary shudder and I feel you like a shadow cross my hands.

Sometimes it strikes me that I have become an entirely different woman from the woman that you knew.

This year I'll spend the week before the anniversary in Virginia. I'll ride in the hunt, then come home to be with the children for the actual day. But leading up to it, I want to be away.

I stay in a small cottage on Bunny Mellon's farm, near the garden by the main house. Over the years, I've come to miss the world I remember from childhood, the wide rolling hills of Virginia, long open fields where I can build a horse's speed to a gallop, riding faster across the swell of space with the sense that if I ride hard enough, I can catch up to those blue dusky mountains in the distance and lose myself there, in the speed where nothing is fixed and there's only the smell of the horses, the saddle blankets, and the tack mixed with the fainter scent of hay and the rich cool damp of the green.

Early that morning, when I arrive at the stables at Rokeby, a crust of frost on the grass snaps under my boots. My breath is white in the cold clean air. I look for the horse I usually ride, Frank, the horse I won the trials with three years before.

Afterward, I'll try to remember what I was thinking when I chose the other horse instead—a dark bay thoroughbred gelding with a neatly braided mane and tail, the one the groom told me used to fly over fences but now might be too settled, too content to follow the hunt.

I lead the horse over to join the others. The hounds pick up the scent of the fox. The horse's girth and stride feel unfamiliar. Then I adjust, and we're swept into the speed and rhythm, the cry of the hounds, the peal of the horn echoing back through the valley while a mist fills in among the hills. We come to the wall, gaps where the rise is low. I move away to find a good place to cross, back the horse up, then urge him forward to jump.

I feel it happen, the jerk as his hoof clips an edge of the wall, and my body flows over his head toward the ground.

I open my eyes. You're somewhere nearby, on the beach. You're with me and we're lying in the sun. No one is there. I know this somehow. No one's looking for us. No one knows we are gone. You're lying beside me, eyes closed, and the sun has shaped your face. You're a man in relief—alien, divine—pulled out of sand, dune grass, light. Your eyes open then, your face turning just enough so you're looking at me, and it is only you again. Young. The way I remember. Your eyes with a kind of forever in them I'd only glimpse from time to time.

"Swim?" *you say.*

The image snaps. Like the vanishing zip on a television screen before it goes dark.

Bunny's face. No, not Bunny. Another woman. Bunny's friend Barbara, leaning over, and a man as well, concerned faces. They tell me I've been out for over fifteen minutes. They have phoned Bunny and she is on her way. Their voices waver like static. I remember the last bad fall I took. That one, too, was this time of year. November.

At Loudoun Hospital Center, Bunny's doctor finds a lump at the top of my thigh.

"You haven't been feeling well?" he says.

"Always cold. Tired. I was unwell earlier this year, in France. I haven't seemed to shake it since."

"Fever?"

"Sometimes at night. Not every night, but some nights."

He nods. "You've been fighting an infection," he explains. He prescribes a heavy antibiotic. After he leaves the room and I'm slipping off the examining table, finding my clothes, I feel a wave of relief. I'd been afraid it was something worse.

So my spirits are light over the holidays. I spend Thanksgiving with the children, celebrating their birthdays, each in turn as always. Colder weather begins to descend—days of biting wind, a dusting of snow. Holiday lights swathe the avenues, carolers gather in the park, Christmas displays in store windows, the smell of roasted chestnuts, pine. I take my granddaughters to *The Nutcracker.* I put up a tree in the apartment, draped with old-fashioned ornaments. Their mirrored surfaces catch splintered fragments off the fire.

Marta helps me load the little BMW with presents, my weekend bag, and extra rolls of wrapping paper, ribbon, bows. As I drive out to New Jersey, where I'll spend Christmas with Caroline's family, John, and Maurice, I listen to the cassette of Carly's duet with Sinatra. Then I pop that tape out and pop in another. It's Carly's voice I want to fill the car—that big, bold poet voice, carving hunger out of nothing. I hum along, tapping the steering wheel, even as I hit the tunnel and the line of cars ahead slows. A few years ago, I was passing through this same tunnel in my car. I'd let my friend William drive. We got caught behind a tractor trailer. William was so tentative, stuck behind that truck. He'd edge out, then edge back in, refusing to cross the solid double line to pass, although there was no oncoming traffic. "You're not going to let us spend the next half hour like this, are you?" I asked as he edged out again. "Oh, for God's sake, William. Just gun it."

. . .

In the Caribbean after Christmas, I'm with Maurice when I'm struck by an agonizing pain in my back and groin, a swelling in my neck that doesn't abate.

We come home to New York early.

The diseased cells are anaplastic—what the doctors call "primitive," which sounds like it might be early and a good thing but which I learn is neither. In a way, I'm glad I didn't know this until now. I didn't have that word—*cancer*—with me over Christmas. I didn't have that word traveling with Carly's voice and all those gifts piled into the car as I drove through the Lincoln Tunnel toward my children.

It strikes me as extraordinary—the way I am floating up there in a corner of the ceiling in the doctor's office, the way one word can change the shape of everything.

"So all those push-ups I did were sort of a waste of time," I say.

They map a course of treatment.

"We think it's curable," the doctor says.

Define think, I almost say.

"I still want to work," I tell Maurice quietly as we wait to take the elevator down.

He is next to me in the living room when I tell John and Caroline. I brace myself for the sudden devastation in their faces but can't bear it when it comes. They cry and hug me, their arms as tight around my body as they were when they were small—these two extraordinary beings, each the split half of my heart, and for a moment I feel the careful walls I've made weaken as my children's grief and fear wash into mine.

. . .

"I've decided it's just something else to get through," I tell Arthur Schlesinger on the phone. "I'll wear a turban and start a new trend. The nurses are good to us. When I have scans, Maurice and I sneak in before seven in the morning. I wear a hooded cape and wait outside in the car. He checks to make sure the waiting room is clear before he walks me in."

I listen to my voice recounting this, like it's happening to someone else. I think suddenly of Clint Hill. Where is he now?

"What do the doctors say?" Arthur asks.

"I've been through hard things before, as you know. Now I just need to get through this."

Hanging up the phone, I go into Caroline's old room, the one I use for yoga. The walls are as Caroline left them, one filled with black-and-white photographs of Jack. Everything is as she left it, the school notebooks and horse-show ribbons, every knickknack on the bureau and the shelves, as if my daughter, fifteen again, might walk in, throw herself down on the bed with a question and her father's eyes and that mane of dark-blond hair.

"Why should I be a public figure?" I overheard her complain to a friend once. It was not the question I found thrilling but the defiance in my daughter's voice—an anger I recognized that she would sharpen to carve her own life. I roll my yoga mat out, leave the overhead off. I lie down and pull my knees into my chest, the curve of my spine pressing into the floor, feeling vertebra by vertebra, those slight interlocking knobs of bone with just enough space between them.

I never quite did what they wanted, did I? I wasn't who they thought or who they needed me to be. I chose to fail them. Even during those four days, I was not brave. . . .

I listen to the tiny pop of vertebrae as they release. My legs rise, lifting over my head, the long exhale as the bones of my cervical spine shift.

I was not strong. I did not hold the country together. In a way, I was barely there. To me, it was not about dignity or majesty or theater. It was never the way they told it. I only did what I thought was right, and I did the best I could. I did what anyone would have done to honor the integrity of someone they loved.

I never loved anyone the way that I loved you.

. . .

Doris Kearns Goodwin once mentioned to me how remarkable it was that I'd been able to raise my children in such a way that each developed as a free, independent spirit even as the three of us shared such a deep bond.

I smiled and said, "It's the best thing I've ever done."

I could have added, *I've often felt it was the only thing.*

I talk with my friend Nancy Tuckerman about how to present my illness to the press.

"You don't think we should say anything about the stage, do you?" Tucky asks.

"You could say *early stage.*"

"Is it?"

I smile. "Well, I only recently learned about it, so in that sense at least."

Tucky studies the draft. "We could say *apparently early.*"

"Yes, that's good. I like that. *Apparently.*"

The world has divided my life into three:

Life with Jack.
Life with Onassis.
Life as a woman who works because she wants to.

My life is all of these things, and it is none of these things. They continue to miss what's right in front of them. What has always been there. I love to work. I love books. I love the sea. I love horses. Children. Art. Ideas. History. Beauty. Because beauty blows us open to wonder, and wonder is what allows us to shift and love and ache and grow and change. Even the beauty that breaks your heart.

. . .

I am in the shower when the first strands of hair fall out. A slight dark nest in my fingers. I put my hand to my scalp and pull.

I go to work with Band-Aids on my hands and arms. Once there is a bruise from the infusions that I watch bloom and fade— a lopsided exploding star.

John has moved from his downtown apartment into a hotel down the street from me. He visits every day. I ask if he remembers me teaching him to ski when he was a child. He fell and started to cry. Bobby skied up and said sternly, "Now, you stop that. Kennedys don't cry."

"This Kennedy cries," John had lashed back at him.

"Do you remember that?" I ask John, even knowing that he

must, whether or not he does, because it's a story I've told so many times.

"How happy you made me that day," I say.

...

The proofs of Peter Sis's new book are in. *The Three Golden Keys.* It has the kind of magic I love, the story of a balloonist who lands in the ancient city of his childhood and goes home. The streets of the city are empty and dark, and he comes to a locked door where a cat is waiting for him.

The art is extraordinary.

"Just let it be dark, Peter," I'd said to him before he started. "Because every good fairy tale—no matter how lovely—has a dark, violent shard at its heart. That's where we learn who we are. Be as free as you want with this book. If it's going to be dark or scary or strange, you do it."

And he has. It's a haunting story, lit with an unruly, luminous flare.

I start to write him and find I don't quite know how to say what I want to say. I'll call instead, I decide. But then he'll ask how I'm doing. They all ask now: *How are you? How is it going?* These are questions I learned to answer without really answering years ago. It's harder now.

I'll tell Peter we must start thinking about his next book.

I start to dial, then hang up. I'll try another day.

...

It snows, a blizzard, ten-foot drifts. The office is closed. The snow tapers off. The wind shifts and blows off the clouds; the sky rushes in. Caroline comes over, and we take the girls outside to play, their little selves stuffed into snowsuits. We cross the street to the paths through the park. We tramp through the drifts and pack snowballs. "GrandJackie, catch!" Rose shrieks.

We spill back into the apartment, their little cheeks red, lips blue, wet clothes in puddles on the floor. "Just leave it," I say. That careless mess feels like a handwriting that is theirs, and I want it to last.

Caroline makes the girls cinnamon toast and big mugs of hot chocolate. They stir in the marshmallows, sticky streaks down their faces. A brief squabble over a cookie. "There are more," I say, but their fingers are grasping after the last one on the plate, which has a crooked extra band of icing, and the light is in their eyes, that sudden fight mixed with laughter and the smell of chocolate and falling bits of snow blown into the sunlight pouring down through the long windows. Sunlight strikes their cheeks, their mouths, their chocolate-smeared chins. Sunlight bright on their dark hair.

A funny twitch like a blade against my throat. This is the life I will miss.

That night in bed, I close my eyes and feel my granddaughters' hands again as they were leaving, kissing me goodbye, their sweet small fingers through my hair.

. . .

I begin to work from home. Maurice sets up an office for himself in my apartment, so he's nearby if I need him. I still try to go into the office for Wednesday editorial meetings. I wear a beret to cover the wig, and I bring edited manuscript pages to be sent off to writers, my typed memos attached, pencil scrawl along the margins.

There is less of me now.
Each day.
Less.

I write letters to friends: *I shall look forward to our doing something together when all this first part is over. . . .* I write to Louis Auchincloss: *Your beautiful letter. I was touched by your writing it.*

All will be well, I promise. . . . I write to John Loring: Everything is fine. Soon we can have another festive lunch at Le Cirque. Six desserts each. Seeing you is always like champagne. . . . I write to one of my authors, Ruth Prawer Jhabvala: *Isn't it wonderful the way our friendship is growing?*

Finally, because I haven't been able to pick up the phone and call him, I write Peter Sis: *Your book is magnificent. Each drawing looks into the well of an artist's mind. . . . It is like nothing I have ever seen before.*

I write these letters on the same blue stationery I've had for years, *1040 Fifth Avenue* embossed in white. Blue for the sea and the sky, white for the shell and the bone and the breath that continues to rise. That which is left over.

I fold the letters, envelopes sealed and addressed. I set them with the mail to go out.

Outside, spring has begun. The trees melting into themselves, buds like tiny fists coming slightly apart, grass smudged in the warmer air, color blending into color, even the streets and the edges of buildings starting to blur.

. . .

The scans say they have gotten all of it from my neck and chest and abdomen—all but a tiny crumb that has run off and escaped to my brain. They can drill a hole in my skull, they tell me.

"If it can work, that would be fine," I say.

I begin to divide my things. Boxes of papers and notes, bunches of letters bound in ribbon. Things I haven't looked at in years. Some I'll keep. Others not. There are many letters in the pile of *Not.*

Once in a while, reading through them, I'll stop and remember who I was on a particular day. It will hit in a rush, right down to the sounds and the smells, those older layers of my life still there.

Maurice comes into the room. He glances at the fire, then at the heap of papers to be burned by the chair where I sit, the astrakhan blanket over my lap. He stops, a question in his face, as if to ask, *Are you sure?* I smile at him. He touches my shoulder and heads in the direction of the kitchen.

Novalis once wrote that fiction arises out of the shortcomings of history. But I've come to realize no matter what truths I leave for the world to rifle through, they'll concoct the stories of my life they want to tell—to worship me or tear me down, their ice queen or their whore.

The world does not need more of me than it thinks it has.

I'm nearing the end of a stack of papers when a loose sheet falls out. I look more closely—my handwriting from when I was younger. *These are the bones of desire.* A few lines crossed out. The paper is torn. Only a fragment. I wonder why I would've kept it. For a moment I can't place the context, then I do. A day years ago; we were not yet married. In Georgetown, at the corner of N Street, as Jack said goodbye, he touched my waist, leaned in, and kissed me briefly on the cheek. Something so pedestrian—a boy, a girl, a street corner. I'd filled pages, I remember now. Far more than just these lines. I start to shuffle through that pile, then untie the next and go through that too, but I find nothing else. I leave the papers strewn around. No neat ribboned bundles now, no order. I stand up, thirsty, but my head is light; I sit back down.

One night years ago, at a dinner party, you were talking to Ben Bradlee about biography.

"What makes that kind of writing so fascinating," you remarked, "is the struggle to answer the single question: What was he really like?"

In history, you told me once, we turn toward what was lost because we crave the dream of a world that might have been.

...

I write out a will.

For Bunny Mellon, the eighteenth-century Indian miniature *Lovers Watching Rain Clouds*.

For Maurice, the Greek alabaster head of a woman.

For Alexander Folger, a copy of Jack's inaugural address, signed by Robert Frost.

The White House things still in my possession will go to the Kennedy Library; the furniture, knickknacks, and other tangibles to Sotheby's to be sold. My books I'll leave to the children. My books and my houses and some money. And the vastest sky. And all the time in the world, which, when sooner turns to later, is the only currency we have.

...

In April, Carly invites me to lunch at her apartment on Central Park West. Joe Armstrong is there, as are my friends Peter Duchin; his wife, Brooke Hayward; and Ken Burns. I ask Ken about the documentary he's finishing on the history of baseball.

"Is it true that Carly's going to sing 'Take Me Out to the Ball Game'?"

"Could we have it any other way?"

I laugh. "We could not."

Joe asks how I'm feeling.

"It's a nuisance," I say. "Four more weeks, this treatment will be done, and I'll get my life back. I'm going to spend the summer on the Vineyard." They go on talking. I half listen, settling back into the sofa. I'm tired. But Caroline is bringing the children to visit tomorrow. I look forward to that. There are so many things, it seems, to look forward to. Carly is laughing now at something Joe said. Her extravagant strong-hearted laughter lights a room. I love how Carly laughs—without caution or distance or fear. We've talked together about how you can't live your life on egg-shells and live it well.

A few years ago, Carly and I were sitting in this same room. We'd decided to go to the movies. She was flipping through the listings, theaters, and showtimes. We were looking for something in the late afternoon, planning for dinner after.

"What about that new film *JFK*?" Carly said.

"I don't actually think I could see that," I said. Her head snapped up, eyes wide, horrified. Her hand flew to her mouth.

"Oh, Jackie, I'm so sorry. I just forgot. I can't believe I forgot."

"And you have no idea how much I love that you forgot."

"I've dreamt in my life dreams that have stayed with me ever after, and changed my ideas: they've gone through and through me, like wine through water, and altered the color of my mind."

Catherine Earnshaw said this in Brontë's Wuthering Heights.

It's a passage I've always loved. It's different to me now because of you.

How simple it's become.

That transcendent mythology that was ours.

Who we were, what we wanted, what we dreamed and made, believed, and failed to be.

Once, desire clung to us like heat
 We were bodies of light falling through time

. . .

I wake to the world in white and beige, unfamiliar faces. The room comes into focus. A window, a shelf, a chair; Caroline is there, stepping out of the white-beigeness to tell me I collapsed at home. I was brought here. John is coming. He is on his way.

Maurice, I notice then, is here too, behind Caroline, who has sat down on the edge of my bed and is holding my hand.

"Could you call the office, please, Caroline," I say. "Call Scott and ask him to let Peter Sis know I won't be able to make our appointment today but that we will reschedule soon."

Sometimes, looking at our daughter's face, I see through the woman she's become to the girl with the wind in her eyes. I see through that inimitable strength and penetrating intellect shaped out of a deep and lasting sorrow, honed by what she remembers and what she has endured.

She has your easy grace—that casual ferocity and burning faith. But in her, it's tempered with restraint, more aware and more humane. From the time she was young, she seemed to understand that the present moment is a thing to take our time with.

. . .

"When may I go home?" I ask, first a nurse, then the doctor.
"When we've figured out your fever."
"I'm sure I can have a fever at home."

It's deep in the lungs now, the doctor explains. I sit for a moment in silence when he tells me this.

"No more treatments, please. I want to go home."

I see the children every day for the rest of that spring, as I have since January. Every night after supper, I phone Caroline's house, good-night hugs and kisses to Tatiana and Rose.

No one tells you it happens like this: a funny ripple at the edges of things—a gnawing away—like a new country sliding over the familiar. Stitches coming undone.

How would I describe it?
It's not what you'd expect—
The severing is a thing you can feel.
The day is made of walls, and walls are air.
You are of the air. And not.
You are the slant of evening light against a tree.
A cool breeze moving now through a cracked window, turning the page.

It's not what you'd expect.

Not as you came to understand it growing older, but how you might have dreamed it as a child.

You are a thousand selves, and that other sky is here.

. . .

One Sunday in May, I wake up to bright light flooding in.

"Let's take a walk in the park today, Maurice," I say.

That afternoon, we cross Fifth Avenue with Caroline and the children.

"Isn't it something?" I remark as we pause to let a raft of bicyclists pass. "One of the most glorious springs I can remember, and after such a terrible winter." I lean on Maurice; the girls are ahead, Caroline pushing the stroller with baby Jack. Runners and more cyclists flow by, shreds of conversation, light on bare shins, forearms pale, a woman in yellow shorts on Rollerblades, a Frisbee tucked under her arm. The grass is just so bright.

I feel my breath catch—so much effort, these small steps, this distance. Maurice glances at me.

"I'm fine," I say with a smile, and he touches my hand. We continue walking. The path splits, then merges again. A bench up ahead in the sun.

"Do you want to sit, Mom?" Caroline asks.

"Not yet. We'll find another spot, farther on, where the girls can play."

"We can stop here for a while, then find another spot too."

But Tatiana and Rose have skipped ahead. They've made up a game—part hopscotch, part tag—their dark hair bright, little jackets swinging open and flapping behind them like cropped wings. When they've drifted too far ahead, their mother calls them. They pause at the sound of her voice. Dark heads bent together, they confer with each other and wait as Caroline starts toward them.

And the park is a green lake all around. The girls seem to shimmer there, at the edge of it, at the top of the rise; they are tall and straight and strong, their bodies small pillars of fire. Their mother has almost reached them. She nods. They turn then and they run.

It is really only this:

   The world is alive to me because of you.

ACKNOWLEDGMENTS

My father's faith in me has never wavered. His love is an inspiration; his support for this novel, our family, and my creative life, beyond measure.

Kim Wright Wiley was with me in this book when it was only the flash of an idea, years before I had the voice and rolled up my sleeves to begin. I will always be grateful for our long conversations about women, art, motherhood, identity, vision, time. An incomparable writer and friend, she read each draft, each page.

Also, and essentially: gratitude to Karen Deutsch, Stephen Kiernan, Jessica Keener, Emily Franklin, Barbara Shapiro, Holly LeCraw, Drew Moran, Carolyn Foley, Elizabeth Lane, Anna Dokoza, Jane Ritson-Parsons, Derrill Hagood McDavid.

Jack, for his presence and his keen understanding of the flow between history and story on the page; Ivan, for his intuitive grasp of voice and heart. Peggy and Maureen, for their friendship and one revelatory conversation over dinner once I had a rough working draft that shifted the way I went back in to revise. Annie Philbrick, for lending me her magical house-of-no-worries in Vermont when I needed the space to write; Topher Kerr, for a singular insight in August 2022 about where the thematic and emotional might intersect.

My mother's passion for reading, for novels, poetry, language, and stories—along with her curiosity about Jackie—inspired mine.

Arrow and Oriana—small infinities—who remind me of the power of women over the long throw of time. Carlin and Nicole, for their love and care.

Kim Witherspoon, fierce and trusted advocate, and her exceptional team at Inkwell, especially Lyndsey Blessing and William Callahan.

At Random House, inestimable thanks to Rachel Rokicki, Alison Rich, Ayelet Durantt, Michelle Jasmine, Matthew Martin, Luke Epplin, Benjamin Dreyer, Rebecca Berlant, Donna Cheng, Monica Rae Brown.

And Kate Medina—for her beautiful and generous intelligence, her guidance and friendship of twenty-five years, her integrity and grace—I am so deeply grateful.

Again, and always, to my boys—Jack and Ivan:

You are my wind and stars, and the reason I chose this particular story.

SOURCES

For readers who want to learn more, the following sources were critical to my work on this novel: *Jacqueline Kennedy: Historic Conversations on Life with John F. Kennedy*, foreword by Caroline Kennedy, interviews with Arthur M. Schlesinger, Jr., introduction and annotations by Michael Beschloss; *America's Queen*, by Sarah Bradford; *Dreaming in French*, by Alice Kaplan; *Jacqueline Bouvier Kennedy Onassis: The Untold Story*, by Barbara Leaming; *Mrs. Kennedy*, by Barbara Leaming; *The Fitzgeralds and the Kennedys*, by Doris Kearns Goodwin; *An Unfinished Life*, by Robert Dallek; *Mrs. Kennedy and Me*, by Clint Hill with Lisa McCubbin; *Five Days in November*, by Clint Hill with Lisa McCubbin; *Profiles in Courage*, by John F. Kennedy; *Make Gentle the Life of This World: The Vision of Robert F. Kennedy*, by Maxwell Taylor Kennedy; *Jackie as Editor*, by Greg Lawrence; *Reading Jackie: Her Autobiography in Books*, by William Kuhn; *JFK: Coming of Age in the American Century, 1917–1956*, by Fredrik Logevall; *Portrait of a President*, by William Manchester; *The Death of a President*, by William Manchester; *One Brief Shining Moment*, by William Manchester; *Four Days in November: The Original Coverage of the John F. Kennedy Assassination*, edited by Robert B. Semple, Jr.; *The Irish Brotherhood: John F. Kennedy, His Inner Circle, and the Improbable Rise to the Presidency*, by Helen O'Donnell with Kenneth O'Donnell, Sr.; *Upstairs at the White House: My Life with the First Ladies,* by J. B. West and Mary Lynn Kotz; *The Eloquent Jacqueline Kennedy Onassis,* edited by Bill Adler; *All Too Human,* by Edward Klein; *Camera Girl: The Coming of Age of Jackie Bouvier Kennedy,* by Carl Sferrazza Anthony; *As We Remember Her: Jacqueline Kennedy Onassis in the Words of Her Family and Friends,* by Carl Sferrazza Anthony; *The Kennedy White House: Family Life and Pictures, 1961–1963,* by Carl Sferrazza Anthony; *Grace and Power: The Private World of the Kennedy White House,* by Sally Bedell Smith; *The Onassis Women: An Eyewitness Account,* by Kiki Feroudi Moutsatsos with Phillis Karas; *These Few Precious Days,* by Christopher Andersen; *The Residence: Inside the Private World of the White House,* by Kate Andersen Brower; *Come to the Edge: A Memoir,* by Christina Haag; *Jacqueline Bouvier Kennedy Onassis,* by Donald Spoto; *The Private Passion of Jacqueline Kennedy Onassis: Portrait of a Rider,* by Vicky Moon; *One Special Summer,* by Jacqueline and Lee Bouvier; *The Odyssey,* by Homer translated by Robert Fagles; *The Iliad,* by Homer translated by Robert Fagles; *The Greek Way,* by Edith Hamilton; *Stride Toward Freedom,* by Martin Luther King, Jr.; *The Power of Myth,* by Joseph Campbell with Bill Moyers; *The Firebird,* by Peter Sis; *The Best-Loved Poems of Jacqueline Kennedy Onassis,* selected and introduced by Caroline Kennedy; *A Family of Poems: My Favorite Poetry for Children,* by Caroline Kennedy. I also pored through vintage issues of *Life* magazine and *Look* magazine that spanned the 1940s, '50s, and '60s as I was creating the world of this book.

Several visits to the John F. Kennedy Presidential Library and Museum were invaluable, as was the online site www.jfklibrary .org. I found the transcript from the forum "The Literary Life of Jacqueline Kennedy Onassis" particularly compelling, and it inspired several scenes in this novel and more essentially a sharper understanding of the depth and nuance of Jackie's character and mind, along with her passion for books. The online archives of *The New York Times* were essential as I was drawing together a clearer sense of history and news reporting during the span of years covered by this novel. James Reston's piece "Why America Weeps: Kennedy Victim of Violent Streak He Sought to Curb in the Nation," published in *The New York Times* the day after John F. Kennedy's assassination, was particularly inspiring. Daniel Mendelsohn's excellent "J.F.K., Tragedy, Myth," published in *The New Yorker,* was an article I read and returned to several times. Steven Levingston's brilliant piece "John F. Kennedy, Martin Luther King Jr., and the Phone Call That Changed History," published in *Time* magazine, helped shape my understanding of the conversation and events around that phone call. *The Washington Post* archives were also important to my research, including the piece "The Young, Tough Guys Behind the Election of John F. Kennedy," by Vincent Bzdek, as was *The Atlantic*'s JFK Issue, published in the fall of 2013 and including the articles "The Legacy of John F. Kennedy," by Alan Brinkley, and "The Man and the Myths," by James Bennet. Multiple articles that provided insight into artist Elaine de Kooning and her portrait of Jack Kennedy include *Smithsonian* magazine's "Why Elaine de Kooning's Portrait of JFK Broke All the Rules" and "A President, Seen from Every Angle" in *ARTnews*. G. Wayne Miller's "Sunset Days of Camelot: JFK's Last September in Newport," published in *The Providence Journal,* helped as I was building those scenes. The archives of *Vanity Fair, The New Yorker,* and *Esquire* magazine were also critical—particularly, in *Esquire,* Norman Mailer's several pieces on Jack and Jackie Kennedy, including "Superman Comes to the Supermart," "An Evening with Jackie Kennedy," "Enter Prince Jack," and "Jackie, the Prisoner of Celebrity." Other writings of Norman Mailer focused on JFK were helpful, including "An Open Letter to JFK from Norman Mailer," published in 1962 in *The Village Voice,* and Mailer's *The Presidential Papers*. The lines of poetry on page 450 are from Anne Carson's poem "The Fall of Rome: A Traveller's Guide."

ABOUT THE AUTHOR

Dawn Tripp is the author of the novel *Georgia,* which was a national bestseller, a finalist for the New England Book Award, and the winner of the Mary Lynn Kotz Award for Art in Literature. She is the author of three previous novels: *Game of Secrets, Moon Tide,* and *The Season of Open Water,* which won the Massachusetts Book Award for Fiction.

dawntripp.com

ABOUT THE TYPE

This book was set in Fairfield, the first typeface from the hand of the distinguished American artist and engraver Rudolph Ruzicka (1883–1978). Ruzicka was born in Bohemia (in the present-day Czech Republic) and came to America in 1894. He set up his own shop, devoted to wood engraving and printing, in New York in 1913 after a varied career working as a wood engraver, in photo-engraving and banknote printing plants, and as an art director and freelance artist. He designed and illustrated many books, and was the creator of a considerable list of individual prints—wood engravings, line engravings on copper, and aquatints.